One Winter's Night

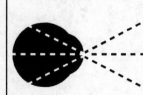

This Large Print Book carries the
Seal of Approval of N.A.V.H.

One Winter's Night

A REGENCY YULETIDE COLLECTION

Jo Ann Ferguson
Karen Frisch
Sharon Sobel
Shereen Vedam

THORNDIKE PRESS
A part of Gale, Cengage Learning

GALE
CENGAGE Learning·

Farmington Hills, Mich • San Francisco • New York • Waterville, Maine
Meriden, Conn • Mason, Ohio • Chicago

GALE
CENGAGE Learning®

LIBRARY OF CONGRESS CATALOGING-IN-PUBLICATION DATA

One winter's night : a regency yuletide collection / Jo Ann Ferguson,
Karen Frisch, Sharon Sobel.
pages cm. — (Thorndike Press large print clean reads)
ISBN 978-1-4104-8450-5 (hardback) — ISBN 1-4104-8450-5 (hardcover)
1. Christmas stories, American. 2. Love stories, American. 3. England—
Social life and customs—19th century—Fiction. 4. Large type books.
I. Ferguson, Jo Ann. II. Frisch, Karen, 1955– III. Sobel, Sharon.
PS648.C45O57 2015
813'.0108334—dc23   2015030965

Published in 2015 by arrangement with BelleBooks, Inc.

Printed in Mexico
1 2 3 4 5 6 7 19 18 17 16 15

TABLE OF CONTENTS

Yule Be Mine

BY JO ANN FERGUSON

Chapter One

Cornwall
Two Weeks 'Til Christmas

When Lady Priscilla Flanders Hathaway felt their carriage dip down the steep road to the house on her husband's estate in Cornwall, she wanted to jump to her feet and dance. She was exhausted after the long journey down from London and the whining of Daphne, her older daughter, who did not want to leave her suitor behind for the Christmas holidays. Daphne's complaints had begun moments after they had left their home on Bedford Square and had not eased through all the long miles west into Cornwall. To make matters worse, her younger daughter, Leah, had spent this final day of their journey suffering from an appalling case of carriage-sickness after eating too much dessert at supper the previous night. Then, she had to contend with her son, Isaac, who never missed a chance to needle both his sisters, even when one was as sick as a cat. The final straw was when Neville, her husband, fled to

7

the box ostensibly to assist the coachee on the last day's long hours of driving. However, Priscilla knew Neville had been desperate to escape the bickering, complaining, and threats of being ill in the carriage.

If he had stayed inside, she might have escaped to the box herself. She loved her children, but after so many days, she was tired of their company.

"Mama," complained Leah, "how much farther do we need to go?"

"Not much." She leaned her younger daughter's head against her shoulder as the carriage lurched. "See? We are beginning the descent toward Shadows Fall."

Isaac lifted the curtain on the window, even though he could not see anything through the night. Clouds had evolved into mist before midday, slowing their journey west. The chill gnawed into Priscilla's bones, warning that the upcoming winter might be as harsh as the previous ones.

"Put that down," Daphne cried. "Do you want to freeze us to death?"

He did, but grinned at her. "You know, Mama always did warn you that if you kept making such silly expressions, your face might freeze that way. My dear, dear, dearest Burke," he said, imitating Daphne's words and tone perfectly, "would run in the other direction if he saw his dear, dear, dearest Daphne now!"

"Mama!"

Priscilla sighed, not surprised that her son continued to tease his sister about her infatuation and preoccupation with Lord Witherspoon. The young marquess had been calling on Daphne for almost two years. She had been enamored with him from the beginning, but had come to understand that neither her mother nor her stepfather would allow her to become betrothed when she was only sixteen. With every passing day, Daphne became less subtle in her hints that her suitor was eager to offer marriage. Her hope that he would propose for Christmas had been dashed when Neville announced that they would spend the Yuletide in Cornwall.

Before Priscilla could chide them both and remind them that during the holiday season they should set aside their hoaxing and annoyance, the small door on the top of the carriage opened.

"Hold tight," Neville said in a deep voice. "We are watching for patches of ice."

"We will," Priscilla called back just before the door swung shut again. She wrapped her arms around her two younger children and motioned for Daphne to brace her feet against the floor, so she would not be thrown if the carriage took a strong lurch to the side.

No one spoke, and Priscilla held her breath as the carriage continued down the steep hill. At least the house and its extensive gardens were between them and the cliffs that dropped sharply into the sea. Then, the carriage's floor grew level as they slowed.

"We made it!" shouted Isaac when the vehicle came to a complete stop.

"Never any doubt," Neville said as he opened the door to Priscilla's left. "Are you ready to see the house now that the repairs are done?"

Priscilla smiled as he handed her out, then turned to assist her daughters. She found it difficult *not* to smile when Neville was nearby. In the year and a half since their wedding, her love for him had only grown. Her late husband, Lazarus, had counted Neville as one of his best friends, and she was sure that he would have approved of their marriage. Neville's handsome, chiseled features still made her heart beat a bit faster, and the twinkle in his eyes, often as mischievous as her son's, delighted her.

"It's cold," Leah said. "Let's get inside."

"Go, go, go!" urged Neville with a chuckle. He offered his arm to Priscilla. "Just watch out for the ice."

"There isn't any ice!" Isaac had already rushed to the door and then back to them.

"Imagine that." Neville gave a wink that Priscilla could see in the faint light from lamps hanging by the front door.

As Isaac ran to the door again, she asked, "Was there any on the road?"

"That road can be dangerous in this weather. Mists off the sea and cool air ice it up quickly."

"But this evening? Did you see any ice this evening?"

"Not exactly, but the warning served its purpose."

"By frightening us?"

He gave her an innocent expression that did not seem to suit him. "I thought your ears might need a rest, and it sounded much quieter inside the carriage."

"Is that guilt from abandoning us to ride outside?"

"Where I could keep out an eye for ice that could endanger everyone in the carriage?"

Priscilla laughed. Getting a straight answer out of him at a time like this was impossible, but she had to appreciate his concern for her, even if he had an unorthodox way of showing it.

"Ah, Neville, you are always thinking of others, aren't you?" she asked.

"No, but I am always thinking of *you,* Pris."

She linked her arm with his and walked toward where the children waited by the front door. Her happiness wavered when the door remained closed. During their most recent visit, she had urged the butler and house-keeper to engage more staff. The repairs to the house, a multi-year project, should have been finished a few weeks ago. That had allowed plenty of time to make sure one of the footmen was always at the front door which should be opened whenever a carriage stopped in front of the house.

"Odd," murmured Neville, who seldom showed any distress. Even so, she felt his arm tense. He had held down many positions before he inherited his family's somewhat blemished title, including serving as a boy in a great house like Shadows Fall.

Or so she thought, because Neville, though unashamed of his past that also included stints in the theater and as a professional gambler, preferred not to speak of his life before he met Reverend Mr. Lazarus Flanders and began on the path to becoming the man he was now.

He reached past the children and opened the door. Inside, the circular entry hall was dimly lit. She thought she heard him mutter about incompetence, but had no chance to ask.

Shouts erupted around them. A hand grasped Priscilla's arm, spinning her away from Neville. Shrieks came from her daughters, and she heard Isaac yell a word that even Neville would not speak in her presence.

Her children! She must protect her children! Neville would try, but she knew him too well. He would be in the middle of the attack, fighting with every skill he had honed during his years of rough living.

An arm wrapped around her middle. She was hoisted from her feet. She swung back her right one. Hard. The arm loosened from her waist as a groan rumbled from her erstwhile captor. That told her exactly where he stood. She drew back her arm and drove her fist into the surprisingly lush and soft flesh of the man's gut.

All around her, the sound of scuffling was loud in the space that reached several stories up toward the roof. She called for her children.

Suddenly, the entry hall was flooded with light. From the stairs, Stoddard bellowed. The butler, who had begun his service at Shadows Fall before he was ten years old, could rattle the very stones of the estate with his shout for Keel, one of the footmen. He held one lamp on the stairs. Coming from deeper in the house, the housekeeper, Mrs. Crosby, appeared with another lantern. Keel, a lanky young man in a footman's livery followed her and glanced warily at the butler.

Priscilla looked around in astonishment. Her son sat on a man who was sprawled on the floor while Neville had her daughters pushed behind him, his fists threatening a man who cowered with his arms over his head. Two women had their hands pressed over their mouths. Not a hint of color brightened either face.

Then, one gave a cry and rushed to the man

13

lying senseless with Isaac on his chest. Priscilla rushed over and plucked her son off the man.

A moan came from where she had been standing moments before.

"Oh, my!" Priscilla stared at the man on his knees in the middle of the entry hall.

His hands were clamped over his belly, and he looked as if he was about to cast up his accounts. Pricilla had seen enough sickness already that day with Leah.

Then she heard a laugh.

Neville!

She whirled to see him bent forward, his hands on the thighs of his black breeches, as he surrendered to laughter.

"What is so funny?" she demanded. "If this is your idea of a jest, Neville —"

He straightened. "Not mine, but I daresay it was someone's." He looked around the entry hall as the man came to, mumbling obscenities. "I may have forgotten to mention that a few friends had discussed celebrating my elevation to the peerage."

Only a few weeks before, Neville had been awarded a baronage by the Prince Regent, for reasons neither man had disclosed. The one-time Sir Neville Hathaway had become Neville, Lord Hathaway, and the lands belonging to this estate had become part of his baronage along with some property in the Lake District far to the north.

14

"Forgot to mention?" Priscilla scowled as the man on his knees pushed himself to his feet. "Do not try to lather me with such tales, Neville Hathaway! I know you too well, and I know you never forget anything of import."

"Especially when it has to do with celebrating," called the man who had just stood. She was not surprised to hear his German accent. Neville had friends from apparently everywhere and at every level of society.

The man beside the German nudged him in the side with an elbow, and the German's face became a sallow green that warned he was again struggling not to be ill.

Priscilla looked hastily away, so quickly that she caught the hint of a smile on Mrs. Crosby's usually staid face. It was masked so fast that Priscilla wondered if she had actually seen the housekeeper smile.

"Honestly, as sure as my name is Neville Hathaway, I truly forgot to mention there might be guests awaiting us."

"Lying in wait would be more accurate." She put her arms around her daughters who were staring wide-eyed at the strangers.

"Forgive us, my lady," said the man with the German accent. "I fear our enthusiastic greeting was mistaken for something more sinister."

"Shall we leave this discussion until everyone is settled?" Neville asked coolly.

"Don't think that I shall *forget.*" Priscilla

was curious why he had failed to mention that he had asked others to Shadows Fall. She had assumed they would have a quiet Christmas week *en famille.*

"I shan't, Pris." He winked at her as he turned to give instruction to Stoddard and Mrs. Crosby, the housekeeper, who had watched the antics with their usual aplomb. "But first, introductions . . ." He gestured toward the German man. "Allow me to introduce *Graf* Jakob von Zell."

Priscilla hoped her face was not bright with a blush as she greeted the *Graf,* which she knew was a title equal to that of an English earl. Realizing that, the fact that she had struck him like an unmannered street urchin was horrifying. Yet, he had grabbed her as if she were a doxy plying her trade on the street.

"Von Zell, my wife Priscilla, Lady Hathaway."

He clicked the heels of his brightly shined boots together and bowed. *"Es ist mir eine Freude, Sie zu treffen, meine Dame."*

She knew enough German to guess that he was expressing his pleasure in meeting her. "*Graf* von Zell, I must ask you to forgive me for striking you."

"Nonsense! I have come to see that English women possess a courage that is exemplary." His accent was not so strong that she had trouble understanding him. "Perhaps if our own women were so strong, Napoleon would

16

not have overrun the Black Forest and claimed it for his own."

"But that region no longer is considered a part of the French Empire." She looked to Neville for confirmation, hoping that the tide had not turned again on the Continent and the French emperor had regained control of the lands along the Rhine.

"And, Pris," Neville continued with a quick frown that let her know he did not wish to speak of the war now, "allow me to introduce Vicomte Antoine de Romilly and his lovely wife Eveline along with their son, Jean-Paul, and beautiful daughter, Lisette."

"Welcome to our home," she said.

"Thank you, madame," the vicomte said in a charming French accent that instantly identified him as having been born and raised not far from Paris.

As his daughter, who was probably around Isaac's age, giggled, he turned to the tall and thin couple who stood beside the French family. Puzzled, he added, "And I am unsure who . . ."

"Forgive me," the *Graf* hurried to say. "May I introduce my friends Herr and Frau Bernard Tolbert, who hail from distant Montreal in Canada. I hope it is no problem that my dear, dear friends asked if they might travel here with me." He turned toward Priscilla.

"You have nothing to ask forgiveness for." She shot a scowl at Neville, but it was futile.

He simply grinned more widely as he spoke with the vicomte and his family.

Mr. Tolbert, a handsome, dark-haired man, offered a courtly bow in her direction. His nasal French accent was quite different from the vicomte's. "It is a pleasure to meet you. We are amazed by your estate in such a wild place."

"And that says a lot coming from a man from Montreal," the *Graf* said with a chuckle.

As she greeted her unexpected guests, Priscilla tried to commit each name to memory. It would be intolerable if, as their hostess, she forgot their names. She drew her children forward so they could be introduced. A sharp glance at Isaac wiped the grin from his face. Later, she would speak to him about how foolish she had been when she struck the *Graf* and that laughing about it would be impolite. Not that *she* felt like laughing. Treating a noble in such a manner was unconscionable, but, as she watched her children politely speak with their guests, she knew she would do the same in a heartbeat to protect them. Still, she needed some time to regain her own composure.

It might be simpler if she could understand why these people had gathered at Shadows Fall during the fortnight before Christmas. Had they truly journeyed through the snow and cold simply to toast Neville on being raised to the rank of baron? She was curious why they had not waited until Neville took his seat in the House of Lords at the beginning of the new year.

Neville edged around their guests to stand by her side. "Pris, you look as guilty as a knight of the pad ready to face the hangman. To own the truth, you look far guiltier, for no highwayman worth his salt would show any expression other than innocence."

"I am not accustomed to welcoming guests by striking them in the stomach." She appreciated his efforts to ease her embarrassment, but it was to no avail.

"It is, in the case of *Graf* von Zell," Neville said in a falsely officious tone, "a target that would be difficult to miss."

She bit her lip before a laugh burst forth. Trust Neville to focus on the most outrageous fact!

All her yearning to laugh vanished when a whoosh of cold air announced the door opening again and she heard a sharp, but instantly familiar voice ask, "What is this muddle?"

She recognized it instantly. Whirling, she gasped, "Aunt Cordelia!"

CHAPTER TWO

Cordelia Emberley Smith Gray Dexter McAndrews frowned as her gaze swept the entry hall, and her scowl deepened when she met Neville's cool smile. His hope that her marriage to his good friend, Duncan McAndrews, would mellow the old tough had been dashed over and over, but each time Pris's aunt made an appearance, he dared to believe that she would change. Duncan was no dour Scot, and he enjoyed a good laugh and an excellent dram. Why couldn't he have been a better influence on his exacting wife?

He looked past Pris's aunt, but the doorway was empty. "Where is Duncan?"

"He wished to spend the Yuletide with his family," replied Aunt Cordelia. "I wished to spend time with mine, so that is what we have done."

He leaned over to give her a kiss on the cheek because he knew that, despite her sharp words which were usually aimed in his direction, she appreciated a welcome from *all*

20

members of her family. When he married Pris, her family had come along with her as part of the "for better or worse." Her children were the better. Her aunt's sharp tongue was the worse.

As introductions were made and baggage brought in to be taken to the family's rooms, Neville was relieved when his guests offered to delay their tea until their hosts were able to join them. Pris led them all up the stairs as if nothing out of the ordinary had happened. Her aplomb would be envied by an ambassador, and a few words to her children conveyed her determination not to let her aunt discover what had occurred upon their arrival.

Neville was not surprised that she had a maid show Aunt Cordelia to her rooms before steering the children up the stairs to where they would sleep. No one would dare call it the nursery. Daphne was still in a miff at the idea that *she* would be consigned to the children's region of the house.

Pris's foresight in getting her aunt settled proved invaluable when Isaac demanded that his mother show him how she had taken the *Graf* to his knees with a single blow. She quieted him by acting as if she had not heard his question. Leaving the children to clean themselves up from the journey, she told Leah that she need not join everyone if she still felt ill.

21

"I am fine, Mama!" Leah replied, appearing shocked that Pris would even suggest such a thing.

Pris nodded, but had a pensive expression when she walked back down the stairs with Neville. He asked her what was amiss. She glanced up toward the door leading to the rooms they must never call the nursery and put her finger to her lips.

He tamped down his curiosity. Even so, it was difficult to keep his questions to himself until they entered the grand master suite of Shadows Fall. It was a room that was both medieval and contemporary at the same time. Pris had done an excellent job incorporating a few feminine elements amidst the masculine lines of thick rafters and stone floors. The tester bed had posts which were the diameter of ancient trees, and the bed-curtains were a lush dark green velvet made to keep out the winter cold. The dressing table looked delicate compared to the bed and the huge cupboards. Two chairs faced the great hearth where a fire struggled to batter back the chill.

As soon as he closed the door, Neville said, "Tell me what has you bothered, Pris."

"Leah."

"Really?" He hid his shock at the answer he had not anticipated.

"Yes. Before we arrived here, she complained endlessly of stomach cramps. Now she acts as if she never had a sick day in her whole life." Pris untied her bonnet that had somehow remained on her head during the melee in the entry hall. As she removed it and set it on the dressing table, her lush blond hair tumbled down around her shoulders, and his breath caught as it did every time when they were alone and she freed her hair from its prim knot.

She cast him as quick smile, showing she had heard his sharp intake of breath. Pris missed very little.

"Maybe she is feeling better," he said when he realized she was waiting for a response from him.

She undid the front of her spencer and frowned. "I'm puzzled by the abrupt change."

"I did notice her staring at the de Romilly boy. Do you think she is intrigued by him?"

"Knowing Leah, she might simply have been envisioning how she could prove that she could run faster or climb higher than he can." She shrugged off her coat and placed it on the back of one of the chairs. Going to the dressing table, she sat and began to wind her hair with the ease of practice into a bun at her nape. "Or maybe not. Leah is at the very age Daphne was when she started paying attention to boys as something other than annoyances."

He grimaced at their reflections in the glass. "By all that's blue, Pris, what have we ever done to deserve having two daughters who draw boys to them like bees to the honey?"

"I daresay I have no idea what *I* have done, but then I am not the one who entertains the children with outrageous stories of my adventures in the past."

He was about to retort with a teasing rejoinder when a knock was placed on the door. He called for whoever it was to enter. As he had expected, it was a maid coming to check on the fire. He suspected after seeing Stoddard dress down Keel for abandoning his position by the door that all the servants would be even more conscientious than usual. Pris greeted the girl with warmth, asking how her family fared. Other baronesses might act as if the servants were invisible, but, at heart, Pris was still a parson's wife, concerning herself with everyone whose path intersected hers.

That was one of the aspects of Pris he loved, because it had allowed her to look past the rumors of his past — some true, some exaggerated — to open her heart to him in spite of her aunt's many, oft-expressed objections to Pris marrying him. He held out his hand to her as she came to her feet. Drawing her to him, he surrendered to his craving to kiss her. His hunger for her tasty lips and her soft curves grew stronger with each passing day. When her arms curved up his back, he wished they were alone in the manor house, so they could spend the rest of the two weeks

24

leading up to Christmas curled up together in their bed.

The maid closing the door behind her as she let herself out of the room was a reminder that both he and Pris had obligations. Later, they would have time alone. She promised him that with a searing kiss, and he smiled as he walked with her out of the bedchamber. Later could not come soon enough.

As Neville led the way down the stairs to the ground floor, he heard a soft clattering against the windows on either side of the heavy door. Pris went to look out. He joined her and muttered an oath when he saw snow. In recent years, winters had been long and hard. The cold arrived sooner and remained deep into what should have been spring. It looked, if the snowflakes fluttering past the windowpanes were any sign, as if this winter would be the same.

"Are all your guests here?" she asked.

"If anyone else planned to come, they would be foolish to attempt the hill in the storm."

She shook her head at him. "Trust you not to know exactly whom you have invited."

"I didn't *invite* anyone. A few friends decided opening my house and entertaining them would be a good introduction for me to life as a peer."

"Excuse me, Neville, if I don't believe your

pose as a victim of your friends' enthusiasm."

He laughed along with her. "You know me too well."

"You still surprise me."

"I hope that will never change. It would be the definition of *ennui* if there were no surprises for us."

As if in answer to his words, a voice called from a room that opened off the entry hall. "If ye're lookin' fer me, I'm in 'ere. 'Bout time ye came to greet me."

Neville glanced at Pris. When she shrugged, clearly as unfamiliar with the voice and its low accent as he was, he walked into the parlor. The room was grand. Too grand for his taste, but he had acquiesced when Pris reminded him that he needed a place to welcome guests of higher rank than himself. If he had known that his guests would surge over them in the entry hall, he would have dug in a bit more on his discomfort with decorating the room in the gilt and white and gold satin to match the sparkling lines in the marble around the fireplace. His feet sank into the thick rug that had cost him the equivalent of a year's wages of his whole household, but he had to own that the space truly befit a baron.

His gaze alighted on a pair of legs hanging over the arm of a winged chair. Filth from the scuffed boots dropped onto the rug. That disturbed him far less than the young man's lackadaisical attitude as Neville, keeping Pris close to him, rounded the chair to face him.

"Stoddard did not alert me to the arrival of another guest," Neville said in lieu of a greeting.

"Probably coz I did not announce meself to 'im." The young man's thick accent identified him as hailing from the north of England. He looked to be in his mid-twenties, but he might be younger. The hard life of the poor aged one prematurely.

Neville folded his arms over his chest. "Need I announce to you what your eyes should show you?"

"Wot's that?"

"There is a lady present. Did you fail to take note of that?"

The young man arched a brow. "Naw."

"Then get on your feet."

"Why?" He draped an arm over the back of the chair. "No need fer all of us t'be standin' now, is there?"

Stretching out an arm, Neville caught the young man by the lapels of his road-worn coat and jerked him to his feet. The young man's fists flew toward Neville. With ease, Neville avoided them, shoving the young man away from him and Pris as if he weighed no more than a piece of fluff. The young man stumbled and almost fell on top of a low table. As he steadied himself, he started to storm toward them.

27

Pris stepped between Neville and the young man. Holding up her hands, she said, "Let us start this anew."

"After I peg 'im in the daylights," shouted the young man.

"Nobody is going to strike anyone." She glanced over her shoulder at Neville. "Nobody." Looking back at the young man, she asked in that calm tone which never failed to take the bluster out of everyone and remind them of their best manners, "Do you understand?"

Her tone worked yet again, astounding Neville who knew he could never copy it. The young man still scowled, but he nodded reluctantly.

"Good," she said. "Shall we start with introductions?"

Stepping around her, Neville said, "I am Lord Hathaway. You are . . . ?"

"Jamie Hathaway."

"Hathaway?" Neville reappraised the young man. In spite of the black hair needing a good wash and his worn clothes which should be tossed into the rag bag, he could see something of his less-than-illustrious family in the young man's face. The raw features and the determination in his eyes, perhaps, or maybe the expression that Shakespeare had described so well as *a lean and hungry look*. The bard had gone on to have Julius Caesar add: *He thinks too much; such men are dangerous.*

28

If this young man presented any danger to Neville's family, he would quickly find himself on the far side of the front door, snow or not. "I have never heard of a James Hathaway."

The young man grinned, revealing two missing teeth on the right side of his mouth. Neville wondered if he had lost them through disease or in a fight. Reaching under his coat, he pulled out a wrinkled piece of paper. "Guess not, but I'm yer closest male relative, m'lord."

Taking the page, Neville opened it to find it was a letter from a solicitor. In the over-flowery language that Neville despised, the solicitor took line after line to explain what the young pup had said with a handful of words. He handed the letter to Pris to read.

He clasped his hands behind his back and affixed young Hathaway with the expression-less countenance that had served him well in other bizarre circumstances. He had known there must be someone in England or else-where in the world who was his closest male relative, but he had not given the matter any thought since he married Pris. His assump-tion that his heir would be the son she gave him had come to naught when she had not become pregnant.

So far, he reminded himself. She had given Lazarus three healthy and intelligent children.

He pushed those thoughts aside. He and Pris had years yet to have a child they shared.

"I must say," he said, "I am no more surprised to see you here than I was to see the family's representative who came to inform me that I was now the baronet."

"But ye're a baron, aren't ye? So I get to be a fancy m'lord one of these days. Right?"

"You clearly have had a long journey to get to Shadows Fall." Priscilla's gentle voice halted Jamie Hathaway from saying more. As if unknown relatives dropped in on them every day and spoke so casually of assuming the title once Neville was dead, she continued, "I shall have Mrs. Crosby ready the green guest room for Mr. Hathaway's use." Looking at young Hathaway, she added, "I assume you wish us to continue to address you so."

The young man blinked, clearly shocked by her genteel words.

"Or would you prefer for us to call you Jamie?" she continued when she received no answer.

"I guess ye should. It's what I'm used to, ma'am."

"My lady," Neville corrected in the same quiet tone Pris used.

"So this be yer lawful blanket," Jamie said, his grin returning.

"Yes," Neville said. "She is my *wife.*"

"Those her kids I saw out in the hallway when I came in? A boy and a girl?"

"I suspect you saw guests of the household.

Lady Hathaway is the mother of three children, two daughters and a son."

A puzzled frown ripped away his bravado to reveal an uncertain young man behind it. "Then why am I your heir?"

"You are my heir — for the time being — because Daphne, Leah, and Isaac are the children of Lady Hathaway and her late husband."

"No bantlings of your own?"

"We are recently wed."

Jamie waved his hand. "Babies don't come solely from marriage beds."

"Heirs do. For now, you are my heir presumptive."

"What side of the blanket a babe is born on doesn't matter so much, not where I grew up."

"The coast of Northumberland, I would wager."

"How did ye know that?"

Pris smiled. "Lord Hathaway has an acutely keen ear after years of learning dialects on the stage."

"Ye were a spoutin' chap in the theater?" Jamie looked from him to Pris and back as if he waited for them to laugh at his gullibility for swallowing such a tale.

"Among other things." Neville motioned toward the door where a very subdued Keel waited to escort their newest guest to his room. "Someone will come to show you the way down for supper, but if you want something to eat in the meantime, let Keel know and a tray will be brought to you."

"Lor'," Jamie breathed, clearly overwhelmed by the change in how he would live, at least until after Epiphany.

Neville knew that Pris would never toss the young fool out before the holidays were past. Family connections, no matter how thin — and Jamie's were so thin they were almost see-through — were sacred to her.

Once Jamie was led away by the footman, Neville turned to Pris.

She did not wait for him to speak. "His grin tells me he is being honest." She ran her fingers along the back of the chair. "It reminds me of yours. A bit naughty and a lot of wisdom about things that a peer should have no knowledge of."

"And more than a bit rough around the edges."

"I daresay you were once the same."

He held out his hand to her. As she took it, he said, "How kind of you not to point out that I still have a few rough edges."

"I shall leave such appraisals to Aunt Cordelia."

With a groan, he said, "Spare me her tuition into what I need to know as a peer."

"I would if I could."

Before he could respond to her heartfelt words, he heard, "Ah, here you are."

32

Vicomte de Romilly stood in the doorway until Neville motioned him to enter. The Frenchman was the epitome of refinement and proper manners. Neville doubted if even Aunt Cordelia could find fault with how de Romilly bowed over Pris's hand.

"What can we do for you, de Romilly?" Neville asked as Pris gave him the folded sheet. He secured it under his coat, then added, "I am sorry for the delay. We were on our way to join you for tea."

"I must speak to you first. Alone." As he straightened, his eyes were wild with unrestrained emotions.

"If you will excuse me," Pris began.

"No, my lady. Stay. You are our hostess, and you should know of this threat, too."

"Threat?" Neville asked, his voice dropping to a growl. "Hasn't there been enough foolishness for the day?"

"I do not speak of what happened in your entry hall." He wrung his hands together. "I need your help, Hathaway. Someone is trying to kill me."

CHAPTER THREE

Priscilla put her hand on the vicomte's arm and drew him to sit on the closest chair. When she heard the thump of the door closing, she glanced at where Neville had been standing. The door reopened, and he came back in.

He mouthed a single word. "Stoddard."

She nodded as she sat facing their guest. The butler would keep anyone from getting close enough to the door to eavesdrop. She assumed Keel had been given the task of escorting Jamie Hathaway to his room.

She bit her lip, hoping Jamie was not involved somehow in the threats against the vicomte. The young man's arrival might not be simply coincidental. Jamie had not explained how he knew Neville was in Cornwall. That was something they needed to discover as soon as possible because she had learned that coincidences were seldom what they appeared to be.

"Now," Neville said as he drew her down

to sit beside on him on a white satin settee, "start at the beginning, de Romilly, and explain why you think someone here is trying to kill you."

"Not here." The vicomte's voice shook like a twig in a high wind. "In London. That is why we had to leave posthaste."

"And I thought you were here to celebrate me being elevated to a baron."

"Neville," Priscilla warned in barely more than a whisper. One look at the vicomte was enough for her to accept that he believed what he was saying. "You made a request of our guest. Allow him a chance to answer."

"Thank you, my lady," the vicomte said. "*Mais oui,* I came here to celebrate with you, Hathaway, but I also knew it was imperative to get my wife and family out of London where I am being stalked. Coming here seemed as good a place as any, because it is almost as far as I can get from London without falling into the sea."

"So you came here where your enemy could endanger *my* wife and *my* family."

De Romilly's face grew gray. "*Mon Dieu!* I did not consider that. We will leave immediately."

"You will not." Priscilla jumped her to her feet. She put her hands on his shoulders when he started to rise. "Haven't you noticed that the weather has taken a turn for the worse? It is snowing. However, you are correct. We are close to Land's End, and nobody can come to the house unnoticed."

"Well, almost nobody . . ." Neville drawled.

She fired him a quelling frown as she sat again. Now was not the time to own that Jamie Hathaway had managed to sneak in without anyone being the wiser. The Hathaway family seemed to live by different rules, rules backed up by the skills they gained at an early age to keep them alive.

"Why don't you tell us why you believe there is a threat?" Neville asked.

"Don't you believe me?" The vicomte sounded frantic.

"It doesn't matter what we believe. What matters are the facts."

Priscilla was about to frown again at Neville because of his unsympathetic tone, but halted when the Frenchman squared his shoulders, clearly pricked by Neville's sharp words.

The vicomte's voice became steadier. "You know that I believe France exchanged one tyrant for another when we allowed Napoleon to replace King Louis."

Neville nodded. "You confided that in me more than two years ago."

"I thought my opinions were known only to the few I could trust. I have not told my children, because they might slip and reveal the truth."

"But you think someone you don't trust has learned of your leanings."

36

"Yes."

Priscilla said, "You live in England. You are amongst those who despise Napoleon as much as you do." She glanced at Neville. "For the most part." She knew there were some crazed people who believed the blasted Corsican had been vilified by the British government and should be allowed to make all of Europe a part of his empire as long as he left the British Isles alone.

"I don't worry about the English," Vicomte de Romilly said. "I believe the threat is coming from the *émigré* community. When my parents and other aristocrats fled the guillotine with their families, there were a few who held onto the dream of returning in glory to France."

"But they could have gone back any time after the Revolutionary government had been pushed aside by Napoleon," Neville said, leaning forward with his elbows on his knees.

"They also want their lands and titles back."

Neville gave an ungracious snort. "All they need to do is offer to fill Napoleon's coffers or flatter him in some new way, and they could have all they wished."

"Or rid him of his enemies," Priscilla said softly.

The vicomte looked at her with new respect. "Quite so, my lady. Those desperate enough to regain their hereditary titles and estates will agree to any task to gain the

37

emperor's favor on their petitions."

"Fortunately, you and your family are the sole members of the French aristocracy here," Neville said. "I will speak to Stoddard about making sure that your family's rooms are subtly guarded night and day."

"Subtly?"

"I think it would be for the best if your enemies were unaware that we are watching for them."

When she saw the Frenchman about to argue further, Priscilla said, "Please listen to Neville. He has handled similar situations before with great success, Vicomte de Romilly."

"Please call me Antoine, my lady," he said, standing so he could incline his head toward her. "When I have come on my knees to plead for your assistance, it seems silly to have you address me by my title."

"I agree, if you will call me Priscilla."

He bowed in her direction. "I am honored . . . Priscilla."

Neville rolled his eyes as he set himself on his feet. "Now that we are all the best of friends, I must ask that you give me some time to consider what to do." He waved the vicomte to silence. "Nobody is coming to Shadows Fall until the snow passes. If the one threatening you is underneath this roof already, the storm will delay their plans. They would want to be able to make a quick escape if they were successful. That gives us time to consider our plans, so you and your family remain safe for the time being."

"*Oui,* that is sensible."

"If you would be so kind as to tell the others that we have been delayed and will be with them shortly . . ."

"*Oui,*" Antoine said again before walking to the door, opening it, and shutting it behind him.

"He believes what he is saying," Priscilla said into the silence that settled in the vicomte's wake.

"Yes."

"Do you believe there is a real threat?"

"Unfortunately, yes. We both have seen that not all the battles in this war against Napoleon are fought on a battlefield."

Priscilla stood and went to the window that offered her a view of the sea. Its gray waves were almost lost in the storm. Without turning, she said, "The household here will have good intentions about protecting the de Romilly family, but what if someone slips in as Jamie did? We need help."

"True, but who would you ask, Pris?" As she faced him, he said, "We are not in London or even your quiet cottage in Stonehall-on-Sea, where the charleys and the constables are eager to keep the peace. Through the years in this part of Cornwall, the constables have made it their goal never to step outside of a public house while ale is available. Otherwise, they might be called upon to do their duty. Only a beef-head would chance having to bring either smugglers or wreckers to justice when both have powerful allies among the gentry and the peerage."

"What about the justice of the peace?"

He shook his head. "I already checked with Stoddard when I went out to ask for a guard on the door. Apparently, the justice of the peace is enjoying the holiday with family in Plymouth."

"So we are on our own?"

"It would seem so." He put his arms around her and drew her closer. "Be honest, Pris. Do you want to take the children and return to London?"

"A slow, cold trip when the roads are covered with snow."

"But, most likely, less dangerous than staying here."

She rested her cheek against his shoulder. "One thing I have learned since you came back into our lives, Neville, is that danger has a way of following us wherever we go. If we leave, we must make sure the others all have a way to return to Town. I would rather be here with our familiar and faithful servants than in an inn with strangers who might have among them a possible murderer."

"I would prefer that you stay so I know you are safe, but I would not stand in your way if

40

you wish to go."

"I know." She edged away from him and wrapped her arms around herself as the chill beyond the walls settled in her center.

"Is something else amiss, Pris? You seem distracted."

"I am," she said without thinking.

"Why?"

She did not hesitate. With his clear insight, Neville would know instantly that if she devised some half-truth to avoid speaking the whole truth. With a smile she hoped did not look forced, she said, "Neville, our simple family holiday has turned into an international assembly. Even without that, between your family and mine, it is not going to be a peaceful Christmas."

"How long do you think we can keep Jamie and your aunt from meeting?"

Her laugh was genuine. "Not long enough."

"Does it bother you, too, Pris, that Jamie has arrived at the very time when a friend comes to tell me that he and his family are being threatened?"

"Yes. I thought of that as soon as Antoine appeared. You know I don't believe in coincidences."

"Except for the fact that sometimes they exist."

"I know, and I find that inconvenient when we are trying to solve a puzzle."

"Dashed inconvenient."

She glanced toward the closed door. "We must join our guests. If not, they will come looking for us, eager to find out what is wrong."

"True. We don't need to create panic among them. I don't know the *Graf* well, because he is a friend of the de Romillys'."

"And you don't know the Tolberts at all."

"Not yet, but I intend to learn as much as I can as soon as possible."

"And as politely as possible." She smiled.

He chuckled. "For you, Pris, I vow I will do so as politely as possible." He wrapped his arm around her waist and drew her into his embrace.

She offered her lips for his kiss. Even when he was distracted with a mystery, as he was now, he still kissed her thoroughly. Combing her fingers up through his dark hair, she leaned into his mouth. She savored the sweet flavor of his lips and the strong, enticing caress of his hands as they slid up her back.

Too soon he released her. He gave her an apologetic smile, and she nodded. They would find time alone soon. She promised herself that.

"I will let you know what I discover," he said, his fingers lingering on her face.

"Go ahead, Neville. I need to speak with Mrs. Crosby about keeping a close eye on the children. With Aunt Cordelia busy with our other guests, I can talk to our housekeeper without my aunt overhearing."

She thought he might protest that they needed to stay together, but he only nodded and gave her a quick kiss on the cheek. She smiled weakly when he told her to hurry to where the tea must have already been served, but that smile vanished the moment he closed the door.

She sank to the chair where Antoine had sat only moments ago. Staring into the roaring fire, she realized that she never had imagined that she would find it difficult to speak to Neville about anything. He was blunt about his past, and he readily acknowledged and accepted that he shared her heart with her late husband. He offered his opinions when she had to scold the children, and he acted the part of the protective father whenever Daphne waxed poetic about her beloved Burke Witherspoon. They had solved many crimes together, encountering some of the lowest aspects of humanity.

So why did she find it impossible to ask if he was disappointed that she had not become taken with a child of their own?

CHAPTER FOUR

Twelve Days 'Til Christmas

"What is that?" Aunt Cordelia put every bit of her outrage into those three words.

And, for once, Priscilla understood her aunt's shock. She stared at the snow melting off an evergreen tree in the middle of the stone floor. She could not imagine why the *Graf* had brought it indoors. When he leaned it against one wall of the solar where she had gathered their guests for some quiet conversation, she saw it had been cut just below the lowest branches.

Overnight, the snow had piled up several inches outside. A chill clung to the house even though every hearth held a roaring fire. The family and their guests had spent the morning and the hours after luncheon sitting as close as they dared to a fireplace. Even Aunt Cordelia, who always was concerned with her appearance, had pushed aside the screen so the heat could reach her.

Neville and a couple of the servants had

been busy outside during the morning hours, but had retreated back inside when the day did not grow any warmer. He had, she knew, been checking for any signs of intruders. He might have been setting up warning signals or traps, because he had talked about both last night when they were in the privacy of their rooms, but she had not had a chance to speak with him since he returned just before the midday meal.

Graf von Zell walked into the solar. He shrugged off his greatcoat, sending snow in every direction. He bowed toward Aunt Cordelia, then swept out his hand as if he were about to announce the king's arrival.

Instead, he answered Aunt Cordelia's question. "This is, *Frau* McAndrews, a *Tannenbaum.*"

Aunt Cordelia looked baffled and did not correct him on how he addressed her.

"We can see it is an evergreen tree," Priscilla said, "a *Tannenbaum* as you say along the Rhine, but why have you brought it indoors?"

"Because it is a tree for Christmas."

Priscilla looked at her family, then back at the German. "But we have selected a Yule log, and it will burn far longer than a tree of this size. The branches on the Yule log have already been cut off, so the fire won't flare when burning needles and twigs. Forgive me for sounding ungrateful, *Graf,* but I am fearful of putting that tree in the fireplace."

"As I would be." His smile broadened. "But that is not the purpose of this tree. It is a *Christmas tree.*" He emphasized the words as if doing that and speaking slowly would help them understand. "Your Queen Charlotte has had evergreen trees for Christmas parties for quite a few years, or so I am told."

"We seldom are invited to royal parties," Neville said in his driest tone.

"And there are reasons we never shall be." Aunt Cordelia turned her glower from the *Graf* to Neville whose face remained placid.

Before her aunt could begin a long litany of Neville's shortcomings, real and perceived, Priscilla said, "*Graf* von Zell, if you would be so kind as to enlighten us further."

"Gladly, my lady." He bowed his head in his crisp Teutonic manner. With his wide smile, he gestured toward the hewn tree. "For more than two centuries, people in the *Schwarzwald* have brought evergreen trees into their homes for Christmas."

"*Schwarzwald?*" asked Leah softly.

"The Black Forest," Priscilla whispered as she drew her daughter down to sit on the arm of her chair.

Graf von Zell must not have noticed their murmurs because he continued to explain in excruciatingly specific detail how the residents of the regions around the upper Rhine River had started the custom by setting spruce trees up in the village centers, using them much as English children did a May-pole. They danced around it and sang and flirted. A sharp frown from Priscilla kept the *Graf* from going into further details of those flirtations and what ensued.

"In more recent times," he hurried on, "the *Tannenbaum* has been brought into the house."

"People clearly realized it was easier to dance and flirt inside where it is warm," Neville said under his breath.

Priscilla bit her lower lip to keep from laughing.

The *Graf* glanced at them, then added, "The trees are decorated with candles to remind us of the stars that shone on the night Christ was born. The candle at the very top symbolizes the special star that brought the Magi from the East."

Priscilla drew in her breath sharply as she thought of what could happen if one put candles on a dead tree with two rambunctious boys and one hoydenish girl in the house. That was not a safe combination. She had insisted on lamps, rather than simple candles, throughout Shadows Fall to prevent accidental fires.

She was about to say as much when Isaac asked, "Do you leave it by the wall like that?"

"No," the *Graf* said. "Its base is inserted in a bucket of soil so water can be added each day to keep the needles alive through Christmas and the week that follows."

"At least the whole idea is not utterly mad," Neville said with a chuckle. "I have heard of these trees, but I never have seen the sense in having a lit tree indoors."

"The *Kinder* love it, especially when gifts are placed near it or on its branches." He smiled at the children who grinned back with excitement. "That is why I have brought it to you, Lady Hathaway. I trust you will allow us to keep it indoors, so I may acquaint the *Kinder* with more of our traditions while I celebrate my homeland's freedom from that tyrant Napoleon."

Priscilla did not like being backed into a corner, and she narrowed her eyes as she stared at the German. His smile faded when she did not give him a quick response. She guessed he had been ready with a list of reasons why she should agree. He had not expected silence and a quelling glance.

"Oh, Mama, say yes," Leah pleaded. "Say that we may have a *Tannenbaum* for Christmas."

Priscilla looked at her younger daughter and smiled. "On one condition."

The *Graf* swallowed a soft groan, but hastily composed himself as he realized he had divulged too much with that single sound. He must have expected more of a battle to keep the *Tannenbaum* in the solar. She wondered if he was more disappointed, as the sound suggested, than surprised. Perhaps he had become so used to war, he had forgotten that people could work together.

"Anything, Mama!" Isaac bounced from one foot to the other in his excitement.

"You must promise that no candles will be lit unless there is an adult in the room, and that all candles must be snuffed out before the last person goes out of the room. If the tree is left alone with the candles lit for even a second, it will be removed."

"And," Neville added, "it shall not return."

The children eagerly agreed, promising to be responsible and on their best behavior while the tree was in the house.

Graf von Zell folded his arms in front of him, looking like a jolly gnome from one of the German fairy tales. Aunt Cordelia harrumphed and strode out of the solar, her heels clicking out her disgust. None of the excited children — and even Daphne was as eager as the younger ones to enjoy such a unique custom — took notice of Aunt Cordelia's exit.

Priscilla did and exchanged a glance with Neville who grimaced, then just as quickly grinned. He knew, as she did, that her aunt would not let the matter rest. She would be livid that she had not been consulted on the issue of the tree in the house and insulted that nobody had heeded her warning to have it removed immediately. Aunt Cordelia was always determined to get the last word.

The children must have realized that as well because Leah stood and motioned to her brother. "Mama, we want to go and see the Yule log. It is out behind the stables. Can we?"

"It will be coming into the house on Christmas Eve night," Priscilla said, glancing at the windows where frost had twined its colorless vines against the glass. "It is so cold outside."

"We will be quick." Isaac looked at his sister. "Won't we?"

"Very quick," Leah assured her mother.

Knowing that they were accustomed to lots of fresh air, she nodded. "As long as you are quick."

"Bundle up in your warmest clothes." Neville tweaked Leah's nose. "Especially a scarf to cover this. I was concerned mine had frozen so hard that it would melt away when I came back inside."

The children laughed. With anyone else, they would have found such teasing demeaning because it made them sound like infants. Not with Neville. Perhaps it was because they knew he teased everyone, babe or grandparent, urchin or prince, in exactly the same manner.

"Could Jean-Paul and Lisette join us?" Leah asked.

"If their parents are agreeable. I trust you

will all come in before you get frostbite."

Leah nodded, but Priscilla caught her rolling her eyes as she rushed off with her brother to retrieve their outer wraps and boots as well as the de Romilly children. With every passing day, Leah was acting more like her older sister.

Neville must have noticed that, too. He gave Priscilla a wink before he crossed the room to examine the tree that the *Graf* had brought in. Soon he was in an intense conversation about the proper size of the bucket and where they would find unfrozen dirt to pack into it to keep the tree standing upright.

When the pail and dirt were brought, the men struggled to get the evergreen tree upright. Only when Stoddard appeared with a footman and a pair of men from the stable as well as several hand-sized stones were they able to prop the tree so it stood straight.

"Beautiful," Priscilla said when the men stepped back to view their work.

"And it only took more than a half dozen of us," Neville said as he looked down at his hands that were stained with sap from the tree. He grimaced when his fingers stuck together.

Standing, Priscilla tugged the bell pull. She sent the maid who responded for warm water and soap for the men to clean their hands. The maid nodded, but looked toward the tree with a skeptical expression that suggested they all had taken a knock on the head.

A rush of footsteps came toward the solar. She turned as Leah raced into the room. She was tugging little Lisette de Romilly behind her so swiftly that the child's feet barely touched the floor.

"Mama!" she choked out. Tears were frozen to her reddened cheeks.

"What is it?" Priscilla started to bend to look her younger daughter in the eyes, then realized she did not have to any longer. When had Leah grown so tall? "What is wrong? Where are your brother and Jean-Paul?"

"Gone."

"Gone where?" asked Neville.

"Over the cliff."

CHAPTER FIVE

Neville did not hesitate. Shouting to Stoddard to send for de Romilly and Tolbert, he motioned for the footman and the stablemen to follow him, then ran toward the door that opened closest to the cliffs. Leah chased after him. He paused only long enough to shove his arms into a thick coat and his hands into gloves. The pine sap on his skin made the leather fit oddly, but he did not care.

"Show us where," he said to Leah.

He took the hand she held out to him and matched her best pace through the snow. The glacial wind tried to batter them back to the house, but he bowed his head and kept going. When Leah began to struggle, he put his arm around her shoulders and held her close so she stayed as warm as possible. He did not want to think of two young boys at the bottom of a cliff where both the wind and icy water could be battering them. Two boys who might be badly hurt or worse by the fall.

"Why were you so close to the cliffs, Leah?"

he asked as he glanced back to see the *Graf,* the vicomte, and Tolbert coming out of the house. He waved to them, motioning for them to hurry. "You know the danger. Isaac does, too. Why risk it especially when there may be ice beneath the snow?"

Shouts came from behind them. He looked over his shoulder again and saw a quartet of footmen hurrying to catch up. Each of them carried a length of rope along with a large cloth bag.

Pris! She must have sent the footmen after them along with the supplies they would need. Not only rope, but most likely bandages and other items they might have to use to save the boys. He had no doubts that she would have been running by his side if she had not felt the vicomtesse should not be left alone.

"There!" Leah's voice was almost swept away by the wind, but Neville looked at where she pointed.

It was a narrow, open strip between the top of the cliffs and an evergreen copse where von Zell probably had cut down the tree he brought into the house. Warning the others to be careful, he edged forward to where the ground had broken away. He looked over the edge and breathed a sigh of relief when he saw both boys sitting on a ledge halfway to the bottom where waves struck the stone over and over.

Jean-Paul waved up to them and shouted, "*M'aidez!* Help me! Help Isaac and me!"

Neville ordered Leah to step back among the trees where she would be out of the wind and away from the edge of the cliff. He had the footmen tie the lengths of rope together. He lashed one end around a cluster of trees. De Romilly grabbed the rope and dug his heels into the snow.

"What can I do?" asked Tolbert.

"Hold onto the rope like de Romilly is. Help him keep it taut."

Tolbert hesitated, strain crossing his face, then nodded and went to stand in front of the vicomte. He seized the rope and did not look back at the Frenchman behind him. It struck Neville as odd. Both men spoke the same language as England's enemies, but both were allied against France. And yet now, they barely looked at each other. Strange, in Neville's opinion, but he had no time to think about the situation.

"Step aside, *Graf.*" Motioning von Zell back because he was in the way and showed no sign of helping with the rope or with the supplies the footmen were unpacking, Neville made a loop with a slipknot, so it could be pulled over a boy's head and tightened around his waist.

"Be careful!" Leah pleaded as Neville inched toward where the ground had collapsed beneath the boys.

He nodded, but said nothing. He concentrated on making sure the earth would hold him before he put his weight on each step forward. When clods broke away and tumbled down, he heard the boys shout a warning to each other and to him. He dared not go any farther.

He tossed the loop over the edge, letting the rope play out through his fingers, though it was difficult given the way his gloves clung to his sticky skin. He shouted for the boys to put the rope around them, one at a time, and give a tug when it was tight around the waist.

"All set!" came back a young voice. Isaac's. Just the sound was such a relief that a grin rushed across Neville's face.

He did not allow himself time to rejoice that his son was well enough to shout. Instead, he motioned for the four footmen to take hold of the rope behind him, so they could draw each boy up slowly. They could not yank the boy up too quickly, because that risked dashing him against the rough wall of the cliff. Pulling one hand over the other and keeping the rope from rubbing the edge of the unstable cliff, Neville heard excited shouts when Jean-Paul's head rose above the cliff. Neville was not surprised that Isaac had sent the other boy up first. Pris's children had inherited their determination to put others before themselves from both her and Lazarus.

He lifted the boy onto solid ground, whipped the loop off over his head, and flung the rope back down the cliff. His respect for the vicomte rose when de Romilly warned his son to stand aside until Isaac was safe, too.

Within minutes, Neville was hugging Isaac who had suffered nothing more than a few scratches. Jean-Paul had scraped his arm from wrist to elbow, and blood stained his sleeve. Otherwise, both boys were unharmed.

"How are they?" asked Tolbert as de Romilly embraced his son. "That was quite a fall. They should be more careful."

Isaac puffed up and was about to answer, but Neville put his hands on the boy's shoulders and squeezed gently. Looking back at him, Isaac was puzzled. Neville shook his head slightly. This was not the time to get into a quarrel with one of the men who had aided in the boy's rescue.

"They are surprisingly well," Neville said, smiling as if no tension crackled in the air. "Surely you remember getting into mishaps when you were a boy, Tolbert."

"I spent most of my youth helping with my family's business." His voice was still stiff and disapproving. "I had little time for antics, especially dangerous ones. Boys should be kept busy so they do not get in trouble. Children in England have too much time to play instead of working as they should to improve their families' circumstances."

Neville was unsure how long the Canadian would have gone on if de Romilly had not walked toward them. As he listened to Tolbert, something at the back of his mind fussed at him. The man's accent? It was quite different from de Romilly's, but that was to be expected considering the two men had been born and raised on opposite sides of the Atlantic. No, it was not the difference in the way the two men spoke that niggled at him. So what was it?

He still had no answer when the vicomte stepped forward to thank Tolbert and the footmen for helping him and Neville save the boys. Tolbert accepted the gratitude coolly before he launched into the same lecture he had offered to Neville and Isaac. That the vicomte was no more interested in listening than Neville had been was made obvious when de Romilly excused himself and his son. As they walked back to the house, Tolbert followed, still prattling.

"You were lucky," Neville said, ruffling Isaac's hair after the rope was untied from the tree and the footmen were on their way back to the house with his sincere thanks. "You know better than to be so close to the rim of the cliff. You could have been killed."

"We stayed away from the edge, Papa Neville," Isaac asserted, standing straight, but still more than a foot and a half shorter than Neville. "We aren't stupid."

"I didn't say you were stupid. I said you were careless."

Isaac shook his head, then winced. "We were not careless either. Listen to me! Jean-Paul started to tumble off, and I grabbed for him to try to keep him from going over. We both went over." He looked toward his sister who gave him a bolstering nod, then added, "Jean-Paul told me he was pushed."

"Pushed?" Neville stared at the two young-sters. "Do you believe him?"

"Yes," Isaac and Leah said together.

"Why? Did you see anyone?"

They looked at each other, then back at him as Leah said in a strained whisper, "I am not sure, but when I heard Jean-Paul scream and turned around, I thought I saw someone in the trees."

"Who?"

"I don't know. Someone in a dark coat. The trees are too close for me to get a better look. But there was someone there. You have to believe us."

"I do believe you." Neville said nothing more as he steered them back toward the house.

Someone in a dark coat. That could be anyone in the house or beyond it. The threat that de Romilly had sensed in London might well have followed them to Shadows Fall. If so, none of them were safe.

■ ■ ■ ■

Pulling off his boots, Neville sat back in the comfortable chair in the bedroom he shared with Priscilla. She smiled indulgently at him. The chair was hideous, looking more like a haven for mice than anything to be found in a baron's house. She was unsure where it had come from, but guessed it had been in the house when Neville first came to Cornwall and began bringing the old house back to its former glory. Maybe she should ask Stoddard. If anyone knew the truth, it would be the butler, because he had been at the house most of his life.

"You look as if you have been run over by a dray. Twice," she said with a smile as she drew the chair from her dressing table so she could sit beside him.

"To own the truth, Pris, I would rather have that happen than face our houseguests again." He rested his head on the back of the chair and closed his eyes.

"You invited them."

"No, *I* invited de Romilly and his family. The *Graf* was standing nearby when I spoke with de Romilly and considered himself invited as well, and he brought the Tolberts with him." He opened one eye. "However, you invited your aunt here."

"You know you enjoy trading words with

Aunt Cordelia." She laughed, but the sound had a caustic edge. "And she, like most of our guests, invited herself."

"If this is the fate of a baron, I need to find a way to get rid of this title."

Slapping his arm, she said, "That is as unlikely as you and Aunt Cordelia calling a truce. You are far too proud of your new title and new life."

"Which feels too much, at the moment, like my old life." He sighed as he locked his fingers together under his head. "I should have known that a whole year could not pass without someone in this family having a brush with death."

"Thank heavens the boys fell where they did. If they had not been able to grab onto that ledge to save themselves . . ." She shuddered and pressed her hands to her face.

Losing someone else she loved was too painful even to consider. It had been almost four years since Lazarus died, and she could not forget the seemingly endless tunnel of pain she had been lost within for months. Only her children had kept her from wandering endlessly in her grief.

And then Neville had come back into her life, bringing her back to looking forward to every day instead of dreading getting out of bed each morning. He had restarted the part of her heart that she had been sure would never beat again after Lazarus's funeral.

Fingers, so much broader than her own, drew her palms away from her eyes that burned with tears that she had refused to shed while among the others. Without a word, he brought her to her feet and settled her on his lap. She turned her face into his shoulder and breathed in the scent of him. She loved him so much, because he had never let her down. Not once. She desperately wanted to say the same about herself, but if she could not give him the son he needed, she would have to admit that she had failed him in that vital matter.

No, she would not think of that. Not now. Not when Isaac and Jean-Paul could have been killed today.

As if he could hear her thoughts he said, "The children are united in their belief that someone pushed Jean-Paul. A man in a black coat is the only description Leah could give me."

Shifting so she could meet his eyes, she whispered, "The children are always truthful, unless they think they can elude trouble by embroidering their story. They would not tell an out-and-outer about something like this."

"Then we have to believe that a man tried to push de Romilly's son to his death."

"I don't want to think that is possible either."

He ran his finger from her cheek to her chin before tipping her lips toward him. "If you want to know the truth, Pris . . ."

"I do!"

"The truth is that I don't want to think of anything right now other than *this.*"

She told him her agreement with her lips against his.

Eleven Days 'Til Christmas

When she invited the women and the children to help her prepare boxes to be delivered to the poor on Boxing Day, Priscilla was not the only one pleased to have something to do now that the snow was finally starting to let up. She had played so many hands of whist in the last two days that she cringed at the idea of enduring another.

Getting the boxes ready also kept their guests from wondering why burly men from the stables and the grounds were seen often in the house. If the guests were curious, they kept those questions to themselves. She was grateful that eccentric reputation and secretive past could give them an excuse if anyone asked. But no one did, not even Aunt Cordelia.

So they continued on as if the incident on the cliffs was no more than two young boys being careless. She felt oddly divided in her roles as gracious hostess as well as that of protector, keeping a close eye on the de Romilly family and her own. When she had gotten the idea to pack the Boxing Day boxes earlier than usual, she had hoped it would lighten her mood as well as entertain her guests.

It had been an unqualified success. Even Isaac and Jean-Paul, who wrestled and ran about whenever she or the vicomtesse took their eyes off them, were enthusiastic about packing boxes. The spirit of competition between them was properly funneled into which one could carry the most boxes into the stillroom where they would be stored until they were distributed.

That was, if the snow held off long enough for the wooden boxes to be taken to the parish church.

"Does it always snow like this in Cornwall?" asked Eveline, the vicomtesse. "I had been led to believe the winter weather here was more like the southwest of France. Cool, but not cold."

"As had I," snapped Aunt Cordelia. "Another clanker told to us by *that* man."

Eveline stared in bafflement at Aunt Cordelia, but Priscilla knew exactly to whom her aunt referred. Aunt Cordelia had taken it as a personal insult when Neville was raised to the peerage. It was, she was fond of saying whenever Priscilla was near, just another sign that the Prince Regent was as insane as his father.

Determined to keep the discussion on safe topics, Priscilla smiled at Mrs. Tolbert. "I suppose this is nothing new to you. After all, I have heard stories of how frigid a Canadian winter can be."

"We know how to dress properly when we go out-of-doors." The tall, slender lady added nothing more.

Aunt Cordelia hated silence, so she began to talk about how the family had prepared Boxing Day boxes when she was a girl. Priscilla was glad — for once — at how her aunt could take control of a conversation and steer it to where she wanted it to go.

"Mama!" said Leah, intruding into Priscilla's thoughts. "Did you hear what I said?"

Priscilla turned to her younger daughter and smiled as she put her arm around her daughter's slender shoulders. "You mentioned something about Jean-Paul."

"Yes!" She slipped out from under Priscilla's arm, then tugged on her mother's other one.

Unsure what Leah wanted, Priscilla went with her toward the kitchen stairs where they could speak without anyone overhearing them. "Is something amiss? I know you and Isaac were worried you wouldn't have anyone your own age at Shadows Fall, so the surprise visit has turned out quite well."

"But Jean-Paul is worried."

"Worried?" She held her breath as she waited for her daughter's answer.

"Jean-Paul is fearful that someone intends

to hurt his papa or *maman.*" Leah's trusting eyes rose toward her. "You won't let that happen, will you? You and Papa Neville will watch out for all of us, won't you?"

With gentle hands, Priscilla framed her daughter's face. "You know that Neville and I always do our best to make sure that good people are protected from bad ones."

That seemed to satisfy her daughter, or maybe it was simply that Leah's attention was caught by her brother announcing that he had filled two more boxes. Jean-Paul grinned a challenge before he picked up two wooden crates and headed with care toward the stillroom with them. Isaac grumbled something, then lifted the two boxes he had packed. The top one wobbled, but he managed to steady it without putting the boxes down. He followed Jean-Paul, each step measured.

"Isn't he amazing?" Leah's gaze was on Jean-Paul.

Priscilla silenced her groan as Leah rushed to the table, picked up another box, and hurried after the boys. Since the incident on the cliffs, Leah had made every possible excuse to stay near Jean-Paul. She had praised him to anyone who would listen . . . except Jean-Paul himself. Somehow she had convinced herself that she was the target of the man in the dark coat and that Jean-Paul had been willing to sacrifice himself for her.

"Why does young love have to be so self-deluding?" she murmured to herself.

Daphne came up beside her, bringing more clothing to sort for the boxes. With a laugh, her daughter said, "Mama, I remember overhearing you tell Uncle Neville the same thing about me not too long ago. Leah is suffering from calf-love, but it is just as precious to her as your love for Uncle Neville is to you. Or it is, until she sets her sights on another young man."

"It's not easy for a mother to watch her children grow up. Part of me is thrilled for the adventures ahead of you, but the other part of me wants to keep you as little children who cuddle on my lap."

Daphne laughed again. "I don't think you want that, really. Even Isaac is almost as tall as you now."

"Logic has nothing to do with matters of the heart."

"That is exactly what I have been trying to tell you since we came down from London. I want to be here with my family, but I want to be with Burke, too."

"I know." She did, because she had been younger than her older daughter was now when she fell in love with Lazarus. He had delayed asking her to marry him because she was an earl's daughter, and he was a parson in a country parish. It had taken her time to convince him that such matters were less important than the longings of their hearts. Fortunately, her father had acquiesced, glad to see her with a good man.

Now her daughter was in love with Lord Witherspoon, who had inherited his title as a marquess quite young. Unlike other men his age, he seemed more concerned about matters of his estate and family than in gambling and horse racing. Priscilla should be grateful that her daughter had fallen in love with such a down-to-earth young man.

And she was.

If only she could persuade herself that Daphne was of an age to marry. The Season would begin within a few months. She would see how Lord Witherspoon and Daphne got along after being separated for almost four months. Sometimes, ardent letters led to unrealistic expectations that could not be met face-to-face.

Her thoughts of her daughter's future vanished when shouts came from every direction. The women froze around the tables. Priscilla pushed past them, though it was like trying to make her way through a maze of statues. Her daughters followed her as she burst out of the door.

The icy cold clawed down her throat when she drew in a breath. Sending Daphne inside to collect their coats and gloves, she stood in the snow-covered kitchen garden and tried to decide where the shouts had originated.

Voices seemed to be coming from every direction, distorted by the wind, buildings, and stone walls.

"I think they are beyond the rose garden!" Leah cried, looking toward the left. At the same moment the door bumped into her back, nearly sending her sprawling in the snow.

Isaac and Jean-Paul rushed out, shouting questions that Priscilla did not have answers for. She held out her hands to the children. She normally would have chided her daughter when she saw Leah grab Jean-Paul's hand as well as her own. Now that was the last thing on her mind. Holding Leah's hand as well as Isaac's, she hurried them out of the kitchen garden. The children were arguing that the voices came from two different directions. She ignored them and strained to listen.

The cold wind buffeted them, but once they were out of the walled garden, she could tell the voices came from the right, closer to the stables. She rounded the corner of the house where a tower had stood before collapsing during their first visit to Shadows Fall. She saw men running with shovels toward the far end of the stables. The men must have been clearing the road to the gate.

Both Isaac and Jean-Paul pulled away and raced to join the men. Shovels were pressed into the boys' hands. They began digging at a tall pile of snow that must have fallen off the steep roof.

"Hurry!" Priscilla heard someone shout as she and Leah got closer. "If he is still alive, he needs air."

Alive? Someone was under all that snow?

"Take care," shouted Neville. "You don't want to jab him with a shovel, especially if he's hurt."

Grateful that he was not the one needing rescue, she hurried toward the massive pile of snow. No extra shovels were available, so she waited impatiently. When one of the older grooms lagged, she stepped forward and took his shovel without comment. She began lifting the heavy, wet snow from where he had been working. She paused only when Daphne offered her a coat and gloves. Handing the shovel to her daughter, she drew on her outer wear as quickly as she could and then spelled another man who was groaning with every shovelful he lifted. He pressed his hand to his lower back as he stepped away.

Nobody spoke. They worked at a fast, but not frantic rate. As her arms began to ache, someone took her shovel. She stepped back, but then rushed forward again when a triumphant shout announced that the man beneath the pile of snow had been found alive.

Running to where Neville bent toward the ground, she gasped when she saw the vicomte lying on the ground, gasping for air. Men were pulling large snow boulders off him, and she glanced up at the stable roof. What had caused the snow to slip at this spot?

She pushed her curiosity aside as two stablemen rushed forward with a broad plank. They knelt by the man.

"Don't move, de Romilly," Neville said when the vicomte tried to sit as he was lifted onto the sturdy board. "We have sent for a doctor. Mr. Prouse should be here by the time we get you inside and in your bed." He glanced across the vicomte to Priscilla with an expression she easily understood.

Gathering the younger children and Daphne, she herded them back to the kitchen as she listed the tasks that needed to be done before the doctor arrived. She sent the boys to alert the servants to have more wood brought to the vicomte's bedchamber. The girls, along with the vicomte's daughter Lisette, were given the chore of working with the kitchen staff to make warm drinks for the men who had helped with the rescue.

Priscilla tossed aside her coat and assisted Eveline out of the kitchen and to the stairs that led up to the wing with the guest bedrooms. She was pleased with the vicomtesse's calm, knowing how difficult it was to maintain her own composure so her children were not frightened more.

On the upper floor, servants rushed about their tasks. None of them met Priscilla's eyes. She hoped Eveline did not notice that, because it suggested that the vicomte's condition had taken a turn for the worse.

The door to the guest bedchamber was open, and Priscilla let Eveline enter first. The vicomtesse grasped Priscilla's hand, pulling her into the room.

Even though the room was large, it seemed cramped with more than ten people in it and the dark red draperies closed. Flames blazed on the hearth, adding to the suffocating warmth. Neville stood by the large bed along with Mr. Tolbert who watched the vicomte intently. Priscilla was astonished to see Jamie Hathaway seated in the room. Where was the *Graf* von Zell? Since their arrival, he had been at the center of any upheaval.

Priscilla released the vicomtesse's hand, staying beside Neville as Eveline moved closer to the bed. When Eveline's husband drew a deep breath and released it as if he slumbered peacefully, Priscilla closed her eyes and murmured a quick prayer of thanksgiving.

Neville gave her shoulders a gentle squeeze. She opened her eyes to look up at him. There had been too many times when she feared he would die. Each time, her prayers had been answered and he had survived. But today . . . Surely today was just a case of the vicomte being in the wrong place at the wrong time.

Right?

As if she had given voice to her uneasy

thoughts, Neville said softly, "He will be fine. The heaviest snow missed him."

"Missed?" she whispered as her stomach sank. "So you believe it was no accident."

"I don't have enough information to determine that one way or the other."

She understood what he did not want to say while others were in earshot. He was suspicious, but he needed to uncover the facts before he could accuse anyone. Later, she would find time to speak with him alone and discover how she could help. Christmas would not be easy to celebrate if they had to look constantly over their shoulders in fear.

In less time than Priscilla had expected, the doctor was being ushered into the bedchamber. Mr. Prouse was a squat man who was almost as wide as he was tall. The buttons on his stained waistcoat fought to keep it closed, and his hastily tied cravat was so loose that it flapped in front of him as he scurried like a well-fed mouse to the bed.

Eveline started to protest, but Priscilla assured her that, in spite of his appearance, Mr. Prouse was one of the most skilled doctors she had ever met. Kindly, Priscilla told everyone else to leave. As she walked out with Neville, he asked the doctor to give him a report after he finished his examination, then strode away along the hallway. She did not ask him where he was bound. She knew. He was on his way to find answers.

CHAPTER SIX

Eight Days 'Til Christmas

The daylight was fading into gray clouds that stripped the color from the land and the sea. Light came through the windows of the house, but did not reach far into the bleak, early winter twilight where random snowflakes twirled. The wind off the sea was ruthless, clawing through Neville's woolen coat. For the first time, he wondered if they should have remained in Town instead of coming to Cornwall for the Yuletide. The threat to de Romilly had become one to his own family when Isaac fell off the cliff.

Neville stood on the stable roof, balanced with care. The roof was as slick as the patches of ice by the kitchen door, so, even a day after the snow had crashed down on de Romilly, he had not been able to examine it as closely as he would have liked. But he had seen enough.

"How long do you intend to remain out

here?" Priscilla called from the base of the ladder.

"As long as I must." His tone was as grim as his expression as he inched down the roof.

"The light will be gone soon."

"And any clues may be as well."

"It was no accident," she said.

He gave her a tight smile. "You did not make that a question."

"Should I have?"

"No."

"What did you find?"

"Just what I surmised."

Priscilla steadied the ladder until Neville reached the ground. As soon as his boots were settled in the snow, she asked, "And what did you surmise?"

"Someone hoped to kill de Romilly. It might have succeeded if no one had seen the snow knock him to the ground." He pointed with the shovel toward the peak of the stable's roof. "See there? A lot of the snow higher up remains in place. While that is not unusual, what is unusual is that the line of snow that slipped away is in a straight line and within reach of a man who would want to push it off from the door on the upper floor."

"What did you find up there?"

"Nothing to identify who was behind this." Neville shook his head. "Nothing to tell us if this is connected to what de Romilly believed was happening in London."

Pris watched him lower the ladder. She rubbed her gloved hands together. "And the attack on the boys out on the cliff?"

"I would prefer to believe they are not connected." Neville carried the ladder into the stable, then said, "Wishful thinking leads only to more opportunities for one's enemy to attack."

He held out his hand to Pris, whose cheeks were bright from the cold, and stared up at the stable's roof. "I find it hard to believe any hired stalker would leave the comfort of London to come to the wilds of Cornwall, especially in such inclement weather."

"But now Isaac, the vicomte's son, and the man himself have been attacked."

"True, but I stand by my opinion that a hired killer would prefer sitting by his fire, waiting for a more palatable opportunity. After all, the vicomte and his family are only visiting here. One would assume they plan to return to London, so why chase them here? Only someone desperate would be too impatient to wait."

"Are you saying what I think you are saying?" she asked.

"If you think I am saying that de Romilly's enemy may be at Shadows Fall, then I am saying what you think I am."

"One of our guests perhaps . . ." She looked at him. "But which one? I have noticed that the *Graf* was nowhere to be seen when the

76

snow fell on Antoine."

"And he offered no help when we were rescuing the boys." He sighed. "However, being lazy is no reason to accuse a man of twice attempting to murder someone."

"He is not our only guest."

His thoughts went instantly to Jamie Hathaway, who had appeared at Shadows Fall despite the bad weather. Was there a reason why the young man had come all the way to Cornwall instead of presenting himself at Neville's house in London? Yet, it made no sense that Jamie would target the de Romilly family. That would gain him nothing. The only way Jamie would advance was for Neville to be dead, and he would be a fool to attempt to kill Neville. The heir was always a prime suspect.

He stretched his taut shoulders and grimaced. When he saw Pris glancing at him with concern, he said, "The snow is heavy."

She rubbed one of his shoulders. "I could massage the knots out for you later."

"I would like that." He gave her the leering grin that always made her laugh.

Until today. Her pretty eyes were dull with anxiety.

He gave Pris a quick kiss on her crimson cheek before she hurried back to the house. Not moving, he watched the shadows play along the snow still on the stable roof. Someone had shoved the snow off with a pointed spade like the stablemen used to clean the stalls.

None of the stablemen were under suspicion, because they had been shoveling the road at the time of the accident. The only one not shoveling had been nearly caught in the avalanche from the roof himself. No one could get the snow sliding and then reach the ground in time to be at risk. Asking if someone else had been in the stables would be a waste of time. With so many guests at Shadows Fall, nobody would have noticed if someone was missing.

A dead fall that was clearly a dead end.

Angry shouts erupted into the afternoon. Another attack on his guests? De Romilly was confined to his bed, finally awake but too groggy to answer questions. Who was being attacked now? De Romilly's wife? His children again? Pris and their children?

Neville's heart contracted painfully at that thought, and he sped toward the front of the house even before he realized he had taken a single step. As he neared, he discovered the shouts were coming from inside. From the entry hall.

The door was ajar, so Neville pushed through. It bumped into Mr. Tolbert, sending the thin Canadian almost into the newel post of the staircase. He collapsed to sit on the floor. Neville took one step inside, but halted when his foot encountered something far softer than the floor.

He looked down and saw von Zell sitting on top of a man who was face down on the tile. He doubted the poor man, whoever he was, could breathe beneath the rotund German.

"What is going on?" Neville demanded, looking from one startled face to the next.

The *Graf* gave a grand gesture toward the man beneath him. "I found him sneaking around the house. One cannot be too careful in times of war, as we learned during the French incursion. And we've had far too many tragic incidents here already."

"Get up!" Neville ordered all three men, wishing that von Zell would refrain from bringing the war into every conversation when Christmas was only days away. But once Christmas was past, everyone would leave, including the potential killer. That would make it impossible for him to be found before another attack on de Romilly and his family.

He heard Tolbert struggle to his feet as Neville gave the *Graf* a hand. They looked down. A groan came from the man on the floor. His head hanging down, he used his arms to push himself up. As he drew his feet beneath him, Neville was not the only one to tense, prepared to keep the man from fleeing.

Then the man turned to face him.

A single word burst from Neville. "Wither-spoon!"

The young marquess, who had such a *tendre* for Daphne, wiped blood away from his broken lower lip. "Hathaway, I cannot say that I am fond of your welcoming committee."

"Leave him be!" Neville ordered as von Zell and Tolbert started to jump forward. The two men halted, exchanging a puzzled frown.

Neville ignored them while he sent a footman for clean water and cloths so Wither-spoon could wash away the dirt and blood from his face. Another footman rushed into the parlor and returned with a generous glass of brandy.

As the footman handed it to Witherspoon, Neville asked, "What happened?"

"I think it is quite obvious," the young marquess said before downing most of the brandy in a single gulp. "I came in and was set upon by those two addlepated beef-heads."

Tolbert puffed up at the insult, and the *Graf* called for his gloves to be brought so he might slap Witherspoon across the face in a challenge to a duel to repair his sullied honor.

Neville ignored them both and aimed a glance at the footmen to order them to do the same. Witherspoon was reputed to be an excellent shot, and Neville was unsure how furious the young man might be. Perhaps furious enough not to fire into the air so honor could be satisfied. Not that it mattered. Neville had no intention of allowing his guests to meet for grass for breakfast, especially when they would have to tramp through the snow.

"Why didn't you identify yourself?" Neville asked.

"It is not easy to do so while trying to ward off blows." He sipped again, wincing as the alcohol seared his lip.

"I hope you will accept my apologies as well as theirs." Neville motioned with his head for the other men to join them. "There have been some strange events taking place here, and everyone is jumpy."

"Strange events?" The young marquess laughed humorlessly. "That in itself is not peculiar, Hathaway. Such events seem to happen around you and Lady Hathaway with disturbing frequency."

"I have noticed that as well. Dashed inconvenient at times."

Witherspoon's lips tilted in a real smile. "I need to remember that in the future and check on the situation before I call."

Neville decided the best answer was to fall back on etiquette. How Pris would laugh if she heard his thoughts at the moment! But he wanted to return to his investigation, so he quickly introduced the men.

As they struggled through their apologies,

which Witherspoon graciously accepted, Neville led the way toward the solar where they could discuss recent events. He paused only to tell a maid to take word to Pris that they had another guest.

"The solar? Must it be the solar?" asked Tolbert, surprising Neville. Tolbert enunciated each word with care, but with an odd nasal accent.

Neville could not help wondering if that was the way one spoke in distant Montreal. He had met several Canadians during his time in London. Anyone from Montreal? Again, he pushed the question aside. No time to think about such things now.

"Are you unwell?" Neville asked, because he could not imagine any other reason for a guest to second-guess his host in such a way.

"No." The answer was grudging.

Even more puzzled, he asked, "Do you have a problem with the solar?"

"Certainly not. It simply seems odd that one would wish to sit in a room with so many windows when it is winter outside. We would not do such a thing in Montreal." For a reason Neville could not fathom, Tolbert cut his eyes toward von Zell, but added nothing more.

Neville curbed his irritation at the ridiculous conversation. When he saw Witherspoon trying to hide his grin, quite unsuccessfully, he turned on his heel and walked toward the warmest public room in the house. He had spent enough time in the cold air while on the stable roof, and he wanted to enjoy the roaring fire that always burned in the solar.

He was glad he had his back to his guests as he thought of his conversation with Pris. No one with a bit of sense would be lured out of a warm house to travel to Cornwall without a very good reason. The low crowd who would take money to rub out a man were always loath to leave London. Their haunts were the cramped streets, and they considered the countryside too open and country folks too eager to find out their business.

As he walked into the solar, he heard a shocked gasp behind him. Witherspoon had stopped in the doorway, pushed forward a half-step when the others bumped into him.

"Do," the young marquess asked, staring across the room, "the strange events have something to do with what is in front of me?"

"In front of you?" asked Neville. "What do you mean?"

"Maybe you should start your explanation by telling me why you have a tree in your solar."

Priscilla heard Lord Witherspoon's cool comment as she neared the solar. She stepped into the room, interrupting the *Graf* who had started to explain, from the beginning and in infinitesimal detail, the history of bringing evergreens inside for Christmas and how those traditions had been put in danger by the French invasion of the Black Forest. Vexation crossed his face, but his smile quickly returned as he bowed toward her.

Walking to the marquess, she said, "Lord Witherspoon, you should have let us know that you were calling."

"A message from Town would not have arrived any more quickly than I would." His twinkling eyes reminded her, just for a moment, of Neville's, and she understood how easy it had been for her daughter to fall in love with the young man.

Neville's sparkling eyes had enticed Priscilla's heart time and again. Like mother, like daughter. She almost laughed at her silly thoughts, but she maintained her welcoming smile.

"Quite true," she said, refraining from mentioning that he could have sent a messenger ahead before he departed from London. She suspected that he could not wait the length of time propriety demanded before he set off on his journey to Shadows Fall.

And he was not the only one who had no patience.

"Burke!" came an eager shout from the solar's doorway.

Everyone hastily moved aside as Daphne rushed into the room, her arms outstretched.

She skidded to a stop when she realized she and the marquess were not the only ones in the solar.

Color rose up her face. She curtsied prettily and said, "Welcome to Shadows Fall, Lord Witherspoon."

"Miss Flanders." He took her hand and bowed over it. He started to raise it to his lips, but then glanced toward Priscilla and Neville. He released Daphne's hand with obvious reluctance, unkissed.

Taking pity on her daughter and her beau, Priscilla urged everyone to go to the dining room where their midday meal would soon be served. Mr. Tolbert and the *Graf* took their leave, but before she and Neville could make their way there as well, Jamie Hathaway stormed into the room.

He was dressed in the best fashion, and she could not help wondering how he had paid a knight of the thimble for such a well-made dark green coat and elegant silver waistcoat that would be more at home at a grand assembly in Mayfair than a country house in Cornwall. Boots that reached to his knees were clearly new because they had no creases in the leather, and even the most skilled boot polisher could not have achieved such a shine on well-worn boots.

Priscilla noticed her daughter staring at him in astonishment, and she quietly cleared her throat. Daphne lowered her eyes, a flush brightening her cheeks. Not that she could fault her daughter. The outward change in Jamie was astounding.

"Where is t'blasted fellow that pushed 'is way into t'ouse?" the young man demanded as if, by donning his finery, he had already taken his place as lord of the manor. Clearly, he had not been otherwise altered by his new clothing because his accent was as thick as ever. "No need for the ladies t'fret. I'll brain 'im and tell 'im to run 'arum scarum from t'ouse."

"Silence!" Neville said, kneading his temple in the sure sign that he had a headache.

Priscilla smiled at Jamie, hoping to ease the strain in the room. " 'Twas only a misunderstanding, and the matter is taken care of now. Thank you, however, for your eagerness to jump to our defense."

"Who's 'e?" Jamie jerked a rude thumb in Lord Witherspoon's direction.

She could not help but notice how both young men's eyes narrowed as their gazes locked. If they had been rams, she had no doubt they already would be charging, each, ready to lock horns. Her daughter looked dismayed, and Priscilla guessed that Daphne had not been blind to the glances aimed at her by Jamie since his arrival.

Stepping forward, so he could block Jamie from a view of Daphne, Lord Witherspoon introduced himself in a tone that suggested he was only speaking to Jamie as a favor to his hosts.

"A marquess?" Jamie sniffed. "Some 'ave everything handed t'them at birth. The rest of us got to work 'ard t'get wot we need."

"Who are you?" Lord Witherspoon asked in the coldest voice Priscilla had ever heard him use. Clearly, he was not pleased at what he saw as possible competition for Daphne's attention.

"James Hathaway, heir to 'is lordship."

The marquess eyed him up and down. "Odd that you discount me because of my birth when it seems that you expect your birth will eventually give you an advantage as well. May I suggest that you learn to think before you open your mouth? That may be a new habit for you, but it will serve you well."

"Wot . . . ?" Jamie obviously struggled to determine if he had been insulted.

"Ah, you are already learning." Lord Witherspoon offered Daphne his arm. Together, they walked from the room.

Jamie fisted his hands and started to follow.

Priscilla moved in front of him to block his path. He tried to edge around her, but she refused to let him.

When the young man put up his hand to take her elbow and shift her aside, Neville growled, "A word of advice. You may want to rethink doing that, Hathaway."

Jamie lowered his hand quickly. Obviously,

he *was* learning.

"Another word of advice, Jamie. You would be wise to take care what you say to Lord Witherspoon," Priscilla said with a cool smile. "You may think you are quite the bruiser and skilled with your fists because of your past experiences in the rougher sections of the north, but the marquess has studied boxing with some of the best gentlemen of the fist in London."

"And that makes 'im think 'e's the chief cock of the walk?"

"It makes *me* think you would be wise to consider what may occur if you continue to taunt him, daring him to darken your daylights."

Jamie's eyes widened at her easy use of London street cant.

"If you had more brains than guts," Neville said quietly, "you would know that Lady Hathaway seldom will act as you expect her to. However, she will always act with good sense, so you would be wise to heed her words."

"Mama?" Leah's voice came from the doorway.

Jamie frowned over his shoulder at her daughter. Apparently, Neville was not pleased by his heir's reaction, because he grasped the younger man by the arm and steered him past Leah. Her daughter stared after them, which gave Priscilla a chance to conceal her thoughts. If she had given Neville a son, her husband would not have to put up with Jamie's antics. Was Neville's frustration because of the young man's unthinking words and actions, or did Neville's thoughts mirror Priscilla's?

"I have not seen Jean-Paul," Priscilla said quietly.

"How did you know I was looking for him?" Leah seemed honestly puzzled.

Priscilla had to fight back her smile. No doubt, Leah thought she was being circumspect about her calf-love for Jean-Paul. "A lucky guess, I would say."

"Did I see Lord Witherspoon going up the stairs?"

"He has come to call."

"From *London*?" She rolled her eyes. "He must be completely enamored with Daphne."

This time, Priscilla could not conceal her smile. "He has been calling on her faithfully."

"Is he staying for Christmas?"

"I suspect so."

Again, she rolled her eyes. "And all the way through to Twelfth Night, like earlier this year?"

"I doubt any Twelfth Night will be like the past one." She shuddered as she recalled the events that had reeked of murder and manipulation. "Come along. We have already delayed the midday meal, and we should not leave our guests hungry."

Leah did not move, and her nose wrinkled. "Just don't make me sit by the Tolberts."

"Why not?"

"They shouted at me earlier."

Priscilla halted and looked at her daughter. "Why would they shout at you? Were they upset over something?"

"Not upset." Leah looked down at her feet. "I must have startled them when I came in here earlier. You should have seen the mess they made when papers flew in every direction." She grinned. "Fortunately not on the hearth."

"Fortunately. I trust you helped them gather up the pages."

"I offered. I even picked up a couple and handed them to Mr. Tolbert. He near ripped them out of my hand, and then he told me that they didn't need my help. All they seemed interested in was having me leave." She shrugged. "So I did."

Priscilla hid her smile. She suspected Leah had been relieved not to have to remain in their company any longer than necessary.

Leah ran to the *Tannenbaum*. "Look! Some of the Tolberts' pages must have gotten ripped up. There are small pieces of paper snagged in the tree branches." She plucked them off, tearing them more than they already had been, handed them to Priscilla, then glanced out of the room. "Isaac, wait for me!" She hurried after him.

90

Looking down at the crumpled and ripped strips of paper Leah had pressed into her hands, Priscilla frowned. What remained was shredded. Only a word or two in a row was readable, and they were in French.

She was able to pick out Napoleon's name on several of the scraps of paper as well as the Marquess of Wellington's name and some other officers whose names were not as recognizable. Only that they were captains. Otherwise, she saw only words like *movement* and *transport* and *location.*

Folding the pieces closed within her fingers, she hurried out of the room. She needed to find Neville without delay. Even if the writing had not been in French, the few words she could read suggested a discussion of tactics for either the French army or the English one or both.

She glanced back once at the *Tannenbaum.* The *Graf* had mentioned that gifts were placed on it. She might just have been given one.

The first question was: To whom did the page belong? The Tolberts? The vicomte or some member of his family? Someone else altogether?

The second question was: Did these scraps have something to do with the attacks on Antoine de Romilly and his son?

CHAPTER SEVEN

Seven Days 'Til Christmas

Priscilla despaired at ever having the opportunity to speak with her husband alone. Usually, in the country, she asked for the evening meal to be served in a simple buffet style in the dining room.

But Aunt Cordelia would have none of that. Every meal must be grand. She would accept nothing less, even though she was not the mistress of Shadows Fall. A trio of footmen walked along the table, offering mushroom soup to the diners and making sure no glass went empty. Both de Romilly children sat at the far end of the table with Priscilla's younger children. The vicomtesse had not joined them, because she would take her meal in her husband's chamber.

Daphne had used Priscilla's delay in reaching the dining room to secure a seat next to Lord Witherspoon's. On the opposite side of the table, Jamie watched them, a scowl marring his face. But neither Daphne nor the marquess seemed to be aware of him or anyone else at the table. So far, Aunt Cordelia had not made a comment about how they made lamb eyes at one another, and Priscilla held her tongue. To remind her daughter, however obliquely, of her duty to *all* their guests could set off another round of scolds from her aunt. That would lengthen the uncomfortable meal even further.

Looking along the table to where Neville sat at the far end, Priscilla could not help admiring her husband. He was, without question, the best-looking man at the table. His black hair and eyes of the same color were striking. The stern lines of his face could alter swiftly from a smile to a scowl or vice versa, but anyone assuming that they could discern his true feelings by reading his expression was in for a rude awakening. He had learned much during his years upon the boards, and he could display any emotion with the skill of the finest thespian.

As he was now while he looked interested by what *Graf* von Zell was saying. Pris doubted her husband cared about the latest agricultural reports along the Rhine and how much better the harvest was sure to be now that Napoleon no longer controlled the region, but he nodded at the appropriate moments. He probably was grateful, as she was, that the *Graf* was not prattling solely about Napoleon and the war. Neville glanced in her direction, and she arched her brows. The shadow of a grin flickered across his lips, but it was gone before the *Graf* could notice.

Then Neville's brows lowered, and she knew he had seen the disquiet on her face. She might be able to hide her feelings from her family and guests, but his keen eyes had discerned the truth, even as *Graf* von Zell chattered on without a break.

A thought tightened her throat. Could the pages belong to the *Graf?* He talked so often of the war and how he relieved he was that Napoleon had lost parts of his empire. She had to look at the few words more closely.

When Neville hooked a finger and Stoddard came to lean down, she guessed he asked the butler to hurry the service. Neville gave her a taut smile before turning his attention back to *Graf* von Zell as if there had been no disruption.

Only Aunt Cordelia was upset when the footmen seemed to add wings to their feet while they offered the next course to the diners. Her veiled comments led to no change, so she looked across the table to where the Tolberts sat in silence. "Are you related to Guillaume Tolbert?" she asked as she spooned a generous serving of vegetables onto her plate.

"No," Mrs. Tolbert said softly.

Aunt Cordelia was undaunted by the terse answer. "Really? Then you must know him.

Didn't you say you lived in Montreal?"

Mrs. Tolbert stared down at her plate, and Priscilla wished she could say that Aunt Cordelia was not being rude . . . for her. But to do so would embarrass her aunt.

"I know Guillaume Tolbert mentioned that his family lived somewhere in Canada when I met him at church in London."

"He lives in Quebec," Priscilla supplied.

"Canada cannot be that large a place." Aunt Cordelia gave a genteel shudder as she added, "After all, how many people of good breeding could endure living in such a primitive place?"

"Montreal is known as a fine town," Neville said, joining the conversation much to Priscilla's relief.

"Yet it is still a small settlement, isn't it?" She aimed the question at the Tolberts, but Neville answered.

"Montreal is probably smaller than Mayfair, most certainly, but far larger than Bedford Square. I daresay, not even my darling Priscilla who is so warm-hearted, knows everyone on that single square."

Across the length of the table, Priscilla mouthed, *No more, Neville.* It was too late. Aunt Cordelia, as always, was ready to take umbrage at anything Neville said. Even his commonplace comment on the weather could bring a sharp retort from her aunt.

"My niece was in mourning when many of

them moved in," Aunt Cordelia said. "I thought her late husband was a friend of yours. You could honor his memory by refraining from making such unthinking remarks."

Gasps came from around the table at the stern dressing-down, but Neville was undeterred. Leaning forward, he gave her aunt his most charming smile. "Ah, so we are in agreement, aren't we, Aunt Cordelia?"

She bristled. "Agreement? In what way?"

"Neville . . ." Priscilla said.

He paid her no mind as his smile broadened. "We agree that there are reasons why one might not know one's neighbor as well as others would assume."

Someone snickered. A child giggled. Aunt Cordelia sputtered.

Priscilla tried to catch Neville's eye. Baiting her aunt would gain them nothing but . . . Understanding bloomed inside her. He hoped to vex Aunt Cordelia enough so she would rush through her meal to be done with him.

"I will never understand you Americans," Aunt Cordelia said with one of her characteristic sniffs that said more than her words.

Mr. Tolbert flinched, then hurried to say, "We are Canadian, not from the United States."

Aunt Cordelia waved aside his words. Priscilla turned the conversation to how different countries celebrated Christmas. The *Graf* was all too eager to discuss his country's customs . . . again!

Neville silenced him by asking the Tolberts if they thought the war with the United States would have any impact on how Christmas was celebrated in Montreal this year. "With all the skirmishes along the St. Lawrence River, I would suspect that trade has been curtailed." He shook his head in disgust. "We hear of the strangest events. One about four British soldiers being captured on one of the islands in the river and how the Americans are raiding from their side of the river."

"The last letter we received from family," Mr. Tolbert said precisely, "spoke of the Americans capturing Akwesasne, an Indian settlement, about a day's travel from Montreal. That happened at the end of October. We have not heard from them since, but assume the Americans have continued their forays into Canada."

"That is disturbing," Priscilla asked. "You must be very anxious for your families."

"No one can rest easily in wartime," interjected *Graf* von Zell, clearly unwilling to be left out of any conversation. "When the French invaded the Black Forest . . ."

Priscilla stopped listening and focused on trying to eat. Her stomach was taut, and she found it almost impossible to swallow. Neville got his wish when her aunt declined dessert. Priscilla barely tasted her own while she waited for everyone else to finish and excuse themselves.

At last, she and Neville were the only ones in the dining room. He stood, drew back her chair, and offered his arm. He said nothing while he escorted her out of the dining room and upstairs to their private chambers. She was as silent and waited while he sent their personal servants away with a warning that they should not come back for at least an hour. She saw the knowing glances and sighed. She would prefer to spend the next hours in her husband's arms, but she doubted that would happen.

As if she had spoken aloud, he slipped his arms around her and drew her against his firm chest. He kissed the top of her hair and, when she tilted her head back, he captured her lips. She lost herself in the thrilling moment. Each time he kissed her was as if he were doing so with the eagerness of their first time. She delighted in the brush of his skin on hers.

"What has you distressed even more than before our meal, Pris?" he whispered.

She was tempted to say it was because he had stopped kissing her, but she drew out the tattered slips of paper and handed them to him. He took them to a nearby table and smoothed each piece out. She watched as he shifted them, arranging and rearranging them to try to make some sense of them.

He grumbled a curse under his breath. "I hope this is not what it appears to be. The small bits of information I can read suggest more than a common knowledge of British troop movements on the Continent and elsewhere. If this intelligence reached Napoleon and his generals, it could be disastrous."

"I agree." The words were bitter on her lips. She had been holding out hope that when Neville examined them, he would reach a conclusion different from hers.

"Was the page torn by accident or by design?"

"I don't know." She quickly explained how Leah had plucked the pages off the *Tannenbaum* after startling the Tolberts earlier. "If the two events are related . . ."

"And connected in some way with the attacks on the de Romilly family, we are in trouble."

Again, she agreed. "But we cannot be certain that the page belonged to the Tolberts. All of us have been near the tree. The *Graf* brought it in."

"And he is clearly obsessed with the outcome of the war, though he has made no secret of his leanings. Why would he *help* the French?"

"I have no idea." She stared at the bits of paper, wishing she could see a pattern that she had missed before. "As far as the tree, even though the *Graf* brought it into the

99

house, I daresay everyone has examined it, including members of the staff." She frowned. "There may be more pieces hidden among the branches. If we search, we may find more clues."

"But we cannot tip our hand. Examining the tree closely might attract attention we don't want."

Priscilla thought for a moment, then smiled. "Then let's make sure we get attention to assist us."

"How?"

She smiled. "Kiss me, and I just may tell you."

He took her arm and tugged her around the table and into his arms. "Don't tell me on the very first kiss, Pris, so I have an excuse to kiss you again and again."

Her laugh vanished beneath his lips.

Neville decided Pris was a genius. Her plan to have the children decorate the *Tannenbaum* with candles the next day in preparation for Christmas Eve was brilliant. The task gave both of them the chance to pick any bits of paper out of the tree and stash them away in the candle box which she held while supervising the youngsters. He was glad that Pris had insisted on counting out the candles before they were brought into the solar. As quickly as the children were lashing them to the branches, they would have gone through several dozen in quick order. He cringed at the thought of the tree erupting into a fountain of flame when so many candles were lit.

"We need more candles," Isaac said.

"No," Pris said firmly, closing the top of the box to keep in the small strips of paper they had collected while the children fitted the candles. "Not before Christmas Eve. *Graf* von Zell told us that the candles were meant to symbolize the stars that shone in the sky the night the baby Jesus was born. We will light the candles on Christmas Eve."

"But," insisted Isaac, "the stars the night before were the same as that night."

"Save for the one that guided the Magi," added Jean-Paul while his younger sister nodded vehemently.

"So why can't we light all of them except the one at the top of the tree?" asked Isaac so quickly that Neville would have believed that the boys had practiced the request beforehand. Rather, he knew, the boys' minds were in perfect harmony in their eagerness to see the *Tannenbaum* alight.

All the children looked expectantly at Pris. Without a word, she handed each of them a final candle to place on the tree. They complied, but glanced with curiosity at each other, clearly uncertain as to whether or not she had heeded their pleas and would give in to their request.

Before they could ask the question or Neville could bend to pick up another piece of paper that had fallen from the branches, a scream rang through the solar. The children froze.

Pris's face blanched as she choked out, "Daphne!"

He had no idea how she knew the screamer was her daughter, but Neville did not hesitate. He ran toward the door and got halfway across the room before he was slammed into by a jumble of arms and legs. Pushed back against a chair, he jumped aside as Daphne, now standing in the doorway, let out another shriek.

She feared her beloved Witherspoon was going to be hurt. The marquess was ducking under a fist thrown by Jamie Hathaway. It nearly struck Neville's nose.

"That is enough." He stepped between the battling lads. He pushed his recalcitrant heir away from the marquess. Frowning at both, he said, "Witherspoon, while this young cabbage-head can claim blissful ignorance, I had thought you were well enough schooled in the canons of Society not to resort to fisticuffs in the house, most especially the solar where the ladies gather."

"No gentleman," Witherspoon fired back, showing the breadth of his anger, "should be expected to endure such comments without an attempt to teach the speaker the cost of that lack of respect."

"Ye call yerself a gentleman, do ye?" Jamie spat. "Thought gentlemen were supposed t'be polite chaps. Ain't nothin' polite 'bout ye intrudin' when I be talkin' t' Miss Flanders."

"Talking? You had your hands all over her! No wonder she screamed."

"She screamed coz ye almost pegged 'er with yer fist."

Neville had heard enough. He put a hand on each young man's shoulder and pushed them farther apart. Looking at Daphne, he asked, "Did Jamie do anything untoward with you?"

"No." Her eyes were as wide as saucers, and she wrung her hands in front of her, clearly overmastered by how the situation had spiraled out of control. "Mr. Hathaway has been nothing but polite to me."

"See?" crowed Jamie and stuck his chin out at Witherspoon as if begging for the marquess to strike it. "Told ye, m'lord."

"Silence!" Neville roared, annoyed at having to deal with two young fools. "Gentlemen, though I use the term liberally at the moment, please excuse yourselves and find a place — separately — where you can regain your cooler heads."

Jamie swore vividly, and Neville hoped that the children were unfamiliar with the cant. When Leah clamped her hand over her mouth to silence a giggle, he knew that had

103

been wishful thinking. Even so, he did not relent in his stance until both his heir and the marquess stomped off in opposite directions.

"Daphne," Pris said in that tone that brooked no debate, "take the children to the kitchen. Cook planned to make fruit pies today, so there will be samples for you to try."

Without waiting for an answer, Pris marched across the room, slipped her hand onto his arm, and walked with him toward the door. He felt her fingers tremble. She must be upset at what she had witnessed. He definitely was. The house seemed to be collapsing into chaos.

CHAPTER EIGHT

Six Days 'Til Christmas

Priscilla drew on her gloves and looked around the entry hall. She missed the Sundays when she and her family could walk down the road to the parish church in Stonehall-on-Sea. When the children were small, she had been responsible for making sure they looked their best when they arrived for the Sunday service, because Lazarus had been busy with preparations and last-minute corrections to his sermon.

Was she feeling nostalgic because it was Christmastime, or was she wishing for a simpler time when the only puzzles she had to deal with were how to keep three young children quiet during their father's sermon? Nothing was simple now. No matter how many ways she and Neville had shuffled the bits of paper from the *Tannenbaum,* they had discovered nothing new.

Though the fragments seemed to suggest someone had information on British troops and their locations, without being able to read the complete document, they must take care not to assume anything. They also did not have enough facts to confront the Tolberts. The fragments might not belong to them, even though Leah had startled them into sending papers flying through the solar. Leah had said those were full pages, not torn ones. Anyone could have gone into the solar, ripped a page and tossed it into the fire, not realizing that some pieces would flutter away and get caught in the tree branches.

Ah, it had been so much simpler in the past! Or had it? Maybe she was painting her memories with a warm blush instead of remembering how outrageous Aunt Cordelia could be in her outrage that Priscilla had married a mere parson. And how the children had tried her patience to its limits and beyond some days. And how Lazarus could be away for a week or more at a time when his parishioners needed him, even if she could have used his assistance, too. She had tried never to complain, especially when he came home exhausted and sick with whatever illness he had been infected with while tending to his flock.

"I miss him, too," Neville whispered as he came to stand beside her. "Lazarus always loved this time of year, and he made it so much fun for everyone around him."

"How did you know what I was thinking?"

she asked.

"You have a special look on your face when you are thinking back to the time before Lazarus died. It is a mixture of both happiness and grief, but more happiness than sorrow." He ran his gloved fingers along her cheek. "I know how I feel when I find myself missing him, and I realize how much deeper the grief must be for you."

"But the happy memories counteract that more with each passing day." She stroked his face as he had hers. "He would be so happy to see what an important part you now play in our lives."

He grinned. "So he would not act like a young lion as Witherspoon and Hathaway are doing? Snarling and snapping at each other as they both try to gain control of the pride."

"Or maintain their own pride in front of all of us."

"Most especially your daughter."

She rolled her eyes as Leah had. "You do not need to remind me of *that.*"

"Don't worry, Pris. Daphne has plenty of chaperones, including your indomitable aunt. No one, not even a lovesick young swain, would dare confront your aunt."

"You did."

"I am the exception that proves the rule." He gave her a self-satisfied grin that widened when she slapped his arm playfully.

Trust Neville to tease her out of her dismals!

"Mama," Daphne said from behind her. "May I drive to church with Burke?"

She turned to her daughter who was dressed in a bright red coat that was the perfect foil for the white bonnet trimmed in green she wore on her blond curls. Not a tress was out of place, and Priscilla guessed that Daphne had gotten ready for church with Lord Witherspoon on her mind.

"You may go with him, but not unchaperoned."

"Of course!" Her quick agreement told Priscilla that her daughter had hoped everyone would overlook that little detail, so Daphne and Lord Witherspoon could enjoy an intimate coze on the way to the chapel in the village. "I planned on having Leah and Jean-Paul come with us."

Two daughters in a closed carriage with two young men they were sweet on? Priscilla smiled coolly, amazed that her daughters thought she would give countenance to such an addlepated idea. "You must take Isaac and Lisette with you as well."

"Those little kids? You know Isaac tattles about everything he —" She halted herself and stared at the floor.

"Isaac has been asking for some time with Lord Witherspoon. You know how he admires your friend."

Daphne's head jerked up at the word *friend,* a word she clearly took umbrage with for it did not match the intensity of her feelings for the young marquess. She composed herself with an admirable speed. "I am sure that Burke will enjoy talking with Isaac on the way to church."

"And on the way back."

She opened her mouth to protest, then nodded. "Yes, Mama."

As her daughter walked away, Priscilla motioned to a footman. She gave him quick instructions to pass along to the coachee of the children's carriage. The conveyance was not to leave either Shadows Fall or the church until she had determined all planned passengers were inside.

"You are a tough one," Neville said with a hushed laugh.

"Only a worried mama."

"One and the same, I am led to believe."

She did not reply as the rest of their guests came down into the entry hall. She was pleased to see Antoine had recovered enough to join them. The vicomte's steps were tentative, and he leaned a bit heavily on his wife, but he wore a genuine smile. She guessed he was glad to be on his feet again.

Watching the other guests, she saw no sign of any reaction other than pleasure that the vicomte had come downstairs. Was someone as skilled as Neville at masking emotion, or had she and Neville wrongly allowed two accidents to persuade them that the de Romilly family was a target at Shadows Fall?

When Neville asked the vicomte and his wife to ride to church in their carriage, she guessed he hoped, as she did, that they could get some answers. They needed them to prevent something else dreadful from happening.

Priscilla listened while Neville spoke to Antoine and Eveline about commonplace topics. The weather, how excited the children were about Christmas that would be arriving on Saturday, the upcoming Season in London. She hoped he remembered how short the drive into the village was.

As if she had reminded him, Neville said, "I hope you feel well enough to answer some questions, de Romilly."

The vicomte exchanged a glance with his wife. "There are parts of the accident that I do not recall even now that I have regained my senses."

"I am sorry to hear that."

"Don't be. I would prefer not to think of those long minutes that I am told I was under the snow."

Eveline gave a soft mew of despair.

Reaching across the carriage, Priscilla took the vicomtesse's hand. "He is safe now. That is what matters."

"Oui." She added nothing else as she pulled her hand away and slipped it around her husband's arm.

Neville leaned forward. "You say you felt threatened in London, de Romilly. Were you ever attacked there?"

"No. It was more of a feeling and glimpses I caught out of the corner of my eye of a man lurking nearby. At first I thought it was a criminal intent on lightening my purse, but then I realized it was always the same man."

"How did you know that?"

"He always wore a black coat and the same cap pulled down low to shadow his face."

Frowning, Neville said, "There are many black coats and caps in London. How could you be sure it was the same man each time?"

"I just am. I cannot explain it further, Hathaway."

"That is not much to go on."

"I realize that, which is why I brought my family all the way west in hopes of getting them away from whoever has been skulking after me."

"But," Priscilla said softly as the carriage entered the village, "a man with a black coat was seen when your son said he was pushed off the cliff. Though no one matching that description was seen when the snow fell off the roof and onto you, there are not any real witnesses to that act other than a stableman who was thinking only of eluding the ava-

111

lanche from the roof. Your enemy may be here."

Again, Eveline made a soft cry and pressed her hands to her lips as she glanced fearfully out the window.

"We may not be able to discover the identity of your enemy," Neville said, "unless we have some idea of why he is hunting you. Who are your enemies?"

"I have no more than any man who has fled his country and lives in exile." Antoine kneaded his fingers together. "None of them are men I would consider capable of murder."

"Everyone is capable of murder. All that is needed to tip a good man into becoming a killer is a reason to make him throw off his humanity. Everyone has that tipping point, and it is different for each of us. Some of us pull back from the edge of darkness. Others rush into it, giving themselves up to evil gladly."

Priscilla bit her lower lip as she saw the other couple stare at him in astonishment. Antoine agreed to give thought to who might wish him dead, and Eveline shrank further into herself, obviously horrified at the very idea.

The carriage pulled to a stop at the lych-gate at one side of the churchyard. No one spoke as Neville stepped out, then helped the others, cautioning them to watch the path to the church's porch carefully because it might be icy.

Letting the vicomte and his wife go ahead of them, Priscilla turned to Neville. She kept her voice to a whisper as she asked, "From which play did those words come?"

"I should have guessed I could not bamboozle you, Pris."

"You are often at your most eloquent when you are borrowing words you once spoke on stage."

"It was a silly play that had only a single performance before it was wisely consigned to oblivion. I played an English soldier in the story of the expulsion of the Acadians from eastern Canada. If Moses Kean had not been performing as well, I doubt I would even remember a single word of it. He watched our practices. Because he was such a skilled mime, he could do all the parts and all the accents." He chuckled. "He had us all laughing so hard we could not speak when he aped the lines of a female Acadian, speaking the whole scene holding his nose shut."

"You miss the theater so much."

"I certainly do, but now I have a greater role to play."

"What is that?"

He bowed before offering his arm. When she put her fingers on it, he said, "Your loving husband. That role I never intend to surrender." He gave her a swift, sizzling kiss

113

before they followed the others into the gray stone church.

Inside, it was damp and seemed even colder than it was outside. Priscilla knew that was impossible, but, within minutes of sitting, her bones ached with the chill. The heat box by her feet quickly gave up any attempt at giving off warmth.

She listened to the sermon with half an ear. Mr. Hammett was far from an inspiring speaker, even with a subject as glorious as the miraculous birth in a stable and angels singing in the sky. He seemed to believe that he would be rewarded for speeding through the sermon like a neck-or-nothing rider. The first time she attended this church, she had been fascinated with how long he could talk without taking a breath. She had not been the only one to notice that, for she had heard Isaac, after each service they went to at this small church, announcing exactly how many times the parson had paused to breathe before hurrying on.

A quick look to her left showed her that the *Graf*'s head was bouncing up and down as he fought sleep. Beside him, the Tolberts stared at their feet, snuggled close together to ward off the cold. The de Romilly family sat in the pew behind her, Neville and the children, so she could not see how they fared. In front of her, Aunt Cordelia, as straight as a soldier at attention, commanded the pew she shared with Lord Witherspoon. Jamie sat as close to the back of the church as he could.

When the service was finished and they all stood to exit the building, Priscilla realized how wrong she had been when she thought the interior of the church was colder than the windswept cliffs. She was grateful for Neville's arm around her. She was doubly glad to have him close when raucous shouts and laughter came from the tavern across the road from the church. The salt from the sea had erased the name on its sign. Two men came out, shouted, "Happy Christmas" in their direction, and reeled along the road. When one slipped and fell, both of them laughed.

Aunt Cordelia gave a sniff loud enough to catch the men's attention. The one who had fallen somehow managed to get to his feet and tipped his ragged cap in her direction. Priscilla swallowed her laughter as her aunt stormed to her carriage, but that was not the only indignity her aunt had to tolerate. Her carriage horse was favoring one leg, so she had to share the Tolberts' carriage. The lanky Canadian and his wife seemed oddly perturbed by the fact. Or maybe not so oddly, because they had already felt the sharp sting of her aunt's tongue.

The children clambered into Lord Witherspoon's carriage with Daphne. Before the door closed, Isaac called, "Ten." His grin was far too wicked for such a solemn outing.

"I believe I counted eleven," Neville replied before Isaac pulled the door closed.

"Eleven what?" asked *Graf* von Zell, baffled.

" 'Tis a silly game my son plays with Neville," Priscilla said before Neville could launch into an explanation which would embarrass the parson if he happened to overhear it.

"As silly as the games Wellington and Napoleon play as they taunt each other on the Continent?" The *Graf* chuckled, but the sound contained no humor.

Neville hissed, " 'Tis no subject for a churchyard on Sunday."

Graf von Zell looked instantly apologetic. Priscilla waved aside his elaborate request for her to forgive him. It did no good. During the ride back to Shadows Fall, the German groveled in abject dismay, giving no one else a chance to speak.

The day went downhill from there. Neville would have preferred to spend the snowy afternoon with his family, drinking hot chocolate and teasing one another about gifts they had made for Christmas, but *Graf* von Zell decided he could not create a noxious cloud with his cigar without engaging Neville and Witherspoon in conversation.

While they sat in the solar and stared at the hearth and the unlit tree, von Zell lamented how long it took newspapers to come down from London. "I welcome whatever tidbit of

116

news you have, Witherspoon," he said. "Surely, there must have been some topics of interest in Town. Or from the Continent, maybe? Word of actions against Napoleon's troops, perchance?"

"How long have you been in England?" the marquess asked.

"Why do you ask?"

Neville arched a single brow when Witherspoon looked at him, shocked by the *Graf*'s sharp tone.

Footsteps came toward the door, and Neville looked up in hopes that Pris had sent a servant with a request that would allow him to make his excuses and depart. If so, he would have to find a way to take Witherspoon with him. Only the worst cad would leave the marquess alone with the German.

The Tolberts appeared in the doorway. Tolbert's eyes widened when he noticed the three of them in front of the fire.

"Oh, we did not realize anyone would be in here." Tolbert spoke, as always, with that nasal emphasis on his words. The man's accent continued to unsettle Neville because he knew he had heard someone else speak that way, but could not recall who or where.

He tried to decipher the glance passing between the Tolberts. It was impossible because their faces were once again bland with polite smiles. Why had he failed to notice before that they always wore those expressions? Maybe it was because they were what Pris's aunt would consider the perfect guests, never asking for anything and seldom offering an opinion. He found such people to be boring . . . and usually hiding something.

"Come in," Neville said, standing and motioning for the Tolberts to join them.

Young Witherspoon stood. "Hathaway, if I may have a few moments of your time . . ."

Surprised, Neville set himself on his feet. "Of course." To the others, he added, "Excuse us."

The entry hall was close, so Neville led the way there. After sending the footman off, he faced Witherspoon.

"Something is amiss," the marquess said without a preamble. "I thought I should mention that, as you and Lady Hathaway might not have noticed."

"What have *you* noticed?"

"That man who apparently is your heir vanished right after church."

Neville had not expected that answer. Resting one elbow on the post at the bottom of the stairs, he regarded Witherspoon with narrowed eyes. He had seen before that Daphne's young man had more insight than the usual cub his age. He almost smiled. If Pris discovered he was thinking of Witherspoon as *Daphne's* young man, she would remind him that neither had the marquess offered for her daughter nor had Daphne accepted such a proposal.

"Jamie Hathaway comes and goes," he said. "He does not feel comfortable with genteel folk yet."

"Aren't you curious where he goes?"

"Not really. No one cared a whit where I was until the previous baronet did everyone he owed money to a favor and died. Suddenly, I was the most popular man in London, especially with his debtors."

"I don't mean this in jest."

"Nor do I."

Witherspoon seemed taken aback for a moment, and Neville reminded himself again that the young man always had been assured of his place in Society. As the oldest son of a marquess, he had been sent to the best schools and taught his duty and the privileges that would be his as the next marquess. Burke Witherspoon had never lived without a roof over his head or a meal waiting for him whenever he was hungry.

As Neville had.

The young man cleared his throat before saying, "I thought you would like to know that he is gone."

"He will be back."

"How do you know?"

"We Hathaways are like bad pennies. We always turn up again." Neville took pity on the younger man. "If you want my advice, ask yourself, if Jamie is not in the house and a certain young lady of your acquaintance is, why you are talking to *me?*"

Witherspoon chuckled. "Well said, Hathaway. If you will excuse me . . ." He strode away at a pace only slightly slower than a run.

Neville pushed away from the newel post. There was a certain lady of *his* acquaintance that he would like to spend the rest of the day with, holding her close and caressing her. Yet, when he went to look for Pris, he found her sitting with the de Romillys.

He doubted there was any polite way he could tell their houseguests that he would appreciate it if they made themselves as scarce as Jamie had. He would be doubly grateful when they took their leave along with their problems.

Two Days 'Til Christmas

The house creaked with the cold wind off the sea on the night before the night before Christmas. Neville walked along the passage that led to the rooms he shared with Pris, glad that the past few days had been without incident. He opened the door and saw she had already gone to bed. He grimaced. He loved watching her brush her golden tresses that fell all the way down her back.

But she was not asleep, he was pleased to see. As he walked into the room, she put down the book she was reading. He sat on a bench at the foot of the bed and smiled at her as he tugged off his left boot.

"I hope your day was better than mine," he said as he set the boot on the floor and reached for the other one.

"Other than reminding the boys that they had to wait one more day before we lit the candles on the *Tannenbaum,* it was an uneventful evening." She sat up and folded her arms on her bent knees.

Undressing, he said, "I assume Witherspoon kept you company."

She laughed. "He did mention that you suggested he get to know the younger children better."

"That was not exactly what I suggested." With a chuckle, he went to the closest lamp and, after checking that the hallway door was securely closed, doused the light. He turned down another lamp. As the room darkened, the wind rattling the window panes seemed even louder. "I said only that he should worry less about Jamie and more about spending time with Daphne. He went off to find her without another word."

"Maybe, since he is here, you should speak with him about his experiences in the Lords."

"Do you think I cannot handle that lot after I have learned to deal with pickpockets and murderers?"

"I think you can handle anything, but polite words can hide bad intentions."

He drew the draperies closed on the three

windows before turning back to the bed. "The Beau Monde has its treacherous shoals, but I have learned to navigate them."

"Yes, you have." She shook her head. "I don't know why I am fretting about such things. Perhaps to avoid thinking about why someone tore up that page and the scraps ended up in the evergreen tree."

He rested a folded arm on one of the bed's uprights that supported the tester and smiled down at her. "So you haven't completely lost your thirst for knowledge?"

"Why would you say that?"

"You have shown a marked lack of curiosity about why I was raised to a peerage."

"I cannot imagine anyone who deserves such an honor more." She nestled into the pillows and watched as he snuffed out the other lamps until the one beside the bed was the only one lit. "And I assumed that you would reveal the truth when you felt the time was right."

He drew back the covers enough to slip beneath them. The brass pan at the foot of the bed was not as warm as his sweet wife. Leaning on one elbow, he lay on his side and gazed at her shadowed beauty. Even after being married to her for eighteen months, he still wondered at the twists and turns of fate that had made her his wife. He had depended on fortune to smile on him for so many years during his youth, and he had thought it had given him its greatest gift when he inherited his family's less than glorious title. But, for some reason that he would never fathom, good luck had one more prize for him: a loving wife who accepted him as he was and loved him in spite of that.

Her fingers curved along his cheek as she whispered, "I trust that you will tell me when you can."

Trust. Did she have any idea how precious her trust was? Almost as wondrous as the love she had offered him.

"I have wanted to tell you, but I cannot." He buried his face in her blond hair that had escaped from the braid she wore to bed each night.

She caught his face in her hands and tilted it toward her. Smiling, she chided, "Oh, Neville! You are just trying to whet my curiosity when I was not at all curious before."

Had that been his intention? Had he been bothered that she had not asked as others had? He had brushed aside those queries with a jest or had simply changed the subject.

Trust.

There was that word again. She trusted him.

And he trusted her as he did no one else he had ever met, even her late husband.

"Maybe I can tell you a little," he whispered as he leaned onto his back and drew her head onto his shoulder. As she curled up against him, he fought his longing to kiss her. If he did, she was sure to accuse him of trying to keep her from asking more questions. Yet, he longed to kiss her so much. He would make the explanation quick.

"All right," she murmured, her breath caressing his neck.

It was becoming more difficult to focus his mind on anything but her. Exerting every ounce of his willpower, he said, "I was made a baron because of favors I did for the Prince Regent. Before you ask, the favors I did were not what would be deemed exactly legal."

She laughed. "That is no surprise."

"He was grateful that I handled the matter swiftly and with no fuss. Once a reasonable amount of time had passed, he decided he could offer me a peerage without anyone connecting the past with the honor he granted me."

"Again, that is no surprise."

"I no longer shock you, Pris."

"Only in how much you love me, because I wonder what I have done to deserve such devotion from a wonderful man like you."

With a single fingertip, he tipped her face toward him. "You must promise not to breathe a word of it to anyone else."

"Or?"

"I will have to silence you." He leaned closer. "Like this."

He captured her mouth, sampling her lips

with appreciation. Slipping his arms beneath her, he drew her even closer as he imagined how he would explore every inch of her tonight. Her fingers slipped up to rake through his hair and to hold his lips to hers.

Pressing her more deeply into the pillows, he sprinkled kisses across her soft cheeks. Her eager breath caressed his face, its heat igniting the embers within him into flames. She drew his mouth back to hers, and he reached for the buttons within the ruffle under her chin.

A distant thump intruded.

Had a window blown open?

If so, he did not care. The cold would not bother them when they were in each other's arms.

More thumping.

"The door," Pris whispered, her voice unsteady.

He cursed under his breath. "Go away!" he shouted, then bent to meld his lips to hers again.

His only answer was more knocking on the door.

"By all that's blue," he muttered as he flung back the covers. "Wait here, darling."

"I wasn't planning on going anywhere. At least not without you."

Her soft teasing almost convinced him to ignore the rapping. Almost. But it was clear that whoever was at the door was not going away.

He pulled open the door. His eyes widened when he saw Stoddard on the other side. The butler wore a bright blue dressing gown, shocking Neville, because Stoddard was seldom seen out of his pristine work clothes.

"What is it?" Neville demanded in a tone he seldom used with the servants.

" 'Tis Mr. Hathaway, my lord."

"What has that presumptuous puppy done now?" He heard Pris throwing back the covers. "It had best be something good for you to intrude at this hour."

Stoddard did not bat an eye as he said in the same unruffled tone, "It is far from good, my lord. A messenger has come from the village. There has been an accident."

"Is he hurt?" asked Pris as she came to stand beside Neville.

"The messenger said that when he left to come here, Mr. Hathaway was still senseless, my lady."

"I hope it is not another so-called accident," she said.

Neville agreed. Up until now, the incidents had been aimed at de Romilly father and his son. If Jamie now was a target, the problem might be far vaster than they had imagined.

"Where is the messenger?" he asked Stoddard.

"Waiting to travel back with you to where

Mr. Hathaway can be found."

Neville did not hesitate. Jamie might infuriate him, but the lad reminded Neville too much of himself a couple of decades before. Telling Stoddard to have a small, closed carriage brought around to the front of the house, he turned to redress.

Pris already was doing the same. He swallowed his groan of longing, but once they brought Jamie safely back to Shadows Fall and got him settled, they could return to their own bed. He hoped the messenger had over-exaggerated the situation, so it would not take long in the village.

And that the worst he feared would not prove to be true.

CHAPTER NINE

The carriage slid toward the edge of the road. One wheel caught in the snow, and the carriage began to tilt. Neville tightened his grip on the reins as the horses regained their footing.

Blast and botheration! If Jamie was still breathing, Neville was ready to change that situation as soon as they found the lad. The night was cold, and his wife had been so warm in bed.

He had sent the messenger on ahead to let the publican in the local tavern know that they were coming to retrieve Jamie. The messenger had been reluctant to share too many details, probably because he feared he would be blamed for the bad tidings. All he revealed was that Jamie had been left unconscious after a fight. If he knew what injuries young Hathaway had suffered, he refused to say.

Beside him, Pris murmured, "If the storm worsens, we may have to stay in the village."

"In that dreary public house?" He grimaced.

"How high and mighty you have become, Lord Hathaway, that you disdain a roadside tavern."

Her soft laugh eased his frustration. A little bit. A very little bit.

"Not all of them, but you must own that one is disgustingly low in character. While I have been known to spend a night or two at such places, I don't want my wife doing the same."

"Good, because if we get stuck here, I think we should beg the parson's indulgence and stay under his roof."

"An excellent thought, but first let us see what state Jamie is in."

She patted his arm, saying nothing more as he concentrated on keeping the carriage on the narrow, steep road. Once they reached the top of the hill, hedgerows marked the boundaries of the road, making it easier for him to guide the horses.

Not a light was visible in the village as the carriage entered it. Neville guessed honest people were asleep while the ones who flouted the law were up to no good somewhere along the shore. Inclement weather would not put a halt to the work of the smugglers, and wreckers waited for nights like this one when a careless captain might run his ship up on the rocks below the cliffs.

Glowing stripes and dots marked the public house's windows. Whatever had been hung over the glass was torn and pitted, letting the lamplight within escape.

Neville halted the carriage in front of the building that might have been the oldest in town, even more ancient than the parish church. Its roof dropped sharply toward the ground, and the stone walls were covered with ivy that had withered beneath the merciless winter wind.

He did not suggest that Pris remain in the carriage. It was too cold for her to stay outside, and it would be a waste of his breath anyhow. Pris still acted as if she was a parson's wife, expecting to find welcome or at least acceptance at any door.

Handing her down, he whispered, "Stay close."

"That is an order I am happy to obey."

"For once."

When she did not reply to his jesting, he drew her gloved hand within his arm and walked to the tavern's front door. The odors of stale ale, rotting fish, and unwashed bodies greeted them when he opened it.

Neville kept Pris close to him as he pushed aside an inner door. They stepped onto a floor of slate and brick and wood and anything else that could be used underfoot. Opposite the door was a huge hearth where the fire made the room over-warm. Smoke hung in the air, warning that the chimney was not drawing as it should. Mismatched tables were scattered around the room. He saw a tea cup under one table leg and a platter under another. Both were badly chipped, and he wondered how often they had to be replaced.

"Need somethin'?" asked a rumbling voice from his left.

Behind a makeshift bar that was little more than some boards placed on top of dusty crates, a bearded man stared at them. The gold earrings hanging from his ears told Neville that the man had once been a sailor. His wooden leg clumped as he pushed his way to the end of the bar.

"Word arrived at Shadows Fall that Mr. Hathaway needed help."

The man squinted. "Aye, ye be that new baron, ain't ye?" Without giving him a chance to answer, the publican pointed toward a table in the middle of the public room. "There." His finger trembled as he pointed to a man whose head was lying on the table while his arms and legs sprawled out in every possible direction.

Did the man think Neville would blame him for Jamie's behavior? The Hathaways might have a tarnished reputation among the *ton,* but they were renowned for being able to hold their liquor even after a long night of imbibing. Apparently Jamie did not possess that attribute which had been the sole source

131

of pride for most members of the family.

"Did he hurt anyone in the fight?" asked Neville, crossing the room to where the young man was face down on the sticky tabletop.

"Fight? 'Tweren't in no fight." The publican grimaced. "Jes sat there a-drinkin', then fell on 'is face on the floor while some of the other boys were enjoyin' a battle-royal. When 'e tumbled over, that put an end to a good fight. A few of the boys propped 'im up where ye see 'im. 'E ain't the fightin' type from wot I seen. Tries t'talk 'is way out when 'is mouth gets runnin' away with 'im. If'n 'e were a local lad, the boys wouldn't abide with 'is ways, but 'e's from Shadows Fall."

"We appreciate you contacting us," Pris said before Neville could blurt out that the only way Jamie would ever learn to control his mouth was to be taught a few lessons. Painful ones, if necessary. "Lord Hathaway will remind Mr. Hathaway how being a careless chatter-box can cause trouble that leads to making a mess in one's business or home."

"Thank ye, m'lady." A smile rearranged the many wrinkles on the publican's face. "That be right kind of ye to consider m'place, but, unlike some of the boys, 'e didn't cause no damage tonight." He grimaced. "Other than castin' up 'is accounts on a few of the boys who weren't 'appy 'bout it."

Neville paused only long enough to pull

out some coins. He placed them quietly on the bar, knowing that they would pay several times over for any damage caused by the other participants in the night's events. The publican snatched them up as Neville followed Pris to the table where his heir rested in a stupor. He pulled the younger man's arm over his shoulder and hoisted Jamie to his feet. The dead weight almost made Neville's knees collapse beneath him, and Jamie's head hit his shoulder with a clunk that sent pain resonating through him.

"Let me help," Pris said.

"Stay back. I can do this."

"Nonsense." She put her arm around Jamie's waist and shifted some of his weight toward her.

Neville heard the publican snicker as they half-carried, half-dragged Jamie from the tavern. The man did not even come from behind the bar to hold the door for them. It bumped into Jamie's head hard enough so, if the young man had been awake, the blow would have knocked him senseless.

Outside, they used the slippery walk to slide him along through the cold rain that must have started while they were in the tavern, and struggled to keep their own feet under them. He heard Pris panting with exertion by the time they reached the carriage. Telling her to step back, he leaned Jamie against one side of it. He upended the young man as if

133

he were a bag of flour. Jamie fell into the back of the carriage with a thunk.

"Can't do it," the young man murmured.

"Can't do what?" Neville glanced at Pris. "That sounds a lot like a guilty conscience. Is this pup the killer we have been looking for?"

"He is still unconscious," Pris said as she stepped up into the box. "He cannot be aware of what he is saying."

Maybe so, but that did not keep his heir from going on. "I can't do it. Don't want to be a m'lord." He mumbled something else, then fell silent.

"Oh, my!" Pris whispered.

"Oh, my indeed." Neville rolled the younger man onto his back, then tilted Jamie's head so rain did not run into his open mouth and choke him in his drunken stupor. "That sounds like someone who is considering clearing the path to a title for himself."

"But you have not been the target of the attacks."

"Are you sure? Isaac was there with de Romilly's son, and the vicomte and I have similar coloring and height."

"But Antoine has been threatened in London."

"Or perhaps he's the victim of an overactive imagination." He looked down at Jamie, then slapped him lightly on the cheek.

Jamie groaned and opened one eye. A broad grin washed across his face. "Uncle Neville!"

He pulled himself up and slung one arm over Neville's shoulders. "Want a drink, Uncle Neville? Buy us a round or two or six." He roared with laughter at what he clearly thought was a witty jest. "Ye be the fine baron with the plump pockets. Let's drink t'yer good 'ealth and long life. Keep yer title, and tell my mum I don't need it. Not now. Not ever. Don't want yer title, Uncle Neville. Jes want another drink."

"I think you have had enough," Pris said gently.

"Don' listen t'er." Jamie's words slurred even more. "Did ye know she used t'be a parson's wife?" He made a rude noise.

Neville had heard enough. Shrugging off Jamie's arm, he shook his head in disgust as the young man fell back into the carriage and began to snore.

"And you thought he might be the one stalking Antoine and his family?" Pris asked from the front seat.

"Obviously a mistake on my part. He is just a frightened young fool." Neville climbed up into the carriage and picked up the reins.

Pris did not reply. In fact, she remained silent as he drove back to the road leading down to Shadows Fall.

"You are quiet, Pris," he said when he turned the horses onto the steep road.

"I feel sorry for Jamie."

"Because he will eventually inherit a title

and the family's holdings? Maybe it isn't the life he expected, but he is not the first to feel as he does. An accident of birth changed my life in ways I could not have imagined years ago. Now it is his turn to accept it as I had to."

He expected Pris to reply, but again, she said nothing. He wondered why. It was unlike her not to reply when he spoke in such a taut tone. His attempts to draw her into a conversation failed; then he had to focus on the road so the carriage did not skid off course.

Something else was wrong. Something that deeply bothered Pris. He wished he could guess what it was.

When Priscilla walked into the bedroom she shared with Neville, the lights were blazing. Stoddard must have ordered all the lamps to be lit after she and Neville went to the village. The butler could always be depended on to do his duty.

She wished she could say the same thing about herself. She sighed.

"That sounds bad, Pris." Neville entered their bedchamber and closed the door behind him.

"Just tired," she said as she shrugged off her coat. She tossed it over the back of a nearby chair.

He crossed the room in a few long steps.

Putting his hands on her shoulders, he asked, "Why don't you tell me what has been bothering you? The truth, this time."

"You think the fact that a man and his son, as well as Isaac, have nearly been killed is not something that should bother me?"

"No. Events like that make you angry, Pris, because the answer to the puzzle eludes you when you believe you should grasp it right from the beginning." He bent so their eyes were even. "Why won't you be honest with me?"

She drew away from him, half-surprised that he released her. She had not thought he would be so willing to let her go before she gave him an answer.

"It isn't easy to speak of," she said without looking at him.

"I assumed that, because, whatever it is that eats at you has been on your mind for weeks now."

Slowly sitting on the window seat, she gazed up at him. "I cannot hide much from you, can I, Neville?"

"Your heart lies next to mine," he said, kneeling beside her. "When yours is filled with uncertainty or pain, how can I help but feel it, too?"

She ran her fingers through his damp hair, and drops of melted ice fell onto his shoulders. "I am sorry."

"I should be the one apologizing. I have

known you are unhappy, and yet I have done nothing because I feared 'twas I who made you unhappy."

"You? Why would you think something absurd like *that*?"

A wisp of a smile curved along his lips at the shock in her voice. "I am asking you to be honest, so I must be honest as well. I thought I had done something to fail you, Pris."

"You have not failed me." She allowed herself a quick smile. "I doubt you ever could. 'Tis myself I find to be a disappointing failure."

"You?" he asked in the same astonished tone she had used.

"I have failed you and Jamie."

His eyes narrowed. "What does that young fool have to do any of this?"

"He is your heir."

"A fact I am all too aware of." He sighed. "I can see that he is going to be a problem for a long time."

"Because I have failed you."

He shook his head. "I do not follow you, Pris."

"If I had given you a son by now, Jamie would be relieved of the duties he clearly doesn't want, and you would not feel responsible for him finding his place amidst the *ton*." She stood and went to her dressing table. Staring down at the silver brushes on its top, she said, "I guess I never gave the matter much thought until you were raised to the peerage. It is different now, Neville. You are a baron, and a baron needs an heir."

"I have one." His mouth twisted in a wry grin as he stood and walked to where she stood. "One that is definitely an unpolished diamond in the rough, but no man gets to choose his heir. It is the hand dealt to him."

"That is not what I am talking about, and you know it."

He drew out the bench by her dressing table. As she sat, he plucked the pins out of her hair to let it fall in thick waves down over her shoulders. He picked up her brush and began to run it in slow, even strokes through her hair. She closed her eyes as she savored his gentle, steady touch. On her lap, her clenched fingers loosened their tight grip on each other while she let herself relax.

When he spoke, his breath caressed her as sweetly as his fingers. "Pris, it is not like you to worry about such matters. If we have a child together or not, nothing could ever change the love I have for you."

"But you must want a true heir."

"To see you grow round with my child would be a pleasure beyond what I could describe, but so is spending every day with you. I know I have been given a great and precious gift that many would say I did not deserve, and I am grateful that you love me.

You have welcomed me into your family as your children have. To ask for more would prove I am as greedy and ungrateful as I have been labeled by your aunt."

She laughed softly. "You know Aunt Cordelia has affection for you."

"The affection of a cat for a mouse it is about to snack upon."

"You, a mouse, Neville? Somehow, that is not how I envision you."

Putting his hands on her shoulders, he slowly spun her to face him. "And how do you envision me, Pris?"

"As the man I love." She rose into his arms and welcomed his kiss. For now, as they savored each other in the waning hours of the night, she wanted to forget everything and everyone else.

CHAPTER TEN

One Day 'Til Christmas

It was snowing. Again!

Neville stood at the window in the office he seldom used and stared out at the storm. The view of the sea had vanished behind the rapidly-falling snow. This morning, Pris had been so busy with the events of Christmas Eve that he had barely seen her. She had announced at breakfast that she was taking the children caroling through the house as well as out to the outbuildings. The faint sounds of their singing occasionally reached him as well as applause from the staff, but no one had come to serenade him yet.

Now he could hear nothing. It was as if he was alone in the great house.

A sharp noise rang through the house and through his head.

A scream!

He ran out of the room, even as he thought to himself that there had been too many screams in the house in the past few days. He had hoped they would get through the day before Christmas without more.

The screams continued unabated. He followed the sound. Something tickled his throat.

Smoke!

As he ran through the entry hall and toward the older wing of the house, he saw smoke billowing out of the solar. Choking, hot, thick smoke. Through it, forms were visible. Tall ones and shorter ones.

The children!

He rushed through the smoke and shouted, "Get the children away from here! Now!"

"I'm trying to," Pris replied. She held the hands of Isaac and the little de Romilly girl and was using them to try to herd the older children away from the smoke.

He was not surprised to find her in the very midst of disaster. If anyone was in trouble, she cared nothing of her own safety.

Grasping the arm of a woman beside him, he had no idea whom it was until she cried out in French. "Antoine! He is in there!"

The vicomtesse!

"Are you sure he is in the solar?"

"Yes . . . No . . . I don't know." The vicomtesse wobbled, and Neville steadied her. "He said something about looking more closely at the *Tannenbaum*. Now he is in there!" She screeched, and Neville knew it had been her screams that he heard.

Footmen rushed forward with buckets of water. Neville grabbed one and tipped it over his head. Grabbing another bucket, he shouted for the footmen to bring more and get the women and the youngsters away from the smoke.

He drew in a deep breath, then coughed. Foolish! All he had inhaled was smoke. Ducking his head, he rushed into the solar. He heard Pris cry out in dismay, but he could not turn back. Not until he was certain de Romilly was safe.

The smoke swirled around him, swept back slightly by his motions. Wiping water out of his eyes, he inched blindly forward. He listened for the crackle of fire. He did not hear that sound. Was the fire out, or was its noise drowned out by the buzzing in his head as he tried to hold his breath? He cursed when his shin banged into a low table. He edged around it, calling de Romilly's name.

Why hadn't the vicomte fled when the fire started?

Maybe he could not.

The thought wrenched through him. If the fire was no accident, whoever had started it might have made sure that the vicomte could not escape before the smoke smothered him.

"Hathaway! Is that you?"

Hope thudded in his heart for a single breath; then he realized the voice had no French accent.

143

"Witherspoon!" he shouted back.

"Over here!"

He stumbled in the direction of the marquess's voice. He hit two chairs. Something crashed to the floor and shattered. The smoke thickened, and the water streaming out of his eyes blurred his vision further, but he still saw no flames. What had caused all the smoke?

A hand seized his sleeve. Threads snapped as he was tugged sharply to his right.

Through the smoke, he could see Witherspoon beside something that looked lumpy and uneven.

Neville squatted and realized the chunky shadow was a senseless man. De Romilly!

Taking a deep breath of the air that was clearer near the floor, Neville stood. "Can you get him out by yourself?" He coughed between words.

"I think so."

"There are footmen in the hall. Call them to help you."

Witherspoon bent to put his hands under the vicomte's arm. He began to tug him out of the smoke-filled solar.

Neville pressed his sleeve over his nose and mouth as he groped his way farther toward the wall that should be right in front of him. Had de Romilly been in the room alone, or was someone else in the solar?

He would never be able to tell while smoke

144

filled the room. Feeling glass beneath his out-stretched hand, he fumbled to open a win-dow. His fingers seemed clumsy, and he knew the smoke was clogging his brain. But he refused to give up.

The window flew out of his hands as a gust of wind swirled into the room, covering him with icy pellets even as the smoke surged out. Pushing back from the sill, he lurched to the next window. This time, he was able to open it more quickly. He worked his way around the room, coughing so hard he had to pause as he gagged, but he managed to open all the windows in the solar.

Tears ran down his face as he sagged against the wall and scanned the room while the smoke was pulled outside. From the hallway, he heard shouts. Someone was being sent for the doctor.

He wiped his blurred eyes. By the hearth was a smoking mess pocked with pools of melted wax. It was, he realized with astonish-ment, the remains of the *Tannenbaum*. The tree must have caught fire, giving off all the smoke, but the fire had not spread when it collapsed onto the hearth. If it had fallen in the other direction, the whole room could have gone up in flames.

But how had the tree caught fire? Had it been an accident or another attack?

A glass was shoved into his hand, and Pris said, "Drink it!"

He complied and winced as the brandy seared his throat that was raw where smoke had clawed at it. He cleared his throat, then took another drink. This one went down more smoothly.

Nodding his thanks to Pris, because he could not trust his voice, he knelt to examine the remains of the tree. It had stood too far from the hearth for a random spark to set it afire. He got up and strode out of the room. He needed some questions answered, and the place to start was with the apparent victim of so many disasters at Shadows Fall.

Trying to console the vicomtesse was futile, Priscilla decided. She continued to weep, no matter what Priscilla did or said. Even the de Romilly children could not soothe her. Priscilla finally sent them off to join her own children, because Eveline's sobs were distressing Jean-Paul and Lisette further. To say nothing of Aunt Cordelia, who sat with *Graf* von Zell in the room attached to the bed-chamber the de Romillys were using. Lord Witherspoon stood next to Daphne, neither of them speaking. Jamie glowered at both of them, black circles around his eyes. He winced at every sound, no matter how soft, and she knew he suffered from being cup-shot.

Only when the inner door to the guest bedroom opened and Neville invited them in did Eveline's crying ease. She jumped to her feet so quickly Priscilla nearly was knocked off the settee.

"Pris?" asked Neville, holding out his hand. She stood.

Aunt Cordelia did, too, but sat again with a sniff when Neville said that the vicomte wished only to see his wife and their hostess. The sniff somehow conveyed an insult to the French and their bizarre manners.

Paying her aunt no mind, Priscilla went into the bedroom where the vicomte was sitting, his feet propped on an upholstered stool. He started to stand when she entered, but she waved him to remain in the overstuffed chair.

"Tell her," Neville said quietly. "Tell her what you told me."

The de Romillys exchanged a swift glance, a mutual apology if Priscilla read their expressions correctly. Antoine motioned for Priscilla to sit. She obeyed when it became clear that he would not comply with Neville's request until she did so.

"My lady," the vicomte said, his accent thicker than usual, "Hathaway has asked me questions last Sunday. I answered him as I thought I should. Today, I was honest."

She nodded when he paused, but said nothing. What could she say?

"My family came to Cornwall because of the danger stalking us in London. That you know. What you do not know is that I brought some important information with me that was delivered to me by allies on the Continent. Important information for the English war effort."

"Troop movements and such?" she asked, looking toward Neville whose face was set in a blank mask. His eyes were bright with strong emotions, however.

"*Oui.* Hathaway told me how you found the bits of paper I tried to destroy when I felt I could no longer safeguard them and my family both. I intended for the information to burn, but when the Tolberts came in, I had to leave the solar before I could be sure the information was completely destroyed." She thought of the Tolberts having many pages with them, and she wondered if they had planned to burn those, too, before Leah walked in. "Why didn't you burn them here?" She cut her eyes toward the hearth in the bedchamber.

"I intended to, but there were always too many people about after I was almost crushed by the snow off the stable roof. I had hoped slipping away to the solar would allow me to be rid of the information, and it would no longer be connected with my family. When I heard you had found the remnants of those scraps, I knew I must make sure no other pieces were found. I went to examine the tree while you had the children and the servants busy with caroling. I had only begun when I was struck on the back of the skull." He touched his head gently and winced. "I don't remember anything else until Witherspoon dragged me out of the solar."

"So you didn't see who hit you?" she asked.

"*Non,* so I cannot tell you who did that."

"But," Neville interjected, "you can tell her who interrupted you when you were burning the information."

The vicomte nodded with a scowl. "I was interrupted by von Zell. I think he is the one after the information to take back to his French allies."

"But he is German!" Priscilla choked out.

"He is from Baden in the Upper Rhineland, a region that early became part of the France's Confederation of the Rhine."

"Baden?" Neville asked. "He speaks only — and endlessly — of the Black Forest."

"Perhaps to confuse us?" Antoine suggested.

Neville strode to the door to the sitting room. Opening it, he fairly leaped across the room and grabbed von Zell by the lapels. He lifted the man from his chair.

The *Graf* stammered out a demand to be released. Neville did, setting him on his feet with more force than was necessary. The *Graf* growled a curse.

"The fire is his fault, isn't it?" asked Aunt Cordelia who clearly believed she had stayed out of matters long enough. "*That* man

149

brought *that* absurd tree into the house." She was clearly determined to have the first word as well as the final one.

Graf von Zell regarded her with the same distaste he would an unsavory plate of food. "Madam, you wound me by suggesting that I would do anything that would bring harm to my new friend, Lord Hathaway, and his family."

"What about the de Romillys?" Priscilla said as she walked into the sitting room. "Would you harm them to gain favor with your apparent allies in Napoleon's government?"

"Was meinst du?" He had lapsed into German, but quickly returned to English. "What do you mean? I hate Napoleon." He glared at each person around the room. "I was a captive of the French for many months, and I grew to despise them even more than I did before they took control of my homeland." He pulled up his sleeves and pointed to scars on his wrists. "You can see where I was bound by those beasts for so long that the rope seared my skin." His nose wrinkled as he looked past her.

When she turned, she saw the vicomte and his wife had come to stand in the doorway.

"I normally do not enjoy being in the company of the French," the *Graf* snarled as if even saying the word were distasteful. "However, they are your guests, my lady, and

I respect that. I give you my word that I would do nothing to bring harm to them while they are under your roof."

"Only under their roof? What about outside?" asked Aunt Cordelia quietly.

"You insult me. My battle is with the self-proclaimed emperor of France. Not French citizens who fled from earlier tyranny. I stand for what I have always believed in." He hooked his thumb in his lapel. "As your William Pitt once said, 'The poorest man may in his cottage bid defiance to all the forces of the Crown. It may be frail, its roof may shake; the wind may blow through it; the storm may enter, the rain may enter — but the King of England cannot enter; all his force dares not cross the threshold of the ruined tenement!' That is how I feel about Napoleon. He shall not have what is mine."

Priscilla had no reason to believe him, save her own instincts that told her the *Graf* was sincere. Even though she trusted those instincts, she said, "Tomorrow is Christmas. It is time to put aside political disagreements."

She watched as both the French couple and the German *Graf* nodded. There might be a temporary truce between them, but that still did not answer who had attacked the vicomte and his son.

Suddenly, her hand was seized, and she was pulled toward the hallway door.

"Excuse us," Neville called over his shoulder as he shoved her, quite inelegantly through the doorway, then quickly followed. He shut the door, grabbed her hand again, and hurried her along the corridor before she could even react.

When she started to ask him if he had taken leave of his mind, he urged her to wait until they could not be overheard. She nodded, her curiosity growing as fast as the snow piles had outside their windows.

He led her into their rooms. After he searched the room and their dressing rooms to be sure they were alone, he said, "I know who has been threatening de Romilly and is behind the attacks here."

"Who?"

"*Graf* von Zell's friends."

"The Tolberts?" She shook her head. "But why would they be trying to halt Antoine from delivering his information to the English authorities? They are from Montreal, which makes them English subjects as well."

"No, they are not from Montreal."

"What? How can you be certain of that?"

"The 'how' I am certain is the key." He put his hands on her upper arms and drew her close enough so he could lean his forehead against hers. In a whisper, he said, "Something about their accent has seemed off to me ever since I met them a fortnight ago. I got thinking about it again when we went to church with the de Romillys, and I quoted that now-forgotten play."

"The one about the Acadians?"

He nodded. "I put the final pieces together while von Zell was quoting William Pitt. Remember how I told you that Moses Kean had watched the practices for that play? He was a great mimic, and one of the people he mimicked was William Pitt with the very quote that von Zell used. That was when I recalled as well how he had mimicked the accent of the characters in the play. The Acadians."

"Who were expelled from eastern Canada by our government."

"Many of them went to live in French territory on the Mississippi River, but some went to England's American colonies. They joined in the revolt against the British government along with the English colonists. When France sold their Mississippi River Valley possessions to the Americans, all of the former Acadians became American citizens."

"So if the Tolberts are descendants of those former Acadians?"

"They are likely on the American side in this double-sided war we are fighting."

Priscilla ran to the bell pull and rang it as hard as she could. Within a minute, a footman stood in the open doorway.

"Find the Tolberts and ask them to meet Lord Hathaway and me."

"In the dining room," Neville added.

The footman said, "I cannot deliver your message."

"Why?" she asked, grasping Neville's hand as sickness filled her.

"They are gone. They left Shadows Fall with all their things more than an hour ago."

CHAPTER ELEVEN

Priscilla heard Neville curse, but she said, "They left while we all were dealing with the fire in the solar."

Her eyes locked with Neville's in the moment before he pushed by the footman and ran out into the hallway. She followed. She heard questions fired at them, but did not pause to answer. By the time she reached the entry hall, Neville had sent another footman for his coat and gloves.

"I hope you asked him to bring my outer wraps," she said, "as well as your own."

"Of course. I had no doubt you'd come after me, so I figured it would save time in the long run." His smile vanished. "We must find them before they can disappear completely. We have seen in the past that Americans have a great grudge against Britain."

She nodded, unable to forget the very first murder she and Neville had endeavored to solve. Americans had played a part in that fiasco too. "Even if we are mistaken —"

"Which I would wager we are not." He looked out a window. "At least, the snow will slow them down."

Priscilla did not answer that their pursuit would be slowed by the weather as well. As she pulled on her wraps, she hurried with Neville out into the storm. She hoped they could overtake the Tolberts before it was too late.

Ten minutes later, her fingers were so numb that Priscilla could barely feel the reins. The horse she rode slowed, and she raised her head to discover that Neville's horse had halted. Ice lashed at her face. She pulled her scarf higher as she saw a rider coming toward them at a wildly unsafe pace. The man stopped inches from Neville's horse.

"M'lord, what are ye doin' out in such a storm?" asked the man, putting his fingers to the brim of his hat. "M'lady, too?"

"We are searching for some guests who have gone missing," Neville replied, and she was awed anew by how easily he spoke the truth, but not the whole truth. "The Tolberts. A man and a woman, both tall. They have odd accents."

"Frenchie ones?"

He nodded.

"They be at the tavern in the village. Got themselves stuck in the snow."

"Thank you. Excuse us. We need to stop

them before they try to go farther."

The man chuckled. "No 'urry, m'lord. Mason said their carriage isn't goin' nowhere. One of their horses sprained a leg, and that carriage can't be pulled by a single horse in all this snow."

"Mason?" Priscilla asked, trying to keep her teeth from chattering.

"Our ale-spinner in the village."

She guessed he meant the publican at the tavern, but did not bother to confirm that as she set her horse to the best possible speed to keep up with Neville. The man followed, too, clearly curious why Neville was intent on stopping his guests from leaving.

The village was bright with lamps lit by almost every window. She hoped it was because it was Christmas Eve and not because the lights were meant to lure a ship in on the rocks or signal to smugglers. She pushed those thoughts from her head because the village looked peaceful and even beautiful with the fresh snow glittering in the lamp-light.

Priscilla handed her reins to the man who had met them on the road. He offered to take their horses as well as his to nearby shelter. Nodding when Neville said they might need their mounts quickly, the man vanished with the horses into the storm.

As they had only the night before, Priscilla walked into the tavern with her hand on

Neville's arm. This time, the public room was far from empty. A half dozen men stood or sat around the room. Trays held empty beer tankards as well as a few full ones. At the center table, the lone woman sat. Mrs. Tolbert!

"Lord Hathaway!" she cried, jumping to her feet. *"Oh, mon Dieu!"*

Scowls appeared around the room when she spoke in French. Mrs. Tolbert clamped her hand over her mouth and looked around in dismay.

Neville smiled icily. "Tolbert, or whatever your name is, I know you are here. Step forward. Or do you always let your wife fight all your battles?"

"She is not my wife," Tolbert said as someone shoved him toward Neville. "I never should have asked her to come with me, but I thought a married couple would draw less attention. It would have been a perfect ruse, but she is a fool."

"An Acadian fool, I would say," Neville's expression grew even colder. "Just like you. Or do you prefer to be called a spy?"

"I told you." He gulped when angry grumbles came from the other men. "We are from Montreal."

"If you are from Montreal, then I am the Queen of England."

Neville's retort brought laughs all around,

but the men continued to watch the Tolberts closely.

"I admit, Tolbert," Neville continued. "You fooled me for a while, but every time you opened your mouth, I knew something was not quite right. Today, with the inadvertent help of your *bon ami,* von Zell, I finally realized the truth."

"How could that be?" asked Mrs. Tolbert. "He does not know the truth that we are —"

Her fake husband snarled for to her to be silent. She seemed to fold into herself. Slowly, she sat at the table and listened with a fearful expression.

"Why have you been trying to kill Vicomte de Romilly?" Priscilla asked, looking from one Tolbert to the other. "For the information he carried?"

"He is a traitor." Tolbert gave up all pretenses as fury erupted from him. "For centuries, his kind have been leeches, living off the labor of the rest of the French. They did nothing when the English claimed our lands and expelled us, putting our families on ships that quickly filled with fever. Other ships sank with all aboard, even the smallest babies. Those who lived were banished far from our homes and separated from our families. Then, when the French rose up against these heartless tyrants, they ran like frightened rabbits and, like de Romilly, turned their backs on their homeland. They became our enemies."

"Yours and America's," Priscilla said in the same calm voice.

Tolbert took a step toward her, but was grabbed and held back by several of the tavern's patrons. He struggled for a moment, then stopped. "I have nothing more to say other than you'll be sorry when England is defeated, Hathaway."

"Yule?" asked Neville with an icy grin. "Like the holiday? Are you saying that I'll be sorry? Rather, I think *Yule* be sorry."

Priscilla groaned. "Neville, this is no time for puns."

"It is always time for puns," he said as the patrons laughed.

Tolbert was infuriated. "Say what you will, but you will regret this night when my country defeats yours again."

The men's amusement vanished instantly. Curses sounded around the room as the men realized that Tolbert was both French and American.

"Let's send 'im up the ladder t'bed!" shouted one man.

" 'Ave 'im kick the clouds!" yelled another.

"Time for a Tyburn jig!" called someone close to the bar.

Neville drew off his glove, one finger at a time. "All of these men have comrades in the Royal Navy, Tolbert. Many of them have learned that those friends are now dead after battling the Americans. They would gladly send you to hang."

Mrs. Tolbert screamed and pressed her hands to her throat.

Mr. Tolbert ignored her, other than to hiss, "Silence!" again in her direction.

"But," Neville said, "that doesn't explain how you knew de Romilly had information you could use."

"We have allies within the *émigré* community. Allies who are eager to help the emperor so he will return their titles and their lands and their wealth." He sneered. "Allies you would never suspect, Hathaway. You can hang us, but that will not halt us."

"Who knows?" Neville laughed icily. "Instead of hanging, you may get to see the inside of the new prison on Dartmouth Moor that has been built for prisoners of war."

"Imbécile!" shrieked Tolbert's fake wife as she jumped to her feet. *"Tu es un imbécile!"*

The men gathered in the tavern laughed, because the words needed no translation. They thought Tolbert was a fool, too.

"Bluster all you wish, Hathaway!" shouted Tolbert. "I will gladly lay down my life for my country."

"That is good to know," Neville said with another laugh, "but I am sure officials in Whitehall will want to speak to you before you go off to your glorious martyr's reward."

Tolbert spun to flee out the door.

Priscilla picked up one of the heavy metal trays and, as he passed her, brought it down squarely on his head. He stumbled forward, hit the door, and fell to the floor. He groaned once, but did not move.

Looking across the room to the Frenchwoman, she said nothing as she raised the tray again. The woman obediently resumed her seat and did not move while Neville made arrangements with Mason, the publican, to have the two spies locked up and guarded until the justice of the peace returned after Christmas. At that time, the law would deal with both of them.

Even though it should have been simple, the arrangements took most of the evening. Priscilla was anxious to return to Shadows Fall, so she could spend Christmas Eve with her children. As soon as Neville was assured that the Tolberts would not be able to escape, he rode back with her through the snow.

A soft glow filled the entry hall when they came into the house. Handing a footman their wraps, they walked toward the glow. It was coming from the solar.

On the hearth, the Yule log was burning, but that was not what caught Priscilla's gaze. A gasp bubbled from her lips when she looked at another *Tannenbaum* set by the window. A score of candles were attached to its branches, each one reflecting in the windows like Christmas Eve stars.

"Happy Christmas Eve, Mama," Leah said as she jumped up from where she had been sitting with her great-aunt and siblings. She rushed to hug Priscilla.

"A very happy evening." Priscilla looked over her daughter's head to where the de Romilly family sat close together. "Everything is exactly as it should be now."

The vicomtesse's face shone like the candles as she leaned her head on her husband's shoulder and ruffled her children's hair.

Jamie sprawled on a chair, still in the throes of his discomfort after giving a bottle a black eye last night. He glanced at them, groaned, and put his arm over his eyes to protect them from the light. Opposite him, *Graf* von Zell was admiring the tree, tears of joy in his eyes.

"Well, not everything." Lord Witherspoon rose from where he had been sitting next to Daphne. "There is one more word that could make this evening perfect." He dropped to one knee in front of her.

Neville took a half-step forward, but Priscilla put her arm out to block his way. There were proper times for him to play the protective papa. This was not one of them. After almost two years of asking Burke to wait for Daphne to reach a marriageable age, the time had come to let Daphne make the decision that would change her life. She was old enough, and she had proved that she was mature enough.

Her daughter's eyes glowed with joy when Burke, as Priscilla knew she must learn to think of him, clasped her hand between his. Isaac opened his mouth to make a comment, but Leah clamped her hand over it. She gave him a scowl worthy of Neville himself, and Isaac subsided. His mouth and eyes became complete circles as he realized what he was about to witness.

No one spoke. The only sound was the crackle of flames on the hearth and the soft puffs of their breathing.

"I cannot think of a better time or a better place to do this," Burke began. "I have loved you, Daphne Flanders, since the first time I saw you. You are so fresh and so straight-forward. You did not simper or flirt with every man as the other young misses did. That is why I offered you my heart the very first time we danced."

"And I offered you mine," she said.

He went on as if she had not spoken. Priscilla's smile widened. The poor young man was so nervous that he must fear that, if he paused, he would forget what he wanted to say.

"You were young. I knew that, which is why I acceded to your parents' wish that we wait. But you are now eighteen, my darling Daphne —"

At that endearment, Isaac screwed up his

face like he was about to vomit. Leah slapped his arm, but a grin tugged at her lips. A quick glance from Priscilla stilled them both.

"And I ask you to grant me the honor, the greatest honor I can imagine, and agree to become my wife. Say that you will. Please say that you will."

"Yes," Daphne whispered.

As Burke stood, still holding her hands, a laugh came from behind Priscilla.

Jamie opened his eyes and rolled them, then groaned. "Lor', I didn't think ye'd ever finish, Witherspoon. All that fancy m'lord chatter."

"You would have done differently?"

"I would 'ave grabbed 'er and kissed 'er until she 'ad breath only enough to say yes."

"That sounds like a good idea." With a laugh, Burke spun Daphne into his arms and claimed her lips.

Cheers sounded all around, save for an offended sniff from Aunt Cordelia and a rumbled curse from next to Priscilla. She turned to her husband and smiled. "Neville . . ." She shook her head. "You must accustom yourself to having a son-in-law who will want to kiss his bride."

"If I must."

She laughed. "Yes, you must."

"I can think of one way to keep the sight from disturbing me."

"By not watching?"

"No, by doing this." He pulled her into his embrace and kissed her as the light from the *Tannenbaum* and the Yule log glowed around them.

EPILOGUE

London
Six weeks later
"Pris?"

When he received no reply, Neville pushed himself up in the sumptuous bed and looked to the other side. The pillow there held the imprint of Pris's head, but she was nowhere to be seen.

He pushed back the thick bed curtains and grimaced as he put his bare feet on the floor that still held remnants of the long winter's chill. Where could she have gone when the sun had barely risen over the roofs of Mayfair?

"Pris?"

Again, he got no answer.

Then he heard the sound of someone being sick. He followed it to where Pris was on her knees, throwing up. He dipped a cloth in the cool water on the nearby washstand. Squatting beside her, he dabbed her forehead.

She moaned softly, then leaned back against

him with her eyes closed. "Thank you," she whispered.

"Let me help you back to bed. You must have the grippe that has sickened half of London."

"No, it is not that."

"But you are sick."

"No, I am not sick." She tilted her head to look up at him, her eyes soft and filled with love. "I am in, what Aunt Cordelia would call, a delicate condition."

He stared at her. "How? When?"

"Neville," she said, the strength returning to her voice, "I cannot believe you don't know how babies are made."

Instead of responding to her teasing with a jest of his own, he said, "No, no, that's not what I mean. Are you sure?"

"Quite. I have suspected the truth for the past week, but this morning sickness confirms that Jamie may get his wish and no longer be your heir."

He smiled. "He is happy with the allowance I have promised him, whether he inherits or not. It will grant him a good life in Northumberland or wherever he decides to live."

She squeezed the arm he had slipped around her waist. "You are going to be a father, Papa Neville."

He smiled more broadly at the name her children had given him as a joke; then he buried his face in her hair. He drew in a deep breath of her sweet fragrance as he imagined his slender Pris thickening with their child. She would be more beautiful than ever.

Gently, he lifted her into his arms as if she weighed no more than their child would at birth. Carrying her back to their bed, he leaned her back into the pillows. He bent toward her, then paused.

"You silly man," she said, "there is no danger to either me or our baby for you to kiss me . . ." A faint flush climbed her pale cheeks. "Or to do most anything else."

"I love you, Pris," he said, punctuating his words with a quick kiss.

"And I love you, Papa Neville."

With a laugh, he jumped onto the bed and pulled her into his arms. The kiss he gave her was slow and deep and filled with all the joy in their hearts.

No Room at the Inn

BY KAREN FRISCH

Chapter One

Either he had been given poor directions, or his driver had gone off course between the winding roads and the fierce snow pelting the carriage. Was there not one wise man in the whole of Cheshire, he fumed, who knew the whereabouts of the woman he so desperately sought? Right now, he would be satisfied with a reputable inn where he might spend the night.

Major Arthur Winstead, Marquess of Edgemere, had made decisions during the war that held fewer challenges than this journey. Were they still meandering about the county's northeast corner, or had they crossed the border into Derbyshire? The drifts beyond his window made it impossible to tell whether the carriage was even now traversing road or field. He was relieved when the driver pulled to a stop, leaned back, and opened the trap between them.

"Won't be able to see much longer in this blizzard, m'lord," the driver shouted over the storm. "What's your pleasure on such a night?"

It would indeed take an angel of mercy to find a place of safety. The storm had the disconcerting effect of almost making it seem as if he was in battle again and in need of a strategy. With an impenetrable wall of white blocking the view to his left, Arthur glanced out the opposite window. He could barely make out a gallows signpost swaying in the gale. "What does that sign say? The Jolly Goose and Thyme?"

"Can't see clearly, m'lord," his driver admitted, "but it doesn't look to be one of the inns recommended to us."

It looked anything but jolly, Arthur thought, for no windows were ablaze with welcoming light. He studied the faint outline of what appeared to be an Elizabethan manor house beyond the signboard, its creaking audible now. His hope grew as he watched one window grow brighter, then another, as candles were lit within. It might be only a small tavern on a byway, but it promised food, a bed, and a warm fire.

"I have no thyme but plenty of time, and I am certainly hungry as you must be," Arthur muttered. "Since we have likely missed signposts along the way, I take this as a message for us to pass the night here."

Arthur watched as his driver drew alongside the mounting snowbanks before leaving the carriage to announce their arrival, the wind whistling and the snow swirls piling up on the rug until the door was quickly closed, muting the sounds once again. While there appeared to be no proper courtyard in which to disembark, the place at least offered shelter. With snow blocking any view of the landscape, Arthur leaned back in frustration, gazing into the murky brightness beyond his window.

Nor were there any stars in the white sky. No star in the east, he reflected, to guide him to the woman he would claim as his bride, for better or for worse. The visit would undoubtedly come as a shock to Theo's widow, for she was not expecting him. Then again, after all this time, for all he knew, she might have remarried. Somehow, he doubted it, given the depth of love with which Theo had spoken of her.

With five years having passed since Theo's death, Arthur had no idea what to expect. Their meeting was complicated by the fact that he had never met the woman he was to marry. All he knew of her had been formed by Theo's reverent and loving description, and a portrait in a locket tucked safely inside his coat pocket that portrayed a vivacious beauty.

After Theo's death, he had carried the locket with him while the war reshaped his character and forever altered his future. The image within had blessed him with hope in the most dire of situations until he was almost in love with the picture alone. Unfortunately, he had not known her in happier days. How had the ravages of that painful time changed her, he wondered?

The likelihood that Rosemary Boughman had moved forward with her life made Arthur reluctant to visit so long after he had promised to ease her pain and hardship. Now, five years after Theo's death, he felt inadequate to the task before him. Suddenly, he feared disappointment, suspecting at the end of his search he might find a woman with whom he was incompatible, one who had begun a new life, leaving behind her sad memories of the war and the husband she had lost.

While he still carried the guilt for not coming sooner, his reasons for waiting had been legitimate. He had been responsible for the men in his command for four years after Theo's death. After traveling home, he had been forced to assume responsibility of his family's estate during his father's illness and subsequent death. Still, he was anxious to keep his last remaining promise. It would be the hardest to fulfill.

And so he had chosen to travel just before Christmas, partly because his sisters had given him an ultimatum. If he did not find himself a bride, they would find one for him.

And they had. While Dolly MacAdam would make a perfectly suitable wife, his sisters knew nothing of his promise to Theo, for he had not told them. Instead, he'd left a letter outlining his intentions to be read after his departure.

Was it possible Theo's widow would find his presence an imposition? Christmas had always been the most special time of year. Bringing news of her husband's final hours hardly seemed a suitable gift, but he knew it would be most welcome, for she must still wonder what Theo's final thoughts had been. Perhaps, Arthur thought, he was already too late. He did not know how he would feel if Theo's widow were already wed to another.

In the silence of the carriage, with only the wind to disturb his thoughts, he removed the locket for another look at the widow to whom he was traveling. The portrait depicted a strikingly beautiful, fair-haired, blue-eyed woman. During the war, her image had come to represent far more, symbolizing hopes of future happiness, of marriage, of peace. Despite her delicate features and soft smile, he did not want to marry her or anyone, ironically. The stress of war combined with previous romantic disappointments, one especially, had left him numb.

Yet, despite his reluctance, the time had come not only to honor his friend's wishes, but to make a commitment. With the responsibility of running an estate came the perpetuation of the family through children, and that necessitated marriage. Now that he was safely home and readjusted to civilian life, it was time to put the war behind him and find a bride.

At the very least, he would be relieved of his guilt. With the burden gone, his spirits might be revived. Now that his father had passed, he could keep his promise and atone for past injustices without paternal reluctance. The decision to leave home on such a reckless errand so close to the holidays was unquestionably impulsive. In truth, he wished he might have fulfilled his duty before this.

But first he must find her.

The puzzling discovery that no one recognized her name along their journey filled him with misgivings. Arthur patted his pocket, making sure the letter was still there. He was glad he had chosen to deliver it in person, for her son would want it one day. His face twitched involuntarily. What was he to do with a child? And a boy, no less. With four sisters and two nieces, he knew domestic life only as it related to females with their frills and fripperies. A sigh of foreboding escaped him.

Had he made the right decision in journeying this far, with Christmas little more than a month from today? He offered up a silent prayer that his arrival would not cause her more pain.

Arthur watched with relief as a servant began clearing a path to the front door through the relentless snow. The proprietors had probably abandoned the likelihood of receiving travelers hours ago.

Discouraged, he leaned back in his seat. He would have to wait until tomorrow to resume his search for the elusive widow who appeared to have vanished.

Shortly before the carriage arrived, Rosemary Boughman approached the window in the great room, unnerved by the rattling of the lattice panes. Four hours earlier, the beauty of swirling flakes in the lantern's glow had taken her breath away. The next time she had looked, gusting wind and rising drifts had filled her with foreboding. Now, snow hugged the glass, obliterating her view, and she knew with all certainty no guests would call, for the road fronting the inn would be impassable.

Fighting disappointment, she reminded herself of the fun that awaited Tad when the storm ended. Playing in snow required no investment of funds. She forced a smile and returned to the hearth, lured by the irresistible combination of the fire's warmth and Charley's fiddle. Tad had taken up his flute as well, raising it to his lips with a look of intense concentration to join in the jig

176

Charley had chosen to play. Stepping gingerly over the spaniel and greyhound lying before the fire, she resumed her seat on the settee, clapping enthusiastically when the duet concluded.

"How lovely that was. Sing with me, Tad," she suggested, embracing her son as he returned to her. "A ballad perhaps. Or have you two something else in mind?"

"I suspect the lad has sleep in mind, for the best he can manage is a yawn." Charley grinned, the fire's glow softening his long beard and wrinkled visage. "He rose early with the cold, hoping for snow, and toiled all afternoon helping the servants ready the grounds. He never even had a chance to throw one snowball." The elderly man winked at the boy. " 'Tis a good lad who does a man's job. Tomorrow, you shall wake up to mountains of snow."

"And soon it will be Christmas!" Tad exclaimed.

The fifth, Rosemary reflected, without Theo. Her heart stirred as the boy with eyes so like his father's glanced up at her, his eyelids heavy.

"May we sing tomorrow instead, Mama?" he murmured, laying his head on her shoulder.

"Any song you like, my sweet," she promised, kissing the top of his head. "The sillier, the better."

His eyelids closed once but opened again as she carried him upstairs to bed. He had grown almost too heavy for her to carry. How difficult life had become now that she was alone. While Charley was irreplaceable, a man around her own age would have made life so much easier, not only physically but emotionally. If only Theo had returned from the war like so many other soldiers had. While no man could take his place, she reminded herself, he had done his patriotic duty.

"Mama, do not worry no one has come yet," Tad said softly as she laid him in his bed. "The new sign Charley made has so many colors, it can be seen even in snow."

His words tugged at her emotions. How easily he read her mind. "You are quite right, my love."

Rosemary had not the heart to tell him no travelers would venture out in such a blizzard. Instead, she smiled as she tucked him in, her desire to preserve his optimism stronger than her fear of destitution. She would maintain hope, she vowed, until all signs of it had been taken from them and even afterward. She could always cling to hope.

Charley's words proved prophetic, for Tad was asleep within minutes, leaving her to return to the elderly man and the dogs. The absence of guests for an entire week had left her spirits uncharacteristically low, and she was subdued by melancholy.

The grandfather clock against the far wall startled her out of her reverie by chiming the hour, ticking away the days of winter along with the minutes of her life. The sound added to her sense of gloom, reminding her that if she ventured out right now she would be buried in snow. If this early storm hinted at what was to come, it would be a long lonely winter indeed.

"Where is your usual optimism?" Charley chided her gently. "I did not know you were capable of anything other than exuberance. Do I detect a hint of gloom?"

" 'Tis only a passing sadness." She managed a smile. "At least I have Christmas with you and Tad to look forward to. But I must wait four more months to see the daffodils bloom."

Theo had also loved the sight of daffodils after winter's bitter cold. Rosemary comforted herself, remembering Spain had been warm enough to make life bearable for him at least part of the time. She drew her shawl about her as she moved closer to the fire.

"With such weather, we might not see travelers for another week," she said wistfully.

"You sound as if you enjoy sharing your home with strangers." Charley sounded surprised.

"Of course, we are in need of money, and I wish our inn possessed the warmth and proximity to the village, for it lies so far off

179

the turnpike road," she admitted frankly. "But I find it most gratifying when travelers bring news of London and visiting family nearby, and when our venture meets with their approval."

"You need no approval from others, my lady," Charley assured her. "Yours comes from knowing you have managed to keep your father's house as he wished. One day Tad will own the land his great-great-ancestor was granted for service to the Crown. He will grow up hearing of glorious battles for which his grandfather was knighted in America's War of Independence. And having two knights in a family is an honor indeed. An impressive bloodline for a young boy," he added gently, "with a heroic father as well."

Rosemary felt a lump in her throat. "A father he will never know."

"A father he will know from his mother's stories," Charley admonished. "Tad will remember how valiant you were in saving his grandfather's lands for his own heirs. He has a mother as brave as any knight in the King Arthur tales he loves so."

"Not always as brave as she might wish," she warned.

"But one whose tireless efforts will one day provide for her son. I see no failure there but rather the promise of success."

"I am not convinced of success with our home in such sorry shape." She held her breath, hoping Charley would disagree. Yet if he were to be honest, how could he? "I fear what the future holds."

His hearty laugh startled her. "If you have any fear, you have never shown it. You have proven you are made of the same stuff your father was, and are every bit as brave." He lowered his voice to a tone of tenderness. "He sends his blessing down from above, lass, with Theo's as well. You cannot fail."

Hearing those words allowed Rosemary to push her troubles aside and strengthen her own convictions. How could she wallow in sorrow when she had Papa's chum as a retainer?

"You are right. Oh, Charley." She sighed deeply. "Papa could have had no better friend, nor could I. Thank you for reminding me better days lie ahead. How fortunate I am to have you."

"I am fortunate to be here. By the by, you did an excellent thing allowing Tad to choose a name for the inn. It made him feel part of our endeavor."

"When I asked what we could offer guests, he said it was our welcoming goose and silly rhyming songs. Hence, the Jolly Goose and Rhyme." Laughter bubbled up within her despite the wind that rattled the panes. "Play me a rollicking jig, Charley. I shall warm myself with a dance."

He positioned the fiddle beneath his chin.

"Pretend it is rain drumming out a melody, my lady. Summertime will bring travelers flocking to our door and fortune to follow." A noise from without, faint but unmistakable, made him glance at the snow-shrouded window in surprise. "Perhaps we ought to stoke the fire. It appears we might yet have a visitor."

The merry strains of a fiddle lightened his spirits as Arthur made his way up the cleared walk accompanied by the driver. To his disappointment, the welcome music concluded as the massive front door was opened from within, allowing him to hurry in from the gale.

"Please forgive my intrusion at this late hour," he apologized to the elderly man and young woman who stood before him as clumps of snow dropped from his greatcoat. "I know that here in the country, it is customary to arrive before dark, and I fear I have exceeded that by far too many hours."

"We are happy to offer you a room despite the hour," the woman assured him.

"You cannot know what a welcome relief it is to find shelter. You are most kind." Arthur moved to the fire to warm his hands, grateful for his incredible luck.

"I trust you had no difficulty with footpads tonight," the older man said cheerfully. "In a storm like this, even they dare not be out at their nasty work."

"The only enemy we feared was the snow," Arthur admitted, grinning. "I suspect we left the main road some time ago and came by field and dale instead."

His enthusiasm returning, he watched as the pair bustled about with efficiency, the white-haired, ruddy-cheeked man moving a wing chair closer to the fire while the woman spread a quilt over the back of it. She was far too young, he observed, to be his wife. Noticing her blue eyes, delicate cheekbones, and golden ringlets massed about her thin shoulders, Arthur complied happily when she insisted he sit and warm himself. Dressed simply, she radiated an air of competence and nobility. Her blushing countenance and upturned full lips reminded him of a rosebud in snow and were every bit as welcome.

Why did she seem familiar to him? His gaze wandered down her form, lingering as it went, noting the soft skin on her slender neck and throat down over the generous curves of her body. It embarrassed him to realize he felt something akin to lust for her, especially on such a bitter cold night. He was certain they had never met. He would have remembered such charm and beauty. Yet there was a familiarity about her that held distinctly positive associations. As he studied her, a greyhound and a spaniel pushed their wet noses at him in welcome, vying for attention.

"Come, Maxwell, Millicent," she scolded gently, returning them to the rug before the fire. "Max and Milly are excellent greeters, but I would prefer they not overwhelm you on your first night."

"I imagine it shall be my last, for I will likely set off tomorrow," Arthur said in an apologetic tone. At first glance, the inn seemed the sort of place he would want to linger. "To call at my destination at this late hour would have been unforgivably rude, I fear."

The elderly fiddler chuckled, his step surprisingly spry as he hobbled away. "You shall set off when the weather allows you to, I suspect. I shall have Cook prepare the stew, Rosemary, while you make our guest at home."

Startled, Arthur stammered his belated thanks. Could it be after all his travails he had stumbled upon the woman he was seeking? Surely the name was no coincidence. Although it was difficult to see with her in motion, he tried to absorb every detail of her face as she collected the dogs from his ankles once again, coaxing them with sweet murmurs back to their spots by the fire, their tails thumping all the while. Although her youthful effervescence had dimmed somewhat with age, the delicate features appeared to match those in the portrait in Theo's locket. If she were indeed the same Rosemary, her hair was more golden than he could have imagined and her features far sweeter and more animated.

"Do not trouble yourself overmuch," he told her hastily, "for I am fond of dogs, and I can make do with a roof over my head. But tell me, might you be Rosemary Boughman? The Lady Theodosius Boughman? If so, you are the very person I have been seeking."

Arthur's voice faltered as she paused in the middle of rising, her stare confirming his suspicion. She was far more than his destination.

She was his future wife.

Chapter Two

She lifted her face to his, her brow creased with curiosity. "You need look no further, my lord. I am Rosemary Boughman."

"It is fortunate indeed the storm sent me off course. I was unable to find anyone in the vicinity who knew your name. I suspect we traveled far off course." How fortuitous he had taken the creaking of the sign as an omen. Elated by the turn of events, yet sobered by the revelations he had come to share with her, Arthur reached inside his breast pocket, fumbling for the item he had kept safe since the war. "I should have recognized you from your portrait. I am Arthur Winstead, Marquess of Edgemere. Major Winstead. Your late husband entrusted this to me so I might return it to you."

He watched the color leave her face as he removed the gold locket by candlelight. Her hands trembled as he placed it in them gently.

"You knew Theo," she whispered. She opened the familiar heirloom shakily, as if to be sure her husband's miniature was still beside her own, a fact confirmed by the anguish in her eyes when she glanced back at him. "I know your name from his letters. Forgive me, I did not recognize it at once. Please, tell me everything. Were you with him when he died? I have wanted to believe he did not die alone."

Arthur tried to remain objective as he gazed into those compelling blue eyes that demanded the truth. Instead, he hesitated at the overwhelming prospect of sharing all he had come to tell her. Where was he to begin? She needed to know, painful as it was.

"I was with him on the battlefield at the end," he said softly. "I assure you, my lady, his final thoughts were happy ones. He spoke only of you and your son. He knew that although he would never see him, young Theodosius would be raised by the most devoted of mothers."

Knowing no words could ease her pain, he delivered the news in as reverent a tone as possible. The anguish and eventual acceptance in her face pained him acutely, more than previous instances in which he had delivered such tidings. He watched her raise a delicate hand to her cheek as if either to soften the blow or to recreate a tender moment from the past. No matter how heartfelt, he knew with a surge of anguish, no words of condolence could justify the sacrifice of a beloved husband and father.

"Tad, Major," she murmured. "We refer to my son as Tad."

Remembering the promise he had made Theo, Arthur suddenly felt inadequate to the task before him. Humbled by her emotional strength, he called upon the kindness and efficiency for which he was renowned to offer her belated comfort while trying to quell his own discomfort.

"As Theo's commanding officer, my lady, I can assure you he died a hero. His contributions to our unit were extensive."

He knew by the intensity in Rosemary Boughman's face that his presence had set her mind whirling with questions. Her lower lip trembled as her hands closed over his with so demanding a grip he winced, her fingers insistent, her touch betraying the depth of her pain.

"Thank you, my lord," she whispered huskily. "You have put my mind at ease. There is more I would ask, but it is your comfort we must address first. Perhaps we might speak again after you have eaten."

"I am neither so famished nor so chilled that I would not speak with you now," he said quietly. "How fortuitous our paths crossed while staying at the same inn. I was led to believe you lived locally, but was surprised when I found no one who knew your whereabouts."

As her expression tightened, he recognized the contradiction in his words. He remembered abruptly that her greeting upon his arrival had suggested both service and authority.

"Lord Edgemere, I must dispel your assumption that I hold any title," she said, her cheeks reddening. "I am not a guest. I am the proprietor of this establishment, the daughter of a mere knight. My circumstances have changed since my husband's death."

The deepening in her eyes and distance in her tone warned Arthur of unexpected misfortune. He had no opportunity to question her further as slow heavy footsteps echoing on the stairs indicated the elderly man's return.

" 'Tis all arranged, Rosemary," he announced, out of breath from the exertion. "Major Winstead shall lodge in The Excalibur. Most appropriate for a gentleman who shares the name of the king who wielded that magnificent sword."

"You are guaranteed a comfortable night's sleep there after your difficult journey, my lord," she assured Arthur, her enthusiasm returning, "for it is our finest room and therefore ideal for you. It is also my son's favorite. Perhaps tomorrow, after you are well rested, we might talk more about your experiences in Spain."

Her hospitality could not disguise the subtle

distraction in her manner. Arthur would not rest, he decided, until they had spoken further. He reminded himself he must view her strictly as Theo's widow before he could consider her his future wife, for that discussion would not come until later. His first priority was to answer the questions that troubled her until none were left.

"I should like to hear more about your circumstances before I retire," he urged gently, "especially since you are the widow of the man who became my closest friend during the war."

She hesitated only a moment. "Very well. Charley, please have Major Winstead's dinner delivered to the dining room when it is ready. It appears our guest was Theo's superior officer," she added, a catch in her voice as she turned back to Arthur. "Major, may I present Mr. Charles Broadwell, private in the American War of Independence. He is our retainer here as well as my late father's closest friend and comrade during the war in the Colonies."

Arthur extended his hand, hiding his amusement as the elderly man's polite expression changed slowly, his jaw dropping in awe.

"Major! This is a great honor indeed." The older man startled him by standing at attention and saluting him before resuming his casual pose. "Charley Broadwell, at your service. As Captain Boughman's commanding officer, you know what an exceptional man Rosemary's husband was."

"I do indeed," Arthur said softly. "Theo was the kindest, gentlest soul I have ever had the pleasure and privilege to know. It was an honor even for so brief a time. Knowing him changed my life."

He stole a glance at Rosemary, her gaze downcast but attentive. Charley spoke up intently. "Winstead, is it? Might your father have been a commander in the Colonies?"

It was Arthur's turn to be surprised. "He was indeed."

The old man's smile widened enthusiastically as he chuckled with delight. "I'm proud to say I served under him, and so did Rosemary's father, my chum Humphrey Peltonby. Humphrey was promoted from captain to major and promoted again until he earned himself a knighthood for valor in that honorable struggle. He would've fought Boney himself were it not for his injuries. On our return, he made me retainer here. So grateful was I that I stayed on after his passing to look after Rosemary. I trust your father is well, Major."

"I regret to say he died several months ago," Arthur admitted. "He always spoke with fondness of the men who fought under him."

Within moments, Charley was reminiscing about comradeship and battles with as much affection as if they had been great victories rather than the humiliating defeats Arthur's

father had described. Arthur listened respect-
fully rather than cut short the man's reflections.

"But I shan't keep you, Major, when midnight is nearly upon us," Charley announced
abruptly, "and you're surely in want of food
and needing to talk with Rosemary."

"I would be delighted to reminisce more
tomorrow." Smiling, Arthur shook his hand.
"It is an honor to make your acquaintance,
Private."

He reflected on the conversation as Rosemary Boughman led him silently from the
great room down a long hall with a vaulted
ceiling, the only sound the echo of their
footsteps until they reached the dining room.
Theo's widow took the end seat beside him
at a venerably aged tavern table. Her face
pale in candlelight, she briefly described her
home's illustrious history in the days of Tudor
kings until an aproned cook delivered a
hearty, steaming bowl of stew, setting it
before him with an admonition not to burn
himself before departing.

"You must have traveled a great distance to
deliver this locket," Rosemary said quietly. "I
thank you more than you can imagine. It lifts
my spirits to believe it comforted Theo."

"My home in Warwickshire is not far. May
it comfort you as well, now."

Encouraging him to eat, she held the locket
tightly. From the miniature within, Arthur

had known she was once extraordinarily beautiful. Despite suffering a loss no woman should have to endure, she possessed a delicate loveliness and surprising vibrancy still. While he avoided his sisters' discussions of hair fashions, he knew Rosemary's was outdated, yet the style failed to detract from her appeal. Her clear, compelling blue eyes assessed him with their intensity, reminding him with painful poignancy of his dual reason for coming.

"I would be happy to answer any questions you have regarding Theo's service," he prompted when he finished eating, knowing many widows were anxious to know the truth, yet reluctant to ask.

She hesitated. "I have only the official word from Sir William Beresford along with some notes of condolence from the soldiers — yours among them. I thank you for that."

"It happened in Spain, as you know, at Albuera. While we lost three regiments that day," Arthur said quietly, "Theo saved countless British lives. None of the men he commanded will ever forget him."

He decided to answer her questions as truthfully as possible, employing discretion when necessary, omitting the gruesome details he could not erase from his own mind. Memories of the bleak struggle that had been a slaughter for both sides made him choose his words as carefully as if he were handling the deadliest explosives.

She waited until he had finished, absorbing each answer with calm strength until they had exhausted the most pressing issues. She was, he marveled, as brave as Theo had been.

"I knew what little he shared in his letters, but I always suspected he protected me from the reality," she said quietly. "Thank you, Major, for your honesty. As Tad gets older, he will want to know the role his father played. Knowing the details will help me explain it. I am not surprised Theo put himself in harm's way to save others. He was noble in all things."

Fighting a familiar uneasiness, Arthur was grateful she had raised the subject he had long avoided. Her words had given him strength to speak the truth his father had discouraged.

"If I have any regret, it is that Theo was not able to stand beside me and be hailed as the hero he truly was," he admitted, his words causing him the pain he expected and probably deserved. "Having decided on a bold and successful strategy during our final battle, we had neither time nor opportunity to discuss it with our superiors."

"I remember reading of your heroic actions," she said softly. "I saved the newspapers upstairs."

"You might have read that the plan to distract the enemy with an attack was mine."

His courage must not fail him now. "In reality, the idea was as much Theo's. I was unconscious for a week and could not attend the graveside ceremony. When I finally awoke, I discovered the troops had been told the strategy was my idea."

She studied him uncomprehendingly. "Yet you told your superiors of his contribution."

"I told everyone. Anyone within hearing."

Arthur remembered vividly the moment he learned he was so severely injured that he was not expected to live. His superiors assured him that Theo's accomplishments were recognized at the memorial service. Yet in the discouraging weeks afterward, he had discovered that a living hero was more valuable than a dead one, not only to the unit but to those who would hear the news back home in England. He had done everything in his power to see that Theo received the distinction due him. Nothing mattered more to him than convincing Rosemary of that so he might finally clear his conscience.

"The newspapers felt I was merely being noble. They assigned most of the credit to me."

His heart pounded so loudly he was surprised she did not hear. Her eyes were averted but wary while she paused as if trying to make sense of his apology.

"So the strategy that made you a hero was as much Theo's as yours, but he did not get the recognition he deserved," she clarified, looking back at him. "Is that what you are saying?"

"That is it precisely." He felt crestfallen just remembering. "Had I not been near death, I would have told the troops how Theo ran before enemy lines to set up our plan. How he volunteered to do it. How heroically he risked his life and lost it. I suspect the newspapers felt they might better serve our countrymen by celebrating a living hero."

The bitter truth poured from him helplessly, as if the sturdiest dam had broken. No words were adequate to capture the horror and confusion of that day, for England had no parallel. Tears pricked his eyes as he gave her time to consider the perspective.

"From what Theo wrote me of war, Major, I understood that every man does the best he is able at all times," she said slowly. "You have held yourself accountable. There is no shame. The commander must be saved."

"They told me Theo was honored with great distinction on the field. I understood it to be both memorable and fitting." A final shuddering breath escaped him.

"And of course, you lived," she conceded with a sad smile, "while Theo lies buried on a battlefield in Spain."

"But not forgotten, Mrs. Boughman. Never forgotten. His grave is marked," Arthur assured her, desperate for her understanding and forgiveness. "I hope I might take you there one day. I could bring you to the spot."

She remained silent for so long, he wondered if she might retract her offer of a room. Perhaps she could not be blamed for wanting to do so.

"I hope I have answered your questions," he said gently. "Is there more you wish to know?"

"Thank you for easing my mind, Major. I have only two questions left," she said, her emotions under control. "In his final letter, Theo said he had found a way to provide for me. He did not specify, and I never understood what he meant. Perhaps you might know. Since you were with him at the end, I should, of course, like to know his final words as well."

It was the moment Arthur had dreaded since Theo's death. The answers to her questions were one and the same. He took a deep breath.

"I believe I can answer both, Mrs. Boughman, for they are related. May I take your hands in mine? It would give us both strength." As she reached for his hands, he felt hers tremble. His own palms were sweating. "With his final words he told me how very deeply he loved you, that every word of love he ever spoke to you was true and honest. That the love and the happiness you gave him was what sustained him. He wanted you to know your marriage was the happiest moment of his life despite the circumstances. He knew you would understand."

Her eyes remained open despite the pain he saw there. Tears slid silently down her cheeks. Forced to look away to save her discomfort, he could not keep the huskiness from his voice as he relayed Theo's declaration of undying love. He glanced back furtively and saw she wept in silence, a sniffle and final sigh a minute later signaling her open grieving had ended. It was some time before he could gain control of his own emotions. Still holding her hands, he felt her strength return before his own.

Now he had reached his newest assignment, a campaign on the home front.

"Theo made a request of me, Mrs. Boughman," he rushed on, desperate to make restitution for the pain his words brought her. "It was your husband's wish — his request, in truth — that I see to your comfort in the event of his passing. Those were his last words."

She stared at him, the bewilderment in her eyes paining him. "I do not understand."

A man more experienced at flirtation, he imagined, would have expressed it less awkwardly. But his feelings were below the surface, and his words had always come directly from his core. Perhaps a direct approach was in order.

"No doubt you would find it more appealing to have a partner to help you," he said in a gentle voice. "Theo loved you so deeply he extracted a promise from me to care for you if ever he could not. I have come to honor his wishes."

Embarrassment colored her cheeks. "I appreciate your offer, Major, but that is not necessary. I have my father's home here where Theo and I lived. While recent misfortunes have forced me to open it to the public, it is only a matter of time before we have steady customers. And with Charley to help, I need no business partner. Certainly you cannot mean more than that."

As she withdrew her hands, the finality in her voice left him uneasy. How could he have given so little thought to her reaction? He had not wanted to make her wait for news of Theo, but his explanation had complicated matters. He had expected a woman in need, not a war. She had no need of rescue. This woman had fought and won emotional battles, and had the scars to prove it.

Had he not been tactful enough? His older sisters knew just the right words for the most delicate situation. If only they'd been here. They would probably advise him to be more romantic.

Lowering himself to one knee, he took Rosemary's hand in his. As he struggled for words, he saw the doubt in her eyes turn to defiance before she snatched her hand away.

"Surely you are not suggesting marriage!" She laughed in disbelief. "You cannot be thinking of taking Theo's place. I would not let you even if he wanted you to."

"No one could take his place. Your husband loved you deeply, Mrs. Boughman. So deeply that his final request was that I provide for you and your son if anything happened to him — if you will have me, that is." Arthur kept his voice steady, his gaze focused on her, waiting for her look of disbelief to turn first to understanding and then to acquiescence. Perhaps she simply needed time to adjust to the idea.

After a long moment, she rose from the table, moving slowly away. Her silence unnerved him. He was accustomed to angry outbursts rather than this ominous quiet. Perhaps humor would find its mark with her. He did not hesitate to rush into the breach.

"I have my faults, as does every man, but perhaps one day you might find me agreeable to live with," he said lightly. "Surely I am not so ill-favored physically that I could never appeal to you as a husband."

She turned back to him, her eyes filled with something akin to outrage.

"I am sure Theo liked you well enough," she conceded, "but I barely know you. As I said, this is my home, and I have no desire to leave. I am perfectly capable of caring for myself."

How was he to break through her refusal when his closest friend had made her his responsibility? Theo had led him to expect a gentlewoman, gentle in all senses of the word, ready to acquiesce to an offer prompted by loyalty between friends. Arthur's own extensive military accomplishments had not prepared him for this woman's strength. He fought down a sense of humiliation to think he had made such a blunder on his initial attempt.

Too late, he realized he should have given it more thought. He had actually considered the possibility that the widow Boughman might have remarried, when she had actually remained loyal to her deceased husband since his death. While Arthur had had five years to adjust to his friend's death, Rosemary Boughman had just relived it again. His own insensitivity and callousness embarrassed him so profoundly, he was unsure how to proceed.

"Here, let us leave this for another day," he said quietly. "The hour is late, and I have come merely to fulfill my obligation to your husband. I ask only that you consider the idea."

"Fulfill your obligation through marriage?"

Was it disbelief or hostility he heard in her tone? Whatever he had said wrong initially, he had done it again. "Forgive me, I should have given you a proper introduction, for you know nothing about my credentials. I am reasonably well to do," he said, searching for common ground, "with extensive property in Warwickshire. As my legally adopted son, Tad would inherit when he is of age. If you would but consider it, I would be most agreeable to wait however long it takes. It is my intention to fulfill my promise to Theo."

Rosemary Boughman remained as silent as stone, with no hint of weakening. She left him no choice but to continue, causing him to make what he hoped would not be the remark that would push his offer out of contention.

"It is surely better than existing like this in a ramshackle old inn," he resumed gently, "is it not?"

Her blush deepened to an angry pink, the chill in her voice unmistakable. "This was my father's home, Major, and it is now mine. It has been in our family for generations. My forefathers lived and loved here. And as Charley said, my own father was knighted for valor." She trembled with quiet fury. "He will tell you what a hero Papa was."

Arthur frowned with confusion. "I have no doubt your father was among England's finest. But why do you live like this," he persisted, "forced to open your home as an inn, when you are the daughter-in-law of the Duke of Prestfield?"

"Theo must have spoken only of our happiness," she murmured, resuming her seat at the table. "Perhaps he did not tell you that when we met, his father was already arranging a marriage he considered more suitable for Theo. It was love at first sight between us. Time only strengthened our bond. His father threatened to disown him if he considered the idea of marrying a lowly knight's daughter. After they parted ways, we married and lived here with my father." The sarcasm faded from her voice. "Soon afterward, Theo went to war and Papa died. It was then I discovered I was with child. Theo knew of Tad's birth only through my letters."

With his emotions mired deep below the surface, Arthur suspected he should have waited. Her reaction made him feel as if he had run directly into a stone wall. While he found himself deeply attracted to her physically, in this reverent moment, such feelings of attraction felt out of place. She was so much more enchanting, alluring even, than the picture in the cold metal locket had been. He had expected someone sweet and submissive. But she was not docile. She was a living, breathing woman with needs and desires and strong opinions. And memories, he realized abruptly, that conflicted with her future.

"Theo told me you had a son," he murmured after a moment, his nerves shaken. "But I had no idea, my lady, that the Duke of Prestfield had treated you so dishonorably."

"He never shamed me in public. But he disinherited Theo, and the result is the same. You require rest, Major, after your travels," she announced in a weary tone. "Let us continue our conversation tomorrow."

"I have told you the truth, I swear," he rushed on, his heart sinking at his failure to convey all he hoped to offer her. "Theo made me promise to care for you in his absence. While he never received the full recognition I felt he deserved, I did my best to convince my superiors of his contributions. Please let me honor my promise to him by committing my life to improving yours."

"I wish you had tried harder to convince them." Her tone of melancholy turned acrimonious. "You might have won many victories in the past, Major, but I am quite certain this will not be one of them."

CHAPTER THREE

Upon waking the next day, Rosemary's first act was to reach for the locket she had laid on her nightstand. After all these years, it was back where she'd always kept it when Theo was alive. He had worn it beneath his uniform while he was with his unit so he might feel her near him. Pulling herself into a sitting position, she fumbled with trembling fingers to open it. There it was, safe and sound. The sight of Theo's portrait tucked beside her own filled her with warmth.

The artist truly had captured his character, she reflected, marveling at his intense eyes, straight nose, and upturned mouth. Perhaps if she held the locket to her heart for a moment, she could will her love to bring him back. Having the portrait back made everything right again.

Almost.

Tears trickled down her cheeks. Drawing her knees up, she laid the locket on top of them, tracing the sculpted outline of Theo's cheek with her forefinger. She had almost forgotten how muscular his face was. She remembered the rough, masculine feel of it when she had first run her hand along the slight stubble that tingled against her skin.

The miniature had brought him home, breathing life into memories and resurrecting happiness from ashes that retained their heat. But she would never feel him in the flesh again.

The arrival of his comrade and supposedly best friend had complicated and twisted matters so the whole world made less sense. She had read of Arthur repeatedly in Theo's letters and felt as if she already knew him. She valued his presence without measure, for he had comforted Theo in the worst conditions imaginable. She was surprised she had not recognized him at once, though, in letters, men generally did not give physical descriptions of other men.

Yet they told women a great deal. The moment she saw Major Winstead, Rosemary had assessed him as a man of endurance, capable and strong. She was embarrassed and somewhat ashamed to admit, even to herself, that she had been attracted to him the moment he stepped through her door. He had managed to make it to the shelter of her home in last night's blizzard when no other travelers had.

But was Major Winstead's appearance an

unexpected blessing or a disruptive threat? Along with the locket, he had given her a firsthand account of Theo's passing. For that, she would be forever indebted to him. While he might have done more to bring Theo's heroic decisions to the attention of his superiors, a ceremony with his troops present would be exactly what Theo would have chosen as a final farewell. Her resentment was already fading.

But she would not consider a proposal of marriage, if that was what Major Winstead intended. No one could take Theo's place after the sacrifices he had made to be with her. And the major's opinion of her home offended and infuriated her. He did not have Theo's understanding of what it meant to her and Tad and how she had fought for it. Her battle was fought far from Albuera, and she had won.

At least his stories had resurrected the Theo she knew and loved. The Theo who faced challenges calmly and directly and sought solutions, refusing to yield until the matter was solved. If only she could seize this feeling and hold onto it before it slipped away, as she knew it must. How desperately she needed Theo now.

But the moment passed. Her mind struggling with reality, she turned, expecting to grasp Theo's hand. He should be sitting beside her, ready to fold her into his arms, reassuring her that the difficulties she had faced in his absence would soon be a memory.

Instead, the bright white at the windows hurt her eyes, and the blustery wind blew away her precious vision. The new day swept Theo into the past and tumbled Rosemary back to the present, leaving only the locket as a stinging reminder of her loss.

To avoid facing Major Winstead so early in the day, Rosemary decided to first consult the kitchen staff on the day's menu. She had gone only a few steps before Tad's enthusiastic chatter caught her attention. To whom was he speaking? She had raised her son to respect the guests' privacy. She followed the boy's voice around the corner, startled to see a patch of light on the hall carpet from an open doorway. Apparently, the major was awake.

Approaching the doorway, she found Tad leaning against the bed, toy soldiers spread on the bedspread, while Major Winstead reclined beneath the covers. He was shirtless but for an elegant silk robe open to reveal a chest that proved that he had taken excellent care of himself physically.

It had been a very long time since she had seen a man half undressed. She found her attention aroused along with an emotion she could not define. His offer of marriage the night before had unlocked a need she had not recognized, one that went beyond the maintenance of her home. Flustered, she took a step backward.

"Forgive me, Major," she apologized in a formal tone before addressing her son gently. "Tad, we have discussed the matter of disturbing guests, especially this early."

"There is no need to apologize," Major Winstead replied in a jovial tone. "Tad has been sharing his impressive collection of soldiers with me. He has made me feel right at home."

"How thoughtful of him." Rosemary attempted to conceal her flustered state, more concerned at the moment with Tad's introduction to the major than her differences with him.

"See, Mama?" Tad exclaimed, glancing shyly at Major Winstead. "The bright colors in our signpost brought us a guest."

"It is all thanks to Charley's carving and your clever thinking," she said fondly, stepping forward to ruffle his perpetually tousled hair. "Major Winstead arrived last night after you were asleep. He fought alongside Papa in Spain. Did he tell you?"

Tad nodded, taking her hand. "Papa led the troops, Mama," he said softly, his eyes wide with excitement mixed with awe. "He fired a cannon."

"Papa was very brave," she said, keeping

her smile steady. "Among the bravest. Shall we leave Major Winstead in peace while we prepare his breakfast?" And allow him to dress properly, she reflected.

"I look forward to getting to know Tad better," the major said cheerfully. "Perhaps we shall play outdoors today. The sun is bright, and the snow is piled very high. Ideal weather for snowball tossing, is it not?"

"Yes!" Tad exclaimed. "We shall have a snowball fight."

As Rosemary continued down the hallway with her excited son, she glanced out a window. Major Winstead's assessment was accurate. Clearly he would not be leaving today, even if she wanted him to.

The snowstorm had left the road impassable, Mrs. North told Rosemary as she arranged eggs and ham on a plate for Tad in the kitchen. Winking at him, the cook warned he would find the snow waist-high, making him even more boisterous.

After pouring Tad some chocolate and getting him settled, Rosemary continued to the dining room where breakfast was laid out. She was surprised to see Major Winstead already seated, chuckling as Charley described how marching with the military had kept him fit. They rose to greet her before continuing their exchange, chatting as she prepared her breakfast from the sideboard.

"How fondly I remember my old comrades," Charley reminisced, shaking his head. "We celebrated triumph and hardship alike. The worst of it, after the loss of life, was the food. We were issued hardtack from the French and Indian War." He chuckled. "Practically had to drop a cannon ball on it to soften it enough to eat. I admit there was a man or two we might have traded for food."

"It left much to be desired. Some consider good food worth a whole brigade," Major Winstead agreed, flashing Rosemary a mischievous grin, his features softened by the morning light through the window.

His congenial manner with Charley as well as with Tad gave him an undeniable charm she found difficult to ignore. While she respected his courtesy toward Charley, no force on earth could undo or soften the ruination war left in its wake. Knowing there was no interrupting veteran soldiers while they reminisced, Rosemary ate in silence while Charley described what a luxury tobacco had been during wartime. Hearing Tad's cautious footsteps in the hall, she opened her arms to her son. He ran into them, although his eyes strayed shyly and with great anticipation to Major Winstead.

With Tad content to cuddle and listen politely, Rosemary decided to do the same. Charley was at his best when entertaining guests, whether playing his fiddle or engaging them in conversation. What did it matter, she told herself, if her home was old and needed repairs? Basking in the morning sunshine with Tad snuggled against her on this bitter winter morning, she realized how fortunate Major Winstead had been to find comfortable lodgings along the deserted stretch of road in such a storm.

She loved the house with its history and memories. It had surprised her to realize she did not mind sharing it with the world after all. Bundling Tad closer, she realized the topic had changed while her thoughts wandered.

" 'Tis most kind of you to seek out Rosemary at this time of year especially, considering our cozy corner of England is a bit out of the way," Charley was saying.

The major paused, a hint of discomfort shadowing his features. "I intended to call sooner, but my father's illness delayed my coming. With the holidays approaching, I wanted to find Mrs. Boughman as soon as possible, to share the news of her husband's military contributions so she need not spend another Christmas with questions. Knowing is always better than wondering."

And yet, Rosemary thought bitterly, it had been five years since Theo's death. What had taken the major so long?

"That's kind of you, Major, taking time away from your family at the holidays. Brave but dangerous, defying the women," Charley

212

ventured, grinning.

"And occasionally, wise. I left at the first sign of the season, while the pies were undergoing consideration. Those kind of details are best left to the women." The major smiled. "Might I ask precisely where we are located? I could not tell in the fierceness of last night's blizzard."

"You are in the hamlet of Woodhollow End, seat of the famed Peltonby family for centuries, along the road between Wilmslow and Congleton." Charley gave Tad a wink. "It might mean nothing to you, being a stranger here, but we are near one of Tad's favorite places."

"Near Alderley Edge!" the boy said eagerly, turning to Arthur. "Did you fight battles like King Arthur did?"

"I fought in battle, but with different weapons. We will have plenty of time to talk about my experiences," Major Winstead promised. "Tell me about Alderley Edge."

"It's a magical place." Tad squirmed out of Rosemary's lap and ran around the table to Arthur and Charley. "It is where King Arthur and the Knights of the Round Table are supposedly buried. You can see all of the Cheshire Plain from there."

"That is so, my boy. You see, Major," Charley continued, gathering the long-legged child into his lap, his tone deliberately suspenseful, "it is rumored that King Arthur and his knights lie sleeping in a cave within Alderley Edge's sandstone cliffs. The spot is very special to Tad, who possesses a great fondness for the Arthurian legends." He turned to the boy. "And the major has something else in common with King Arthur, Tad. They share a name. He is Major Arthur Winstead."

Rosemary could not resist a smile as she watched Tad's eyes light up at the revelation.

"Were you named after the king?" Tad gasped in awe.

"No. I was named for my father, whose name was also Arthur," the major explained. "He was not a king, but he commanded an army during America's War of Independence. The very army in which Charley fought."

Tad's eyes widened. "Charley said you fought in Spain," he pressed eagerly.

"Fighting today is very different from the way it was in King Arthur's day, Tad," Rosemary said, compelled to speak as she pushed the bitterness of last night's conversation from her mind. "The weapons and strategies are more sophisticated."

Arthur returned Tad's smile. "I am sorry to disappoint you, but I fear I am Arthur in name only."

How enthralled Tad was, Rosemary observed. Studying the sincerity in Major Winstead's demeanor, she wondered whether he was truly as valiant as he appeared. To wait five years after Theo's death before approaching her implied careless indifference. A timely letter describing the details would have gone much further in helping her understand the loss. By now, she had adjusted to her widowhood and had no desire to marry again.

Worse, he appeared not to fully appreciate the effort she had put into her home. He saw its flaws rather than the pageantry of its early years. Even here in the dining room, the four of them filled only a corner of the two-century-old dining table. He could not know, she thought with an acute pang, how she had fought to keep it.

"Mama, may I be excused to get some of my toy soldiers?" Tad asked hopefully. "Major Winstead might be able to tell me more about them."

"What a fine idea, Tad. Why don't you go upstairs and collect them? Quietly, please." Before she had finished her suggestion, he had run from the room, shoes clattering down the hall.

As the conversation returned to war in Charley's day, she considered Tad's future with a pang of bitterness she knew was both uncharacteristic and uncharitable. Why had not Major Winstead, a man without a wife or children, been taken instead? Ashamed of harboring such spite, she felt her cheeks color at her own callousness. She'd heard from Charley that before he'd retired last night, the major had insisted on paying extra for his stay. She should be grateful. Besides bringing cherished news of Theo's final hours, he had given her desperately needed funds that would help them get by when last night's storm had taken business away.

She would remain civil during his visit, for he was no more than a guest. If their new venture was to succeed, she reminded herself, she must extend hospitality to all. Marriage, however, was out of the question. While her status had changed, her heart had not.

Abruptly, Charley raised the matter of chores. "As this is the largest snowfall of the season, I imagine Tad will want the chance to destroy at least some of its unbroken surface," Charley announced cheerfully. "Before the staff clears the walks entirely, I shall see to it that the lad has a chance to enjoy it."

And then he excused himself, his abrupt departure leaving Rosemary inconveniently alone with the major. If Charley thought their differences could be bridged this quickly, she thought irritably, he was mistaken.

"It has been some time since I have had this fine a breakfast, even in my own home," Arthur Winstead said with a guarded smile. "I want to thank the Jolly Goose and Thyme for extending to me the finest hospitality I can remember."

"Rhyme, Major," she corrected him. "It is the Jolly Goose and Rhyme. According to my wise and imaginative son, our animals' friendly greetings and our instruments and songs are what we offer travelers."

"Both of you are talented and charming, then. It is no less than I would expect from Theo's family." As his smile faded, she observed a depth in his earnest eyes that hinted at pain. "During the most difficult time of my life, Theo became the closest friend I shall ever have. While I did not know you then, at least now I have met you. Perhaps you could call me Arthur. May I call you Rosemary?"

"I prefer to be addressed as Mrs. Boughman." Her manner could be no firmer. Could her desires, she wondered, be any clearer?

"You may still call me Arthur," he countered with a tentative smile.

"I shall address you as Major," she declined, intent on retaining her aloofness even as his face fell, "for that is your role in my life."

"Fair enough," he resumed after a pause. "I apologize for our unfortunate beginnings last night. I intended to withhold nothing, for you deserve to know the truth."

"Theo's heroic actions do not surprise me," she admitted, grateful while reticent. "I will share your recollections with Tad when the time comes. I appreciate your coming all this way."

The look of relief mixed with concern that softened his features was not lost on her. "I ask your forgiveness for not coming sooner, but I knew nothing of your circumstances. Theo rarely spoke of his father. I knew only how happy you were."

"There was nothing more to tell, Major. Our happiness was all that mattered. As the younger son, Theo naturally became a soldier. He loved England above all."

"That was evident from his actions." She knew from his hesitation that he sought a diplomatic way to broach a subject he knew would offend her. "I hope that in time, you might consider my offer, bearing in mind that I was Theo's closest friend and that my seeing to your happiness was his final wish."

Of all times for him to enter her life, could any be worse than Christmas? Her happiest memories with Theo revolved around December, when she and Tad still lit a candle for him. For their wedding, the few Christmases they shared together, the discovery that she was with child. Firm in her resolve, she rose from her chair. "I appreciate your thoughtfulness, but I regret you have come all this way only to be disappointed. Having known the deepest love imaginable, I have no need of a marriage without genuine affection. Now if you will excuse me, I must tend to household matters. I assume you have other pursuits that require your attention."

He seemed to fumble for words. "A bit of correspondence, perhaps."

She withheld a sigh of relief, glad to be free of him temporarily. "Then while Charley and the servants are widening the paths to the stable and barns, I will be addressing matters in the kitchen," she said. "That is where you shall find me, should you need anything."

Gazing out the library window, Arthur was relieved to see that the sun had dulled and the sky paled soon after, for it made departing today unlikely and gave him an excuse to linger. Winning Rosemary's trust, he acknowledged, would require more patience than he had anticipated. And perhaps more insight.

He had not given much thought to women, frankly, since Pamela's defection.

In what had been especially unfortunate timing, his occasional companion Pamela Adair had dashed his faith early in the war when their letters had crossed in transit. His had requested her to wait so they might resume their courtship, while hers had announced she had become engaged to another in his absence, a gentleman far less patriotic. Her curt dismissal of his devotion convinced him that women were far more complicated, devious even, than men.

Yet a costly misunderstanding had nearly jeopardized his own purest intentions last night. Captivated by Rosemary's remarkable beauty, he had assumed Charley was the proprietor and she, a mere tavern keeper's daughter. Had he been able to take her between the sheets in this drafty, aging tavern, she would have satisfied his desires, warming him up on this cold winter evening.

His simple raw lust had turned to guilt when he discovered that his hostess, beautiful and warm and inviting, was Theo's widow. When, he wondered, had such great irony accompanied such poor timing? The woman he had come to wed, the widow of his best friend, was the most beautiful one he had ever laid eyes upon, and tender-hearted as well.

While it was one thing to marry for honor, it was quite another to lust after his dead friend's wife.

It had been a long time, he realized, since he had lain with a woman. Not since he had sought consolation in Portugal before leaving duty. When he was finally home in England, he had found comfort with the discreet mistress of a friend. And then duty had called again, in the form of responsibility to his elderly and ailing father, with a pain too deep to be erased in a woman's arms. The reminder of war and his lost comrades, the lives of friends who remained and had either moved on or enjoyed relationships too superficial to have depth or significance, had stolen his taste for female companionship.

Yet none had sparked his interest like the beautiful woman who toiled downstairs. She had the loveliest sky blue eyes that sparkled like a sunlit lake when animated. And he'd wager she had the softest skin . . . Her shawl had slipped a bit as she arranged the afghan over the back of his chair, and he'd caught a glimpse of the creamy expanse of flesh beneath. He longed to run his fingers along the delicate skin of her throat, to entangle his rough fingers in her soft golden curls.

Out of habit, he reached into his vest pocket before he remembered the locket was no longer there. He had become so accustomed to carrying it that he often removed it simply to look at her picture and be reminded that the promise of happiness that awaited him at war's end. But he hadn't anticipated Rosemary's reaction to his arrival. With marrying again not among her plans, this delicate but most determined woman had her heart set on turning her ramshackle home into a successful inn.

For the families of men who did not return, Arthur knew, life would never be as easy or as comfortable. And those who had returned were so changed, they could not resume the same carefree relationships with friends they had left behind, those who remained ignorant of the horrors of war. He found the focus of their lives to be shallow and their pursuits unfulfilling. It prompted him to seek companionship elsewhere, spending more time with his sisters who expected him to resume life by seeking a partner without knowing there was already one he had promised to care for in the absence of her late husband.

He could not deny his attraction to Rosemary Boughman. She was even more beautiful in person than in the hand-painted miniature, more vibrant and colorful, her blue eyes alive with emotion and love for her son. While he had promised Theo that he would look after her, how did he expect her to find Arthur a more enticing husband than the one she had loved and lost?

He heard the scraping of shovels outside and the grunts of servants frustrated by the depth of the snow, distracting him from his reverie. Perhaps he might join them to lighten their load. His promise to Theo was one he intended to keep, despite obstacles from the one who would benefit most, ironically. She was clearly in need of assistance, financial help as well as manual labor. He had both to spare. Doing the honorable thing meant that he must convince her to marry him, and not only for reasons of honor. He could not deny his strong physical attraction to her.

Leaving the library, Arthur retrieved his greatcoat and boots and headed for the kitchen exit, prepared to toil. He had not been outside a full minute, shovel in hand, before the door opened and Rosemary confronted him. He hid his amusement at her chagrin, noting that the severity of her expression did little to mar her beauty.

"A walk tomorrow might be possible, Major," she cautioned, "but I must advise you we are over a mile from the next house, with no additional help to shovel us out."

"I intend to shovel snow from your walkways," he informed her.

"I am afraid I must object, Major." She gave him the stare of disapproval he expected. "First, you are a guest in my home. Second, snow will leave velvet collars in a sorry state, and your Hessians will be ruined. Third, the task of clearing snow is hardly worthy of a marquess."

Slow and steady would earn the victory, he reminded himself. He would be as patient as necessary.

"I am perfectly fit and well rested. I faced greater physical challenges in wartime. I shall do whatever I must to prove myself worthy of you, Mrs. Boughman," he said cheerfully, ignoring her look of alarm. "I would hope, in exchange for my help, we might speak yet again on the topic I introduced last evening. Shall we say half-past three? Perhaps my efforts on behalf of your inn might enable travelers in need of shelter to find it more easily."

Let her argue with that, he thought as he headed into the drifts without turning around. The senses honed in battle told him she was probably watching, still annoyed.

He was glad she could not see the grin on his face.

Chapter Four

The sun emerged again, giving the snow a glittering quality that hurt the eyes. Not only had the servants cleared a path to the front door, Arthur observed, they had also flattened the snow on the road fronting the inn using a board and rope to pack down snow. Impressed to see the staff had the workload well in hand, he noticed Tad had come outdoors and decided the boy would probably enjoy some company.

"What do you say to having a bit of fun?" Arthur teased him, seizing an extra board from a shed. "You shall ride while I pull."

He enjoyed the delight in Tad's laughter as he lifted the child and sat him down on the makeshift wooden sled. As they flattened mounds of snow, the delighted boy's giggles and whoops restored Arthur's own energy. While pulling Tad, he caught a glimpse of Rosemary in the kitchen window, watching intently, no doubt indignant. But it was Christmas, and this was a major snowfall even for this region. He wondered if she was still watching fifteen minutes later when he engaged Tad in a fierce snowball fight. He felt invigorated as snow went down his collar, to Tad's delight.

While walking, he saw seasonal supplies kept in storage, including winter shoes for the draft horses and a set of runners that could replace the carriage wheels should anyone need to travel. He was relieved to find the animals safely housed in barns. Given Rosemary's isolation, he was suddenly grateful that serendipity had sent his carriage off the main road.

He went indoors when the servants insisted, for Tad had tired himself out, and Arthur rewarded the boy's efforts with hot chocolate from the kitchen. The child, he mused, managed to capture the essence of both parents equally. He had his mother's piercing blue eyes and blond curls, but the set jaw, straight nose, and square chin were the image of Theo. The combination created an altogether winning and charming countenance.

With the storm putting the house in an uncommon state of turmoil, he enjoyed Charley's company over dinner. Confiding the graver aspects he had spared Rosemary, Arthur described Theo's heroics in battle along with Arthur's frustration at his father's reluctance to change public belief.

"Perhaps I am looking for some sort of

redemption," he admitted slowly, determined to clear his conscience, "but after witnessing such a courageous tactical maneuver on Theo's part, I cared not if my own reputation was sullied, for England's was preserved."

"Do not trouble yourself with past injustices, lad, especially in the heat of battle," Charley said gently. "Theo would have understood and forgiven you."

"I confess I knew nothing of Theo's differences with his father until Mrs. Boughman told me. I am disappointed she rejected my offer, but I suspect she needs time to adjust to the idea. I have every intention of keeping my promise." Arthur shook his head. "What must I do, Private, to convince her of my sincerity?"

"Lad, I believe you take your responsibility to Rosemary and Tad seriously. I value my service to the Crown more than me life, but once I was transported back to England —" Charley shook his head. "I've been home long enough to know nothing in life is as important as family, 'specially since I've none of me own. But I have Rosemary and her boy, and I respect her wishes. I must warn you, she has run this property alone for a long time, and she has her own ideas about how to spend her life."

"I had hoped she would be more receptive to the idea of marriage," Arthur admitted. "Indeed, I expected it."

"I know it seems unusual," Charley agreed. "But give her time."

Rosemary could not have made it clearer that she came prepared to do battle. After greeting her in the sitting room, Arthur seated himself in a chair as she directed, noticing she waited until he had chosen a seat before taking the one opposite him.

"I must compliment you again," he began truthfully, "on an excellent night's sleep. Between the fine bedding and savory food and drink, you have created a hostelry of which your husband would have been proud."

"Thank you, Major." His sincerity seemed to defuse her resentment. Had he not already committed to delivering a marriage proposal, she might have persuaded him with the depth and beauty of her blue eyes alone. "For some time, I suspected we might be forced to open our home as an inn. I knew we could also entertain. Night after night, I have told Tad bedtime stories of knights, dragons, and legends in these parts. And Charley's music and carving provides a bit of cheer. You saw our signpost. After Theo's death, the inn became the most likely prospect for our survival. Poverty, you see, is the dragon I fight."

"Sometimes hope is born of misery. And your sign was most welcome in last night's blizzard," Arthur said quietly, choosing his words carefully. "I believe in signs, Mrs. Boughman. I hope yours will give you a good livelihood. Innkeepers are traditionally a respected part of the community. Surely you must be as well."

She gave him a wan smile. "People in these parts have long memories, Major."

"Perhaps not as long as you think. If you recall, I found no one who knew your name."

"Or would admit to it," she countered. "Much has happened in the five years since Theo's death. He, of course, never knew we had fallen upon hard times. I am glad it did not happen while he was alive. I would not have wanted him to worry."

"I wish I had been able to call sooner," Arthur admitted frankly. "I was unaware you were living in such poverty, forced to open your home to the public."

"If it was so important for you to share your glory with Theo, why did you not approach me until now?" she demanded, her tone cautious.

"I would have done so without hesitation, Mrs. Boughman," he explained. "I have been home from the war less than a year."

It would take all the discretion he could call forth, he thought, to deflect the guilt she had directed toward him. While her unspoken accusation stung, he refused to feel penitent for respecting and honoring the wishes of his dying father.

"My father was seriously ill," he resumed quietly. "He was perhaps pleasantly surprised that I had lived up to his expectations and helped win the war, something he was not able to do in the Revolution. He felt he had failed as a commander, and England's loss affected him profoundly. I believe that is why he found it difficult to share the glory I had earned. I suspect he lived for my victories, as if I had restored our family name and reputation. In refusing to let me relinquish the honor he felt I had earned, he was thinking only of our family. He died three months ago. It was my intention to make amends to you before this year was out."

"You are hardly coming to claim a blushing young bride, Major. I am a widow. My past and my future are here," she said, sitting upright as if to make her slight form appear more imposing. "The war took my husband from me, but not my means of survival. I believe we have done well enough without you."

"It is clear to me that you have not, my lady," he said softly. "What your husband envisioned was an arranged marriage between us. Even if you do not desire the comfort of a husband, Theo wanted Tad to be raised with a father. I realize now, it is probably because he did not get along with his own. Theo considered it the most important role in a man's life. He chose me to play that role."

Why the devil was his insistence, combined with cold, hard truth, not enough to convince her? He had watched Theo take his final breath. She could not know that her husband's emotional suffering outweighed the physical. She knew only that his death left her as sole supporter of their young son, dependent on an aging home to save them from ruin.

"While you see fatherhood as an obligation, I am certain that is not what Theo intended. You feel a sense of responsibility, but not love." She paused, a catch in her throat. "For five years, I have viewed myself as a mother and a widow and now as an innkeeper. I already fell in love with a man who married beneath himself. I do not intend to do it twice. Why would I, when I knew perfection the first time?"

"Because Tad needs a father, and you need someone to help you run this inn." Studying the determined set of the blue eyes that were colder than ice now, Arthur recognized the formidable challenge he faced. He decided to tell a slight fib, for his sisters did not know the whole truth, and he felt a pang of guilt as he recalled their disappointment at his departure. "My sisters in Warwickshire are hoping I will return in time for Christmas with a wife and child."

"And because of that, you expect me to marry you." Her eyes blazed with fury, yet

231

the catch in her throat threatened tears. He watched her emotions turn from anger to despair. "Theo will never receive credit from those who knew him. His father will never know of his bravery, for he does not recognize us as his own. Even Tad is not recognized by his grandfather."

That was news. If she had told Theo, Arthur thought, stunned, he had never mentioned it. He had intended to visit Theo's father, the Duke of Prestfield, while in Cheshire. Now he had another topic to discuss with the man. "I did not realize. Perhaps that is why Theo never spoke of his father. I am sorry. Please allow me to make it up to you. By accepting my offer of marriage, you would be fulfilling Theo's final wish."

"Marriage," she echoed bitterly. "You are a pale substitute for my husband, who risked everything for me — reputation, inheritance, lifelong security. I appreciate your words regarding his final hours, and I regret you have had to come such a distance in this weather, but I can offer you nothing more than hospitality."

What was he to do next? Arthur reconsidered his words in silence. While others considered him a hero, clearly Rosemary believed he paled next to Theo. Calling upon the fortitude he had relied on in battle, Arthur remained patient. Heroes persevered, he told himself. He would persist for her sake until he found another way to her heart.

"Have you truly never considered the possibility of remarrying?" he asked gently.

He watched her fingernails grip the arms of her chair, her tone clipped with frustration. "Marriage requires familiarity with each other. You do not know me, and I do not know you."

"Yet I made a commitment to Theo to protect you," he countered, his tone sharper than he intended, "and the promise must be kept."

"I am not accustomed to being ordered, Major. The only orders I take are from our guests."

"Of which I am one," he reminded her bluntly, no longer able to hide his frustration. "Your husband and father are gone. It is clear you cannot continue to run this inn on your own."

He watched Rosemary's face turn white, then red. Before she could reply, a knock at the door startled them both. The door opened and Charley appeared, smiling with anticipation.

"A guest has arrived by horseback, my lady," he announced, "and he wishes to stay the night. I shall have a room prepared to welcome him."

Rosemary stood up at once, relief and triumph in her face as she turned to Arthur.

"You arrived too late last evening to enjoy

our entertainment," she said coolly. "Tonight you will see how we intend to make this inn a success and why it is so important to us."

CHAPTER FIVE

"Two miles is not far on horseback," the newly-arrived gentleman told Rosemary with an apologetic smile, seating himself in the chair she indicated. "But in last night's blizzard, I could not travel even that far to my sister's. I daresay the poor woman who took me in felt a bit put out. I am glad she directed me here and that my horse was able to push through."

"Even those in the tiniest cottage could not be so cold-hearted as to turn a traveler away in such a storm," Rosemary assured him kindly. "We are glad you have come, Mr. Wiggins. Now that you are here, you shall be well provided for."

Watching from a corner chair, Arthur was struck by her efficiency as she instructed Joseph to take the guest's knapsack upstairs while dispatching Mrs. North to prepare tea. Rosemary delivered orders as promptly and with as much confidence as any officer he had encountered in Spain.

The guest's arrival meant the roads were beginning to clear. Even in snow, Arthur guessed, the journey to the duke's residence would be under two hours. The visit would give him an excuse to remain and attempt to convince Rosemary to accept his proposal. If nothing else, having the chance to observe her proved she could be kind to travelers, if not to him.

Yet by the following morning, he found that the presence of another guest gave Rosemary a strategic advantage, for she was able to focus on someone other than him.

"Having a second visitor in as many days is encouraging, Major, is it not?" she asked him after he had finished breakfast. "I am certain others will follow and help make our inn a success."

While he remained doubtful, he understood her desire to prove him wrong and seized the few chances he had to observe her throughout the day. As an innkeeper, she was as decisive as a major but with a feminine touch. She ensured every spoon was polished until it shone and every detail in Wiggins's guest chamber passed her inspection. The diminutive woman made the large, drafty home as cozy as a cottage. Her kindness filled the emptiness, making the public rooms warm and inviting. In the absence of relatives, visitors became her family.

Having spent the morning reminiscing with

Charley, Arthur sat by the fire afterward to catch up on news, finding only an outdated newspaper, an oversight he attributed to the storm. Rosemary startled him at one point by laying her hand on his shoulder when he had apparently dozed off.

"Take heart, Major," she said with mock sympathy. "Soon the roads will clear, and you shall be on your way again."

As if this irony could bring him comfort, when she was the reason he had come. When one strategy did not work, Arthur reminded himself, a commander tried other options. He would press his suit with Theo's widow until he succeeded. She required patience, he told himself. Steadfast patience.

One advantage of having Rosemary preoccupied, Arthur discovered, was that he was able to get better acquainted with Tad. He had not expected to be so captivated by the child, whose gentle nature and wry sense of humor reminded him so much of Theo. His friend's son became a looking glass, through which Arthur attempted to gain insight into the boy's mother.

"I understand you chose the name of the inn," Arthur began, "and a fine one it is. You certainly do have a friendly goose and dogs to welcome guests and, of course, horses. I imagine you like animals," he said, as they lined up Tad's soldiers together in the library.

"They keep me company when we have no

guests," Tad admitted. "Most of the time it is lonely."

"I suppose it can be fun to be an only child," Arthur countered. "I have four sisters who are always telling me what to do. Should I send one your way, so you can see what it is like to have a sister?"

Tad giggled, his dimples making his face cherubic. "Yes, please, sir. Please send a nice one."

"One day you might have brothers or sisters," Arthur suggested cautiously, watching for his reaction.

Tad brightened before his face fell. "I would like that. But Mum says I can't now that Papa is gone. Mum never had any brothers or sisters either."

Arthur berated himself for having raised the topic to satisfy his own curiosity. Hoping to lift the boy's spirits, he changed the subject. Listening intently, he heard tiny scraping sounds that he was certain did not belong in a library.

"Perhaps mice might make good companions." Arthur leaned toward him with a confidential wink. "I think I hear a few running about."

"I like mice," Tad said frankly, his eyes wide. "Mrs. North is afraid of them. But Mum says the mice need a home, too."

Arthur found it difficult to keep from grinning. Any other woman of her station would have run from the tiny intruders. "Your mum is a kind and remarkable woman."

"It's like with Squire Maxwell and Lady Millicent," Tad said, moving his soldiers into place with a glance at the tail-wagging tan greyhound and brown-and-white spaniel who had tagged along with them. "Max grew up here, but Milly just wandered in. We kept her since she didn't belong to anyone."

"Your home seems like a happy place," Arthur said.

"It's the best in the whole world," Tad replied solemnly, turning away from his soldiers briefly to gaze at Arthur.

The truth was in his eyes, Arthur saw. It gave him insight enough into Rosemary to know his battle had just begun. He attempted to broach the matter of marriage again in the late afternoon when he encountered her in the hallway leading to the kitchen. How beautiful her face was in the waning light through the window, he thought, and how delicate her features.

"Let me ask you again," he pressed, hoping she would know the kindness in his tone was genuine, "for perhaps I did not make it clear how deeply I respect your attachment to Theo, and it is clear that Tad is your greatest concern. While we are not yet well acquainted, we shall become so very shortly. Are you certain you do not wish to marry for Tad's sake alone? I would happily consent to such an arrangement."

To his dismay the smile on her face widened with something akin to affectionate humor.

"I am certain, Major," she assured him. "But if you truly want to help, help me here. See that pitcher of water by the door? I will thank you for carrying it upstairs, if you would be so kind, in case our guest requires water during the night. It may be left on the table outside Mr. Wiggins's door. As you appear to be headed in that direction, I trust it will be no inconvenience."

A moment later, Arthur felt his indignation rise as he stood alone in silence. Did she imagine he was accustomed to taking orders? It had only been a matter of months since he had issued commands to soldiers on battlefields who did his bidding without hesitation. Nowhere had anyone taken for granted his willingness to assume the role of servant. He considered leaving right now. Obviously, that's what Rosemary was trying to goad him into doing.

Yet he looked forward to the evening's promised entertainment, for the idea left him somewhat merry. With grudging acceptance he realized her request was both practical and sensible.

Remembering his promise to Theo, he retrieved the pitcher from the table, headed toward the staircase in the great room, and carried it upstairs carefully so as not to spill a drop.

The music, storytelling, and reminiscences they shared several hours later gave Arthur insight into the life Rosemary had created. With Charley and Tad joining her, the trio chased the cold from the great room with ballads and melodies and laughter, warming both visitors with a combination of song and story entwined in the music of Charley's fiddle, Tad's flute, and Rosemary's lilting voice.

The melodies ranged from humorous to wistful, including a familiar war song that reminded Arthur of his own mortality. Had she chosen it for him? It seemed as if she had. His wealth and status could not remove the emotional scars, for the worst of the memories had returned with him. Yet Charley's stories would have made even the most world-weary visitor laugh as Arthur's reactions shifted between laughter and sentiment.

Rosemary wore a pale blue dress that flattered her with its elegant detailing. While he refused to think of her as a wench, the neckline was low and the waistline high enough beneath her bosom to show that her figure rivaled that of the finest tavern keeper in England. Since the first day she had worn her hair upswept, but tonight it flowed about her shoulders as it had on his arrival, making her look feminine and vulnerable.

Wiggins entered into the spirit of the evening, raising Tad's level of excitement by announcing his Christian name was also Arthur, making the boy feel even more privileged to be in the presence of two gentlemen by the name he so revered.

"I remember my father singing these same songs," Wiggins exclaimed as they concluded a military melody. "I was a lad of twelve or thirteen when he fought in the American war. What memories these lyrics bring back."

Two songs later, Wiggins joined them in singing, leaving Arthur the odd man out. Despite Charley's encouragement, he refrained. His military service was too recent to put him in the spirit to sing.

"I haven't had such a roaring good time since I was Tad's age," Wiggins exclaimed at the end of the evening, laughing as he tried to catch his breath.

Arthur felt compelled to add his compliments as well. "Your singing, my lady, is remarkable," he told her sincerely. "Your voice is clear and sweet and, if I may say so, full of heart. And Charley and Tad's music is as cheerful as one could wish for on a cold night. Truly your entertainment rivals that of the finest country inn."

She beamed with pride. "Thank you, Major. It is our routine and our comfort, and it is more valuable to us than gold. I hope our performance proved to you that we have a growing enterprise here."

The only thing growing, he realized, was his doubt. Each time he had tried to make her consider practicalities, suggesting the house was rather small and too far from the road, she reminded him that she could charge less and give more personal service. As for its placement, she pointed out that it was where her ancestors had built it.

By morning the roads had cleared sufficiently that Wiggins was confident he could make it to his sister's without difficulty.

"I shall remember this stay for a long while," Arthur Wiggins told her fervently before departing. "It brought back memories. I will call again. And next time I shall bring my sister. I suspect she would have a jolly time, just as I did."

It was clear how much Rosemary enjoyed entertaining, Arthur acknowledged, as her visitor continued to thank her profusely for her uncommon hospitality. The same hospitality, he conceded, she had shown him. Despite its drawbacks, if she continued this way, she would develop a reputation for hospitality that would spread quickly.

With Woodhollow End blessed for days afterward with sunshine and melting snow, Arthur had a chance to spend time with Tad while the servants removed the hard-packed drifts that refused to succumb to the warmth. Tad declared Arthur his new best friend, and Arthur found himself charmed by the names Tad had given each of the animals, all of whom he could tell apart, even the sheep.

But it was Rosemary he had to win over. She emerged from the main house after Tad went inside for hot chocolate while Arthur was wandering the grounds, assessing the condition of the buildings. While he watched unobserved, she loaded buckets with chicken feed, earning his full respect before he could rush forward to carry her load.

"Too much falls on your shoulders, my lady. Allow me to help," he offered gently, knowing she could not afford to hire additional servants. He accompanied her into the barn, where she scattered grain for the chickens.

"Thank you, Major, but I am perfectly capable of seeing the animals are provided for while Polly and Martha clean and Mrs. North cooks dinner to the level of perfection I wish," she said simply. "Charley and Sam and Joseph do everything else. In this respect, I am no one's obligation."

"No one could possibly see you as such," Arthur protested, falling in step with her. After some pleasant exchanges, they returned into the bright sunshine where he broached the subject uppermost among his concerns. "I understand you hesitate to ask for assistance from the duke, yet is it not a grandfather's responsibility to provide for his grandchild?"

Rosemary hesitated as if trying to excuse Tad's grandfather from accountability. "The duke associates me with the circumstances that led to Theo's death. I cannot fault him, for I share his loss. He is not obligated to see to our well-being. Nor are you, for that matter." She shrugged, the sunlight on her bonnet giving her a most appealing femininity. "I have chosen the course of my life, and I am satisfied with it."

"I do not wish to diminish Theo in his son's eyes, but Theo is no more real to Tad than a knight of legend. The boy needs a father," he continued gently. "I ask only that you reconsider. Think of his future if not your own."

How could she remain so maddeningly detached? Arthur wondered in frustration. As she gazed at him, the sunlight made her cornflower blue eyes dance.

"But remember his attachment to the Arthurian legends, Major. Here he is able to visit the cliffs at Alderley Edge and imagine what once was and what might be. You propose to take him away from the only home he has ever known. Tad deserves to grow up here, surrounded by the history of his ancestors." Removing her gaze from the chickens, she gave him a glance that was both shy and — dare he think it? — congenial. "I am able

245

to give him hopes and dreams, you see, if not a lot in the way of material things."

A more stubborn woman he had never met. Frustrated, he could not let the subject drop. "There is a way you can give him all, Mrs. Boughman. I can ensure a future that would provide for his material needs as well. Were you to accept my offer, I would know with all confidence that your future and his were secure."

He watched the stubbornness in her eyes soften to gratitude. "It is I who must ask your forgiveness," she said softly. "I spoke out of turn the night you arrived, before I knew you. I understand Theo was recognized with appropriate gratitude at the graveside ceremony. You need not feel guilty."

He hesitated, searching for the words to seize this opportunity to persuade her. "As I explained, it is not enough merely to honor Theo on the battlefield. I wish to provide for you and Tad by easing your burden."

"You came here out of guilt, expecting to redeem yourself by fulfilling a promise. But marriage is not a suitable way to repay a debt. Frankly, Major, I would marry only for love. I regret having to disappoint you, but I could never love another as much as I loved Theo."

Conveniently choosing to overlook his proposal, she returned her attention to the chickens. He had never met a woman, Arthur marveled, who possessed such beauty and serenity even dressed in work clothing while feeding chickens. He found himself not only captivated by Rosemary, but quite convinced Theo had been extremely wise in choosing such a devoted wife.

Later that morning, Rosemary continued her indoor routine by cleaning the pewter tankards in the great room, the ticking of the grandfather clock monitoring the pace of her life, a constant reminder that chores took up the better part of her day. She already missed Mr. Wiggins, for without visitors, there would be no entertaining tonight. At least the scraping of shovels and the sun shining meant that the roads would soon be clear again for travelers.

Stretching to reposition the mugs on the high mantel, she paused in her work as youthful squeals beyond the windowpane drew her attention. Moving to the window for a glimpse of her son, she jumped as a snowball struck the window and Major Winstead came into view. *Just look at him,* she thought with exasperation. While she believed he had gone out to shovel, he had no shovel in hand, and his collar was filled with snow. There was Tad, running alongside him, getting just as wet. Her son was growing so fast, she thought wistfully, that soon he would require a more formal education.

"Look at them," she complained to Charley,

her eyes on the pair. "To think I warned them both. They shall catch their death of cold. Their necks are wet."

"Probably sweat from their exertion. The sun will melt the snow. Maybe you should join them before it does." Charley finally raised his eyes from the newspaper he was reading when she remained in the window. "Upon my soul, Rosemary, the major is a good and noble man. Might I remind you he saw to it that Theo was held up to the troops as a hero? He ensured they will never forget."

"Yes, but he lacked the courage to stand up to his father, even to do the right thing," she countered. "His father might have understood had he stated the truth more firmly."

"And sometimes even fathers do not listen to what they do not want to hear. Mothers as well," Charley said, his eyes returning to the newspaper. "Perhaps you might try letting go of the past. If we are to be open to the public, we need to look forward, not back."

Rosemary ignored his admonition. Instead, she watched Major Winstead jog by her window again, Tad clinging to his shoulders tightly with the major grasping his hands securely as they ran with great abandon. Major Winstead must possess considerable strength, she thought as she studied his broad shoulders, to carry the boy's weight so securely. He had not yet slowed down, and it was their third trip past her window.

"I do not require his help in marriage, for I am still a young woman," she argued.

"Not as young as you once were, my dear," Charley reminded her gently, his words making her frown. "You are approaching your late twenties, although you are still very beautiful. He cannot help but notice that."

Whatever did Charley mean? She had never considered how Major Winstead perceived her, if he looked at her at all. Now she wondered, her heart thudding with suspense. Did he see a woman who had once been vibrant but was now too preoccupied with her child and with innkeeping to tidy up herself so she was more than just presentable? She was once considered a beauty, but that was before she had known Major Winstead. It all seemed so long ago now, she thought, her spirits sagging under the burden of housekeeping chores.

But she must focus on visitors and how to draw them in. Christmas was only a few weeks away. The holiday represented the perfect time for her to earn money from her venture.

Yet while assessing the snowdrifts through the window later that morning, she nearly dropped the vase she was cleaning when a rapid motion cutting across the snowdrifts startled her. Craning her neck to look, she saw Major Winstead dash by with Tad astride his shoulders, bouncing as he went. Whether

Tad was pretending to be riding a horse or the major was bouncing him deliberately, she could not tell. But the major had certainly won Tad's heart. The childish shrieks and laughter cut the stillness and brought the servants to attention, for she heard chuckling throughout the house.

Anxious for Tad's welfare, she moved closer to the glass. Major Winstead must be very fit. He'd been carrying Tad around for more than an hour. The military, she thought, had certainly left him in fine physical condition. Arthur had hold of Tad's legs and was deliberately bouncing him on his shoulders, apparently just to hear him shriek. For a brief moment, she feared the boy would be safer on a runaway horse. Yet his squeals of glee and abandonment touched her heart.

This, she thought, was what childhood was meant to be. Somehow, Major Winstead understood that. When, she wondered, had she forgotten? Every time she sent the boy outdoors, she realized with sudden guilt, it was to do chores.

Perhaps, she thought, the merriment did as much for the former soldier as it did for her son.

When evening came, Rosemary retreated early to her room where she dropped onto her bed, too tired to open the book she had brought upstairs from Papa's library. Despite the welcome sunshine, the day's chores had exhausted her. She had lied to the major when she was feeding the chickens to convince him she was as capable as he believed her to be.

How could she have been so foolish? She had refused Major Winstead's offer of marriage and help without fully considering the consequences. His strong physical presence would have helped her tremendously about the inn, for he was capable of the heavy lifting that she was not. His unwavering devotion to Theo had finally found its mark with her, she realized.

In addition to being unfailingly polite and excessively kind despite her rudeness to him, he was also ruggedly handsome in a most masculine way. There was an undeniable appeal in his thick dark hair and his perceptive, earnest brown eyes. She had dared to look directly into them while they fed the chickens together, allowing hers to linger there. The strength of his arms filled her with yearning. It had been a very long time since she had felt the protection of a masculine embrace.

She had never realized how small she was physically until she had undertaken the renovation of her home. His height had been noticeable the moment he stepped across her threshold. And while she performed physical labor daily, her capabilities had limitations as did those of the servants, as loyal and willing as they were. Furniture was heavy. Wide planks held considerable weight. She enjoyed knowing that the major was there, if help was needed.

But she could not love again. If she were to remain loyal to Theo, she would have to be steadfast in her rejection of his closest friend. She had loved her husband so deeply, she sometimes found herself wandering at night, awakened by the random creakings of her home. Habit prompted her to check, in case Theo had returned somehow.

But he had not. Nor would he ever.

Her heart was frozen in time, and she had wrapped herself in memories that kept her from moving forward.

Soon the roads would clear. Major Winstead had told her of his intention to visit the Duke of Prestfield before he departed. She had never considered the duke a father-in-law, for he had never behaved as such. Major Winstead would do his moral duty to inform him of Theo's contributions, but his call would not change matters.

In time, happiness might return, she reminded herself as she glanced at the mantel clock and saw how late it had grown. The ticking of the clock reminded her that every second lessened the hours until Christmas . . . and that there was so much work to be done before then.

Seeking comfort, Rosemary reached for the

locket on her nightstand that held Theo's image. But memories no longer solved her problems, she realized before she could open it. She laid it back down without a glance. Reaching for the book instead, she did not react quickly enough as the volume slipped from her grasp and fell. She picked it up and saw with dismay that the impact had broken the spine. But not her own, she vowed. Never her own. She had a strong backbone and an even stronger will.

Yet this time, the thought failed to convince her. In utter frustration, she rolled onto her stomach and buried her face in the folds of the linen where she wept in silence.

Life had been simpler, she thought, when she had only a deceased husband and happy memories.

Should he feel amused or offended, Arthur wondered? Here he was, offering wealth and comfort and warmth, yet Rosemary chose to stay in this drafty tavern, content to live in the most meager of circumstances.

He was watching through a window the next morning when a shed door split in half as she attempted to close it. She could not possibly go on like this. In the face of her stubbornness, he marched outdoors to confront her, his exasperation overflowing. He was barely able to extend brief pleasantries before broaching his concern.

"Supporting yourself by running an inn is an admirable goal, if that is what you wish to do," he conceded shortly. "Yet even you must recognize the many drawbacks here. Is not the home rather small and far from the road for such a purpose?"

"Here I can give more personal service and charge less than larger inns," she replied smartly. "As for its placement, I told you I cannot change the spot where my ancestors built it."

"Is this all you want Theo's son to know?" he demanded impatiently. "I can give Tad opportunities to study and to travel. To see London and the Continent. That is what Theo would have wanted for his son. Profitable inns are not run this way. They are not dilapidated like this."

He knew he had overstepped his bounds, but he had to make her see the truth even as her face tightened with fury.

"We take this endeavor seriously, Major," she retorted. "We clean. We offer excellent meals. We take time to make paths through the snow in case travelers need a place to stay."

"You create paths, but it is not likely you will have many guests," he said bluntly. "There is too much work that must be done here."

He saw her stiffen before her face crumpled and quickly hardened with defiance. "My ancestors made imprudent decisions, Major," she acknowledged quietly. "Lost wagers, youthful impulsiveness, and misspent years have taken their toll on the property and on their descendants. They are not my fault, but they are the responsibility I inherited."

There it was again, that tenacity on her part. It was clear she was devoted to the ramshackle house, for it was home. He could stand it no longer.

"Here, let me do that," he demanded, taking hold of the broken door. But how was he to fix it? It was not likely she happened to have extra wood handy. Seeing an unused rope, coiled inside the shed, he grasped it and leaned the broken half against the hinged part of the door so he might lash them together. It was a temporary fix, but it might hold until he found a better solution.

To his surprise, three more guests came the following day, making him question his judgment of the inn. Rosemary was at ease with both wealthy and poor, from traveling soldiers to local folk. She entertained guests with kindness and attention, and they responded with compliments rather than complaints. They felt comfortable in her presence because she made them so. The advantages were obvious.

She would be, it occurred to him, the perfect wife.

Theo had never seen this side of her, Arthur realized abruptly, for he had known her only as a wife, not as an innkeeper. The realization made it even more critical that Arthur stay to help.

She had judged him correctly, he saw now. He had not looked forward to marriage, for he had looked upon her, not as a person, but as a responsibility. If she had not left this drafty, cold, rambling house after all this time, it must matter deeply to her. So deeply she was willing to sacrifice everything to keep it and raise her son here.

He was a slowtop not to have realized it before.

Checking on the stable later that day while Rosemary was occupied elsewhere, he saw how decrepit parts of the property had become. While the horses were comfortable enough between straw and blankets, boards were missing, robbing the enclosure of respectability. Yet when he considered her fierce pride, he felt humiliated to realize how his comments must have hurt her. She was such a tiny woman, overwhelmed by this great Tudor house, dwarfed by its demands for restoration.

Yet when he assessed the inn with a critical eye, his overall impressions were positive. Wayfarers were greeted with a blazing fire in the great fireplace, excellent fare and strong ale, and unparalleled service. Rosemary served the first dish at dinner as was customary of a proprietor. The sheets were warmed and scented with lavender before bedtime. The potential was evident everywhere he looked.

Arthur knew what he must do.

Ironically, he thought, it all came down to chance. Not that he was a betting man, yet being here felt rather like being at White's. The inn represented a chance of security for Tad and Rosemary. He was suddenly convinced it was not too much of a risk to take. He announced his intentions to Charley when Rosemary was out of hearing.

"If she will not wed me as Theo wished and help is truly what she wants, help is what I shall give. It is certainly what she needs. I have made an appointment to speak with her tomorrow morning. I intend to make myself useful by staying to assist her." He glanced about the home's Elizabethan interior. "Doing repairs, for instance. There are places that require work, potential problems even."

"You're a true friend and a gentleman, Major," Charley said, his eyes crinkling even as they filled slightly.

"She is as committed as the best soldiers in my unit. With such determination, the inn is far from a losing proposition. I believe she has the spirit and the forethought to make a success of it." He sighed, having accepted the inevitable. "If she prefers that I help her with the inn rather than marry her, then that is how I shall serve Theo's memory. Ultimately, the result is the same."

Charley shook his head. "You deserve commendation you will probably never receive, Major, especially since she refuses to marry again."

"Fighting her will not bring anyone victory. Theo would have wanted me to help." He grinned. "I had been seeking a sign. I did not expect to find it in a rundown inn."

Arthur realized, too, that he was already more than a bit in love with her. Too bad he had already admitted defeat . . .

Arthur arrived early the following morning for his meeting with Rosemary. But when she failed to appear at the proposed time, he wondered if she had chosen to be uncharacteristically late. Perhaps she would not come at all or would refuse his offer. He sat for many moments thinking the worst. So, when she finally arrived, he was relieved and delighted to see she wore a stylish dress in a becoming shade of rose with burgundy detailing. She waited until Martha had delivered the tea tray and left before turning to a discussion of small matters to clear the air. Noting her relaxed posture and conversational mood, he decided it was time to discuss matters of importance.

"With the snow cleared away, I had a

glimpse of some of the gardens and statuary on the grounds," he began casually. "You have taken remarkably good care of the property."

She blushed so deeply the rose in her cheeks matched her dress. "After Mama died, Papa was responsible for the entire property. And I was so young —" She shook her head. "Perhaps in time Charley and Tad and I shall be able to restore it to its original grandeur."

"But you have more rooms than you might ever have guests," he countered gently.

Her smile widened with amusement. "I might. One cannot know until one tries."

How could such a petite woman remain so confident in the face of overwhelming odds? Genuine obstacles blocked her success, but perhaps she perceived them differently than he did. The earnestness in her eyes made his heart turn over.

"You have made the inn a real home, Mrs. Boughman, and you have earned my respect," he said frankly. "I hope I might have the chance to earn yours as well."

"Thank you, Major. I would not mind if you were to stay longer," she confessed, her tone surprisingly warm, "for winter roads can be treacherous, and there are few accommodations nearby. My only request is that you accept, without judgment, my decision to continue the business of innkeeping and to remain a widow."

Her words stung, yet he felt he must persevere. "I could not judge you, my lady. It is neither my place nor my desire to criticize someone who loves her son so deeply she would trade the respect of others to provide for him. Your determination is most admirable."

Her high cheekbones blushed that becoming shade he found so charming. He smiled to think he had said something that pleased her for once. He continued, anxious to settle the matter.

"I would like us to call a truce. If you will not accept my offer of marriage, at least allow me to stay and help with the house."

Rosemary paused. "To fulfill your duty, you mean."

"If that is how you wish to see it." Arthur spoke cautiously. Perhaps these would be the words that would open her closed heart again and allow him to enter. He already felt his duty to her would never be done. He wished he might stay forever.

"Very well then," she agreed cautiously, a half-smile teasing her lips. "We shall declare a truce."

"Before you accept, Mrs. Boughman, I wish to suggest another proposal as well. As you have mentioned, the more recommendations your inn has, the more income you will gain as a result. Since this is the busiest time to travel, I suggest we make a detailed list of improvements to be made. I recommend a deadline in the third week of December so we finish in time."

She stared at him as if assessing his sincerity. "And as you are fulfilling your perceived duty to Theo, I shall tell you when you have succeeded. Is that acceptable to you?"

So this is how it was to be. His hope that she might agree to marry him dimmed at her words, yet he must be content with her compromise. As long as she allowed him to stay, there was a chance he might make his way into her heart.

And in the end, now that he was going to make the necessary repairs to the inn, his actions would help improve the quality of her life and Tad's, if nothing else. But would she dismiss him when she decided he had done enough? He focused on her lovely eyes, pleased to see how attentive her gaze was.

"It is more than acceptable," he replied politely. "I believe Theo would have considered the arrangement most appropriate."

Was it his imagination, or had he just seen her visibly relax?

"Thank you, Major Winstead," she said with a sudden smile. "I imagine Theo would be quite surprised by all we have done here, Charley and Tad and I, and what we shall do with your help, don't you think — Arthur, if I may call you that?"

It was the first time she had used his given

name. The sound of it on her lips thrilled him. "I do not think he would be surprised, Mrs. Boughman," he said frankly. "But he would most certainly be proud. I look forward to starting."

He dared not overstay his welcome, having procured her agreement at last. Rising, he bowed slightly and turned toward the door, only to be startled by her unexpected reply.

"I am delighted to hear you feel that way. And please," she said, a quiet urgency in her voice, "call me Rosemary."

"Arthur has announced he will remain here to help make improvements to our home," Rosemary told Charley when she found him in the library, her spirit buoyed by the news. "While I have decided not to marry him, I have accepted his offer of help with our business venture."

She had expected him to be overjoyed. Was it her imagination, or did Charley's face fall when he discovered the proposal she had accepted was for repairs to the inn?

"You of all people know I would trade my life to have Theo back," she continued. "But having Arthur here brings back too many memories from a part of my life that is gone."

She paused, having said all she considered necessary. Her expectations were dashed when the concern returned to Charley's face.

"It is not what you think, Rosemary," he

said gently. "Major Winstead is not trying to take Theo's place. He is an honorable man who was devoted enough to Theo to honor his promise to provide for you." Charley's tone became stern. "And as sure as I am that more snow is on the way, I am certain the major's offer of marriage is motivated only by kindness. He has already overpaid us for his stay and refuses to take any back. If you want my advice, Rosemary," he added with a meaningful stare, "and even if you do not, I would advise you to marry him."

"I do not want his charity." Her defiance sounded hollow even to herself.

"Want and need are very different things, my lady," he cautioned. "You cling to a memory. Think of Tad. You could find no one closer to his father than the soldier who was with him when he died. Major Winstead is a living hero to the boy. I fought under his father, and so did yours. He is a respectable man like your father and his were."

"Except his father tried to keep him from telling the truth about Theo's final battle," she countered.

"Sit down, Rosemary."

Charley's tone told her he would tolerate no argument. She took her place on the windowseat as he hobbled over and sat beside her. He took her hand in his, his face red. Emotion embarrassed Charley. It humiliated Rosemary to have been the cause.

"I am going to tell you what your father would say if he were here. And I want you to listen. There is no reason why you should not honor your husband's wishes — his last wishes. Major Winstead's father was trying to preserve his son's image. The major waited out of respect so he would not offend his father while he was alive. That is all there is to it."

Rosemary failed to keep her lip from trembling. To admit she needed Arthur's help was to admit that she had failed Theo. "But we have always taken care of ourselves. There is no reason for me to marry again."

"I've lived nearly eighty years, Rosemary," Charley said gently, the corners of his eyes crinkling as he smiled. "You knew Theo for one year and were married for two. From my perspective, you know him more as a memory than as a husband. You have spent more time mourning him than you were married to him."

Tears welled in her eyes, but she remained silent.

Charley paused, regarding her cautiously. "You and Theo had a wonderful life together and a precious son to show for it. But the years are flying by, and it is time to move on with your life. If you do not consider the people around you, you will have many more lonely years ahead of you." His smile held both sadness and affection. "And that is not a happy prospect."

Her beloved Theo had been gone for half a decade. It seemed impossible. She could hardly account for those years. How little, she wondered abruptly, had she accomplished in that time?

"I know you loved him, Rosemary. We all did. But you know better than anyone that all our prayers will not bring him back." He cleared his throat and patted her hand, prepared to issue a new order. "Major Winstead has made you an offer that is not only heartfelt but generous. I advise you to accept it. If your father were here, he would tell you the same."

Still, she did not relent. When she had remained silent just long enough that even she knew she was being unreasonable, her beloved Charley rendered her powerless to argue.

"It is your decision, Rosemary," he said in a tone of finality. "But Major Winstead will not be here forever unless you accept. If I were you, I would take his offer before he retracts it. Do not allow pride and stubbornness to prevent Tad from having the father he needs."

CHAPTER SIX

"I am glad Major Winstead has come, Mama," Tad told her the following morning as he rose from the floor of the great room where his soldiers were spread before the fire to cuddle with her in the chair.

"Are you?" She smiled as she wrapped his curls about her fingers. "What is so special about him?"

"He keeps me company," Tad confided in a tone of sincerity that stabbed at her emotions. But it was his next remark that took her completely by surprise. "I think it would be nice to have a sister."

Flabbergasted, she had no idea he had ever considered such a thing. "A sister? What gave you such an idea?"

"Uncle Arthur has four." Tad giggled. "He says he would give me one if he could."

So now he was Uncle Arthur, she thought. When had that come about? She was relieved, for Tad's words indicated Arthur was not necessarily still thinking of marriage. But he was working his way into the family through her son.

"I already picked out a name," Tad continued, to her chagrin. "Theodora. It's the girl version of Theodosius. Or maybe Althea."

While the likelihood was too remote for serious consideration, Rosemary's heart stirred with yearning. In the early years of her marriage, she had desperately wanted more children so Tad would not grow up alone. But she could not have more children unless she was prepared to consider marrying again.

And the most likely prospect for that role was Major Winstead.

She had seen how tall and strong he was when they were standing together in the warm sunlight. She had even seen his emotions laid bare. He was a handsome, brave soldier. Sitting beside the frosty windowpane reminded her how frigid her bedsheets had felt in last night's chill. Arthur must be as cold between the sheets as she was, she mused. Did he awaken in the night and think about her in such a way? She blushed just considering the possibility.

How was she to achieve her dreams, she realized suddenly, if she continued to close doors? Arthur had offered to marry her, even after seeing the reduced circumstances in which she lived. Even after she had continued to argue with him. He had kept his promise to Theo to care for her.

And still she had refused his offer of marriage.

Instead, she had convinced herself that it was better to live with the memory of a perfect man than — what had she called him? — a pale substitute. Her heart contracted as she remembered the harshness of her tone. How ungrateful and self-absorbed she must have seemed, putting her own grief first. When had she developed the capacity to be so cruel? At the time, she had wondered how he could possibly expect to make restitution. He could not.

Yet it was not his fault Theo had died.

Her rejection of Arthur out of loyalty to Theo's memory must have seemed incredibly selfish. The major considered Theo his best friend. She tried to put herself in his place, imagining what both men must have endured. How incredibly painful it must have been for Arthur to see his closest friend slain in a plan of his own creation, one he had approved as commander.

He must not only grieve but feel responsible.

Rosemary's cheeks burned with humiliation. Arthur had come to offer her his life in place of Theo's. How ungrateful she must have seemed.

What he'd found was a self-absorbed widow who put her own grief before that of anyone else — even, she realized with growing shame, that of her son.

As she walked about the house while cleaning, she noticed how wide the cracks in the doors had become. And had those splits on the far wall been there all along, or were they new? Somehow, she had become less responsible than an innkeeper ought to be about repairing defects.

She saw that Joseph was already measuring the width of the boards. Undoubtedly, Arthur had gotten him started on the renovation project. Now perhaps she could give her son the comforts and respect she had known in her early years. But could she give him those things without a husband?

Still, could she bring herself to marry for a promise? For an obligation the major felt he owed her husband? Perhaps it was what Theo had wanted.

A small voice from within told her it might be time to accept Arthur's proposal. Charley felt it was. And Charley had never led her astray.

She had kept the major waiting long enough, Rosemary told herself, setting aside the cup of tea Mrs. North had prepared. It was time she took the matter of marriage seriously. Leaving her chores for the moment, she found Arthur writing letters in the library. Seeing the pile of letters laid out before him gave her a twinge of guilt. He had left family

269

and friends to call upon her at the busiest time of year, when everyone wanted to be home. How could she not have seen it until now?

"Good morning, Arthur," she said contritely, wanting to appear every bit as humble as he had upon his arrival. "I am glad to see you have found a space in which to write. I trust you are making yourself more comfortable the longer you are here." She took a deep breath. "I beg you to forgive my earlier behavior. I have been defensive even toward you, when you deserve it least of all. I owe you a very great apology."

When she had finished, she closed her eyes tightly so she would not see the reaction she feared before he could rescind his offer. Her compromise had not been completely fair to him. Her mind was made up. She decided on impulse to tell him that after deeper consideration, marriage seemed far more appealing. She opened her mouth to speak at the precise moment a familiar grin spread across Arthur's virile features.

"I am grateful you are staying to help us," she stammered. It sounded lame even to herself. She was ready for honesty at last. She took a deep breath. "And if truth be told —"

"You need not feel obligated. I have also given the matter much thought. While I am pleased you decided to accept my help, I realize how unfair it was to expect you to be ready for marriage. Perhaps I am not either." He shrugged. "At any rate, I am happy to relieve you of the pressure of a decision. Matters are best left the way they are, at least for the immediate future. They might even be preferable."

Rosemary listened with a combination of relief and dismay as a fond smile spread across Arthur's face. It was astonishing how much more captivating a dimpled grin made his already handsome features. There was even a spark of humor there, if she was not mistaken.

She was unsure whether his turnabout pleased her or not. With her hopes deflated and her spirits descending, she felt a bit disheartened.

"I consider it an honor to accept your compromise," he said, his grin broadening. "I believe Theo is smiling upon us with approval even now. Tell me where to start."

For the first time since he arrived, Arthur thought as he observed the sky later that afternoon, conditions looked promising enough to travel.

"It is a distance, but the weather might finally allow me to travel to the duke's home tomorrow," he told Rosemary. "I would like to get the visit behind me before we begin our repairs in earnest."

"While you are there, you must ask him to take you to the monument the family erected for Theo." He saw sadness in her brief smile. "It is larger and far grander than our own. But ours is another reason I should find it hard to leave here."

Her words startled him. This was the first he'd heard of a memorial to Theo. "You never mentioned a monument," Arthur told her, surprised.

"It is hardly a monument," she corrected herself, looking somewhat embarrassed. "We erected a wooden cross near the gardens. I attended the service at the duke's home and rooted a bit of holly from his tree to plant here. It has flourished under our care." Her smile faded to a wistful expression. "I always bring some holly indoors in winter to make sure it survives another year."

"I should very much like to see your monument," Arthur requested. His spirits lifted at her devotion, for her heartfelt effort was worth more than all the marble in the world.

The tree had indeed flourished, Arthur found when he had finished following her down the pathways that meandered through her lands. Its height and width were more impressive than trees half its age. She must tend it daily, he thought. Its size was without doubt a consequence of love, as was everything within her care.

He watched with loving fascination as her

look of sadness was replaced by blushing confidence. When she spoke at last, her voice held a calm yet triumphant quality. "You should see how lovely the spot is in summertime. The entire property is beautiful. The orchards, the fields of lavender, the rose gardens. It is not as it was in my ancestors' day, of course, but the essence remains." She smiled confidently at him. "In time, with your help, perhaps it shall be that way again."

The next morning, with the weather still clear enough to travel, the decision was made. Arthur confirmed he would visit the duke that afternoon.

"I notified him of Theo's death by letter originally," he reflected, "but I still wish to tell him of his heroics at Albuera personally. Did he contact you afterward?"

"We only attended the memorial service on his property," Rosemary admitted, her smile fading. "While he wished to have limited contact with Tad, he did not accept me. I confess it was I who ended contact for fear Tad would feel the sting of inferiority. All I see of the duke now is his carriage passing quickly along the road. It does not stop here, of course." She paused. "I understand your desire to visit him. I trust, for your sake, it will go well."

"What has prompted your call today, Major?"

After greetings had been exchanged, Arthur

273

seated himself across from Aloysius Bough-man, Duke of Prestfield, determined not only to impart the details of Theo's final battle but also to speak on behalf of Rosemary and Tad.

"As I am sure you remember, Your Grace, it was my sad duty as your son's command-ing officer to send my condolences to you upon Theo's death, along with those of Lord Wellington and all of our troops," Arthur began quietly. While the duke was taller than his son, he noted, Theo had inherited his commanding presence.

After an almost imperceptible nod, Theo's father cleared his throat. "I appreciate your kindness. I remember receiving your letter," he said, his voice softening.

"Theo became my closest friend during the war. He was an extraordinary patriot as well as a fine individual, and I miss him deeply. I believe our friendship would have continued after war's end."

Arthur proceeded to describe Theo's role in the fight at Albuera and of his final hours on the battlefield, adding how he had likely saved Portugal from the French.

"Over twelve hundred British soldiers were slain, wounded, or imprisoned that day. Enemy artillery devastated our troops at Al-buera." Arthur was surprised how steady his voice remained. "We fixed our bayonets and moved forward, prepared to charge. Suddenly, torrential rain fell, blinding us. Smoke went up — hail rained down. We could see nothing. It rendered our muskets useless. Before we knew what had happened, enemy cavalry charged into the confusion. Their spears were everywhere. So many officers were killed no one knew who was in charge."

He shook his head, still in disbelief, as the duke remained silent.

"Theo and I knew if we fell, we would lose not only the battle, but probably all of Portugal. I issued the command for our regiment to form square to stop the cavalry from going around to cut us down. But our infantry needed time to set up. We devised a plan to distract the enemy by leading a small charge against them. It worked. It gave us time to regroup, and it saved us. But — Theo was lost."

Choked with emotion, he hoped that as a father, the duke could see, despite his silence, how his son had played an equally important role in the strategy.

"Because I remained unconscious for so long afterward, I suspect Theo did not receive the credit he deserved," Arthur admitted. "I wanted you to know how selfless his actions were. I did my utmost to convince my superiors of the significance of his decisions that terrible day. But by the time I emerged from my state of delirium, the army was preparing for its next battle and there was little time to honor or to grieve. The slight, if any, was entirely unintentional."

The Duke of Prestfield was silent for a few moments, his emotions unreadable. "It does not surprise me that my son would defend his country with his life. It is laudable of you to come all this way to tell me, Major. I appreciate it."

"It is an honor, Your Grace." Arthur broached the more challenging issue. "I also hoped to speak on behalf of your daughter-in-law and grandson, young Lord Theodosius."

"I understand my son's wife has turned to trade," the duke said dryly. "I thank you for apprising me of this information, but my son was lost to me a long time ago, seven years to be precise, when he was seduced by Peltonby's daughter. He married without either my permission or my blessing." His lips tightened. "The boy will inherit no title from his mother, for the title of knight passed with her father."

But a title could pass to Tad from this grandfather, Arthur reflected, if the duke would but recognize him. How could so eminent a man fail to appreciate his son's efforts on behalf of his countrymen?

"Yet she is a widow now and your son a hero," he protested politely.

"And his widow is still a commoner," the duke replied equally as politely. "Theodosius might have married someone with aristocratic bloodlines."

"Yet his son might possibly become the Earl of Stockton one day, is that not so?" Arthur reminded him discreetly. "Perhaps you did not know Humphrey Peltonby died shortly after your son left for war."

Fearing he had overstepped the bounds of courtesy, he watched the duke's expression darken. "The boy is not among my heirs, as my older son has a child who will inherit my titles," he replied coolly. "I cannot be certain the child is even my grandson. It wasn't until my son had joined the war effort that his wife learned she was with child."

"With the greatest respect, sir, the boy's face is quite as handsome as his father's," Arthur said quietly, "and rather like yours, if I may say so. It leaves no doubt in my mind."

"I did not like the girl," the duke admitted. "She was even more headstrong than my son."

Seeing he would make no headway on the matter, Arthur asked if he might visit the monument to Theo. As the duke led him outdoors into the fading light, Arthur realized he had lingered longer than expected. They followed a path close to the manor house until the duke paused to indicate a marble monument some distance away in a grove of evergreens. In the twilight, Arthur saw with dismay that no path had been cleared to it, an indication that few visited. Nor to his surprise did there appear to be any holly.

He was relieved when the time came to depart, for the encounter had left him heavy-hearted. As he returned by carriage to the Jolly Goose and Rhyme, his emotions were numbed by Theo's father's cold-hearted indifference. Ironically, Arthur had probably become more attached to Tad in the time he spent with him than the boy's own grand-father had.

From the carriage window, he gazed up at the stars, visible now that darkness had fallen. There had been stars to shine over Bethlehem on Christmas, he reflected. If only he had a star of his own to guide him. He remembered the Bible verse often quoted at home: "And now abideth faith, hope, charity, these three; but the greatest of these is charity." Theo had certainly had faith in love, Arthur thought, knowing it transcended wealth. He hoped the duke might one day feel the same toward his grandson.

As for charity, the duke had humiliated Rosemary by offering it before Arthur had unintentionally done the same. No one who knew her, he conceded, would consider her helpless. She was the most determined woman he knew. And while his original intent had been to right wrongs, he had fallen deeply in love with her.

Charity or the lack of it had certainly been

the theme of the day. If only the duke had not been so uncharitable toward Theo's impoverished family. If only Rosemary would not refuse what she saw as charity in his marriage proposal, clumsy as it had been. It was hardly charity, he reflected, to propose to a beautiful and desirable woman. Theo had been most charitable, giving all for the British cause, with hope of returning home when it was over. A hope that never came to pass.

Arthur had believed that telling Rosemary the truth would relieve his guilt. Instead, it had worsened matters. Now, with his own faith floundering, he suspected the only virtue he could promise to keep was hope.

CHAPTER SEVEN

"Tell me his exact words," Rosemary demanded upon his return. He seemed rather laconic, considering he just called upon her father-in-law.

"It is hardly worth discussing. He actually said very little," Arthur said abruptly.

Now he was testing her patience. Rosemary did her best not to interrupt while Arthur relayed the few details he wished to share of his visit with the duke. While it naturally included military concerns, his hesitation told her he was reluctant to discuss what mattered most.

"No doubt you have stirred up unhappy memories for him. I do not know how the duke can ignore the child of a son honored posthumously for valor. He does not deserve such a fine grandson." Choking back her bitterness, she called upon her pride to crush her sorrow. "The duke at least must have shown you the monument. I remember how lovely it was. Appropriately large and suitable for someone of Theo's stature."

"It is," he conceded, "though I suspect it has not been visited in some time. It might surprise you to know the holly that is so abundant here no longer surrounds the monument. While marble is elegant, I find your wooden cross more impressive, for it is heartfelt."

"Thank you, Arthur. While I am disappointed to hear it goes untended, I suppose I should not be surprised." Her spirits plummeting, she moved absently to the window.

She failed to notice Arthur rise behind her until she felt his gentle but insistent grip on her arm, turning her about until they were face to face. Eyes the shade of rich, solid mahogany locked with hers.

"While I called on him to tell him of Theo's heroics, you and Tad were my main consideration." His voice was soft, she thought, and intent on removing her pain. "It is my hope that my visit will make the duke look more charitably upon Theo's memory, and on you and Tad as well. At some point he might offer to help you."

Why had he interfered in something that was not his concern? "I do not want his help," she vowed recklessly, pulling away. "I know what it is to grow up with one parent. It is difficult enough that Tad will never know his father. I will not risk his grandfather spoiling the image I want him to remember."

How could Arthur expect Theo's father to help her, Rosemary wondered, when the duke had no interest in his own grandson? Thrusting the past from her mind, she tried to force her vision into the future. One day her inn would be renowned throughout the countryside, the rooms filled every night, and she would be forced to turn travelers away. There were mountains to climb before they would achieve that kind of success. But every step brought her closer.

"It is unfortunate the duke never contacted you after the memorial service," Arthur reflected after a moment.

"He offered us another home when he called on us, but I refused," she said shakily, her mood subdued. "I wanted Tad to be raised on the land where his father and grandfather lived."

Arthur stared at her. She watched with foreboding as his expression changed to one of bewilderment. "I did not know he had made such a generous overture toward you. Why did you not tell me this earlier? It casts him in a different light."

"We did not hear from him until three months after we received word of Theo's death," Rosemary defended herself. "By then I had to make arrangements. My father had already passed away. With no husband and no connections, I had to consider my options, one of which was to open our home to strangers. And in truth, I was lonely and reluctant to remove Tad from the only home he had ever known. We were happy here, Papa and I. I knew Tad would be as well."

"Am I to believe your father-in-law offered you more but you refused because of your pride?" Arthur demanded in disbelief. "Surely it was not in Tad's best interest to do so. I cannot imagine Theo would have been pleased with your decision."

What right had he to criticize? She fumed in silence. He had not lived through the agony of discovering she was a widow with no means of survival and a young child to support, blamed and ostracized by her powerful father-in-law. When she held in her fury and refused to respond, he appeared to reconsider her point of view.

"But I respect your feelings," he said at last. "I am certain you made the best possible choice at the time."

At least he had the wisdom to drop the subject when she did not respond. He could not possibly know she had already reached the same conclusion. And she was disappointed in herself for having disappointed him.

If it was true that Tad's future was at risk because of the decisions she had made, Rosemary realized with fading hope, she had only herself to blame.

■ ■ ■ ■

Now that Rosemary's mind was made up, Arthur realized, his first order of business was to send word to his sisters. Upon leaving, he had told them in his note that he needed to tend to an outstanding obligation and might not be joining them for the holidays. Then, reluctant to leave them alone on the first Christmas without their father, he left a second note to be read after his departure revealing his true intentions, and that he expected to return with at least the promise of a wife and stepson, if not their physical presence. His spirits fell as he thought how disappointed they would be when he returned without them. But Rosemary had made her decision, and he had no choice but to respect it.

In a carefully worded letter, he advised his sisters that his return had been delayed indefinitely and apprised them of his location. Should any emergency arise, he thought, they would be able to find him more quickly than he had located Rosemary. Lastly, he added his regret at disappointing them but warned he would not be bringing his new family home as expected.

It was hardly fair to raise their hopes at Christmas, after all, only to have them dashed afterward. He was filled with relief once it was written. Sending off the letter allowed him to focus on the most pressing matters, and that meant deciding how best to improve Rosemary's chances of attracting travelers to the inn, starting with repairing the physical structure.

Finally, Arthur thought, she had come to her senses. He was delighted by her sudden clarity in recognizing the need for changes as she took a critical look about the home, prepared to do battle with disrepair.

"More areas needed improving than I realized," she announced, her cheeks reddening. "I am afraid the list I have compiled is rather long."

As she apologized for the number of issues needing to be addressed, Arthur fought to hide his amusement at her sudden look of dismay when he and Charley doubled its length.

"He certainly has his work cut out for him, Rosemary," Charley chuckled. "I believe the major has found the best possible way to keep his promise to Theo."

"I am certain Theo would have approved," Rosemary agreed.

"I am happy to help in whatever way I am able," Arthur assured her cheerfully. "The sooner we start, the sooner we finish. We want to beat the Christmas rush, so to speak."

With so many restoration projects needed to make the inn respectable, he might spend his entire life in Rosemary's home, he thought, even without marriage. While primarily Tudor in age and style, the residence at Woodhollow End was a rambling home, he saw, like so many manor houses that had undergone additions over time. Currently, Charley noted, Rosemary had four rooms to let.

"Don't tell her I said so," Charley revealed under his breath, "but she's never had more than two rented at the same time. And that happened only once."

Arthur found other rooms that could also be used. While they did not have the amenities the furnished rooms had, they appeared to be structurally sound and their appearance could be improved considerably with silk bed hangings, paintings, and china accents.

"Here is what I propose," he announced. "Let us first clean walls and shine woodwork and then appoint the rooms."

"Aye, sir," Charley replied at once. "A solid plan it is."

"I haven't the funds for extensive repairs," Rosemary said in dismay.

"But I have," Arthur reminded her, "and more importantly, you have the drive and desire. In addition, you have the staff, all of whom are devoted to you. We cannot go wrong."

"What shall be our new campaign, Major?" Charley prompted, grinning broadly beneath his mustache.

It was indeed time for a new assignment. Arthur reflected on the task before them. "We have four bedrooms able to be used. One is mine, so you are already on your way to having them all booked," he told Rosemary confidently. "With a bit of work, I suspect we could have an additional four ready by Christmas. Does that sound reasonable?"

As incredulity mixed with hope on Rosemary's face, he kept his expression serious. Better she believe he would tolerate no doubt from her. He expected of her just what he would of any soldier, although it would be daunting to look past her beauty to do it.

To his surprise, he saw her skepticism turn to frank consideration and then to a look of hope.

"We must start right away then," she announced.

Arthur resolved to be candid rather than underestimate the work required. As they discussed what must be done to raise the standards of the inn, he would take direction from Rosemary, he decided, while offering discreet suggestions. He recommended tending to the structural issues first while she decided on improvements to the interior.

"We might start by fortifying the front door," Arthur suggested. "I have felt a bit of a chill managing to creep in."

"We can brace it with wood from the

unused rooms," Charley suggested.

"How may I help?" Rosemary offered at once.

"By tending to Christmas preparations once you have decided on the interior," Arthur said cheerfully, "for the season is already upon us, and the day will be here before you know it."

As the men searched other wings of the home for suitable wood, Rosemary watched in silent indignation, not wanting to intrude upon their progress, but feeling the need to oversee changes made to a home that had seen none in over a century.

Perhaps, she told herself as she noted the threadbare corner of a woolen tapestry that dominated one wall, moving objects from their customary spots to less traveled areas might be a useful occupation. Maybe she should look for decorative objects appropriate for the bedrooms Arthur intended to prepare.

When, she wondered, had she become so resistant to change? Perhaps she should accept his suggestions, put them into effect without another thought, and consider herself blessed.

Arthur had certainly been wise in suggesting she address Christmas preparations. She realized, with sudden alarm, that they should have been started over a week ago. She was relieved to discover Mrs. North had already seen to matters.

"It's already begun, my lady. I've prepared the frumenty," she assured her hastily. "Stirred east to west for the Wise Men, of course. And the plum pudding has its silver sixpence hidden inside for good luck, not like last year when we forgot and had to add it afterward!" She clapped her hand to her forehead. "I hope that isn't why it was such a hard year for you, Mrs. Boughman. Surely the coming one will be filled with blessings, especially with Major Winstead here."

Whether his presence would bring blessings upon her home had yet to be determined, Rosemary reflected. She had no doubt the aromas emanating from the kitchen certainly would. Was it her imagination, or were Charley and Tad and even Arthur finding excuses to visit? The delectable scents of Mrs. North's dishes left everyone in joyful spirits, making the merriment worth the unnecessary bustle near the savory pots hanging over the fire.

It was soon clear they had not spent all their time sampling new dishes. Rosemary was surprised how quickly the entrance door was replaced with one that was sturdier and far grander.

"We doubled the door's thickness by attaching it to one slightly larger to keep heat in," Arthur explained, glancing at her anxiously. "Does it please you?"

He need not work so hard to please her, she thought. "Yes, it is impressive," she replied. "It is done so quickly."

An expression of relief spread across his winning features as he studied the door. "I gave orders and received help, as I am accustomed to doing. The inn must be warm. And since we are expecting guests, or soon will be, I wanted it done immediately."

He turned and eyed her smartly, the triumph in his eyes so direct she wondered what kind of effort she had unleashed on his part. Even Tad contributed to their cause.

"I have decided, Mama," he announced after dinner, "that I shall build a snowman to attract business." He paused thoughtfully. "Maybe a snow family would be better."

"What an excellent idea, Tad," Rosemary exclaimed.

"And may it bring us great success," Charley added.

Tad spent the remainder of the day outside in the snow. When he had finished, a row of snowmen ranging from tall to short flanked the road that fronted the inn.

"This is how we are now, Mama," he pointed out. "Here is Charley, and Major Winstead, and you and me."

"We are all here, represented in snow, to greet our new arrivals," Rosemary said with a laugh.

"He's certainly done a fine job of making

me as heavy as I am." Charley pulled off Tad's hat and tousled his hair, chuckling. "You might at least have taken off a few pounds, lad. I don't want to be any heavier than I am, even the snowy version of meself."

Arthur discovered a bigger challenge when he took a closer look at the great stone fireplace. Even from the outside, it was apparent it needed stabilizing. They waited for a day mild enough that they could leave the fire unlit before they examined it thoroughly.

"Perhaps we might work on it from within," he suggested to Charley. "The snow makes it challenging if not impossible to do from outside. But if we strengthen the stone where it is needed most, we can do a more substantial job when warmer weather comes."

"Aye, Major, that's wise," Charley agreed. "All it needs is a bit of mortar."

"We can, of course, find another way if this will not work." Arthur's voice echoed within the fireplace where he'd hoisted himself for a closer inspection of the damage done by age. He was aware Rosemary was listening. "This tight space was not made for one my size. Perhaps we can get Tad to look up inside."

"Aye, he's small enough to fit," Charley agreed.

"Tad is not a chimney sweep!" Rosemary reminded them sharply. "He is my son, and I treasure him."

Arthur lowered himself from his perch, emerging from the chimney in time to see her wrap her arms around her son and pull him to her. She planted a kiss on his cheek, but he brushed her fingers away.

"Not now, Mama, I have work to do," he told her, in so official a tone it made Arthur grin.

The look of worry that replaced her smile as Tad hurried toward the fireplace tugged at his heart. Her every action, Arthur thought, was prompted by concern for her son. As Charley pointed out to Tad the problem inside the fireplace, Rosemary turned to Arthur, doubt in her eyes.

"I did not realize repairing a fireplace is such a serious undertaking," she murmured. "Are you certain you know what you are doing?"

Amused by her suspicion, he led her to the hearth to point out the weakened stones. "You learn more in wartime, my lady, than how to defend an army."

Even Rosemary admitted to noticing the difference almost immediately once repairs were done. Within a day of the arduous work needed to repair the loose stones supporting the fireplace, she declared her home to be warmer and dryer even in winter's chill.

Arthur was again amused when she felt the need to assert her role as proprietor.

"I should like to check the work if I might,"

she requested.

While he doubted she knew anything of chimney interiors, he placed a tall chair among the cold ashes so she might examine the extent of the work. Realizing she required assistance, he concealed his delight in the sensation of his hands closing about her slender waist as he lifted her onto the chair, for his hand brushed against her ankle as he released her. It felt soft and delicate. He could not help but be very conscious of her femininity.

From within the chimney, her voice echoed as she mumbled some words of satisfaction. When she was finished, he took even more delight in lifting her down, for holding her securely allowed him to slide his hands up the sides of her body. She could not be blind to his attraction. While he noticed she did not struggle, he acknowledged it was unlikely that the caress was to be repeated.

"That ought to keep the dampness at bay," Charley declared triumphantly. "Let's hear the gales try to whistle through now. Ha, not anymore! Keeps out the wind, too, it does."

"Well done, Major," Rosemary said quietly, smoothing her skirts. "I am confident your efforts will provide us with warmth through the winter."

While Arthur had hopes of eliminating the mice, he felt much less confident in the success of that venture. Without telling Rosemary, he set traps in the hallways near the kitchen and pantry. He was surprised to find not only were there no mice the following morning, but there were no traps either. A second effort had the same result.

On a day cloudy enough to require candles, he found excuses to follow Rosemary when she ventured into the kitchen. With Mrs. North's cooperation, he was able to watch, unnoticed, as she stepped around the corner into the hall. There her shadow revealed her true purpose in coming. He saw her elongated arm reflected on the wall as it reached down to remove the traps and leave crumbs in their place.

"You need not sweep up here," she confided to Mrs. North. "It is not a public area, so it does not affect our guests. And you know how Tad loves the mice," she added softly.

"As you wish, my lady," the cook murmured.

Arthur honored her wishes as well, for to do otherwise would be devastating, perhaps more to him, he suspected, than to the mice. Even if she was jeopardizing her own financial venture, there was no other option. Her heart was simply too kind.

He would not wish it any other way.

Even Mrs. North contributed to their economic venture by creating variations of old and trusted dishes. At one point, Arthur observed Tad slipping a bit of a new mutton dish to the dogs. As the meat was gobbled up, Tad interpreted their wagging tails and anticipation of more as a positive sign.

"Squire Maxwell and Lady Millicent approve!" the boy exclaimed.

"What, none for me?" With his hands on his hips, Arthur gave Tad an exaggerated frown that made the boy shriek with laughter.

"All I got to try was a bit from the spoon," complained Mrs. North. "It appears we have been forgotten in favor of the mutts and the rodents."

"Then I suppose we shall have to take Max and Milly's word," Arthur quipped, as Tad's giggling filled the kitchen with its pure joy.

There was no question in Arthur's mind that Mrs. North's dishes would be not only memorable, but would rival the greatest culinary efforts in taverns throughout England. In Rosemary's home, of course, even the mice must be fed.

Oddly, he realized with some concern, what mattered more to him was that no recipe gave him as much satisfaction or filled him as much as Tad's laughter.

The outdoors, Arthur discovered, was as seriously in need of repair as the indoors. Rotting boards needed to be replaced in the stable sheltering the horses and in the barn containing the other animals, but more extensive work would have to wait until spring. In the meantime, they would make temporary repairs.

"We shall breathe new life into the property," he exclaimed, clapping Charley on the shoulder. "I imagine you know a local man who can repair it properly, the way we want it done."

"Aye, and done well, but it might cost dearly," the retainer warned.

"I will see that the cost is taken care of."

As part of his plan, Arthur brought in villagers Charley recommended to perform work that he knew was more challenging in wintertime. Rosemary bristled when she saw laborers she did not recognize on her land, but Arthur set her fears to rest.

"A property like this should grow with each generation," he assured her, his own enthusiasm growing, "just as it is doing now."

He instructed the men to fix up a proper stable that would do until spring, when they would begin work on a more substantial one. Next, Arthur hired a carpenter selected by Charley.

"It will require the efforts of a few hired hands," he reminded Rosemary, "but we need it. One cannot run a respectable inn without proper quarters for horses."

Somehow, Arthur discovered upon retiring that night that he was more motivated than exhausted. Were it not for Rosemary's devotion to Theo, he reflected once he was comfortably ensconced in bed, she would surely have received other marriage proposals before his. Not only was she beautiful and vivacious, he could not remember when he had seen such domestic dedication. The evening before, he had observed her mending bed hangings by candlelight.

More changes were needed, he decided, in order to see to her comfort. He vowed to arrange a special surprise that she need not wait long for, but it must wait for at least a couple of days. He lowered his head into the pillows, determined to sleep before another thought of her enticing vulnerability could consume his thoughts.

A quiet stretch of weather allowed work to proceed more quickly than they had expected. One evening, relieved that the storms had subsided long enough for the workers to make substantial progress, Rosemary took Tad outside to view the horses' new quarters under moonlight. They walked past a brand new pantry window, one Tad had accidentally broken in his excitement two days after Arthur had installed it to keep drafts at bay. Showing no hint of frustration, Arthur had reacted with humor and kindness, replacing it at once so Tad need not suffer the constant reminder.

Could any man, Rosemary wondered, have

been more devoted than Major Winstead, arriving before the holidays, bringing the promise of new hope and permanence? She must not consider marriage a possibility any longer, she reminded herself. Now, after all he had done for her, all she wanted was his happiness.

On their way to the stable, they stopped to laugh at Tad's snow family in the dark, their shapes deformed and sagging now, the glow from the candles in the windows lighting their path.

"Look, Mama," he exclaimed, pointing to the sky, "a star in the east!"

She stepped forward to where he stood, laying her hands gently on his shoulders as she gazed into the darkness at the point of light he indicated.

"It is a bit too early," she reminded him, "for it is not quite Christmas yet. But it shall not be long. And this one, I believe, will bring many blessings."

"We have already had lots of presents, Mama," he said, a note of hope in his voice. "We have faith. We know everything will work out."

Rosemary tried to release the catch in her throat. How had her son made the observation before she had? Her heart overflowed for Tad's grateful nature. "Yes, my love, we do indeed have faith," she assured him.

"And we have hope. Major Winstead

brought it," he added with a giggle. "Maybe it is his Christmas present to us."

A little smile rose to her lips as she felt her heart pound. "It is a wonderful present, is it not?"

"The best, because it is something we needed very much. And we have the gift of charity," he continued, his words making her heart skip a beat. "Just like Major Winstead said."

"The gift of charity?" Rosemary echoed.

Did Tad recognize the difference between Arthur's wealth and their lack? She had been foolish to think he would not compare Arthur's fashionable attire to their own. Her spirits plunged with humiliation. To think, she had once accused him of seeing her and Tad as a duty. Suddenly, she felt sick.

"He says the men from the village have very little compared to us, but we helped them by hiring them," Tad explained. "It's our way of showing charity. Because we have so much. We've always had faith and hope. Now we have charity, too."

Rosemary felt as if a leaden weight had been lifted from her shoulders. She tried to hide her trembling smile. "Major Winstead is correct. This year we do have all three — faith, hope, and charity."

And, she realized with a dizzying sense of awe, they had them in abundance.

■ ■ ■ ■

As if the fates were listening, Tad's plan to attract visitors with his snow family worked promptly, drawing the arrival of new guests the following evening. While the Dawsons preferred sleep to entertainment, Rosemary was delighted to receive payment for their room while Arthur arranged to have their bags taken upstairs.

"We are grateful you and your husband still have room on this bitter night," the wife exclaimed before proceeding to explain their delayed arrival.

Feeling herself turn crimson, Rosemary fumbled for words to correct the assumption that Arthur was her husband but gave up, relieved he was not there to hear. Still, she had to admit, the assumption made her feel warm inside. She had forgotten how good it felt to be part of a couple.

Four hours later, as she lay awake listening to the blustering wind, she was glad all the rooms had adequate blankets on such a frigid night. All but her own, she realized, trying to stretch her thin blanket about her neck. How comforting it was to have someone to cuddle with on cold nights. She envied Mrs. Dawson the warmth of Mr. Dawson's presence in bed. How would it feel, she wondered, her heart pounding, to have Arthur lying beside her?

He would already have brought her extra blankets, she realized, warmth filling her at the thought. The memory of him lifting her onto the chair so she might inspect the chimney made her body tingle in a way she had never experienced. It tingled again now, just remembering.

Had she agreed to his marriage proposal, she thought, she might not be sleeping alone tonight or ever again.

Disturbed to realize Arthur had crossed her mind before Theo had, she could no longer sleep. Instead, she rose and left her room to check on Tad. She was relieved to find him sleeping soundly, his rest unhindered by the gale. She jumped when she emerged from her son's room, startled to find Arthur in the hall. A powerful intensity brought back her most intimate thoughts as he laid a hand on her arm to steady her. As the only two awake with an occupied guest room nearby, they moved closer together, so close that his robe fell open slightly, resting against her exposed neck. They spoke barely above a whisper.

"The wind is fierce," she whispered, shivering. "I hope it has not awakened our guests."

"Let me get you another blanket," he offered at once, stroking her upper arm to warm her. The touch of his fingers made her skin tingle through her robe. "I will give you mine."

"No, thank you," she declined, imagining

the cozy warmth of his blanket. But she was reluctant to leave him without. It would have been more appealing to share it with him, she reflected, her heart pounding despite her embarrassment. "I have an extra one in my room."

"I suspect Mrs. Dawson is awake," he said softly, "but not because of the wind. Mr. Dawson has been snoring. I made sure their windows were sealed tightly before they retired."

Rosemary felt herself relax. "You have thought of everything. Thank you, Arthur."

As he murmured how much he enjoyed being of assistance, she could not help noticing the strength in his arms, evident even beneath his robe. No wonder he was capable of repairing whatever she needed done. In the candlelight, she saw the strength inherent in his face that matched the rest of his powerfully muscled body.

His hand resting on the banister reminded her of how good his hands had felt on her waist. Their eyes met and lingered for a long moment, filling her with a desire she had never known. Reminded of propriety as a feeling of awkwardness swept over her, Rosemary excused herself and returned to her room.

Rather than easing her mind, the encounter kept her awake so late into the night that she regretted not borrowing his blanket.

CHAPTER EIGHT

While the laborers focused on repairing the stable, Rosemary followed Arthur about as he continued to inspect the home's interior.

"Progress on the bedrooms has gone so well," he told her, "I am certain six will be ready by Christmas if not all eight."

"Imagine what that will do for our reputation," she marveled, hardly believing the progress he had made in such a short time. Her home had gone too many years without major changes, yet he had transformed it almost overnight.

His announcement that he would be gone several hours on an errand early the next morning raised her suspicions. Whatever was he up to? He returned just before darkness fell, announcing cryptically that she was to expect a delivery within a few days.

She was still dressing one morning the following week when Arthur knocked on her door and urged her to come quickly. Throwing on her dressing gown, she followed him to an empty guest room, stunned to see silk bed hangings for the newly redone rooms laid out on the bed. The smooth quality and brilliant colors took her breath away.

"Wherever did these come from?" she demanded in amazement.

"Macclesfield is known for being a great silk center, is it not? Full of mills," Arthur said by way of explanation. "We can't have all our efforts going to waste," he said, motioning around the room. "They arrived yesterday. You had retired by the time I finished unpacking them."

Rosemary lifted each set in turn, awed by their considerable weight. She studied the intricate designs in rich red, bright purple, and royal blue.

"They are a wonderful surprise," she exclaimed, overwhelmed by their beauty. "But we do not need seven sets. We had four rooms without hangings, and you felt two of the sets we already had needed replacing."

"I replaced yours as well," he admitted, smiling. "I thought you might enjoy gazing at that light blue should you ever have time to lie abed."

She had missed the final set. They were a shade lighter than the summer sky, the gold threads forming a floral design with birds scattered throughout. Seeing them from the comfort of her bed would be like gazing upon a summer garden each morning.

As she found her efforts to restore the pile more clumsy than effective, Arthur stepped closer to relieve her burden, his hands brushing hers as he did so. The tingling sensation warmed her to the core. She withdrew her hand discreetly, fearing the power in his touch.

As he arranged the draperies, seemingly unaware of his profound effect on her senses, he announced that hanging them would require Joseph's help. Rosemary felt a twinge of disappointment when the chance for their hands to touch again vanished. It had been brief, too brief, and soft as a caress, a generous and kind gesture on his part.

Even loving, perhaps.

It was that spark she needed to feel again. She had not realized the effect of its absence in her life. She fought to hide her emotions, fearing they would be laid bare before him.

"I believe these suit the rooms quite well," Arthur said casually.

Joseph was summoned and hung the draperies about the beds room by room before he departed. Arthur adjusted the folds while Rosemary rearranged the panels, displaying them to advantage. When they had finished, he stepped back to admire them.

"The gold with the red sets off the dark wood to advantage, does it not?" he said cheerfully. "I should find it a comfortable experience indeed to sleep in this bed on a cold night, especially with a wife or husband beside me. Do you not agree?"

Her eyes locked with his for a long moment. The intimacy of their surroundings made her cheeks flame. She was embarrassed to think her emotions were clear in her face. Arthur laughed unexpectedly.

"Your expression says all," he said lightly. "I can see you are pleased. Since I have a personal stake in our venture, I am happy to have contributed something of lasting beauty."

His hands caressed her shoulders with a featherlight touch as he bestowed the briefest of kisses on her cheek before pulling away.

"Perhaps you should try out each bed in turn so you know what your guests will experience," he said in amusement. "It is, after all, the hostess's duty to see to her guests' comfort. A privilege, too, I should think. I shall leave you to try them out in peace and privacy. Let me know if any adjustments are needed."

Chuckling, he hurried downstairs as Charley beckoned, leaving Rosemary fighting to control her blush, her hand still on the cheek he had kissed. He had certainly been unusually attentive while they worked on improvements together.

She realized her dressing gown had slipped open. While she was fully clad beneath, more of her throat was revealed than usual. She

had been so warm under the morning bed-
covers that she had untied the top ribbons of
her nightdress and forgotten to close them.

She was so flushed now there was no point
in tying them, especially since she would
return to her bedroom.

Had Arthur's presence prompted such
heat? Surely it must be the fact that the
fireplace ran more efficiently since he had
strengthened it.

Of course, it could be that unexpected and
most inappropriate kiss on her cheek, in a
bedroom no less, unchaperoned and in her
nightclothes.

Now that she was here, she decided, perhaps she should take his suggestion.

She closed her door to give herself privacy,
as if she had a shred left. Easing herself down
on her comforter, she eyed the sumptuous
bed hangings, delighted with how the golden
threads woven into the silk gleamed in the
lamp's glow. The draperies would shelter
future guests who would lie in the comfortable four-poster bedsteads. She felt herself
relax in the softness of the pillows, her
concerns fading away in the beauty surround-
ing her.

Yet when she closed her eyes, try as she
might to dismiss her cares, the vision that
remained was Arthur's face, smiling so close
beside her, lowering his face to hers with his
warm lips.

She could not let go of the image, nor did she make any attempt to try.

Surely, Arthur reflected, such a reaction indicated some attraction on Rosemary's part, no matter how slight. He knew little of women firsthand, but he had seen his sisters' flushed faces and heightened attentiveness when suitors they favored showered them with attention. The sight of Rosemary in her nightclothes exposed her vulnerability, both charming and heart-wrenching simultaneously.

She was such a frail woman to have taken on the monumental responsibility of running an inn. The folds of her robe and nightdress, while preserving her dignity, were not subtle enough to conceal the soft curves of her form beneath. The image that lingered in his memory stirred something hot and deep within him.

How could Rosemary have seen his early interest as being prompted only by responsibility rather than attraction? Had he been so detached emotionally that she considered his interest in her motivated only by duty? Guilt and regret surged through him as he recalled his initial hesitation at the idea of providing for her. While he still waited to be dismissed by her, his feelings had continued to deepen.

He reminded himself he must be vigilant in his behavior. The mere whisper of scandal could ruin Rosemary's efforts at running a respectable inn. The last thing she needed was a damaged reputation caused by an error in his own judgment. As much as he yearned to tell her of his feelings for her, he had to quell his desire while he was living under her roof.

As if his own doubts were not enough to convince him, the following day brought the delivery of a letter from his sister that confirmed them. Since a betrothal was not imminent and he could not return in time, Meg wrote, they might pay a visit to the inn for Christmas. Just like his sisters, he thought with foreboding, to intervene on his behalf. They hoped he did not mind, Meg concluded, if Dolly MacAdam accompanied them.

His heart sank. The prospect was not what he had hoped for. Had it been Dolly's idea? If she had agreed to come, she must not mind the idea of being courted by him. The fact that she had delayed choosing a spouse but seemed ready to do so hinted that she wanted to begin her family soon — and probably with him, he realized with dismay. Even if he tried to dissuade his sisters, there was little chance a reply would reach them in time.

Perhaps it was for the best, Arthur told himself. While Rosemary had rejected his proposal, he had found a compromise to satisfy his promise to Theo. Contemplating the idea of seeing Dolly MacAdam, a friend of his youngest sisters, he wondered if he might enjoy it. It was the holiday season, after all.

He had never viewed Dolly with marriage in mind. While her interests focused on social matters appropriate for one of her breeding, they were separated in age by nearly a decade. Yet she was certainly pretty enough to turn a man's head and would make a suitable wife for an army officer. Her father had served as a colonel in America's War of Independence, and Arthur had a fair amount of admiration for him.

Another consideration also loomed before him. Once Rosemary's home was restored and attracting guests steadily, his obligation would be complete. It weighed heavily on his heart. He remembered that Rosemary intended to inform him, in her words, when he had fulfilled his duty. His departure loomed inauspiciously before him.

The prospect of having no reason to remain at the inn pained him. Perhaps if his sisters decided to bring Miss MacAdam, it would lift his spirits and give him something to look forward to in the new year.

"We are close to being ready to spread the word that we are open for business," Arthur announced to Charley, Rosemary, and Tad two days later. "Once everything is in place, I shall send one of the hands back to the village with word that the Jolly Goose and Thyme —"

Charley interrupted him by clearing his throat. " 'Tis the Jolly Goose and Rhyme, Major," he reminded Arthur meekly.

"Thank you, Private. The Jolly Goose and Rhyme has been restored to its former or, perhaps even better, its *new* grandeur and is open for business. All that is needed is one person of consequence to stay overnight, and word will spread."

"The Jolly Goose has been spruced up," Tad agreed, then grinned. "The Jolly Goose, spruced. We should add that to the sign so everyone will know how hard we have worked."

"Don't say it too loudly in the presence of your mum," Arthur advised as he laid an affectionate hand on the boy's shoulder, making sure he was within earshot of Rosemary. "For quite some time, she felt it was fine as it was."

He was startled but pleased by her reply.

"I think even Papa would admit it is better like this," she said with a confidence Arthur had not seen previously, as she stood back to assess the exterior. "Your grandfather, Tad, was proud of this property. I suspect it looks much better today than it did even in his day."

Later that afternoon, Charley took Rosemary aside. " 'Tis good news the major might have visitors over Christmas," he said casually "It guarantees we shall have business. A young lady will also be coming along with his sisters. Daughter of a colonel, I believe. I can see why his sisters like her. She would make the major a very suitable wife."

Word of a possible rival for Arthur's affections had made Rosemary's spirits plummet while jealousy soared.

"How do you know his sisters like her?" she demanded.

"He said so," Charley replied. "His sisters might come to collect him at Christmas time, and he expects Miss MacAdam to accompany them. Maybe he figures a betrothal would make a fine present for his family. It promises joy and happiness, after all."

Unable to find a reply that did not betray her sudden devastation, Rosemary had no choice but to find another task to occupy her mind. Perhaps she should reconsider her options. If she had no interest in Arthur's future, another woman clearly did, one who would not hesitate to enter his life in the midst of holiday festivities.

Yet she had bigger concerns. The major renovations were complete, and a few visitors had come and gone, but the lull that followed the Dawsons' departure worried her. She tried to remain optimistic and hide her anxiety from Arthur. What if it did not work out after all? It would be a shame, she reflected, for he had done so much work, and her home looked so wonderful that even Papa would have been pleased.

Then three guests arrived in two groups. She registered a young couple and a single gentleman, all traveling home for the holidays. Here was success, she thought, thanks to Arthur's efforts.

But what would happen when renovations were concluded? He would pack his belongings and return to Warwickshire, as she had requested. And in the meantime, the thing she feared most seemed to have happened.

She had fallen in love.

CHAPTER NINE

Was it possible, Arthur wondered that evening, that the Duke of Prestfield had been unaffected by his appeal? His hope was dwindling that Theo's father would take his rightful place among their visitors.

Arthur had watched lives torn apart by war, parting families and severing relationships. Had not the duke wisdom enough to see the tragedy of sacrificing a relationship with his grandson over pride? It was a far more minor thing than war that separated this family, and therein lay the tragedy.

At least he had the satisfaction of seeing Rosemary glow with joy again during the evening performance for the registered guests, exuding confidence as they entertained in the newly renovated inn. He sat beside her and Charley, listening as Tad sang a trio of ballads.

"Just like a chorister," Charley said in wonder. "There stands a young man of great talent, Rosemary."

Even before the carriage door closed behind the passengers the following day, Arthur realized an opportunity had presented itself. He hailed the driver before he set off.

"Here's something extra for your trouble," he said cheerfully, amused at the stunned amazement on the face of the driver as he studied the amount Arthur placed in his hand. "There shall be more of the same, my good man, when you bring us more customers. And do recommend our inn to other drivers."

After the carriage set off, Arthur confided to Charley his attempt to draw more business to the inn. Three days later, Charley laughed as he watched Arthur offer money to a second driver.

"Rather like being in the captain's pay, isn't it?" Charley suggested.

"Let us keep it between ourselves," Arthur agreed under his breath, "lest the mistress considers the transaction a bit underhanded. I see promoting our inn as good business."

"What precisely do you see as good business?" a suspicious female voice demanded, startling them. "Pray do not tell me this is what I suspect. Did you actually pay that driver to bring us customers?"

As Arthur struggled to reply, Charley piped up, "And ain't it a plum idea, Rosemary! Now let's see how many customers we'll have over the next week."

Arthur saw Rosemary's features tighten as her color deepened. But instead of the rebuke he expected, she sighed. "Let us hope so."

With that, she turned and walked back toward the entrance, leaving Arthur relieved yet slightly disheartened. He had not expected thanks. He was startled to see her stop unexpectedly when she reached the door and glance back at him, a wickedly mischievous smile on her face.

"I shall pay you back, Arthur, every penny," she promised, her eyes twinkling merrily, "as soon as the money comes in. It would not surprise me if that were to happen soon. Thank you from the bottom of my heart for your brilliance. In the captain's pay, posh! Tad's future looks bright indeed."

At first, Arthur saw, there were fewer overnight travelers than expected. But that did not mean there were no guests. Villagers and local folk came to be entertained.

Suddenly, he saw how sensible it had been to put money into the tavern, for it was proving to be an excellent investment. As he watched Rosemary sing with Tad, their joy was obvious. His task, he realized, was complete. Even without overnight guests, Rosemary might make enough from local folk on which to survive. Still, he hoped Rosemary would allow him to stay until he knew for certain that their success would continue.

The following night, more locals came, with one man even bringing a drum. Charley invited Seth Marbury to join them in front of the fire, his addition creating a small band.

"I'll come back tomorrow," Seth promised.

And he did. Seth returned every night afterward, eventually bringing his wife Edith with him. Others began coming as well, until there were so many villagers, Edith Marbury offered to help with kitchen duties on busy evenings. In Edith, Arthur observed, Rosemary had found not only a helper but a friend. Edith's children, two boys and a girl, offered Tad companionship.

Then Arthur noticed a surprising and unexpected development. People began to flock to the inn in numbers each evening to enjoy a pint of ale or to listen to Charley tell war stories while Tad played the flute and Rosemary sang. Listening to their voices harmonizing, Arthur understood what drew them. Visitors came for the warmth and camaraderie.

The musical storytelling trio could not be duplicated, for they were unique, he realized. They had become part of the Cheshire culture and landscape.

And they were family. A family Arthur was not part of. It was bittersweet to think he must leave just as they found success.

Rosemary, he conceded, was as heroic as any knight as she and Tad sang, from ballads and rounds to Christmas carols. Suddenly, he understood what he had failed to see before. She did it not only for survival, but to spread happiness and cheer. He knew the tenants on his father's estate would have loved and welcomed her as much as he wanted her. But she had chosen otherwise.

Here she was loved by poor and gentry alike. Even if her feelings had changed, taking her away would be impossible. He dared not ask. He had indeed fulfilled his duty to Theo.

That was it then, he thought. He had come full circle. He would go home while she remained at the inn where she belonged. She was its heart, an angel who poured her soul into singing to bring joy to others. She made it more holy by including her young son and the man as close to a father as she had. They formed their own trinity.

And, Arthur conceded, there was no room for a fourth.

Rosemary was delighted that travelers had begun to come at least in small numbers. Yet some of her fear returned when she remembered that Arthur had offered money to the carriage drivers. Perhaps the gesture was prompted by a lack of confidence in her abilities as a hostess. Christmas, she fretted, was only a week and a half away. Why were more travelers not passing through?

Still, the local residents more than made up for the absence of overnight guests. They treated her as if she belonged at last. It warmed her heart to see Arthur sitting in the middle of the great room floor playing with Tad, while the guests wandering about referred to him as her husband. She no longer corrected them. And she had a true friend in Edith Marbury. The villagers made her feel so much like one of them that several drank themselves into senselessness one night, and Charley deemed them unable to make it home safely.

"What shall we do with them?" Rosemary asked in exasperation as the drunken men began to nod off in the great room.

"We have bedrooms upstairs," Arthur suggested.

"A capital idea, Major!" Charley exclaimed. "Let's hoist them over our shoulders and get them up to bed."

And before Rosemary could protest, all the upstairs rooms were occupied with snoring villagers.

"Tomorrow, they will return to the village," Arthur confided to her in the hallway, "and they will spread the word about your wonderful entertainment, the comfortable beds, and Mrs. North's scrumptious breakfast. And before you know it, people will come." He sighed with satisfaction. "And now, having given my room to that large lumbering fellow

319

who snores so loudly, I shall go downstairs."

Rosemary was filled with sudden alarm. "But where will you sleep?"

"Mrs. North prepared a cot in the kitchen. Worry not. I endured far less comfortable accommodations in the war."

Guilt kept Rosemary awake. There was so much extra room in her own bed. She spent the night tossing and turning. Should she give Arthur her bed? He was still a guest, after all. No, she decided, he would not accept even if she offered. She struggled to warm herself between the cold sheets.

If only she could invite him to share the bed. She could hardly make such an offer, although she yearned to desperately.

Her fears of his discomfort were ungrounded, she learned the next morning.

"The major said sleeping on the kitchen cot was like being in the army," Mrs. North announced, "but better."

Rosemary felt her cheeks burn. She should apologize for expecting him to stay until all projects were completed, for it was too late for him to return home in time for Christmas.

She did not doubt Arthur had formed attachments during his stay, yet she suspected she was not the object of his affections as much as Tad was. Perhaps he considered it his duty to spend time with her son while under her roof. But love was another matter. While he appeared to enjoy their exchanges despite her rejection, he was unquestionably aware that he could also enjoy children with another woman willing to accept his offer. Someone like Miss MacAdam.

Rosemary swallowed her hopes. She could not deny him the happiness he deserved. The conclusion she reached did not please her but satisfied the requirements of their arrangement. It had become clear she must release him from his promise to Theo.

You have fulfilled your duty, she would tell him. Had she not said, ironically, she would inform him when his mission was complete? Her own words haunted her. *You have done all you promised Theo.* Even if her voice faltered ever so slightly, he might not think anything amiss. He had proven himself a most useful handyman and excellent business partner, ensuring work was done to his strict standards.

There was no longer a need for him to remain. She had received precisely what she had requested from the handsome, efficient major.

But she no longer wanted a business partner. She wanted a husband.

As if the question was not sufficiently disconcerting, Arthur approached Rosemary late that morning with a missive in his hand that filled her with foreboding.

"This was forwarded to me from my superior officer," he said slowly. "Someone discovered a sealed letter that was never delivered. It is from Theo to his father."

Her heart skipped a beat, making her feel suddenly lightheaded. As she absorbed the significance of his news, her tension drained away, replaced by melancholy. Its contents were not intended for her, and she would probably never know what they were.

"This gives me an excuse to call on the duke a second time," he added, "should you have any message to convey."

"I would not know what to say," she admitted in a mournful tone. "Even if I might wish our relations were different, I cannot change the past."

"It was discovered among the soldiers' belongings," Arthur said quietly as he passed the letter across the desk to the Duke of Prestfield several hours later.

Theo's father held it for a moment before returning his gaze to Arthur.

"I shall read it in private. I trust you will understand. Thank you for bringing it." His voice was slightly husky as he placed the letter in the top drawer of his desk. "I take it you are still at the home of my daughter-in-law."

"We have just completed renovations to allow her to open her home as a full-fledged inn. I daresay she will make a success of it yet," Arthur replied, surprised by his interest.

"I understand you visited your daughter-in-law and grandson after Theo's passing."

"My son and his wife lived in her father's home," he said slowly. "After I received news of Theo's death, I made a goodwill gesture toward her and the boy. Though I did not necessarily want contact with her, I would like to have seen more of my grandson. He was asleep during my visit. I had only a brief glimpse of the child, not wishing to awaken him. He was very small at that point. I offered to remove her and the boy to a distant country home of mine, suspecting she did not want to see more of me than necessary. The home was far grander than her current residence, yet she refused, saying she wanted nothing from me. She was proud and, if truth be told, rather spiteful. That was the last I saw of my grandson."

Why had neither of them been so forthright? Perhaps the duke had hoped for an acceptance Rosemary denied him or misinterpreted her grief as spite. If she had not been so headstrong, Arthur reflected, her life might have been different.

"I cannot speak for her, Your Grace, but I know Theo regretted defying you. While he defended his marriage, he always wished he might have made amends for his rash speech. He felt he had wronged you with his outspokenness and lack of respect." Arthur waited, filling the silence when the duke did not react. "Frankly, I suspect his determined nature was what made him such an excellent officer. I believe it was a gift he inherited from you."

The duke was silent for so long that Arthur consoled himself with the thought of his imminent departure.

"Your expression of sympathy gives me comfort," the duke said at last. "I thank you for that and for your discretion. I hope his strength of character continues into the next generation."

Here, Arthur realized, was an opportunity to open a door.

"Your grandson is a bright, thoughtful boy who is already capable of decision-making," Arthur ventured, hoping the grandfather would be moved by his earnestness. "He is musically talented, possessing skill on the flute, and has a vivid imagination, having been raised on stories of heroism by his mother. It is more the pity you could not meet the boy at this impressionable age. He would benefit from your influence."

Apparently, the duke would ignore the suggestion by changing the subject. Opening a drawer, he withdrew a box and handed it to Arthur.

"Some time ago, I received a package as Theo's next of kin," he announced. "Hearing some sort of music from within, I assumed it was an instrument and did not trouble myself further. I have no reason to keep it. I intended to give it to you on your previous visit but forgot. Perhaps you would like to have it. I suspect it will mean more to you."

Arthur departed soon afterward, satisfied he had improved relations, yet was no closer to introducing the duke to his grandson. It was disappointing but not surprising that Rosemary's stubbornness had prevented them from forming a relationship. She could not change her mind now even if she wanted to. And he could not change it for her.

He waited until he was ensconced in the carriage before opening the package. He knew its contents, for he remembered the sound. Within the box lay a familiar tambourine, rusted now but still functional. Belonging originally to an Irishman in their regiment, it had been passed on to Theo after the soldier was killed.

Also included was a note from an officer of Arthur's acquaintance. While the duke hadn't had any intention of reading it, Arthur would not let the gesture go unacknowledged. Written to deliver comfort, the note described the joy the tambourine had brought his unit. Arthur remembered how Theo had stayed with the soldier until his last breath, just as Arthur himself had done with Theo.

The memory caused his throat to contract, but a smile replaced the pain when he thought of the traveling tambourine's next recipient.

"And this very instrument," he said with dramatic emphasis, handing the tambourine to Tad after sharing its history, "was played by your father. He held it in his hands just as you are now."

With that, he released the instrument, letting Tad feel the weight and shape of it. The boy studied it with a look of wonder and reverence. "Papa played this instrument?"

"The very same. It is the one he used to entertain the troops," Arthur told him. "He was musical, like you. He made people laugh and sing, just as you do with your mother and Charley."

"Maybe you can play it with us," Tad said hopefully, holding the instrument out to him.

Arthur was so touched, he was unable to speak for a moment. "I think it best if you play it. Your father . . ." He could not continue.

"The lad has a sound idea," Charley spoke up quickly. "Sound, got that? It popped out in jest, but anyone can play, Major. Won't you join us in a song?"

His eyes focusing again, Arthur could not suppress a grin. Charley considered him capable of successful military maneuvers, but his musical ability was another matter.

"I do not think that entirely true, for it requires a degree of skill not everyone possesses," he replied. "However, with your kind encouragement, I shall try my best. But I believe I shall refrain from singing."

While Arthur's efforts on the tambourine were laudable if not exceptional, he conceded their humor was far more entertaining than his musical ability, which was fortunate since his efforts were required to register guests. They came in a steady flow toward the end of the final week before Christmas.

With the grandfather clock in the great room announcing that time was running out, the holidays approached as rapidly as a runaway stallion. The days went quickly as the list of tasks lengthened.

"Shall we plan a big dinner like your father used to have?" Mrs. North asked Rosemary, unflappable as usual. "The kind I used to cook when your mother was alive. I think I will," she concluded, and without waiting for agreement, she set off to put her plan into motion.

Rosemary worried about feeding all who might decide to make use of the newly renovated rooms before Christmas. It was not a problem she had ever faced before, she realized with a mix of triumph and wonder. It was the best possible problem.

To ensure the inn had a successful holiday week, her newfound friend Edith Marbury offered to help with cooking and serving. There were still six days until Christmas.

"We'd no plans of our own other than being home," Edith admitted. "Here we shall
be part of a bigger family."

At four that afternoon, Rosemary saw her
hopes coming to fruition.

"We have a couple ready to book a room,"
Charley told her under his breath. "You had
best take care of them now while there is
space."

"But we still have five of the eight rooms,"
Rosemary countered. "One is Arthur's, while
two are for Arthur Wiggins and his sister.
Won't it be lovely to see him again and to
meet her?"

"A passing driver sent word that a party of
four wishes to reserve two rooms for tonight,"
Charley confided. "They stopped to dine and
will arrive later. Your reputation has spread,
my lady."

"That is indeed most promising," she
exclaimed, feeling jubilant. "But we still have
three rooms."

"Not quite," he confided with happy urgency. "Two rooms were just booked by a
family whose carriage axle broke. There is
more to tell, but first you must get this couple
settled."

Rosemary's heart pounded. "Is there but
one room left? Does this mean — ?" She
could not finish.

His eyes twinkling, Charley gave her a look
of exultation. "Once you book this couple,

there will be no room at the inn."

"And during Christmas week." Rosemary feared her heart would stop with disbelief. "It is truly a miracle."

Leaving Charley behind the desk, she introduced herself to the young woman who sat by the fire, stroking the ears of Maxwell and Millicent.

"I see your husband has gone with Joseph to tend to your bags, Mrs. Beadle. Fortunately, I have one last room available."

Elated by success, Rosemary had failed to notice Ivy Beadle's manner change at her words. The uncertainty in the young woman's face alerted her to some unspoken concern.

"Thank you. We will share a room." Ivy hesitated. "Though my hair is still up, and — that is, I do not want him to see me in the nightclothes I have brought, for they are not my finest . . ."

Why was she suddenly reluctant? Her hesitation made Rosemary's suspicious. Their behavior upon arriving held the anticipation of those passionately in love. Yet while Ivy's manner and diction suggested her family was among England's peerage, Timothy Beadle's behavior was lacking and his appearance unkempt.

They were not married, Rosemary realized. Ivy had probably eloped with a man of whom her family disapproved. The outer door opened abruptly and Joseph and Timothy hurried in with their bags. Watching Timothy's eyes on Ivy's dress, Rosemary was convinced he had not yet seen what lay beneath but hoped to tonight.

Hesitant to assign them the room, she consulted the reservation book. Impossible as it seemed, one room remained, and it was assigned to Mr. and Mrs. Timothy Beadle.

Even if there was no room left at the inn, Rosemary vowed to separate the pair if it meant relinquishing her own bed.

Chapter Ten

"Please make yourself comfortable," Rosemary said gently as she led Ivy into the sitting room. Indicating a velvet chair, she took the one across from it. Noting Ivy's anticipation had been replaced by worry, she delivered the lie she had prepared. "I realized I have two rooms available, should you require them."

Ivy paled. "Why would we need two?"

"As a mother, I am concerned for your welfare. May I share a personal observation?" Rosemary said delicately. "Your manner tells me you are reluctant. If you are not quite ready, do you not think it advisable to wait until you reach Gretna Green?"

The young woman's pallor, already contrasting sharply with her black hair, grew even whiter before reddening as she realized she had been discovered.

"May I ask your advice?" she begged. "Timothy does not want to wait, and I am afraid of disappointing him."

At least she was honest. "I imagine your mother has no idea," Rosemary said gently.

"My mother died many years ago. My father and elder sister raised me. Delphinia married earlier this year." Ivy's face paled again. "She would be furious if she knew."

Rosemary patted the young woman's hand. "My mother died giving birth to me. I married a man whose father disapproved of our union. Now I am a widow with a son of my own," Rosemary confided. "I know how your sister would feel if she knew your intentions. You are a lovely young woman of breeding with your life before you, while Timothy seems a bit youthful yet."

Memories engulfed her. How much like Ivy's her situation had been, except Ivy's family was wealthy and Timothy's intentions were less noble than Theo's. What an advantage hindsight was, Rosemary reflected. Family disapproval probably made them want each other more. Knowing the pain that would result, she was relieved Ivy seemed receptive.

"You want a man who will love you despite the quality of your nightdress. One who will accept you with all your foibles and imperfections. If your sister were here, she would tell you the same. You must be certain the man you choose loves you for who you are."

As Rosemary finished the thought, her words caught in her throat. She was convinced Ivy's Timothy had never known true love, but Arthur certainly did. The words intended for Ivy applied to her also. Despite her imperfections and headstrong ways, Arthur had never faltered in his support of her.

Ivy's next remark was so unexpected Rosemary regretted her own mistake.

"I would like to find someone wiser and more understanding — someone like your husband," Ivy said bluntly, "for I can see that is how you and he are together."

That, Rosemary knew with all certainty, was true love. She fought to find her voice. "I shall put you in my room if I must, but I beg you to think this through. Please reconsider your options."

She listened while Ivy described her beau as a former soldier with cousins in Cheshire they were to visit before continuing on to Gretna Green. Ivy froze in mid-sentence at a commotion down the hall, her whisper a suspenseful lament. "It is my sister."

By the time she and Ivy reached the great room, Rosemary discovered Arthur and Charley had matters well in hand. They were attempting to compose an agitated dark-haired woman who resembled Ivy and was accompanied by a gentleman.

"I am Captain Nicholas Hainsworth, Earl of Greymore," the woman's companion said in an urgent tone. "My wife and I have come in pursuit —"

He stopped as his wife swept across the hall with a cry of relief to embrace Ivy. Rosemary was relieved to see them cling to each other.

"Oh, I have worried so about you," Delphinia said in a rush, stepping back to brush Ivy's hair from her forehead. "I spoke rashly only because I care so deeply. Please tell me you are all right. Did he — have you — ?"

"We are not married," Ivy said at once. "I — I am inclined to wait."

The earl spoke quietly with Charley before Arthur made introductions and reminded him of a mutual acquaintance. As Delphinia took her sister's arm before departing, Ivy seized Rosemary's hand.

"Thank you for your kindness," she said fervently. "I intend to heed your advice."

"I am certain all will be well," Rosemary assured her, taking Ivy's hand in hers. "It is your sister who needs your reassurance."

Rosemary watched Ivy leave with her family, while Timothy lagged behind. Arthur gave her a conspiratorial glance.

"That young man claiming to be a hero is an imposter, for he could not tell me the name of his commander when I asked his regiment," he said. Then he added in an admiring tone, "You are a fine judge of character, a most important quality for an innkeeper."

"I was ready to give her my room," Rosemary confessed.

"I would have slept in the kitchen again to prevent such an occurrence," Arthur agreed.

How could she not be grateful? His loyalty pained her.

"Our other family has arrived, Rosemary," Charley reminded her, approaching them with a sense of urgency. "They have been served tea and refreshments in the dining room. I believe it is time you met them. Ah, here they are now."

Before he could say more, she was stunned to see Tad return to the great room with a boy about his own age. Both children's hands were stuffed with toy soldiers. Rosemary stared in disbelief. The child was about the same size as Tad and looked remarkably like him.

A group of adults followed them. There was a young man escorting a woman on his arm accompanied by two women who appeared to be his siblings. Rosemary's heart skipped a beat. She had seen Theo's family briefly on one occasion, although they had not been introduced. *This must be Aloysius, Marquess of Lyndgate, Theo's older brother,* she thought, *with his wife Jane.* The women would be his sisters, Rebecca and Catherine Boughman.

The younger had to be Catherine, the sister to whom Theo felt closest and of whom he had always spoken so fondly. As their eyes met and locked with recognition, she was stunned to see Catherine move forward slowly and take hold of her hands.

"I lost my brother in the war," Catherine said slowly, "and your son tells us you lost your husband. Can it be — ?"

"I believe we have met," Rosemary reminded her tenderly. "If I am correct, Catherine, we grieve for the same man."

"We feared you had left the region," Catherine exclaimed softly, her face full of wonder. "Finding you here is like having part of Theo back."

The young woman, her face so like Theo's, burst into tears and threw her arms about Rosemary. They held each other tightly for a long moment, Catherine's head on her shoulder. Overcome with emotion at such a greeting, Rosemary responded in kind, not surprised when Rebecca and Aloysius and then his wife Jane took turns doing the same.

Afterward, she would remember only the hushed apologies that had been so long in coming. Before five more minutes had elapsed, everyone was wiping away tears and laughing and proclaiming holiday tidings all at once, while the two boys played on the rug in front of the fireplace with Maxwell and Millicent hunched down beside them, wagging their tails.

Just when Rosemary thought she could not absorb another shock, even one wrapped in joy, Joseph interrupted their reunion to announce the arrival of another guest who would be making his way inside shortly.

"We have no rooms, Charley," Rosemary whispered in concern. "Or is there one left?"

"This guest might not require a room, for he does not live far," Charley ventured with a smile. "The marquess's family was here long enough, having eaten their dinner while you were tending to the ladies, as well as young Timothy and the Earl of Greymore, that they had time to send word to another family member."

Rosemary felt herself pale. "You cannot mean — it cannot be Theo's father."

"It is indeed. Tad's grandfather has decided to join our reunion." Charley's eyes twinkled. "He is the only one missing, is he not?"

But absent no longer, she saw. The Duke of Prestfield appeared in the doorway, his eyes taking in his family but scanning the great room for someone else.

Her.

The event seemed unreal, despite the many times Rosemary had hoped for such a reunion. Theo's father greeted his family briefly, with a pat on the head for young Aloysius, as he crossed the room slowly. Averting their eyes discreetly to give him privacy, his family turned their attention to one another, speaking softly among themselves of Christmas plans.

"Happy Christmas, daughter," the duke said in a subdued voice, his expression haunted by their history.

"Good afternoon, Your Grace," Rosemary said, tripping over the words in her confusion. "Happy Christmas. Welcome to our home — to this gathering. You are very welcome here."

"My children have made me see the error of my ways," he said, his tone humble. "And my grandson says he has found a fine companion in your son — my grandson. I have faith he is correct."

"Thank you. Tad is a good boy." Rosemary could hardly believe his words.

"I thank you for receiving me, my dear," he continued, taking her hand in both of his, "for I have wronged you and my grandson as well as myself. I do not know if you can find it in your heart to forgive me, for we have lost many years. But if you can, I promise you I intend to spend the remainder of my days making it up to you and your son."

"Your grandson. I would very much enjoy having Tad get to know you," she said softly, in disbelief at the words she was hearing. Could the moment be real? "You are the only grandfather he will know. And I speak not only for him. I wish to know you better also."

"Then let us not lose another moment," he vowed. "Perhaps you will be able to tell me more about those intervening years." His eyes were misty and his voice quavered the slightest bit. "Those years you spent with my son

338

from which I was absent."

"I would be delighted. There is so much to tell you. I harbor no resentment toward you, Your Grace," she hastened to add. Theo's father might not even have known about the death of her own father or the workload she had assumed to turn her home into a tavern. She reflected on the war and the changes it had wrought. While the situation was not always happy, she had somehow managed to remain optimistic and cheerful. She knew a large part of that was due to Tad. "I know, in the past, I have been ungrateful to you and rude as well. It is unforgivable that I brought upon my son the consequences I had hoped to avoid. I wanted him to have a large family with cousins and other generations. By arguing with you, I denied him that."

"I gave you no chance, my dear," he said tenderly. "It is merely a temporary setback. The finest, most effective leaders of our army look for every opportunity to seize a victory. I believe we have done so today, have we not?" Briefly, he glanced toward Arthur. "One of the best is, in fact, with us now. I am sure Major Winstead would agree."

"I know he would."

An involuntary smile of wonder spread across her face. She felt a tightening in her throat as she remembered the likelihood that Arthur would live out his life elsewhere. She would spend hers here, she reminded herself, where she would be happy. She turned back to the duke.

"Do you wish to meet your grandson? He would find great delight in getting to know you. He is most fond of heroes, and I am certain that is what you will be to him. He is much in need of real ones." In what she feared might be a futile attempt to get Tad's attention away from his newfound cousin, she called to her son. "Tad, there is someone very special I would like you to meet."

Arthur watched the scene between grandfather and grandson unfold from a distance. He basked in the jubilation he felt at his part in bringing them together. Of all the repairs to Rosemary Boughman's home, he realized with a sense of triumph, mending these torn relations was the most rewarding.

He discovered the Duke of Prestfield had an excellent singing voice as well.

"I was told as a child that I had a fine voice," Theo's father admitted modestly. "I performed only for the family, of course. I should very much like to hear Tad sing. I would like to think he has inherited the talent from me."

As Arthur saw tears of joy and delight glisten in Rosemary's eyes, he suspected the duke would at some point share with her the contents of Theo's final letter. Had the letter prompted this reconciliation? Whatever it was that turned his heart, the duke had made a wise decision.

It occurred to Arthur that each of the three men whose lives had intertwined with hers for good or otherwise had the same qualities. Theo must have had faith his father would come to accept his wife, and that she would in turn recant her rejection of him. The Duke of Prestfield must always have held out hope that he would be reunited with his grandson no matter how difficult he himself had been and how stubborn the boy's mother was. He had been charitable enough to open his heart.

And whether Rosemary consented to marry him or not, Arthur knew the importance of never letting go of hope. He understood fully the quality of love in all its wonder, even if she spent her life here instead of with him.

He realized the family was gathering together and preparing to sing.

"We have much to sing about," the duke said in a surprisingly jovial tone, "for all our family is here today for the first time." He paused, turning to Arthur. "Will you join us, Major?"

It was late in the afternoon before the family had exhausted themselves with the strength of their emotions. Rosemary was flabbergasted with the changes in her father-in-law, so striking she might not have recognized him had she met him in town. The duke was

341

preparing to head home, but promised to return the following day to visit the grandson he had already spent time getting to know. He would, he promised, have something special for each child, making his departure an event that saddened neither Tad nor Aloysius. Instead, they talked of nothing but their surprises the following day, when they would no doubt be more awake. They were more excited together, both Rosemary and Jane declared, than either had ever been on his own.

After Theo's sisters and brother and his family had retired to their rooms to rest, Arthur approached her once he found the chance to speak privately with Rosemary.

"My father-in-law — how strange that sounds — shared with me the contents of Theo's final letter," she admitted. "Theo's last request was that his father take care of Tad, just as he requested that you care for me. He also asked his father to provide for me."

"He asked us both for the same promise," Arthur said in surprise.

"Perhaps Theo could not be sure his wishes would be honored but wanted to give his father the opportunity." Rosemary shrugged, taking his hand. "Theo knew I would be cared for, for he had asked you as well."

"Maybe he knew one man alone could not handle you and your son," Arthur teased.

"Or he suspected Tad would turn out headstrong like me," she continued, oblivious to his poking fun because she saw the truth in it. "Happily, I suspect he will be more like Theo in temperament."

"I believe Theo wanted his father to have a role in his grandson's life," Arthur reflected, "and he found a way with his final letter."

Overwhelmed by the reunion with its cascade of emotions, Rosemary was relieved moments later when Arthur's presence was required elsewhere. It was the first quiet moment, Rosemary reflected, in a day that had been altogether too hectic. Telling the servants she required a moment to herself, she made her way to the breakfast room, where she sat alone in silence over a comforting cup of tea from Mrs. North. It appeared that Tad's future would be secure after all, she realized with a sense of triumph. She had achieved all she had wished for.

With Arthur's help, she had accomplished all she had had hoped and more. Yet her triumph did not come without a certain melancholy. She could have been wed by now, she realized. She might have been looking forward to a happy domestic future. Instead, her prospects included days like today, though perhaps not quite as busy. There would be travelers calling at the inn, seeking accommodations. She would rarely be alone, for she would have company regularly. While the realization brought her comfort, there was also something lacking.

The mantel clock chimed delicately, another reminder of time passing. Yet another Christmas would come and go, and the coming year would make her another year older. How, she wondered, could she feel such dismay when she should be happy?

Because she had only so many years in which to have children, she realized without thinking. And that required a husband. She had lived her life as if time had stopped.

But it had not stopped. It was hurrying on without her.

The realization of that truth struck her like a flood, washing over her and awakening her to what she needed to do. She must do it immediately, she told herself, rising at once.

As she made her way downstairs, she found Charley on the landing.

"Ah, Rosemary. There are four ladies presently making their way up the walk. These are the ladies who reserved the last two rooms before stopping for dinner," Charley explained cheerfully, "giving us a nearly full house for the night."

Rosemary hastened to the window to peek at the newcomers. What she saw left her slightly lightheaded. A group of women with familiar features was approaching the inn. This time, the faces reminded her not of her son, but of the man she loved with all her heart.

Her throat went dry as she recognized the similar eyes and smiles. The women were laughing, all quite pretty in their own way, which was no surprise since the group comprised Arthur's sisters.

Rosemary's heart beat furiously. How many sisters did he have? And which woman, she thought frantically, was Dolly MacAdam?

CHAPTER ELEVEN

Before Arthur could discuss with Charley the joyous ending of the duke's estrangement with Rosemary, the retainer drew him aside with a haste that startled him, merely to inform him that the women in the dining room had requested tea only.

"Might you see to their individual needs?" Charley requested urgently.

With the servants apparently pressed into service elsewhere, Arthur made his way toward the dining room, approving Rosemary's decision to place paintings and candelabra along the length of the hall. The additions added cheer to what had been a dark, dreary walk when he had first taken it. His eyes lingered on a painting of pink roses before he turned the corner and entered the room.

"Oh, and just look who has been sent to wait upon us," a familiar voice exclaimed. "I certainly hope he does an adequate job of taking our requests."

While he would have recognized the imperative voice anywhere, Arthur was still startled to see his sister Joan seated at the head of the table with his sisters, smiling with anticipation. Having completely forgotten about Meg's letter — how many days ago was it? — he found the presence of his family an unexpected complication.

"Has any decision been made regarding your engagement? We look forward to meeting your bride," Meg announced, a look of anticipation on her face.

With dismay, he remembered notifying them of his dashed expectations. Where was Dolly MacAdam? Alarm surged through him. He had almost forgotten they intended to bring her. She must be freshening up. He would focus on Joan's and Meg's families to avoid the subject.

"Where are William and Henry and the girls?" he asked to delay the inevitable. "And Miss MacAdam?"

Joan broke the awkward silence. "At the last moment Dolly could not come," she said dryly. "She complained first of the megrims and then the sniffles. She always has some excuse. I told her both would be gone within a day, but she declined."

"We suspect it had to do with Major Ryder's return," Lisbeth piped up.

"The rest of the family remained at home. We ate along the way. But perhaps we ought

347

to order," Emma teased, her eyes twinkling, "so our tea can be prepared while we catch up."

"And while we are waiting," Joan continued imperiously in the tone Arthur dreaded most, "you can tell us how the marriage proposal came about and what has been decided."

To distract them, he discussed arrangements for tea and cake first, stalling for time while searching for a way to explain his intentions had fallen through. "Enough about tea," prompted Lisbeth, the youngest and most impressionable. "We want to know about your bride and the proposal. Tell us everything."

Arthur could no longer conceal the truth. How might he adequately express his regret and genuine sorrow? He was surprised by a cheerful voice behind him.

"His proposal was most gracious and kind." Rosemary stepped into the room from the doorway. "Just like everything else he has done for me since his arrival. His generosity knows no bounds."

His four sisters rose with a collective gasp, all speaking at once.

"We wish you all happiness," exclaimed Joan.

"We are so anxious to meet you!" cried Meg.

"Is this Rosemary at last?" asked Emma.

"Was it romantic?" demanded Lisbeth.

"It is, and it was," Rosemary replied softly, giving Arthur a knowing smile. "I look forward to getting to know all of you. I expect we shall be very happy together."

"I cannot tell you how relieved we are," Joan continued. "I am Joan Ambler, my dear, Arthur's older sister. We are delighted. I believe we met your son upon our arrival."

"The boy pretending to be part of our snow family is indeed Tad," Rosemary laughed. Arthur noticed how bright her eyes were.

"I hope you will be happy with us," Emma enthused. "We are thrilled to add you to our family. We hope your presence will allow us to see more of our brother than we do presently."

In stunned silence, Arthur listened, prepared to apologize but finding no need. He watched Rosemary's expression soften, her eyes locking with his for a moment.

"Thank you truly," she said to Emma. "I will enjoy getting to know you all. I know Arthur will make a wonderful husband and father to Tad."

"And maybe he'll give you more children," Meg teased. "We have hope."

Unsure what had just happened, Arthur announced he must tend to their tea and cake. Extracting herself politely from the excitement, Rosemary accompanied him from the room.

"You have performed a charming charade,"

he said earnestly when they were beyond hearing, "and I appreciate your attempts to make the occasion happy. But I fear it will only make it more difficult to tell them the truth when the time comes."

Rosemary sighed impatiently. "Men are so slow-witted sometimes," she continued. "What difficulty will there be, Arthur, when I spoke the truth?"

He frowned as hope replaced confusion. "Does this mean you have changed your mind after all this time? After the doubt you put me through —"

He stopped himself, recognizing the danger in saying more.

"When I saw your sisters arriving, I feared I would faint," she confessed. "My heart leaped when I learned Miss MacAdam could not make the trip. I was never so grateful. I felt God had given me another chance."

"Does this mean you will marry me?" he demanded incredulously, taking her face gently in his hands.

"Only if you will have me," she said softly, "and Tad, of course."

"Of course I will have Tad, and you — I would consider myself the most fortunate man on earth to have you." The hope in her eyes as he gazed into them swept away all doubt regarding his future. "I shall not assume this means you are willing to leave your home, for I have come to understand all it means to you. It even feels like home to me. I cannot take you from the place you belong."

Rosemary responded with words he had never expected to hear. "I think it would be wise for us to create new memories in a new place." As she gazed into his eyes, Arthur could see she was searching for understanding. "Tad and I would live with you anywhere. No one has ever been so loyal to us."

"Or has loved you more, except Theo, of course. I know no one could ever compare to him, and I shall not attempt to try."

"Yet you have done more for me than anyone," she assured him hastily.

He kept his face close to hers, ecstatic to have finally been given the opportunity. "We shall return here whenever you wish. I only know I cannot live without you."

"Perhaps Charley would consent to run the inn in our absence," she suggested. "We will have to ask."

"I have already done so, hoping you would change your mind, stubborn as you are. I know you have the strength and endurance to handle the inn as well as marriage. You will when you are ninety and we have been together many years in marriage, and our children are grown."

He felt his heart stir as he watched her eyes light up. "I want more children," she whispered. "And Tad wants siblings."

"We might have our own child, born here

perhaps, by this time next year," Arthur suggested tenderly, gazing into her eyes. Pausing to reflect, he continued, "Perhaps not here after all, for there is no longer room at the inn. I am a mere marquess, not a carpenter as Jesus was. And yet look. All of your rooms — our rooms — are full."

For a change, the tears she could not hold back were happy ones. Her trembling smile widened as her eyes sparkled. "It appears, Arthur, you have helped bring about a Christmas miracle."

Seeing the love in her eyes made him realize he was wise to have stayed when a weaker man might have run.

EPILOGUE

"We have already had a few guests," Charley told the family upon their return. "I entertained them as best I could without you."

"We had hoped to be the first guests of the new year," Rosemary exclaimed.

"But we are not the last," Arthur consoled his wife, gazing at her with deep affection and surprise. "Would you like this to be an inn always?"

"I believe I would," she admitted. "It can continue to extend hospitality to all. In those lean years, I learned the value of company, the importance of caring for others. And we will always have a place to come when we pass through, assuming we shall be in Warwickshire much of the time."

"At least some of the time," Arthur agreed, winking at Charley. "Besides, it will keep Charley occupied."

Charley chuckled as he watched Tad greet the dogs, squealing with delight at being hit with their wagging tails.

"I imagine Tad was a lively chaperone," Charley said, adding in an undertone, "I hope you did not run into that young couple at Gretna Green."

"Fortunately, we saw neither of them," Arthur said. "We were most happy to take their place."

Rosemary returned Arthur's teasing glance with a shy smile.

"Our wedding vows shall be consummated here," Arthur confirmed in a low voice. "We would not have it any other way. Tad will remember our wedding day for the rest of his life. Now that we are home, however, we shall get to work on our newest responsibility."

"So soon?" Charley said in surprise. "What is it that cannot wait?"

"Producing a sibling for Tad." Arthur winked, taking Rosemary's hand to lead her upstairs as they exchanged a furtive smile.

"Perhaps Tad will have a sibling this time next year," she suggested, a note of hope in her voice.

"If we hurry," he said, squeezing her hand.

DEDICATION
(*NO ROOM AT THE INN*)

In loving memory of Aunt Marian, who lavished upon us the most generous and memorable Christmas celebrations any children ever saw, even after we'd already celebrated at home. Those with nowhere to go at the holidays always had a place at her table.

In the Season of
Light and Love
BY SHARON SOBEL

Chapter 1

"If I step over him on my way down the stairs, he might catch a glimpse of my leg," Miss Violette Makepeace said to her companion. "And if I do not step over him, I might very well kick him into the street. That would not be so very terrible, but I daresay neither action would do much for my reputation."

"Your reputation has withstood a good deal worse," Evelyn Cabot said softly.

"Thank you very much for reminding me of it," Violette retorted, and for the tenth time in as many minutes, looked out onto the snowy scene in Berkeley Square. She regretted her waspish tone almost at once, for scarcely an hour passed when she did not recall her foolish impulse to dash off to Gretna Green with a man she thought she had loved. Indeed, she truly had loved him, until the moment they were intercepted by the brother of the woman to whom he was married. Everything changed for Violette with that dreadful and humiliating revelation, for she no longer harbored dreams of a happy marriage, but instead envisioned a future of living on the margins of respectable society, of being the object of gossip and ridicule. Evelyn, alone of all those she once considered her friends, remained loyal and sympathetic. "But two years ago," Violette continued, "I was imprisoned in my house because of unkind gossip. Now we are forced to remain here because a great lout of a man has turned up drunk on my doorstep."

James Hanford, Earl of Greenlough, was no one's idea of a lout, even though the stories of his notorious behavior were shared among polite society on what seemed to be a daily basis. But Violette was connected to him in ways that others were not, for their families had long been neighbors and his younger brother was married to her older sister, Olivia. Whatever he did in his very public life did not seem to matter very much to Olivia Hanford, who always welcomed her brother-in-law into her home and encouraged him to spend time with her children.

Indeed, Violette could not quite say why it mattered so much to her. Her own reputation, which was indisputably earned, could rival his in every scandalous way. And, as such, she ought to be more forgiving. In her weaker moments, she was prepared to be very forgiving indeed, for Lord Greenlough had intrigued and attracted her for nearly her entire life.

But no one knew that, not even her dearest friend. She looked toward Evelyn, who studied the great, tall man sprawled across the snowy marble steps.

"Perhaps he is dead," Evelyn said solemnly, without any sense of irony.

Violette was pretty sure he was not, but her own sense of irony had been well-honed in the past few years. "Then I suppose there will be an official inquiry," she said, sighing. "I shall have to admit some acquaintance with the fool, and our day shall be utterly ruined."

"Though not as much as the earl's, I suppose."

Violette laughed out loud, for so unexpected was this little display of wit. She looked away from the Earl of Greenlough to her friend and quickly sobered. Evelyn, as always, was quite serious.

"Perhaps we can postpone our shopping excursion for the day after next," Evelyn murmured, though Violette knew the offer was simply her friend's attempt to ease things for her, nothing more. The entire Cabot family was about to descend on the great house of Evelyn's uncle near the Palace of St. James, and Evelyn would have no more time for shopping than she would for a sea journey to celebrate Christmas in the Holy Land.

"I am sure I have nothing on my busy social calendar, but you will be entertaining all the

"Indeed," Violette said, lightly. But, in fact, she was never quite able to reconcile the serious, practical man with the rake who was rumored to have slept with half the ladies in London.

"Well?" Evelyn asked.

"Well, what?"

"Shall you not invite Greenlough in?"

"Oh, yes," Violette said. "I suppose it is the only way we can get him to leave."

She thought to call one of the servants to open the door, but decided to adopt Evelyn's spirit of compassion and approach him herself. She did not need to embarrass him further, after all. But, more importantly, she wished to have a moment alone with him, to see what was amiss, and if she could provide some comfort to him.

She left her friend in the parlor, and walked to the door. Opening it and stepping outside, she regretted not throwing on her pelisse, for the air was quite frigid and a brisk wind tossed about snowflakes like feathers spilling from a quilt. Violette lifted her skirt, just slightly, so her hem would not drag in the snow. Below her, on the cold stone steps, her visitor wore neither a hat nor long coat to protect him from such weather. His dark hair blew about his head, taking on a reddish sheen in the waning sunlight.

"My Lord Greenlough, is that you?" Violette called cheerfully. "Have you lost your way to White's this afternoon?"

He did not respond at first, and so she thought he did not hear her. But then he turned his head and seemed to do the very thing she had scornfully discussed with Evelyn some minutes earlier; he studied her ankles. Violette promptly dropped her hem. But before she could repeat her words, he grasped the sturdy iron rail and pulled himself to his feet, his eyes roaming along the length of her body as he rose to her level.

He looked wretched. His noble aquiline nose was humbled by its reddened tip and nostrils and his gray eyes were swollen and bloodshot. His ascot was wrinkled and stained. That such a strong and handsome man should be brought to this state by alcohol and debauchery was tragic, for all it was self-wrought.

"Lord Greenlough? Are you unwell?" It was a foolish question, for the man looked like he was about to tumble backward into the street and likely concuss himself. He closed his eyes and wavered.

"Oh, good heavens," Violette cried and ran down the remaining steps, catching his arm before he fell. She pulled him closer, surprised to note he did not smell of whisky or of the streets. In fact, he smelled rather nicely of bay rum, the popular gentleman's soap of the Caribbean. She pulled his arm around her, enveloping her body in his warmth and exotic scent. "Where have you been?" she asked, trying to sound stern. In fact, she would not mind remaining like this for an hour or so.

"No further than King Street," he murmured. "I have rooms there, you know."

She did. Something crunched beneath her boot and she looked down to see some shards of broken glass. Her first assessment was correct; he had been drinking.

"May I come in?"

"Did you lose your way? Or did you tire yourself navigating the vast distance between King Street and Berkeley Square, and decide to seek a respite on my front steps, like some weary chimney sweep? And why are you not wearing a coat on this cold December day?" Violette asked in a rush of questions as they stumbled up the steps to her door.

Surprisingly, he laughed, a low, rumbling sound from deep in his chest. "I did not expect to account for my careless habits."

"Well, my lord, someone must take care of you," Violette said, and then realized she would not very much mind being the one chosen for the task.

"And I did, in fact, come to see you, Miss Makepeace," he said.

Though they were shy only one step of their destination, she stopped, and he stopped alongside her.

"Why on earth would you come to see me,

when any small correspondence you may wish to share may be accomplished with a note delivered to my door?"

She felt his body tremble and looked up to see his smile gone, replaced by an expression of utter misery.

"Is it the children?" she asked, in a hoarse voice. Young Wils, John, and Anne were in the care of their nanny and the household staff, and Violette visited them nearly every day. Though she never met the earl there in all the time Wilson and Olivia were abroad, she knew from the children that their Uncle James was a frequent visitor as well. Perhaps he was just coming from their home. "Is it the children?" she asked again more urgently, shaking him.

He shivered again, and it was a moment before she realized it had nothing to do with the wind, which had very nearly died down.

"May we go within?" he asked, his large hand already resting on the door.

"Of course," she said, feeling wretched for prolonging his misery. Her ungloved hand reached for the cold brass knob and she turned it quickly, before very nearly pushing him through the opened door. Thinking that whatever he wished to share might not be for Evelyn's ears, she said, "Come, my lord, let us sit in the library."

But his words spilled out before they could go more than a couple of steps.

"It is Wilson and Olivia. Their ship went down in a violent, late season hurricane in the cursed Caribbean Sea, and all are gone. Our brother and sister are forever lost to us."

An hour or so ago, James thought he might wallow in his grief for days, but the sight of his sister-in-law's delicate sister collapsing against a cabinet in the hall did much to restore his sanity and strength. As he caught her, and kicked open the library door to carry her within, he silently acknowledged that he was to blame for her present state, and had acted selfishly. He, who had demonstrated his strength in sport and in manual labor, who oversaw the operations of several estates and business in Parliament, had now exercised the control of a child by coming to her door and spilling out his sorrow without preamble or the patience to escort her to a chair.

He had always thought her a fragile, beautiful thing, like a dancer on a music box. Whereas her older sister was ever one to challenge the Hanford brothers, Violette Makepeace quietly watched from afar, as if the endeavors of others were better to be observed than joined. And he was always aware of her watching him, even more so as he pulled away from childhood ties and became more adventurous, developing a bit of a reputation. Perhaps more than a bit.

But Miss Makepeace remained contemplative and cautious, and on their occasional meetings, he sensed her aloofness, even her censorious opinion. Therefore, her ruinous elopement to Gretna Green was all the more surprising. He sometimes caught himself wondering about the man she would someday choose to marry and did not doubt the paragon would be of extraordinary worth and impeccable honor. And knew that he, with a history of amorous liaisons churning up the waters in his wake, could never be that man.

He was pretty certain what Miss Violette Makepeace thought of him, and he doubted this intrusion into her home would repair her opinion.

James reached over to tuck a knitted blanket about her shoulders, but she brushed him away. Standing over the large chair to which he delivered her a half hour before, he felt desperate to do something more reassuring than handing her one handkerchief after another, collecting them when they became too damp to do much good. Her companion, Miss Cabot, made certain there was a steady supply of the dainty linens available at hand, as well as a large pot of tea. Now she sat on the far side of the large library with her own cup of tea, watching them and — he keenly felt — judging him.

"When did you first learn of this?" Miss

Makepeace asked, hiccoughing between her words.

"Only this morning, Miss Makepeace. I received a letter from a Mrs. Hamilton of Nevis, who was acquainted with your sister. What remained of their ill-fated ship had been washing ashore in that island's tiny harbor for two days before she wrote me. She remembered the children, and took it on herself to be the bearer of such news," he said. "As I doubted the lady would have known Olivia's family name, I came to Berkeley Square to be certain you knew nearly as soon as did I."

Miss Makepeace sniffed and looked up at him. He had never really studied her before, but in her face, he recognized the delicate features and dramatic coloring of their exquisite niece. Little Anne favored Olivia, but the child was truly a miniature of the lady who now bore so much grief at her sister's death.

Her eyes and nose were reddened and swollen, but it did little to diminish her beauty. As she bit down on her full lower lip, dimples appeared in her cheeks, and her skin was very pale. She blinked once, and again, and for the first time in their long acquaintance, he wondered if her parents had named her Violette because of the extraordinary color of her eyes. He leaned closer to stare into those eyes, wondering if it was just a trick of the light that drew out the indigo reflection, and

Miss Makepeace blushed.

"And yet you took your time about it, sitting like a layabout on my front steps," she said, her hands suddenly trifling with her skirt. "I am sure anyone who recognized you would suspect some mischief here, Lord Greenlough."

She was right, of course. He must have looked like an idiot. In most circumstances, he would hardly care. Many things were said about him that were not true, and years ago, James had decided to shrug off gossip and innuendo. It never seemed to sway the very proper Miss Makepeace, but now he appreciated that she might be anxious to shrug off some of her own. He continued to study her and recalled some of the details of her sad story, even though he had been somewhat dismissive at the time. She had become the favorite of a newly-arrived foreign nobleman, full of pomposity and affectation, happy to regale everyone with tales of his own heroism. James thought him a bore and a very bad card player, but Miss Makepeace had apparently thought otherwise. Well, he did not actually know if she'd ever played whist with the man. But whatever else she thought him, she could not have known he was a married man, until the very moment they were intercepted in a posting inn a half day's ride from Scotland.

Wilson and Olivia did everything they could

to shield her from gossip, and James attempted to reassure them that her disgrace would only be on everyone's lips until the next great scandal on someone else's part. But it raised quite a stir at the time.

Still, he doubted anyone had thought about it in years.

Even so, the lady knew what it was to stir up gossip.

"You may be quite right, Miss Makepeace," James said at last, returning to the current, and much more enduring crisis. "And yet, given the news of this day, we have more urgent concerns."

"The children, of course," she said softly, and reached for another handkerchief.

"They must be told at once. I will go to them if you are indisposed." James straightened his back, demonstrating his resolve, when in fact he dreaded the idea of sharing the news with his nephews and niece. "It is my responsibility, of course, as the head of the family."

Violette Makepeace dropped her handkerchief, smoothed her wrinkled gown and stood to face him. "They are my family as well, all I have remaining. You are their legal guardian, and I know I have no rights to them, Lord Greenlough. But I adore them as does — did — their mother and am prepared to do whatever I can to keep her spirit and love alive in their memory. Please allow me this, my lord." She wavered, and then repeated most plaintively, "They are all I have."

James stood, ready to catch her again if she fell. But this time, and most inappropriately under the circumstances, he would enjoy holding her a bit longer.

"Do you not trust me?" James asked. Her trust might be applied to several things concerning his behavior, he realized. And was grateful she could not know what he was thinking.

"About speaking to the children?" she asked, looking doubtful. Perhaps she knew precisely what he was thinking.

"Of what else could I be speaking?" he asked. "Do you wish to come with me to Curzon Street?"

Her deep indigo eyes looked past him to other places in the room, but he did not know if she truly saw anything, or was utterly distracted in thought. He glanced at her friend Miss Cabot, who frowned and helped herself to more tea. After several moments, he half turned to see what Lady Violette gazed upon, but there seemed to be nothing of particular interest, just some stacks of oversized books, a jar of peppermint drops, and several boughs of Christmas greenery strewn on the large library table.

"I will come," she said, "but we will not share any news of this tragedy with the children."

He faced her again, and her eyes sparkled either with her tears or with pleasure. James dismissed the latter as impossible, until he saw her smile. What nonsense was this?

"They will have to know the truth of it, Miss Makepeace," James said, sounding more severe than he intended. "They are old enough to hear what has happened. Why, Wils is already a boy of seven."

"Wils has just turned six, and all three of them are children. Babies, truly." She studied him, daring him to challenge her. "And please do not tell me that you were of the same age when your parents sent you off to school, with Wilson following a year behind. We can see what has come of that."

"I beg your par . . ." James sputtered. He never had reason to doubt the particulars of his upbringing, nor give serious thought as to how he might like to raise his own children. He supposed he would have some one day, but that day was surely a very long time off.

"They are your responsibility now, my lord. But I hope you will concede that, in some ways, they are mine, as well. We have an obligation to them, but also to our unfortunate partnership. We ought to agree on how we must proceed," Miss Makepeace insisted. Her color remained heightened and her eyes were very bright.

"But surely you must admit that the children must be informed of their parents' fate.

To leave them ignorant of the circumstances would be a very cruel deception and I doubt we would ever be forgiven,"

"Lord Greenlough, I am not such a fool to imagine we would succeed at this for any length of time. I only request a delay."

He understood now. "You wish to consult your solicitor. Of course I understand. There are personal items belonging to your sister that you might desire for yourself or to put in safekeeping for Anne."

"My solicitor will not act on anything until we have proof beyond the despairing letter of an acquaintance in a far-off land. No, I wish to delay because of the season. Our nephews and niece have been anticipating days filled with feasting and gift-giving and all sorts of delights. It is soon to be Christmas and the New Year, Lord Greenlough. Have you been so busy that you have forgotten?"

He refused to admit that indeed, he had. It was never his favorite time of year, for his friends were likely to be at their family estates and what house parties he attended were absurdly sentimental and marked by nostalgia he did not share. If he had been particularly attentive to a woman through the fall, she expected a nice gift, usually including emeralds to match the season. His hosts expected him to participate in endless games of charades. And then there was all that singing.

His beautiful inquisitor frowned as she

looked up at him, daring him to admit he had not looked past this day in early December. He suddenly recalled that she once sat at his own dining room table looking at him just so, several years ago at Evergreen.

"How can I forget the pleasures of the holiday, Miss Makepeace? Were you not with us when we last celebrated Christmas Eve with our little family at my estate in Kent? We only had the boys then, and they sat with us and listened to all the stories we shared about when we were children ourselves." He paused, thinking that nostalgia was not necessarily a bad thing if it was your nostalgia. "And then we went out on Christmas morning to skate upon the lake. I recall you were most proficient."

"I recall I nearly broke my leg. But you know precisely what I mean," she said, leaning toward him. Miss Cabot cleared her throat and Miss Makepeace pulled away.

"No, I fear I do not," he said, perplexed. Why was she reminding him of a long-ago dinner at which she barely spoke to him?

"Lord Greenlough, your grief has made you inattentive. I propose we wait to tell the children the tragic news until after the New Year, when the greenery has been pulled down and the antique silver is back in the cabinets. Let them celebrate this last Christmas, while all thoughts of their parents are still joyous, and they can anticipate their homecoming with excitement. If they learn the truth beforehand, all their Christmases thereafter will be punctuated by the greatest sadness. Their lives will never be the same."

"But that is the truth of it, dear lady," he said. He sympathized with her need to protect his nephews and niece, but to delay the inevitable did not seem fair either. "Their lives will never be the same, as it is."

Violette Makepeace put her hand on his arm, but it was a feather's touch. "Please, Lord Greenlough. Let us give them one last Christmas of happiness and innocence. You and I could do this for them, for the memory of our beloved brother and sister." Her voice broke on the last words.

Not trusting himself to speak either, he remained silent.

"Please, Uncle James?" she said softly.

She hit her mark, as she knew she would. He pulled away, but he was already trapped. "I agree. But I do not see how I am to be their guardian if you are to get your way in all things," he grumbled.

"In all things? Dear Lord Greenlough, you have only acceded to my request in one thing. We have many years ahead of us, and I do not expect that you will always be so amiable," she said. "Thank you."

James was accustomed to women who cajoled, begged, put their best assets on display before getting him to do what they wanted. But his sister-in-law's little sister applied nothing more than logic and the gentle touch of her hand to make him agree to her terms.

Never was he so easily and foolishly seduced into doing what he did not wish to do at all.

Just as they set out from Berkeley Square, it started to snow in earnest, quickly blanketing London in a virginal shroud. Evelyn left for home in her own carriage and offered them transport. But as the walk to her sister's house was very brief, Violette sent her on her way. It was hardly necessary to have her groom bring out the carriage. She'd walk to her sister's house. Would it ever be possible to think those words without feeling the knife-edge of pain that currently cut through her?

Violette adored Olivia, as only a younger sister could. Olivia was lovely and sophisticated, and knew to make the best choices in fabrics, home furnishings, and husbands. She'd married Wilson Hanford when she was only eighteen, but already knew to look past the fact that he had no title. Instead, she appreciated his innate goodness. She was also able to recognize, as many women could not, that the man loved her.

And now Olivia and Wilson were gone, leaving something more precious than any legacy of title and wealth. Their children were what remained of their splendid marriage, and Violette silently pledged to keep their memory alive in the minds of her nephews and tiny niece. She glanced up at her companion, who seemed indifferent to the snowflakes clinging to his eyelashes and falling about his shoulders. He would have to do much to keep Olivia and Wilson's memory alive as well.

"Miss Makepeace," he said suddenly. "Please take my arm. It may have been a mistake to set out like this when the streets are turning icy."

She slipped her arm under his proffered elbow, and he pulled her close. It was not necessarily easier to walk, but she no longer felt the cold of the winter day. Indeed, she was aware of little else but the tall man at her side.

"And you are without a coat," she remarked.

"I confess, I thought nothing of good sense when I ran from King Street to bring you the news I received. I suppose it was lucky I was dressed at all." They walked several steps, leaving footprints in the deepening snow. Lord Greenlough must have reconsidered his words. "I beg your pardon. It is an indecent thing to say to a respectable lady, even worse than lingering on her steps without a care to whom might be passing."

"I thought you were drunk, Lord Greenlough. Your behavior supported that notion, and I saw the broken glass of a bottle on the steps when I helped you inside."

His free hand shifted into his pocket, where he seemed to be fishing about for something. "It was not a bottle that was broken," he said. And then, changing the subject a bit too quickly, he added, "I shall borrow one of my brother's greatcoats when we leave his home. We are much the same size."

And he will no longer need it. Violette trod carefully through the snow as her eyes filled with tears.

"Miss Makepeace, I must ask you to explain something you said back there, in Berkeley Square," Lord Greenlough said.

"If it is about my sister's possessions, I entirely understand the proprieties. By law, they became the property of her husband, and are therefore now yours. Or will be, when the estate is settled."

"You cannot believe I am concerned about such trifles. There are, perhaps, a few jewels belonging to the family, and should be held in trust for Wils to give to his wife someday. But that is not what I mean." They ducked back while a passing carriage splashed icy water their way. "What did you mean when you said it is clear that our going away to school had some effect on us?"

Violette did not answer at first, belatedly having regretted making such a comment. To speak her honest opinion now would be unkind and might have the effect of beating a man whilst he was already down. On the other hand, now that Lord Greenlough had seemingly gotten over his first excesses of grief, he seemed rather sturdy and capable. She would need to rely on his strength as he would on hers, if they were to get through the upcoming difficult days with three young children. She would have to trust him on some things, his honesty among them. And so she needed to be honest as well.

They crossed the street and she would have slipped on the frozen mud if he had not held her even closer to him.

"Your brother was very young when he married. He was but nineteen, when most men wait until they are thirty years or more to settle on a wife," Violette said softly.

"Your sister was much the same age, but they had known each other for years by that time. I believe they settled on each other by the time they were twelve or thirteen. Most people would say it was very romantic," her companion remarked.

"And I do not doubt their love, nor their ability to have made thoughtful decisions affecting their future. But I cannot help but feel that if they had each been happier at home, they would not have been so eager to leave it. My father had already died, and my mother was a sad shadow of herself, no longer able to face the world. And so she remained until her own death, just before Anne was born. Little Anne is named for her, of course." Violette decided to say nothing about her own feelings of guilt in the matter of her mother's death, for Anne Makepeace had finally succumbed to her prolonged bout of depression soon after Violette parted ways, so to speak, with her French suitor. "And in your case, my lord, I am already aware that your parents did not particularly take pleasure in their two sons, and did not have much to do with either of you. Wilson confessed as much to me, soon after Wils was born."

"You have enjoyed a companionable relationship with my brother, it seems. I wonder what else he told you?"

"Many things," Violette said evasively. "We have truly been like brother and sister."

"How very admirable. I assume he spoke of his own brother as well." Greenlough brushed red fingers against his forehead, keeping the melting snow from dripping into his eyes. "If my brother sought to marry your sister partly as a consequence of a great desire to leave our home, why do you suppose I have not yet married? Would it not stand to reason I would have wished the same thing?"

Violette knew she must abide by her own decision to be honest with him. It was essential he knew precisely how she felt, so he might exercise some caution when he was with their nephews and niece. "It is not

unusual for there to be different consequences resulting from one cause, Lord
Greenlough. When it rains, farmers might be
joyous, but the hostess planning a garden
party is utterly disappointed. So it might be
that when parents are indifferent to their
children's upbringing, one child might be
committed to starting his own, happier home
life. And the other wishes to do quite the opposite."

She knew she sounded like a prig, like some
interfering matron who accosted the unsus-
pecting at the door of a church, commenting
on their garments or their absence from
regular services. She was a bit young to be
cast amongst them, but she already had some
experience of life and reason to regret it. She
believed Greenlough regretted very little, and
wanted him to know how she felt.

"And I have done the opposite, I suppose,"
he said, sounding amused. "How so?"

Violette looked up at him in surprise. Could
he be so cavalier that he did not know what
others thought of his behavior and the life he
led?

"Lord Greenlough," she said sternly. "It is
not only I who is aware of the rumors about
you, but all of England. All of Europe, for all
I know. Very little escapes the business of our
gossips, and you have given them ample
material with which to work."

"Yes, I suppose I have," he said, thoughtfully. "It is quite a thing for others to understand one so thoroughly, perhaps even better than one knows oneself. But you have chosen an odd moment to take me to task for this, Miss Makepeace. Do we not have more important things to discuss just now?"

"Here is Curzon Street," Violette said unnecessarily. Greenlough knew the direction even better than did she, for it was one of the Hanford houses Wilson and Olivia occupied. "This is the perfect time to discuss this matter, my lord. The children must be kept innocent of reports of your drinking and gaming and utter lack of morals and so I will never speak of them." Violette paused, not sure how to articulate the real point of her concern. "And I will ask, in return, that you do not speak of my unfortunate liaison with a Frenchman."

"And yet, such lively gossip reported about the two of us did not seem to bother your sister and my brother very much. Why bring them up now?" Lord Greenlough stopped.

"Because we are now the ones closest to their children, and they must be protected from gossip and censure. We must give them a more settled home than either of us enjoyed ourselves."

"So it seems you may be more concerned about rumor than fact, Miss Makepeace."

Violette looked around her, trying to discern her bearings through the curtain of snow. "Why have we stopped? And are you telling me that there is a difference here between rumor and fact?"

"We are at our children's home," Greenlough said abruptly, and Violette felt the knife stab once again, realizing his casual words were now true. Wils, John, and Anne were their children now.

And as they started up the stairs, their footsteps crunching in the untrodden snow, she thought he said, "There is all the difference in the world."

"Uncle James! Have you been swimming?" Wils said suspiciously, looking up from his book. "I would have joined you if I had known."

Greenlough ran his long fingers through his wet hair, until it stuck up in all directions, like spines on a hedgehog. "If I had, I would have invited you. But I am sorry to say this is just the consequence of walking for ten minutes in a rather severe snowstorm. Your Aunt Violette neglected to remind me to put on a hat."

Violette shook her head. She would not take the blame for his current state, particularly since she had stepped out, fully prepared for the wintry elements. "Your Uncle James forgot his hat all on his own, without any interference from me."

This was the second time she called him by

his name, and she rather liked the sound of it.

He turned toward her, grinning, and she guessed he rather liked the sound of it as well.

"Mrs. Belden." Violette looked away from him and faced her sister's housekeeper instead. "Would you be so kind as to bring Lord Greenlough a towel? I fear he is putting this lovely rug in some jeopardy."

"Certainly, Miss Makepeace. It is one of Mrs. Hanford's favorites," said Mrs. Belden. She handed Greenlough a porcelain bowl, perhaps intended for him to catch the water as it dripped off his jacket, and walked briskly from the room.

Violette did not trust herself to speak, thinking only that rugs and the possessions in one's house were worth nothing if the people who lived there were never coming home.

"Who is Lord Greenlough?" John asked, coming close to her side. She hoped she would never be called up to choose a favorite from among her sister's children, but she supposed it would be John. He looked very much like her late father and shared many of Sir Ellis's interests in the natural world, in books, in studying plants that grew in the small London conservatory. John pulled on her skirt.

"Why, Lord Greenlough is your uncle, of course. Did you not know that?" Her eyes met Greenlough's amused ones. "Your Uncle James."

John nodded, as if filing away that piece of information for future reference. "I did not know you were acquainted."

It sounded like something a curious adult might say, as it was laced with just the smallest touch of skepticism. Her friend Evelyn sounded thus, when a man she did not know approached Violette at a dance, or at the theater. And Anne Makepeace had spoken in such a fashion about nearly everyone they met. Or expected to meet. Or never expected to meet but whose name was mentioned casually, in passing.

"Of course we are acquainted, John," Violette said. She had not always answered her own mother's questions, but her nephew deserved an explanation. "I am your mama's sister and Uncle James is your papa's brother. We have known each other for years. We stood up with your parents at their wedding."

"Why have we never seen you together?" Wils said, getting into the game.

"We were all together at Evergreen, only a few Christmases ago," Violette said, but her nephews looked unconvinced. "However, your uncle and I keep very different hours. I am up and about during the day. And Uncle James has night habits."

It was an impertinence, but she doubted the children would recognize that. Of course,

Greenlough knew what she was about. Still gazing at her, he shrugged off his wet jacket, revealing a muscled torso that filled out his white shirt very nicely. She met his eyes and was unable to look away. After years of carefully avoiding him, she could not explain why she was unable to do so now.

But then, in truth, she did not want to.

"Here are towels for you, my lord," said Mrs. Belden. "I've brought an ample supply, as you look to have need of them."

"I am sorry to cause so much trouble, Mrs. Belden," Greenlough said, contrite. The housekeeper pursed her lips, and Violette guessed that dear Lord Greenlough could do anything he wished around the house, and that none of it would be any trouble at all. In fact, Mrs. Belden looked like she would be happy to rub him down with those towels herself.

And no wonder. He handed the older woman his jacket and she promptly brought it to the fireplace, draping it over the screen to dry. Greenlough turned to watch her, at the same time giving Violette an excellent view of his broad back and strong arms, barely concealed by the damp linen shirt he wore. He selected a towel, and raised his arms to rub it through his hair, pulling his shirt out of his waistband.

"And what of your boots, my lord?" Mrs. Belden quickly asked. "They would do well

387

to dry here by the fire, as well."

"I suppose they would, but we will go no further than that. I do not have any more clothes to spare," he said.

"You still have your —" Wils piped up, but Violette hushed him. Greenlough had already removed quite enough.

He sat down on a plain wooden chair, and gestured for the boys to come over and help separate him from his high Hessians. At one time, perhaps only this morning, they would have been polished to a high sheen. But now they looked like sodden tree stumps, discolored and stained. Wils and John seemed to know their business, however, and each tugged on a leg, seeing whose released boot could propel them farther across the room. It seemed like great fun.

"Where is my niece, Mrs. Belden?" Violette asked, a little disturbed by all this great familiarity, of which she played no part.

"She is napping, Miss Makepeace. I've already asked Nanny Lind to bring her down as soon as she awakens."

"Thank you very much, Mrs. Belden. I would like to see her this morning," said Violette softly.

The two women stood for several moments watching the boisterous scene before them. The boys were walking the large Hessians toward the fireplace, detouring to step over their uncle's stockinged toes. Mrs. Belden surely despaired about the track of wet sho-eprints on the floor, while Violette wished she had the utter lack of inhibition to join in their fun.

"Now, that is enough, you little rogues," Greenlough said, when the boys started to pull on his stockings. "I am scarcely decent as it is."

He looked up at Violette, who blushed for truly no reason at all. She supposed he was quite accustomed to teasing women, showing off his fine figure in various states of undress, and acting as if it entirely proper. She had heard about a house party in Greenwich, at which people shed clothing over a game of cards, and how most of the garments were not claimed until the next day. Greenlough attended such events quite regularly, if what she heard was to be believed.

But not even Greenlough would be so utterly indifferent to propriety in the home of his dead brother and in the company of Wilson's children, to intentionally tempt her in this way.

"Do you think you might borrow your brother's garments, in the name of decency?" Violette asked, wishing she did not sound so very desperate. "I am sure he would not mind." Her voice cracked.

Greenlough did not seem to hear her, but Mrs. Belden did.

"What is it, Miss Makepeace? Is there

something that troubles you?" she asked. "I do not recall you ever having visited with his lordship before."

"It is true we travel in entirely different circles, and rarely do they intersect. Today, however, we seem to have been in accord, and recognized each other as we each turned onto Curzon Street."

"And you without a carriage, and his lordship without a coat, in this storm," Mrs. Belden commented. "That two such people, with great presence of mind, should be so distracted is truly a great coincidence."

Violette bristled at the housekeeper's statement. She was comfortable enough with Mrs. Belden, who seemed more a family member than a servant in Olivia's household; that was not the issue. But that the woman should consider Lord Greenlough to exhibit a thoughtfulness equal to her own was somewhat disconcerting. Violette prided herself on her equanimity, her judgment, her discernment, which had only faulted her once. True, it was a rather serious error in judgment, but she had endeavored to compensate for it over the past two years.

But everyone knew Greenlough to be impulsive and reckless. Why, had he not demonstrated his utter lack of propriety on her steps, not an hour ago?

Violette sniffed, disdainfully.

"It is the odor of wet wool that bothers you,

my dear," said Mrs. Belden. "I will remove his jacket to the kitchen, where it will dry and be blocked by the girls. Otherwise, it will shrink to a size fit for the boys."

The boys — all three of them, it could be said — were on their way out of the room. Wils rode on Greenlough's back while John dangled from his arm, like a monkey on a vine. Greenlough made fierce noises as he staggered in a mock attempt to brush them off his body and the boys gleefully screamed. They finally made their way through the door, leaving a broken vase and a spilled embroidery basket in their tumultuous wake.

The two women stood alone in the room still echoing with the sounds of the ruckus.

"It is a wonder no one has broken a limb." Mrs. Belden sighed as she walked toward the yarn now strewn about the room and started to gather it up. "I guessed this is why you usually stayed away during his lordship's visits."

Violette bent down and retrieved a ball of fine cotton thread and a pin cushion. "No, it is as I said; we are customarily on very different commitments for the day and evening. But I believe that will now change."

"Oh, bless you both!" Mrs. Belden cried. "It is your sister's greatest wish!"

"Of what can you be speaking, Mrs. Belden?" Violette thought Olivia's greatest wish was to have ten children. Slowly, another possibility occurred to her, but it was so unlikely she dismissed it almost at once. It was absurd. Why would her beloved sister wish her to tie her fate to a notorious rake?

Mrs. Belden recovered her error — if such it was — almost immediately. "Why, Miss Makepeace, that you and his lordship enjoy the children at the same time," she said.

"I see," Violette said, though it did not make any sense at all. "Well, that is soon to be the case. Lord Greenlough and I have decided to celebrate Christmas with the children. Not merely Christmas Day, of course. And the twelve days that follow. But we wish to help them anticipate the holiday, and decorate the house with greenery, and make presents for all the household. We will do the things Mr. and Mrs. Hanford would do, since they cannot be with us this season."

"I see." Mrs. Belden nodded. "But do we not expect them before Christmas? I received a letter saying it was so."

"I fear they may be delayed," Violette said, and cleared her throat. "There is a property that particularly interests them, and they wish to explore it more thoroughly."

This answer seemed to satisfy the house-keeper, and the two of them spent some time putting the room to rights.

After a while, Mrs. Belden sighed. "You must be terribly, terribly sad."

Violette looked up to where the housekeeper kneeled on the rug, picking up pieces of the ruined porcelain vase. Did she already know the truth of it?

"I am," Violette said simply, testing the waters.

"For your family to live so far away from you, separated by a long sea voyage . . . it will deprive all of you of so much pleasure. Letters are nothing to conversation, and Mrs. Hanford always enjoys conversation. You must miss each other most dreadfully." Mrs. Belden retrieved a toy cannon from beneath a chaise. "Unless, of course, you intend to move to the islands along with them."

"To be perfectly honest, I have never considered it, Mrs. Belden. My life has always been here, in London. I daresay that if I marry, I will have to find a man who shares my interests."

Mrs. Belden nodded and cocked her head to the door.

Wils and John burst through first, yelling something about cutting down trees. Greenlough followed, walking stiffly through the doorway. Violette frowned, thinking he had paid the price for allowing two rugged little boys to climb all over him. But then she realized his problem had more to do with his garments than with any sort of soreness. His clothes — Wilson's clothes — were just too small.

Violette studied Greenlough with a critical

eye, too closely to be considered polite. But had he not tempted her by removing all his garments? Well, some of his garments. At a guess, she would have said that he and his brother were of the same size, but she saw now he was taller, broader, and altogether more athletic.

"Miss Makepeace? Do you not approve of my wardrobe?" he asked, smiling.

She met his eyes, and knew he teased her as he surely teased legions of women far too numerous to count. Still, he must know how he affected her, how he somehow managed to leave her so very hot and bothered.

"I very much approve, Lord Greenlough. Just have a care before you settle yourself upon a chair," she said softly. "It would not be an appropriate time to show off all your assets."

The boys darted between them, and from above came the crying sounds of Anne waking from her nap. Greenlough laughed heartily, and went after the boys, as quickly as his snug trousers would allow.

"Is it always like this?" Violette asked Mrs. Belden.

"Oh no, my dear," said the housekeeper putting a hand to her hair, as if protecting herself in a windstorm. "It is usually a good deal worse."

CHAPTER 2

The snow had stopped, but not before burying the city in its pristine brilliance. The mud, the refuse, the rivulets of waste that were a daily hazard even in the best neighborhoods, were hidden for a few hours, but the most cynical of Londoners knew that it would be only a brief respite. When the snow melted, all would be revealed.

Greenlough thought it an apt image for his own grief. Hours spent with his nephews — and even little Anne — were only a respite from the inevitable revelations that would occur after Christmas. He remembered how he had felt when his own parents were killed in a carriage accident. Miss Makepeace was right to suggest that his parents were reasonably indifferent to his brother and to him, but that did not make their loss any easier to reconcile. Indeed, he was at once possessed of a title and great wealth, but he would have given it all away to spend one more day with them.

Miss Makepeace must understand that, for she had also suffered losses in her past, and her current grief had to be as strong as his own. She loved her sister as he loved his brother. Hell, she loved her sister *and* his brother, as he loved them both as well. She would understand.

Greenlough turned his gaze from the window to his large desk and knew he would accomplish no work this day. He had reports to study and letters from acquaintances throughout Europe, but the reading of them would have to be deferred.

He could think of little else but Violette Makepeace.

How had he not noticed her before? Oh, indeed, he could be said to know her very well and over many years, but that was not quite the same thing as truly recognizing in a person those qualities that make one remarkable. For the first time, he realized she was possessed of a beauty that surpassed that of nearly every woman he knew, and an intelligence that one might overlook if one was preoccupied gazing into her deep indigo eyes. And yet, everything about her seemed to be understated, as if she did not wish for men to take notice of her, nor seek her out.

Yesterday, she had made him accountable for his own behavior, daring to speculate that his parents' indifference made Wilson and him the men they were destined to become.

She was perceptive about several things, for he now had to admit that some of his reckless behavior probably was prompted by a great desire to get his parents to actually pay attention to him. When they did not, he continued on his path, little caring that he did not do at least half of what was said of him. His parents remained indifferent.

Knowing that his own story was unable to be deciphered by anyone who did not look too closely, he now wondered if the same would be said of Violette Makepeace's ruinous adventure.

He did not recall all of it, though it was of great concern to his brother at the time. Sir Ellis Makepeace, her father, was already dead of some lung ailment. He had left his widow and younger daughter with a fine house, but very little with which to maintain it in the style to which the two women were accustomed.

Their resources were conserved to bring Miss Violette out on the marriage mart and James remembered dancing with her on several occasions, at Olivia's request. She was pleasant enough, but at the time not possessed of the physical attributes most likely to impress him. In any case, he remembered he was preoccupied that season, enamored with Lady Marguerite Denton who gave freely of herself until she decided to marry the Duke of Welden, a man thirty years her senior. With Marguerite's betrothal, she became a virgin once again, wearing white gowns to every ball, her lively past remarkably forgotten.

It presented a rather extraordinary paradox, for his part in the affair did not seem to be forgotten, and their exploits, real or imagined, became part of his rather regrettable reputation. Perhaps he ought to consider wearing white as well.

"My lord?"

"Do come in, Blaine," James said to his servant. Though truly, why should his reputation matter one whit to anyone but himself? "Has that package arrived from Portugal?"

"It has not. But there is a lady."

Ah. A package of another sort.

"Miss Makepeace to see you, my lord," Blaine said, a smile breaking through his serious countenance.

Damn the man! He knew just what James was thinking. "Bid her welcome, Blaine," James said, glancing down at his jacket, making certain there were no crumbs from breakfast upon his lapel, and that his pearl buttons were fastened.

Violette Makepeace was already at the door and came through with the determination of a schoolmistress ready to uncover mischief among her charges.

"My lord?" she asked, as she walked past Blaine. For his part, the man ducked out as quickly as possible. Miss Makepeace stopped short, and surveyed the scene about her. James thought his small library rather a fine room; certainly it was his favorite among those he rented. He had brought his favorite volumes along with him, and had furnished the place entirely to his satisfaction. Other gentlemen, in similar circumstances, would have used the space for social encounters. But James rather preferred the wood paneled room for his private work. And, after all, he did have a rather large bedchamber for liaisons.

"Miss Makepeace? You look rather surprised. Did you not expect to find yourself here? Did you set out from Berkeley Square with the intention of arriving elsewhere?" he asked, amused at her expression. "Or are you surprised to find only me?"

He chose his words most unfortunately, he realized. She looked at him then, with her extraordinary eyes, and he thought she was amused.

"I am quite alone," he said softly, grateful for it.

"You are alone no longer," she said, and somehow managed to endow those most insignificant words with all the grace of a promise. Perhaps sensing this, she took a step backward. "That is to say, I am sorry to interfere with whatever it is you are doing today."

"I am attempting to work on my correspondence," he said. "But I am not succeeding."

"I know precisely what you mean. I spent nearly a half hour deciding whether to wear a blue shawl or a green one this morning. I feel quite bereft, lost to all sense of purpose."

"My dear lady," he said, and quickly came around from behind his desk to approach her. He took her hand from where it hung limply at her side, and brought her over to the large chair, where he often read in the evenings. She went without any resistance.

"I know now how it was for you yesterday when you lingered on my steps, indifferent to anything else going on in Berkeley Square — the people, the carriages, the falling snow. I am sorry to have been so hard on you," she said.

James pulled up a stool and sat beside her. "I do not think you were that hard on me," he said, reflecting on their conversation.

She bit down on her lip. "Oh, yes. Though perhaps I was harder on you before you came indoors. I was not very generous in my thoughts."

"I see," he said, though he was not sure he did.

"I thought you were drunk, or perhaps worse," she explained.

"Do you mean, you thought I was on opiates?"

"I thought you were dead," she said bluntly. "But it is not you who is dead. It is . . ."

She could not finish her words, nor did he wish to do so for her. They had each suffered a terrible loss, the very definition of an unspeakable loss. "I know. You need not say it," he murmured.

He reached for her hand again, but this time, he took the bold step of pulling off her glove. He wished to comfort her — to comfort them both — and thick wool gloves were a hindrance to such intimacy. Rather than withdraw from him, Violette Makepeace laced her soft fingers through his, and he thought his heart would stop.

"To have thought such things of me, you must believe every tidbit of gossip that has ever been said," James said. He looked at her hand, at its neatly buffed nails and ink stains in the grooves of her middle finger.

"It is much more amusing to believe it than not," she said. "It is why I hesitated to come to you this morning, and why I was surprised to find you alone."

"Do you find my life sufficiently amusing to risk your own reputation? It is most unusual for a lady to come to a gentleman's apartments."

She raised one brow, the little minx. Was she about to lecture him on his behavior, now that they were entered into a partnership in the care of their nephews and niece?

"Truly, Lord Greenlough, I do not think it so very unusual."

"I am speaking of ladies like yourself," he said, and before he could stop himself, "Violette."

She let out a deep breath, as if she had been holding it in all this time. "I think ladies like me must find their way to your door all the time. But our expectations are quite different, you see." And then, she added, "James."

He did not think any other lady, other than her sister, called him by his given name, and somehow, the one syllable on her lips had all the intimacy of a caress.

"Perhaps our expectations are very much the same, my dear," he said, his voice suddenly hoarse.

She frowned. "Of course they are. We are to share in the care of Wils, John, and Anne, and we wish for them to grow up properly and have whatever they need. But I refer to those other ladies, all those who have come to your rooms, expecting . . ."

"What?" he asked, before he realized she could not bear to speak of such things. She was a lady, but one who had been utterly compromised. And yet here was something that exposed her as an innocent, as she could not even articulate what other women were prepared to do with him, or for him. At least, she would not do so in his company. But his question, uttered quickly in his effort to get her to say what she wished, was already hanging between them.

"Private pleasures, intimate conversations, perhaps. In this season, even a partridge in a pear tree," she finished, and shrugged awkwardly, as if she had given up her store of euphemisms.

He had no idea to what she referred. His quarters here on King Street were small enough, without bringing in flora and fauna to clutter up the place. But then he recalled the old song, with the nonsense about leaping lords and milkmaids, and believed he understood to what she was referring. But did she think his pleasurable liaisons with other ladies had anything to do with love?

She truly was an innocent, in ways Society never troubled itself to consider.

"You must think many, many ladies have come through that door, Miss Makepeace. They have not, if you find that at all reassuring. But even if it were so, please believe that there are none whose company I would find as delightful as yours." He bowed slightly. "Let us begin this conversation anew, Miss Makepeace. You are welcome to my very humble rooms."

"Lord Greenlough." She smiled, appearing somewhat relieved. Even so, she pulled her hand away. "I have been thinking a good deal about our situation. And my thoughts keep returning to that lovely Christmas we spent at Evergreen some years ago. I know you scarcely noticed my presence, but I have very fond memories of those days. My mother was happier than she had been in years. And I quite enjoyed myself, skating, singing, reading." She paused and looked around the room again, but this time he sensed she actually saw what was there. "You have a very fine library there. I assume it was your father's."

"To the best of my knowledge, my father never opened anything other than *The Tatler.* The collection of books was largely compiled by my grandfather, the fifth Earl of Greenlough. I have spent some years attempting to purchase books to fill gaps between the volumes. In fact, when Blaine opened the door, I thought he was bringing me a copy of Shakespeare's *First Folio,* recently purchased from a seller in Coimbra."

"There is a great university there, I understand," she said.

"Yes, even in Portugal there are great universities." James paused for a moment, thinking how much he took for granted during his years in Cambridge, and how a lady of reasonable intellect could never hope for much more than a sensible governess and perhaps an indulgent father with a good library. "And I have a great library at Evergreen. We have established that. Do you wish permission to travel there and peruse the shelves?"

"No, I wish to travel there with you and the children, and spend Christmas together. We have already decided to give them a splendid holiday, and how better to do it than to take them away from London, and let them enjoy the pleasures of the countryside?"

The thought of spending each evening alone with her, after the children were abed, left him acutely uncomfortable. She would wish to discuss hiring a tutor, or moving the children into the house at Berkeley Square, or what he thought of Christopher Marlowe's mysterious death or something of that sort. And all he would wish to do is seduce her.

"How do you know I have not already made plans for Christmas?" he asked.

She looked stricken. Looking up at him with startled eyes, she opened her lips but uttered no words.

"I may have already made very important commitments," he continued, knowing he was being unkind, and not at all sure why. And then in a moment of sudden awareness, he realized he wished to make her jealous, like some green boy hoping to impress the first girl he adored.

And with that awareness came long submerged memory, for when he was truly a boy, little Violette Makepeace had indeed been the first object of his desire. She'd utterly distracted him then, but never more so than

405

she did this day.

"But what can be more important than the children?" she asked, artlessly, indifferent to his desire to provoke her. Or any of his desires, apparently.

She was right, for he realized that dinner with Mrs. Amelia Buttons or going to the theater to see another performance by the lovely Eliza Rushwell was not all that interesting. There were many women in his life, but no one who really mattered to him. But his brother's little children mattered, and looking at Violette Makepeace's anxious face, he knew she mattered to him as well. Even more startling, he realized she was someone who might come to matter even more.

"They have been part of my plans from the start," he lied. "I only thought we would bring Christmas to them at Curzon Street. But your idea for the celebration at Evergreen is an interesting notion."

She clapped her hands together in either pleasure or gratitude. Most likely, both. "How wonderful!" she exclaimed. "When shall we leave?"

Three days later, with very little effort on his part, and a great deal on hers, they left the busy streets of London for the pastoral lanes of Kent. Violette tried to settle herself comfortably in Lord Greenlough's very large carriage, but there did not seem to be much room for five people, though three of them were very small.

Behind them, in another carriage, Nanny Lind rode with Blaine and four other servants, and another carriage followed, replete with the clothing and requisites without which children could not survive away from their own home. Indeed, while other households had items that might prove amusing to young people, Greenlough assured Violette that there was nothing of the sort at Evergreen. And so it was left to her to determine which of their possessions were necessary for several weeks in the countryside, and which could be comfortably forfeited. The third carriage was the result of her perhaps too-generous assessment.

But when her brother-in-law's brother started to protest, she placed her finger on his lips. He ought to have helped if he wished any say in the matter. He did not, however, protest when she said she would ride with the children. And while he might have traveled in comfort surrounded by his books and bags, he chose to share the carriage with them all.

Mrs. Belden, seeing them off at the curbside, could scarcely contain her pleasure at seeing them together.

"He only wishes to be with the children, Mrs. Belden," Violette sternly reminded her. Surely the housekeeper could not imagine he would attempt anything untoward with a young audience, and certainly not with herself. "And we have a whole caravan of chaperones. I could ride in any of these carriages, and it would not matter much."

"Yes, indeed. I am sure it would not." There was no mistaking the housekeeper's mischievous tone.

"I know how to behave, Mrs. Belden." Violette turned as she accepted the helping hand of one of the grooms. She did not wish for Mrs. Belden to see her face, for she was afraid she would reveal too much. In fact, she had already demonstrated that she did not know how to behave, that getting into a carriage with a man was enough to ruin her reputation and mark her as damaged goods for the rest of her life. For two years, Violette had tried to compensate for her misdeed with good behavior, and it had brought her little pleasure. Now, she knew she had nothing to lose, and dared to imagine that she had a good deal to gain. With anticipation, she stepped into the closed carriage, where Lord Greenlough awaited her.

"It is not you I worry about, my dear," the woman said in a low voice, behind her. And then, in a voice intended for all to hear, "We will see you in January! If the Hanfords arrive earlier than expected, I shall send them directly to you!"

The carriage door closed on her last words.

Violette's eyes met Greenlough's over the squirming bodies of their nephews. "Let this be a lovely Christmas for all of us," she said softly, pulling Anne onto her lap.

Though the passing scenes of London were fascinating for the children, their caravan had scarcely left the southeastern environs of the city before the rocking motion of the carriage lulled them to sleep. Violette settled Anne into a cocoon of blankets on the seat beside her, and the two boys sandwiched their uncle, sleeping against his arms. Though Greenlough and she were slightly offset in their seating, it was very difficult to avoid contact with his legs, which were longer than even the designer of his own carriage must have considered.

"Did the book you expected arrive from Coimbra?" she asked politely.

"The *First Folio* is extremely rare and very valuable. It can only be read on a flat surface whilst one uses a glass pointer, so as not place one's fingers on the parchment. As with ancient religious texts, it must be carefully preserved. Indeed, some go so far as to say that our Shakespeare's works are as insightful and as awe inspiring."

Really, he must think her an idiot to lecture her so.

"I am aware of its value, Lord Greenlough. I did not suppose you would open it as Wils drooled on your shoulder. I only wished to

409

know if you would be studying it when we arrive at Evergreen."

He sat up straighter and John slipped down into the cushions.

"That is my intention. I shall retire to my library each evening for study."

Perhaps she was an idiot. Some small hope, undoubtedly placed in her heart by the optimistic Mrs. Belden, had her imagining she might spend time with him in the evenings, perhaps becoming better acquainted. Where that might lead, she preferred not to consider just yet.

She did not know what her expression revealed, but he relented almost at once. "You may join me, of course. You have probably brought some reading of your own?"

"I have, my lord. Something in the spirit of the season."

"Aha. The Bible, of course."

"Aha," she echoed. "*Twelfth Night.* I daresay you will find it in your precious *First Folio.* My own copy of the play, purchased only last week at Marcus Bradley, Bookseller, may be held, read on a blanket spread on a lawn, or in the comfort of one's bed."

"How very quaint, Miss Makepeace. I have never thought to bring a book to bed with me. Other things, perhaps."

Violette did not answer, for she was coming to know him well enough to understand that he wished to do nothing more than provoke her on every point. She did not, however, know herself well enough to stop from saying things that made her such an easy mark. Talk of bedtime activities or the women he entertained had to be avoided, placed under lock and key in the confines of her own too-vivid imagination.

For, while she heard rumors of Lord Greenlough's adventures for so many years, she was coming to suspect they might be somewhat overstated, possibly by the man himself. His willingness to spend Christmas in Kent, in her company and that of the children, was some evidence of that. And his scholarly collection in his rooms on King Street did not seem ordered with seduction in mind. Of course, she had no idea what his bedchamber looked like.

And suddenly, she knew how very much she wanted to be there, preferably with the man himself.

"Well, Miss Makepeace? Have I somehow managed to render you speechless?"

She blushed, realizing she stared at him, but without actually seeing him. She blinked as he came into focus.

"You already know me too well to think it possible, my lord. I am only . . . noticing something about your eyes." She hesitated, because what was uttered as a deflective comment now seemed to have something of the truth in it. His eyes were gray, as were his

411

brother's, and yet something appeared odd. Violette leaned forward but Greenlough, still braced by the sleeping boys, could only stay where he was.

"I believe there is a darker stain in the color of the iris," she said.

"It is a birthmark, and only in the right eye. Whereas some have a blemish on an arm or on the face, a fairy's finger seems to have touched me in the eye at the moment of my birth. Or poked me in the eye, rather. And yet I am lucky to be an Englishman in this fine century, for those of an earlier time, less enlightened, would likely have drowned me before I lived a week."

"It is horrible to imagine it so, and yet I suppose it is hard to dissuade people of their superstitions." Violette sat back, realizing she had edged so close to him, their lips might have touched. "After all, you just spoke of a fairy's mark."

"The season has made me a romantic fool. The boys have been speaking of tree sprites in the winter boughs, and trolls in the snow, and I suppose my cook is preparing all sorts of food without which it would be impossible to celebrate Christmas. It all seems to be such excess."

"It is," Violette whispered, running her tongue over her lips, imagining the taste of his. "But wonderfully so. I hope you can manage to enjoy it even a little, knowing the truth of our losses. And you are neither romantic nor a fool."

"Some might call me romantic, but I am never a fool. I believe I am intelligent enough to understand how the world really works, and the fact that my father also had such a birthmark in his eye predisposed me for bearing the same imprint. It is a circumstance of nature, over which fairies and tree sprites have very little sway."

"Does it ever bother you? Does it give you pain?"

Greenlough looked as if the mere mention of pain was sufficient to induce it. Or perhaps he was bothered by her overt familiarity. But Violette told herself that if they were to share responsibility for the care of the children, she ought to know if he was prone to migraines, or irritation, or anything that might compromise his behavior.

"Do the freckles on your cheeks give you pain? It is no different for me," he said after a while.

She said nothing, for she quite forgot about those odious freckles. Why did she not powder her face this morning, knowing they would be in close quarters? But then, why should she? For he was only her sister's brother-in-law and it would do her well to remember that.

"It is not pain, precisely," he went on, contradicting himself. "But my right eye is somewhat more sensitive to light. It is fortunate that I spend so many hours indoors."

Again, Violette's thoughts went to his possible indoor activities, of which she now realized she truly knew very little. She blushed.

"I am speaking of my research, Miss Makepeace. And my book collecting, of course."

"Of course. Whatever else could you mean?" she said, too quickly. "What is it you research, Lord Greenlough?"

"Many things, though I am particularly interested in optical refraction. In fact, on that day when we became reacquainted, what you thought was a broken bottle of spirits on your steps was a cracked lens, fallen out of my pocket. I am a member of the Royal Society, you know."

She did not know.

"And did we not agree that we would be Violette and James to each other?" he asked.

"And yet, you called me Miss Makepeace not two minutes ago," she added.

"Old habits die hard. I have always thought of you as such."

She laughed out loud, and regretted it when Wils stirred in his sleep and opened his eyes. He looked at them irritably, then closed his eyes again.

"Lord Greenlough. James. I doubt you have thought much of me at all," she said, and told herself she was not being flirtatious. He so rarely spoke to her before, even when they sat in the same room.

Perhaps it was those regrettable freckles that put men off. If so, then they did give her pain.

"Then it has been my loss," he said and, oddly, she did not think he was flirting with her either.

Not knowing how to answer, Violette looked out the window, on the passing scene. They had some hours to go before they reached their destination, and just now, the midday sun reflected off the white snow. Having already abandoned the protection of her bonnet, she reached up to lower one woven shade.

"Your interest in optics demonstrates the very point I made the other day," she said, thinking out loud. She turned back to him and had the sense he had been watching her all the while.

"Please refresh my memory. I can only recall your comments on some of my habits, and therefore suspect you are referring to wine glasses tossed against the fireplace and shattered on the hearth rug."

"I mean that in the way your life is a sort of rebellion against your parents, so your interest in optics may be a consequence of curiosity about your eyes. We become what nature and circumstances make us," she said, thinking it made much sense.

"You may be correct. But right now, I find

I am only curious about you." He gently settled Wils into a more comfortable position. "Well, Violette? Will you not tell me more about yourself? You cannot always be poor Olivia's little sister."

Violette put her finger to her lips and gestured to the children with her other hand.

He stopped, his words echoing in the small compartment. Outside, other carriages rolled past, grinding against the ruts in the road. "I apologize. I must be more careful when I speak of Wilson and Olivia, lest I reveal too much."

"We have set a very difficult task for ourselves this Christmas season," Violette said. "But I will always think of myself as Olivia's little sister, for her decisions very much affected me. She loved your brother from such an early age, she scarcely had the time to know herself or what she might become without him. It is a life for which most women would yearn, but I did not wish the same thing for myself. I wanted to sample other possibilities and learn about many things. I hoped to travel."

"As we are traveling now," he said.

"James, your *First Folio* has traveled more than I have, and has been opened in many more settings. It is far more desirable and engaging as a companion than I." Violette nodded, realizing the sad truth of it. And then she rushed on, embarrassed by what she let him see. "Three years ago, I met a gentleman who intrigued me. I do not think I loved him, but I think we might have been happy together."

"You need not say more," James interrupted.

Violette caught her breath. She did not know if he already knew too much of her story, or did not care enough to learn her history.

"But we are being truthful to each other. And besides, there is not much more to tell. I believed in him, and he betrayed me. Not more than he was prepared to betray his wife and children, but enough to make me a pariah in Society. After all, a lady who lacks the good sense to know she is betrothed to a man who is already married to another, surely lacks good sense in all things."

"And so, happy to prove the harpies correct, you have isolated yourself."

Violette sat up straighter in her seat. "I have been active. I have several friends."

"You have not lived your life, and have deprived yourself of pleasure."

For once, she had no answer. A man whose life was lived solely for pleasure surely would recognize the lack of it in another. And yet, she now knew that there was a good deal more to him than she ever before wanted to believe. And even better — or perhaps, worse — she knew there was a good deal more of herself, a woman who wanted to break free of the prison she had created for herself. She wished to escape, right into James's arms.

"Your sister was ever concerned for you," he added.

"She was not!" Violette protested. This really was too much. "She knew me to be perfectly happy."

"She knew you to be content, which is quite different from any sort of happiness."

"I'm happy," said John. Violette gave a yelp of surprise, for she thought the boy had been sleeping soundly. He rubbed his small hand against his eyes, and yawned.

"I am happy as well," added Wils.

What had the children overheard?

"I am sure you are, and that makes me happy as well," said Violette, grateful for the diversion. But she knew her confession was not yet at an end.

"Well, we are agreed that we are the happiest group on its way to Kent, for I, too, am happy," said James, putting a final punctuation point on the business. But perhaps it was not over for him either.

"And yet, your Aunt Violette is quite mistaken about one thing," he continued. "I cannot imagine having a more desirable and engaging companion than she, anywhere."

The sun was already below the tree line when their caravan arrived at Evergreen. James disliked traveling in the evenings, but the prospect of settling three small children into a country inn was sufficiently daunting to make him overextend his staff and horses — and his own patience — to arrive at his home in one very long day's journey.

It was worth the inconvenience.

As they rode up the long drive, along the river and rows of well-manicured trees, he felt at home as he never did at King Street or at his other properties. Though the rest were finely maintained and full of possessions that belonged to generations of Hanfords, he did not feel the same pride of ownership that nearly humbled him each time he walked the house and grounds of Evergreen. Though he had never really considered it before, perhaps it was the reason he had only invited his family and closest friends here.

His town apartments, a great drafty castle near Inverness, a hunting lodge in Dartmoor, and a fine Jacobean house near Pembroke's estate in Wilton were all excellent places for week-long parties and for entertaining ladies who caught his fancy and who were interested in a brief dalliance. But never were they here at Evergreen. Here, he followed different pursuits and if he entertained at all, he was more likely to welcome in the neighborhood than shut them out. He sometimes wondered if his capable staff here ever suspected what rumors there were about his behavior in

London and elsewhere.

"It is as lovely as I remember it," Violette said softly. And then, she turned to the children. "There is the lake where Uncle James and I will teach you how to skate."

"We shall have to hope the old skates Wilson and I used are still in good repair. If not, we will purchase new ones in the village," James said, recalling an afternoon when he fell through the ice, and abandoned one skate to the floor of the lake.

"I have brought the children's skates, my lord," Violette said. "And nearly everything else they might require for several weeks in the country. Do you not recall we packed a carriage with nothing but their trunks and cases?"

"I hope you did not neglect your own needs in your enthusiasm to see to theirs, Aunt Violette? I should wish for you to have everything you require as well."

She gazed at him in that odd way she had, as if she held a scale to weigh his merits against his demerits. Usually, he sensed that he did not fare very favorably in her estimation. But then there were moments like these, when she seemed to glimpse the hidden parts of his soul. It allowed him to believe she saw something that others did not. He suddenly hoped that what she saw was enough to light the sparks he had kept tamped down up until now.

"I believe I have everything I require, Uncle James," she said.

She spoke for the benefit of the children, who avidly listened to every word they uttered. In another place, from another woman, such words would be an invitation to a seduction, and James would have likely answered that invitation without hesitation

A few days ago, he would have guessed any overture on his part would surely weigh down the scale against him in Violette's estimation.

And now, and perhaps because the possibility intrigued him so much, he sensed she offered an invitation as well. There was nothing to be done in a crowded carriage approaching the final ascent before they arrived at the entrance to Evergreen. But there were days to come, and places where the children would not follow, and words that might only be spoken between them.

And if indeed it proved that Violette Makepeace offered him an invitation to something that invoked his fantasies as no other lady's offer ever had, then he vowed he would do everything of which he was capable, to weigh down her scale in favor of his estimable and rarely appreciated merits.

CHAPTER 3

James's servants greeted her as if she came to Evergreen as the mistress of the estate, and not a lady who once visited several years before, attracting little attention and no particular popularity. But she was, of course, the sister of Mrs. Hanford, so whatever slight status she possessed was enhanced by association. For her part, Violette recognized several of the staff, and most particularly the housekeeper, Mrs. Bligh. The good woman managed everything in James's absence, and took charge even in his presence.

She had the maids escort the children and their coterie to the nursery, where dinner would soon be served. She noted where each of the heavy trunks should be brought. And she explained that Violette would be staying in the North Wing, and James in his rooms in the South.

"You will be most comfortable there, Miss Makepeace," Mrs. Bligh said. "The rooms are among our finest and your windows will face the morning sun. The children will be on the floor above you, but our rugs are too thick for their running about to disturb you."

"I am certain I will be just fine, Mrs. Bligh. I believe I was in the North Wing when I last visited."

"Yes, that is very likely, for Mr. and Mrs. Hanford have their rooms there, and you would wish to be close to your sister." She turned to James. "Will they be joining us on their return, my lord? Your letter was not clear on the matter."

"No, they will not be joining us this Christmas. If my letter seemed ambiguous, it is only because of my own great . . . disappointment. My brother and sister-in-law remain in the Caribbean."

"It is a fierce place, is it not?" Mrs. Bligh chattered on. "I understand pirates frequent the waters, and there are fish that could bite a man in half. The sun is unrelenting, and insects are as large as terriers. I prefer our cold English winters, where we only fear mice scurrying about in the larder. The cats take their job seriously, however."

"I am appreciative of all that the staff does, including the cats. And I should mention that my brother was aware of nearly all the hazards of a warm climate before he set forth from Greenwich," James said.

"Nearly all, my lord?" Mrs. Bligh said.

Violette was suddenly alert. It seemed nothing escaped the housekeeper's watchful eyes or attentive ears, and it would be necessary to have a care in her company.

"But of course, Mrs. Bligh. One can only imagine the surprises at every turn in the uncivilized New World. And yet, that is what is so attractive to my brother; he is an adventurer," said James.

Mrs. Bligh laughed. "Is that not what they say of you, my lord?"

"Oh no. I am much too settled in my old ways, and come to Evergreen for peace and contemplation." He smiled so brightly his gray eyes shuttered in response. "It is why I have only brought eight additional staff, three young children, three laden carriages, Miss Violette Makepeace and —"

"And a partridge in a pear tree," Violette said.

Mrs. Bligh laughed again. "We already have the pear tree — a very small one — in the conservatory. It was brought indoors before the first snow."

"Bless you, Mrs. Bligh. You really do think of everything," James said.

"I do try, my lord. But like your charming brother, I expect surprises at any time." She smoothed down the bodice of her neatly-ironed dress. "Would you like to see your rooms, Miss Makepeace?"

"As I am retiring to mine, I am happy to bring Miss Makepeace upstairs. It would be my pleasure," said James.

Mrs. Bligh looked from one to the other. "Miss Makepeace is in the North Wing, and you are in the South, my lord," she pointedly reminded him.

"I believe I might manage the exercise without undue exhaustion, Mrs. Bligh," he said.

"And dinner will be served in one hour," Mrs. Bligh said, a little more insistently.

"An hour is more time than either of us require, I am sure," he said, and offered his elbow to Violette.

"Miss Makepeace? Will you allow me to escort you to your door?" James said very properly, and leaned toward her. "I believe you are destined for the blue rooms that have been a favorite of other ladies who have visited Evergreen."

Violette waited until they had climbed to the first landing on the stairs and were beyond the housekeeper's hearing before responding to him. "I daresay you have entertained a good many ladies in this house, my lord?"

"Oh, certainly. Lady Marie Eliot and Mrs. Graham George, my aunts, are frequent visitors and occasionally neighborhood guests remain overnight. I suppose it is possible you will remember this room from your last visit, for it is likely you were situated there. Little has changed."

Violette said nothing, surprised and a little embarrassed she recalled nothing about it. She was so certain of her memory in nearly all things, and yet she had no idea to what room she had been assigned when last she was here. But then, three years ago, perhaps all she had really thought about was James. He seemed so aloof from her then, a man whose experience could only allow him to see her as an innocent relation, a young lady with whom he ought not tamper. She was not innocent now. And perfectly willing to be tampered with.

When they arrived at the head of the grand staircase, James stepped to the left, and then stopped short. "I apologize; it is my habit, I suppose. We are to go to the right." He walked around her, turning her as he went, and they walked down the opposite hall to the door at the very end.

"Here we are. Please let me know if the room does not suit, and ring for the servants if there is anything you require." He pulled his elbow away and reached for her hand, bringing it up to his lips to press a kiss upon it. He smiled and opened the door with his other hand. "We will meet in an hour for dinner, when we will have much to discuss."

He released her, bowed sharply, and turned.

Her heart humming, she watched him walk away, until he disappeared in the shadows of the far wing. He was wrong, of course: everything had changed.

Violette was too distracted by James's behavior to pay much attention to her dress or the hour, and though her maid worked efficiently to attend to her hair and her dinner gown, she was twenty minutes late for their dinner together. She came down the stairs with measured footsteps, so as not to arrive in the dining room breathless and overly warm, but was tempted to run and skip every other step. It was very rude to keep her host waiting.

But the look on James's face when she arrived in the drawing room, only slightly breathless, was enough to let her know he would forgive her. His lips parted as his eyes ran down the length of her body. One brow was raised, as if he had a question to ask of her, and one hand reached to her, coaxing her to come closer.

"You ought to wear green more often, Violette. I would have thought blue suited you most admirably, because of your eyes, but that can only be because I have never seen you in emerald." He bowed.

Violette came toward him, into the center of the room. "I did not realize you were quite so expert on fashionable colors, James. But you can expect to see me in much green during this sojourn, for it is the color of the season."

"And of my house," he added.

"Of course; I did not think of that. If I had, I might not have selected gowns as I did, for fear of blending in against the wallpaper."

"I do not think it is possible, for you would be noticed wherever you go."

Violette laughed, mostly at her own vanity in hoping his gestures and words sincere. Was he not a notorious seducer?

"James, there is no purpose in flattering me. If you had ever paid me the least bit of attention, I might be encouraged to think otherwise. But as I am already in your house and about to sit down to dinner with you, and as fate has decreed we work together in the raising of our little relations, you have nothing left to prove. I am here. I look no different than I did three years ago, when last I was here. Come, let us eat, for I find I am quite famished."

One of the servants chose that moment to appear in the doorway, his silence sufficient to announce the purpose of his presence.

James held out his elbow as he did earlier in the day. "I realize I am famished as well, or perhaps it is only that I find my appetites are different from what they are in London."

Violette threaded her arm through his, shaking her head at his effort at seduction. His words were so practiced, so smooth, she would do well to ignore his suggestions. Therefore, she must remember to answer him literally, as if she had no idea what his words might otherwise imply.

"And yet, when you sit down at your table, you may find that well-prepared food will satisfy any appetite, James. If you have the same cook you did when last I visited, you shall eat very well," Violette said. "And if you are as hungry as you say you are, ought we not go in and dine?"

"Oh, I hope to eat very well, indeed. Will you come with me?" he said, and they passed through a narrow anteroom into the large well-heated dining room. At the table surrounded by thirty or more chairs, there was one setting at the head, and one just to its right. James escorted her to her seat and held the chair for her to sit down.

"Is there not a smaller room, James?" Violette asked. "As we are nearly relations, might we not dine in cozier quarters and save the staff the trouble of heating this great room?"

"This great room is famous for those who have dined here, and I thought it appropriate to begin our stay at Evergreen, and recall the history of the place. It was built in the reign of the Tudors, and Henry visited with two or three of his poor wives — though not at the same time. Christopher Marlowe brought his actors to perform *The Massacre of Paris* in this very room, shortly before he, himself, departed for Paris, leaving England forever."

"I thought he was murdered in a brawl in Deptford." Violette frowned, trying to recall the old stories about the playwright who was once more famous than Shakespeare himself.

"So it was put about. But Marlowe is thought to have been a spy, and escaped to Paris and then, possibly, to the New World."

"Very few people would take you for a scholar of history, James," Violette said.

"No, no one does. But you already knew the truth of it when you came to my rooms in London."

Violette was suddenly aware of the servants setting down steaming bowls of soup and pouring sweet red wine into their goblets. What did they make of her presence here, without the company of her dear sister?

"My father often hosted American diplomats in this very room, including the secretary of their treasury. The man was born in Nevis and I suspect my brother first became interested in the Caribbean islands while talking to Mr. Hamilton. It is, of course, one of his relations who sent me that fateful letter."

James did not exaggerate on that claim, for one woman's anxious words forever changed the course of their lives. Violette would have otherwise remained in London this season, dining alone while her cat slept under the table.

"This place has been witness to conversations between famous and otherwise excellent people, James. I fear its claims to glory are much diminished by my presence," Violette sighed.

"Any room is made greater by the presence of a beautiful lady," he said, and reached for his wine.

Violette said nothing until she was certain they were alone. "James, I am not sure what you want of me. Your attempts to flatter are admirable, but I am not one of your susceptible females, likely to succumb to the power of your seduction. That I am in your house and unattached is the consequence of tragic circumstances. Two weeks ago, you would not have given me a second glance if we walked right into each other in Hyde Park."

"Then I would have been rightly labeled a fool. My brother certainly thought so." He replaced his wine glass without drinking any of its contents.

Violette looked at his long fingers wrapped around the goblet, thinking they looked fairly rugged for one who spent his time in libraries, gaming rooms and bedchambers. "And yet you are the older brother," she argued, unnecessarily.

"But Wilson accomplished a good deal more. The three children upstairs in the nursery are his legacy, and far more valuable than a collection of books to enhance one's library."

And her sister's legacy, as well. But when the children were old enough to themselves marry, what would they remember of their parents? The boys would have a watch or a stickpin, and Anne would wear Olivia's embroidered shawl. But would they remember their voices or the touch of a hand? Would they recall how Olivia and Wilson finished the other's sentences and smiled knowingly at each other?

Did her sister and brother-in-law know they would never see their children again? Did they sense the moment when three small children were no longer to be their responsibility, but their legacy?

It was too tragic to imagine. Unable to stop herself, Violette started to weep, using her pressed linen napkin to staunch tears that flowed at unpredictable moments, and could not be explained to those who witnessed them but for James, who understood precisely how she felt.

James cursed himself for being such a boorish host. He thought he was complimentary to his brother's memory, but he somehow managed to open the sluice gates of her despair. With any other lady, he would have gone to her side, pulled her into his arms, and comforted her. At the very least, he would have patted her hand or handed her another cloth.

But Violette Makepeace had already made it clear he was to keep his distance, for she so clearly did not trust his motives or his intentions.

For the first time in his life, he was unsure how to behave in the presence of a lady.

She utterly bewitched him, making him say things that appealed to the vanity of other women, but seemed crass when spoken to her. She made him speak of history, and literature and his damned books, when everyone knew such subjects were not of interest to anyone but gentlemen who sought seclusion in their libraries. Equally troubling, because he had made the fatal error of not paying court to her three years ago, she accepted his current compliments as false.

And yet, the most uncomfortable business of all was the realization that he was incapable of speaking falsely to her. Every word he uttered, every effort he made to get her to yield to him — even the littlest bit — was sincerely felt and absolutely true. She was beautiful. Her gown was splendid. He wanted to have her at his table, sharing conversation and words of comfort. Even more, he wanted her in his bed.

He was glad her tears, achingly sad though they were, stopped him from telling her the reason his brother truly thought him a fool.

"Is there too much spice in the soup, Miss Makepeace?" one of the servers asked. "I shall return it to the kitchen and bring you another."

She hiccoughed, and looked up at the man. Her eyes glistened in the candlelight and her skin seemed almost translucent. James resented the man's view of the bodice of her green gown.

"Not at all," she said kindly. "Please tell the cook that the nutmeg and allspice seem a perfect complement to the flavor. I am only tired from the journey."

She wiped her eyes, which looked lighter as they were ringed by her damp lashes.

"We have much to do, James," she said.

He knew what he wanted to do, but had a feeling that was not on her calendar. He raised his glass again.

"I have a very well-stocked wine vault. What do you have in mind, Violette?"

She made an odd bubbling sound, and he realized she might be suppressing a laugh. Perhaps he knew what to say to her, after all.

"I meant we must prepare your house for Christmas. No matter how beautiful or famous this room, it must look just so every other day of the year. We must bring in boughs of trees and cut little angels to hang from the candelabras and —"

"That sounds very likely to set the whole place ablaze. Could this not wait until Christmas Eve? In the meantime, we might see what we can find in the attic or storerooms. I know my mother once brought home painted tin frivolities from Bavaria."

"Truly? I never think of anything frivolous coming from Bavaria," she mused. The tears were nearly gone and she smiled. "I believe their craftsmen are best known for heavy carved things."

"I may be mistaken, but that is why I suggest we take our time about it. I have no idea what is hidden away at Evergreen."

"Do you mean we might find tree sprites doing mischief among the relics of Christmases past?"

"Truly, I have no idea what we might find, but I look forward to exploring with you and the children."

Whatever James hoped to find, it was not the company of unexpected guests joining them for breakfast the next morning.

After an evening buoyed by yet another truce between the lady and himself, during which she allowed herself to laugh and not rebuff every word he uttered, he decided to dress with extra care this morning. Before he went down to breakfast, he stopped by to visit Wils, John, and Anne. The children seemed remarkably well settled, and were busy playing with toys he remembered from his own childhood. He showed the boys how to set up a line of dominoes, which were promptly set in motion by their little sister. But they vowed to try it again.

He felt the same sort of optimism about his

relationship with Violette Makepeace.

It seemed that everything she knew — or thought she knew — about him was garnered from gossip rags and drawing room conversations. And yet, Olivia must have spoken of some of his qualities: if nothing else, that he was a devoted uncle. In other ways, he did not think his behavior so reprehensible, or that it should matter to anyone but himself. And perhaps the woman who might be persuaded to marry him one day.

There was a thought. He had no idea why it had suddenly entered his mind.

"Dear Lord Greenlough!"

He was so preoccupied he did not realize there were people seated on the side chairs in the foyer. Now they both rose as he arrived at the bottom step.

"Mr. Whittier! Miss Rosella! What a delightful surprise," James hesitated, realizing that in their haste to see him the morning of his arrival at Evergreen, they might have news that would be anything but delightful. "Is all well? Is Mrs. Whittier in good health?"

"Never better, James," said Mr. Whittier. The gentleman had aged since James saw him last, for his hair was almost entirely white and he looked smaller, more frail.

"And you, Miss Rosella? How are you situated? How do the fellows of the neighborhood resist you?"

"In that, they seem to have little difficulty,

my lord. If this is your way of asking if I am already taken, I assure you I am not," she said.

He looked at her, trying to determine if she was pleased or disappointed to utter these words, and if they were intended to reflect on him, as well. Rosella Whittier was one of his oldest friends, someone who used to get into mischief with Wilson and himself. In fact, she was so capable of keeping up with them in all things, it was not until he was ten years of age or so that he realized she was a girl.

Now, there could be little doubt of it. Her features were plain, but her character was such that one noticed her bright eyes, her red hair and her perpetual smile before one put all the features together to some disappointment. She was tallish, which had made her competitive as a child, but possibly ineligible for some men. Not for him, however.

After Wilson married, a few people mentioned that Rosella Whittier was sore at heart because of his defection. James had not even realized that anyone considered them a match. But then, those living in Kent would not be aware of another lady who had known Wilson just as long, one who lived in Berkeley Square. Now James vaguely wondered if anyone held out any hope that he and Rosella might someday grace the altar of the tiny church in nearby Littleton. If they did not, they might do so once they heard word that the Whittiers had come to visit him at the first opportunity after his arrival at Evergreen.

"Rosella did have a beau from Town. He was a very fine gentleman and a scholarly one," said Mr. Whittier.

"But that is quite over, papa," Rosella said, her smile just breaking a bit. "He had more important business in Scotland, it seems."

"Well then, he might be back," said James, for lack of anything else to say. "Have the two of you already had breakfast? Would you like to join me?"

"We had our breakfast hours ago, James. We keep country hours here. But we would very much like to join you, and welcome you back to Evergreen."

"It is settled then," James said. But then, perhaps it was not.

The sound of dainty bells greeted them from above, and he looked up to see Violette coming down the stairs with a silver rattle in her hands. She was not shaking it, but the sway of her body was sufficient to set it in motion.

"Good morning, Miss Makepeace," he said, before she reached the marble floor of the foyer. She nodded briefly, but her eyes were on Rosella.

"Allow me to introduce Mr. Whittier, our neighbor, and his daughter, Miss Whittier," he continued. "Miss Makepeace is my sister-in-law."

"By your name, I assume you are Mrs. Hanford's sister or cousin," Rosella said sweetly. And then, turning slightly to him, "which would not make you Lord Greenlough's sister-in-law at all."

"You are very astute, Miss Whittier. We are only related by the circumstances of our brother and sister," Violette said, and placed a possessive hand on his arm. James looked at her in surprise, and much pleasure.

"And are they here as well, Miss Makepeace? We did not hear that was so," Rosella continued.

Violette tightened her fingers. "Your sources are very reliable, Miss Whittier. Did they also mention how many trunks I brought with me? Or the color of my cape, perhaps?"

Rosella's smile looked brittle. "Not at all. Only the number of children. They are not yours, of course."

"They are my niece and nephews. And they are also Lord Greenlough's, you understand."

"I understand perfectly."

James saw the prospect of a pleasant breakfast quickly evaporate, but his invitation was already accepted.

"Shall we go into the breakfast room?" he asked, a little too quickly.

"Yes, please," Violette said. "I need sustenance after such a late night. You really should have allowed me to go to sleep, Lord Greenlough."

James pulled the minx into the room, with the Whittiers at their heels.

The servants had already set two more places, and as there was usually enough food to feed half the village, he was not concerned they would run short on the kippers or cold beef. He waited for his guests to fill their plates, and then made his selections and sat in his accustomed place, with the two ladies on either side of him. Mr. Whittier sat next to his daughter.

"I would like to meet the children," said Rosella, between sips of her chocolate. "Will their parents join them soon? I have not seen Wilson in some years."

"My brother and his wife are unexpectedly delayed in the Caribbean," James said. "That is why the children are with us here at Evergreen."

"Are they enjoying the warm climate?" Rosella asked.

"My sister and her husband are considering purchasing a property there, so they must enjoy the climate a good deal," said Violette.

Mr. Whittier's crunching down on a biscuit was the only sound in the room for several minutes.

"We are a small party this Christmas Eve. We hope you will join us. And Mrs. Whittier, of course." It seemed to be the polite thing to say, but James regretted the words as soon as they were uttered. Whatever else the holy night represented to the world, he and Violette would probably be utterly consumed by their private sadness as soon as the children went to bed.

Rosella clapped her hands in delight, forgetting that she still held a slice of buttered toast. She daintily picked up her napkin and wiped her hands.

"Unless you have other plans," said James, though it was now fairly clear they did not. "I would not interfere with your arrangements."

"We have none," Rosella said excitedly. "Mother and Father and I expected to do no more than toast chestnuts. They grow in abundance near the posting inn."

"Do bring them along, for I am sure they will be very tasty." James wondered if he had ever willingly eaten a chestnut, as he never liked the look of the things, but the Whittiers must have developed a taste for the grubby nuggets. And they seemed healthy enough.

"Oh, we shall. I intend to bake minced meat pies as well," Rosella added.

"My daughter's a fine cook, James. She'll make some man an excellent wife," Mr. Whittier said.

"I am sure she will," James said agreeably, hoping that his old neighbor did not imagine that a man possessed of his fortune would expect his wife to spend time in the kitchen.

On the other hand, perhaps Whittier wished his daughter to find a position or open a shop. He knew nothing of Whittier's finances or Rosella's expectations.

"Do you add nutmeg to your pies?" Violette asked.

"I do, Miss Makepeace. Do you bake as well?"

"It is an interest of mine, though more scholarly than practical. I am collecting recipes from cooks throughout London, as a guide for young girls wishing to enter that line of work. Of course, the very best cooks are reluctant to share their secrets, as they wish to retain their exalted status. It would not do, for example, for every posting inn in London to serve the Duke of Wellington's little beef delicacies."

James closed his mouth, realizing he was staring at Violette. But what news was this? He never heard of her culinary inclinations before, not even from Olivia.

"Is this a new interest, Miss Makepeace? I never heard you discuss it before." he commented.

She looked down at her hands and once again he noticed the little nub of an ink stain on the middle finger of her right hand. She had been engaged in her project for some time, he guessed.

"Perhaps you and I have had other things to discuss, Lord Greenlough," she answered sweetly. To his left, Rosella Whittier cleared her throat and coughed, but he continued to gaze upon the previously guileless Miss Makepeace. She knew precisely what she was doing, turning his words into innuendo, as he was inclined to do with hers. She was taking his own recipe, adding her own spices, and serving it back to him.

He wanted nothing more than to partake of it, savoring every morsel of it until he was utterly sated.

Violette smiled at him, and ran her tongue over her upper lip. "And of course our sister and brother knew of this interest, for they promised to bring me back the most precious nuts and seeds from the Caribbean. Olivia already sent me several recipes from the islands."

"Are any of them suitable for Christmas, Miss Makepeace? I would be happy to try my luck at preparing them," said Rosella.

"Rosella is an excellent cook," chimed in Mr. Whittier again. "She would make someone a —"

"Yes, I am sure she will," James interrupted, not interested in another recital of poor Rosella's talents. At the moment, he was only interested in Violette's. "But as you are to be our guests, I must insist that you allow our cook at Evergreen to prepare the meal. You will have other chances to impress our small society, I believe. Perhaps you will prepare several musical selections and sing to us?"

"Sing?" Rosella squeaked. "I have never —"

"Rosella has a lovely voice," said Mr. Whittier. "Some day she will make someone an excellent wife."

At James's right hand, Violette Makepeace coughed. He wondered if all this coughing and choking had to do with the conversation or with little bones in the kippers.

"I recall Miss Makepeace has a lovely voice as well," James said, "if she does not damage her throat by her coughing. Would you care for some hot cocoa, Miss Makepeace?"

"I am quite well, my lord," she said, glancing at the servant. "Though I rarely refuse an offer of hot cocoa and sugared cream."

"Do you play as well as sing, Miss Makepeace?" Rosella asked.

"I probably do both as well as any other young lady for whom such skills are considered obligatory. My finer talents lie elsewhere. But perhaps even the children can accompany us on Christmas Eve." She reached under the table and retrieved the small rattle she had been holding when she first came down the steps. She shook it gently and a sweet tinkling filled the breakfast room.

"Even a baby can play this instrument," she said.

"A baby once did," James said, and took it from her fingers.

■ ■ ■ ■

Violette found a comfortable chair by the window, and watched from the drawing room as James cut an irregular path through the grass on the great lawn, accompanied by his old friends. Even at this distance, Violette was able to hear Rosella Whittier squeal with delight as James said one thing or another. And her father, walking several steps behind them, undoubtedly heralded his daughter's extraordinary talent at laughing, something that would be most desirable in a wife.

Violette declined the invitation to take the air with them, noting it too chilled and windy for her to find much pleasure outside. But, in fact, she thought they all looked somewhat relieved at her decision, and she wondered if Mr. Whittier's protestations were just icing on a cake that James already intended to eat. It certainly would explain why the two Whittiers arrived at Evergreen even before the last bags were unpacked and why breakfast at his table was such a family affair.

She was very happy for James. Rosella seemed a good, solid girl, possessed of some talents, if her father had the right of it. She would make a good aunt to Olivia's children, and would probably be as loyal a wife as she was a friend. That she did not seem to be James's type mattered little, for Violette had heard wise matrons note that what a man desired in a mistress was not at all what he would wish to see in the mother of his children.

But who was James's type?

She knew he admired actresses and singers, older widows and women of established character. In whispers, she'd heard gossip about the women he slept with and some unusual sexual proclivities. Scandal and angry husbands followed him like hungry dogs after blood pudding.

And yet, she also knew him to be perfectly at home with his nephews and niece, a thoughtful conversationalist, a generous host, and a polite companion. His interests in books and history and science were quite unexpected, and she saw she surprised him as well, when she spoke of her gathering of recipes. Aside from the teasing suggestiveness of his words, he did not make any inappropriate overtures to her.

And that was the worst thing of all.

If he was interested in Miss Rosella Whittier, why could he not be interested in her? They already shared some interests, wit, and three children. She knew him at least as long as did Miss Whittier, though they had scarcely said five words to each other in all those years. But now she was here, in his home, and surely had some claim.

For all she heard about his past, she realized

she wanted him for her future. And now, after recognizing this absurd change in her own senses, he might be as far from her reach as she had ever imagined.

She looked out the window, wishing to admire his fine form and athletic gait, but the three walkers were gone. She half rose from her seat, straining to see them, but could see nothing but a few peacocks trying to impress one indifferent peahen.

"Is something wrong, Miss Makepeace?"

Violette was so startled, she fell against the windowpane. Turning slowly, gently rubbing her injured nose, she saw James standing at the door.

"Are there trespassers in my garden?" he asked. "If so, I shall get Edwards to shoot them at once."

She laughed. She immediately forgot all her wayward thoughts; she was just happy to have him with her. "Is that how you treat trespassers at Evergreen?"

"No. I usually invite them in for breakfast," he said. James came closer and stood by a large upholstered chair. Knowing he only waited for her lead, she took her own seat, so that he might sit as well.

"Do you consider your old friends to be trespassers, then? The Whittiers seem most comfortable here in your home."

"Old friends are granted certain privileges. Like you. You are an old friend," he said

447

softly, leaning forward.

"If by that, you mean that we were occasionally present in the same room where your brother and my sister flirted with each other while our parents spoke about the weather, then you have an odd idea of friendship, my lord. In truth, I think you were very careful to avoid me," she said, and leaned toward him as well. The birthmark in his eye caught the reflection of the sun.

"I was an idiot. My only excuse is that I was a boy and have matured a bit since then. I've spent half my life looking for pleasure, scarcely aware that I ought to look closer to home."

Dear God. Surely he did not mean what he had just said. But then reason intruded and she decided he meant precisely what he said, and that this was his way of announcing his intentions.

"You refer to Miss Rosella Whittier, of course. I have every reason to believe her father's assertion that she is a lady of many talents, an excellent quality in a wife."

"And I have every reason to know there is another such woman, so close I can see her freckles, with even more compelling attractions."

"James, you cannot mean . . ."

"I do," he said, slipping off his chair, and poised on bended knee in front of her. He looked questioningly as he braced his arms on either side of her. "I do," he repeated, and kissed her.

Violette had been kissed before, but those chaste brushes of one's lips against another's were nothing to this assault on all her senses. James's lips claimed hers, tasting, testing, exploring the contours of her mouth with his tongue, and igniting the heat in her body even while touching nothing but her lips. He smelled of wool and fresh air and pine needles. He tasted of mint.

Her hands, seeking anchorage, found it on his shoulders, and her fingers edged along the fine line of his starched collar to the hair on the back of his neck.

"Please, James," she said.

He stopped, and blinked at her.

"Please, James, no? Or please, James, yes?" he asked.

She looked into his eyes, no longer disconcerted by the almost catlike appearance of the right one. Though he had casually referred to his enjoyment of indoor activities, she saw the sun had left its mark in the creases in the corner of his eyes, which deepened when he smiled. And he was smiling now, causing that tempting dimple to form in one lean cheek. Her gaze dropped to his teeth, which were straight and even, but for a chip right in the forefront.

"Oh, yes," she said, needing more, wanting nothing but this.

His arms came around her and pulled her closer, so she, too, was off her seat, now pressed against his hard body. He held her so her knees did not touch the carpeted floor, and there might have been nothing in the room — or all the world — but the two of them. His lips started an exploration of their own, leaving her trembling and feeling a little wild.

Finally, they just clung to each other, gasping for breath.

"Why did I not do this ten years ago?" he asked, against her damp forehead. "My cursed knees were much stronger then."

"I was a girl of fifteen and would scarcely have known what to do with a man of twenty," Violette said. She reflected that she scarcely had known what to do with her Frenchman, nor had he much patience to teach her. "I am much improved with sad experience."

He laughed in a low voice, coming from deep in his chest. "Do not speak of past sadness, only of present joy. On that subject, I must say you have aged very nicely, Miss Makepeace."

"Like good cheese, I should think," she said. She felt his arms open slightly and she shifted back onto her seat.

"More like intoxicating wine," he said. "I guessed I would not be sipping weak cocoa but am delighted to have opened a bottle of the sweetest Christmas port."

"I suppose that is a compliment, though it does not quite sound like one. Is that how you seduced legions of ladies over the years?" Violette primly smoothed down her dress and studied him.

"I thought we were not to speak of the past," he murmured.

"I do not see how it can be avoided. You are a man with a history. And I am a woman with a sadder one."

James seemed to be studying the intricate patterns in the rug at their feet, and she guessed he could not meet her eyes.

But then he did so, looking up at her, making her unable to turn away.

"It is a history written by others, bearing only some relation to the truth. You and I are writing a new chapter now, and while others may speculate what they wish, only the two of us could possibly know the truth of it."

He looked so serious, this man of books, Violette tried very hard not to smile. But it proved impossible.

"James, everyone knows the truth. You are a notorious rake." She paused, waiting for him to deny it. "Have you not already confirmed it yourself?"

"I may have spoken of some lady of my acquaintance or a party at which I was in attendance. But we have shared much in these past few weeks, and have I given you any reason to believe I have any inclination toward wicked and wild ways?"

He revealed some of those inclinations not five minutes before, but she knew she had met him more than halfway. And he was talking of other things, not the glorious moments they just spent together, but the gossip and rumors and tales of indiscretion told in discreet company.

Violette would not be so easily persuaded, nor so readily flattered, no matter how much she wanted to pursue whatever was wicked and wild about him.

"James, I am your brother's sister-in-law. You are obliged to behave yourself with me," she said.

"Am I indeed? It would not have looked that way to anyone walking in the door a few moments ago. I believe I ought to apologize because it did not feel that way to me either." He reached out, his palm upheld, and Violette placed her hand in his. His flesh was warm and dry and every callus was revealed to her. "I have been thinking about this for a long time."

Violette started to pull away, but he caught her. "You have been thinking about me?" she asked, startled.

James hesitated not at all before he spoke. "Yes, I have. Since I was the sullen boy sitting in your parents' parlor and you would not even look in my direction. But I have also been thinking of what you said the other day, about our characters being the product of our upbringing."

Now she had no desire to pull away, for she sensed here was a moment of some truth.

"I have cared little about what others said about me, for I had so little to lose. I came into my title far too young, and was flattered and cajoled because of it. I misbehaved as a very young man, knowing there would be few consequences. And then, as I grew older, I did nothing to change anyone's misconceptions. I convinced myself that when it was time for me to be a father, I would settle upon a path of domestic responsibility. Now it appears, as with everything else in my life, I have come into my calling far too young."

"Your calling?" Violette was not sure what he meant.

"To be a father," he answered.

"You are not the children's father," she said gently. "And, as you are older than your brother, you cannot be too young."

"Their father no longer lives. And in the time it took to read a letter, I went from being their uncle to being the man who must raise them. I think such responsibility came upon me too soon to be properly digested."

He was quite serious, Violette realized. And with the responsibility that now burdened him, he resolved to put his past behind him, to effectively dismiss it, and set forth on an unchartered path in his life. It was necessary for him to become a family man. And with that obligation came the necessity of securing a family woman.

She pulled her hand away, and this time he released her.

She had had every reason to doubt his intentions. But in the cruelest twist of irony, just when she thought he desired her for himself, she understood he desired her for his household. That behavior which she would have censored had he been exercising it with anyone else, proved absolutely delightful when she was his partner. And yet, he had just told her he was newly resolved to lead an exemplary life.

And this came at the very moment Violette decided she was quite prepared to give herself up to passion and do something that would be considered far from exemplary.

She was younger than he, and for all her indiscretion with a married Frenchman, she had not been very adventurous. James made her desire to experience a bit more of life before she took on the obligations of motherhood. Now that he had given her a taste of the sublime, she also needed time to digest it properly.

There was much she did not understand, but she resolved she would not be married simply because a handsome gentleman finally decided he must settle down to domesticity.

And because she was the first one, convenient and available, on whom his unusual gray eyes alit.

Chapter 4

James tried very hard to keep his mind on other things during the course of the afternoon. With three young children running about the room, throwing pine cones at ancient Greek artifacts and at each other, it should not have been difficult. But for whatever else was happening in the east parlor, it was impossible for his eyes to stray very far from the image of Violette Makepeace standing on a sturdy stool, positioning feathery boughs of greenery across the mantel and along the molding that framed the room.

James would have done it or, even better, directed one of the servants to do it. But Violette insisted that they decorate the house with the children, to better appreciate the traditions of the season. Wils occasionally handed her a bell or a pine cone. John decided pine cones made excellent projectiles, and Anne was just happy to play with the bells.

James did his best to look busy. But truly,

all he wanted to do was watch Violette, her graceful arms stretching above her head, the way her body swayed when she bent the unruly boughs in her hands. Once or twice, she caught him staring at her, and frowned disapprovingly. When this happened, he tried to look industrious, but somehow he sensed there was something more amiss than the fact he had not a clue what to do with scratchy sap-covered branches.

She was angry with him.

The irony of this did not escape him. He was accustomed to women who allowed him every liberty, and never seemed to become irate. And here was one woman with whom he had demonstrated extraordinary restraint and yet she behaved as if she wished to be anywhere but in this room with him.

"Uncle James? How long must we plant these trees? May we go to the lake?" John tugged on his jacket, demanding attention.

"These poor branches have been cut down and will not grow again," James explained. "They have been sacrificed to make Evergreen a place of beauty for Christmas, so we may enjoy the season no matter the weather. But I thought we might go to the lake tomorrow morning, and skate upon the ice."

He got her attention then. Violette paused in her work, with a twist of ivy looped around her neck, and her lips shaped in a surprised little O.

"Your Aunt Violette will teach us all, for I am far out of practice, and will need her assistance as well. I am not sure how she will hold onto the four of us all at once, though."

"We will borrow plain maple chairs from the kitchen, and use them as our partners," she said, turning her back on him and speaking over her shoulder. "It will be very safe. And when the children are tired, they can sit upon the chairs to rest."

"This sounds very strange," Wils said.

"Your mother and I learned to skate thus on the Serpentine," Violette said. "As soon as you are comfortable on your own, you may abandon your partner."

"That does not seem very fair," James said for the benefit of the children, grinning as he spoke.

"And yet gentlemen do it all the time, my lord," Violette said tersely, surely for no one's benefit but his own.

Why was she angry with him?

The children resumed their play, still fascinated with the pine cones. James recalled the wonderful gifts he'd purchased for them before they left London, and thought he might have saved himself a good deal of expense if he had but gone to the park and filled a few boxes with leaves and pebbles and a few good pieces of bark. He watched Wils and John toss a stick back and forth over their sister's outstretched hands, all three of them screaming with delight. He felt sick that he would have to be the one to tell them about their parents when Christmas was past.

But Violette would help him. He did not know why she was so upset, but she would help him with this.

He looked across the room at her, and realized she was in need of his help just now. The last bit of greenery had been anchored and she looked adrift, standing on the stool on the side of the room and looking about for a handhold so she could drop to the floor. James walked toward her, coming up from behind, and put his arms around her in a move that was both secure and far too intimate.

She fluttered her hands for a few moments as he lifted her from the stool, and settled her on the floor, still in his embrace.

"It was only a kiss, my dear," he said in her ear.

Even with a coterie of servants assisting them at every turn, life was infinitely more complicated when and where children were concerned. After breakfast the next day, Violette advised Nanny Lind what Wils, John, and Anne ought to wear to protect themselves against the cold air and spills on the ice. She also had the children's shoes fitted with blades and straps. Though the great house was close by the frozen lake, Violette had the servants pack food and spare mittens for them all, just in case.

This late December day was almost unbearably brilliant, the sort of day that arrives in the heat of summer and the dead of winter, and during which most ladies and gentlemen elected to stay within closed doors and behind thick draperies. Violette's eyes quickly adjusted to the sunshine reflecting off the fallen snow, as she guided the children to the lake.

"Where is Uncle James?" John asked, blinking up at her.

Uncle James had disappeared around the time she and the servants were suiting up the children.

"There he is, wearing his funny spectacles," Wils said, and Anne laughed, prompted by nothing more than the word "funny." Such, Violette already knew, was all that was required for a three-year-old to find amusement.

But, in fact, Greenlough's spectacles were funny. Even absurd.

"What on earth are you wearing?" Violette asked as he came up to them.

"Wool stockings, a scratchy sweater I purchased in Ireland a few years ago, a scarf knit by one of the housekeeper's —"

"You know very well what I mean, my lord," Violette said. "What are you wearing on your face? We are not likely to find time to read books while we're skating on the ice."

"Nor would I attempt to read books through heavily tinted glass, dear lady." He looked down at the children and the spectacles slipped off his nose, which his young audience found uproarious. After righting them on the bridge of his nose, he turned back to Violette. She knew he studied her but, disconcertingly, she could not see his eyes.

"I call them my sun-dimmers. There is nothing wrong with my vision, except in the brightest sun. Years ago, James Ayscough tinted glass to aid against the glare, and his blue and green lenses are very pretty. I have not found them all that helpful, however, and I have been experimenting with other tints."

"Black, my lord? You might as well strap chunks of coal over your eyes, for all you can see."

"That is a most hideous image," James commented, fairly enough. "And I very much admire your red cape embroidered with blue flowers, your elegant brown bonnet and your green dress. Are those ribbons along the edge of the hem?"

Violette scowled at him.

"I can see perfectly well through my darkened lenses, as I have just demonstrated. Shall we proceed to the lake?" He promptly turned on his heel and started back to the house.

Violette laughed along with the children,

who ran after him and turned him in the right direction. They adored him and if she was honest, she did as well. After years of considering him someone she ought to avoid, and then being a person herself whom others avoided, she found him irresistible.

They walked down through the well-tended hedges and formal gardens to the lake. Though it looked very much a part of nature's landscape, Violette's experienced eye was able to appreciate that it was as artistic a creation as the Serpentine, though even more beautiful in its setting. An elegant Palladian gazebo stood directly across the frozen expanse from the house, and a small conservatory was nestled amongst beech trees.

"Are we to have a theatrical production, Miss Makepeace?" James asked, above the chatter of the children.

"Do you mean, for our Christmas Eve entertainment in a few days, my lord? I did not think you would wish it."

"You are quite right. There are several things for which I wish, but that is not among them."

Violette glanced at him, but could not see his eyes behind his lenses. Nevertheless, she knew what he meant, and felt her cheeks go warm.

"But I only meant our present seating arrangement," he continued.

Violette paused, still confused, until she saw

the chairs. Set up as if awaiting the entrance of a singer and her accompanist, two rows of plain maple chairs faced the lake.

"I shall embarrass myself sufficiently without the presence of an audience," she murmured. "Whatever was the footman thinking?"

"I daresay he only thought to please you. If you asked for three chairs, he undoubtedly thought you would be happier with ten. Most men are perfectly willing to take a lady's requests to extremes."

"Would you be willing to skate with me upon the ice, with the children holding hands between us? That is a simple request."

James cleared his throat. "I would be willing to skate the length of the Thames to the Channel, across the water to France and up the Seine to Paris, if I could but be with you."

"Now you are being silly," Violette said and would have laughed, but no sound came out.

"No, silly is wearing coal over my eyelids. I am quite serious about the prospect of traveling with you anywhere you wish."

These were not the words of a man looking to find a convenient wife who would be willing to take on the care of three children. Nor were they the words of a rake, a man who flitted from one woman to the next. They were the words of a man Violette was coming to love, who had the ability to both arouse her and calm her, making her feel safe.

"Let us see how we manage on this very small lake, and if our abilities have improved since I was here last," she said quietly, as she sat upon a chair. The children closed in around her, clambering to be the first to test the frozen waters.

The children were so exhausted from their ice-skating adventure, they barely made it through their dinner in the early evening. James did not mind that so much, but he wished he did not feel so weary himself. His legs and back pained him and he had twisted his ankle while showing off his prowess in skating along sharp curves. He was sorely tempted to retire to his own rooms, and bathe in a steaming tub of salt water. It would do wonders for his much abused body.

But there were other cures with which he was familiar, and one sat not ten feet from him, reading a small volume of verse. Violette could not know he watched her, for she seemed utterly indifferent to his presence. She pushed a stray curl off her cheek and tucked it behind her ear. And as she read, her tongue teased the tips of her front teeth, as if trifling with a rough edge there.

"I very much like what you have done to this room," he said.

Violette closed her lips.

"It is a fine enough place as it is, but now it looks very festive with the boughs and candles that have been awaiting Christmas," he tried again.

"I am sorry, my lord. I was engrossed in John Donne."

James felt a little flush of jealousy, which suggested something about his disordered state of mind. Anytime a man resented the intrusion of another, long dead, he became a candidate for the asylum. But if ever he met a lady who could drive him there, it was Miss Violette Makepeace. She flirted with him, pushed him away, laughed with him, and frowned upon him, all in a matter of minutes. As was true on the ice this morning, he could never be certain where he stood.

"You have decorated this parlor most becomingly," he began again.

"You might have offered to help, rather than stand watching me the whole while. I did not expect to be on display."

"If I expected that you would be on display, as you say, you would not have needed to decorate at all. Your presence in the room would have been sufficient."

"All men say things like that when they want a woman to do something for them."

"But you have told me that I am not like most men, to my eternal regret."

Violette closed her book and put it on the table next to her. "No, you are not. But I find I do not regret it at all," she said softly.

James quickly forgot about his aching back

and his sore ankle. "You have taken me to task for my lack of regard for my reputation. You have suggested I am unreliable, irresponsible, and altogether a bad sort. Are you now telling me you may have judged me too harshly?"

"I ought not have judged you at all, my lord. You have proved yourself to be a gracious host and a most solicitous uncle."

James felt his racing heart slow to a more tempered pace, and his fingers loosened their tight grip on the arm of his chair.

"So, you have reassessed the situation for the benefit of the children," he said. As was her habit and his, she reversed his expectations and even his hopes.

"Oh no, James." Violette's fingers twisted nervously in her lap. "I cannot say it is for their benefit. What I now feel is entirely for myself."

If ever there were words capable of redeeming a calculated sinner, they were these uttered from her sweet lips.

He was out of his chair in an instant, pulling her out of hers and into his arms. Her anxious fingers found their way to his hair as her body stretched against his. His lips covered hers, open and warm, and everything sad that brought them to this place was forgotten in the joy of the present. Evergreen was his home, the only place other than the Royal Observatory to which he truly felt an attachment, and now Violette was here with him, bringing delight to what had been simple pleasure. It felt as if nothing else mattered.

But for the fact they were in the parlor and any of the servants could walk in with the coffee service at any moment.

With extraordinary effort, James pulled away.

"But you have, perhaps, not improved upon your opinion of me, I see," Violette said. Her lips were reddened and her eyes were still half closed in the dream of lovemaking.

"I only misjudged in thinking you still a girl, too quiet and delicate for this rough world. No one ever thought your history with your French rogue had anything to do with your own behavior, but that you were too easily tricked by a man of experience."

"And yet my experience has not made me cautious, as you see," she said happily, and shrugged. Her shawl slipped off her shoulder and he seized the brief advantage to kiss her bare skin.

"And my experience has not prepared me for you." James paused, thinking about his words. No woman had ever intrigued him as she did, no woman had ever made him imagine he might love her.

There were things he wished to show her, and do with her.

"Come, let us go to another place," he said,

before he thought through his scheme.

"To your chamber, do you mean?" she whispered.

Of course she would think it, but that is not what he meant.

"There will be time enough for that, my dear Miss Makepeace. For this place, you must change out of your slippers into sturdy boots and wear your warmest cloak."

She looked surprised, but ready for whatever he proposed. "Are we going on a journey, then?"

"Yes, I rather think so," he said, and grinned in perfect contentment.

Violette held his gloved hand as they walked carefully down the icy steps of the broad terrace and through the dark garden, where snow-covered shrubs glistened in the moonlight. He knew where he was going, and she did not, and so it made perfect sense to follow him, even if he led her down a path to perdition.

She already was a ruined woman and was perfectly happy to be ruined and ruined again, for she hoped his intention was to thoroughly compromise her. For all his professed concern about his brother's children, he clearly did not mind if they associated with an aunt of blighted reputation.

He turned suddenly and caught her by the waist. "It is particularly dangerous here and I do not believe your boots are up to the task," he said, lifting her as if she were as light as Anne, and placing her on more stable ground. He paused for a moment, staring down at her, and then thought better of whatever he had in mind.

"We are almost there," he said.

"Are we going to the pavilion?" Violette asked, her teeth chattering, though not from the cold.

"An open colonnade with a frozen fountain in the middle?" he asked. "I'm not sure even I could warm you there, though I'm tempted to try."

Indeed, Violette was tempted to have him try, but said nothing as they continued on their way. She watched his legs bend exceptionally high as he stamped his way through the snow, and she stepped carefully in his footsteps.

She thought briefly of the others in his past, and the one notorious man in hers, knowing that every liaison brought with it an unspoken promise that somehow this time, this passion, this person would be different from all others. Violette now dared to believe it again. But even if she proved an utter deluded fool, she wanted to have him now, and not concern herself with the morrow.

They continued silently, surrounded by the sounds of the season. The snow crunched beneath their feet, and a stiff wind whistled through the bare branches of the beech trees. An owl hooted across the lake, and was answered by a mate somewhere nearby. Ahead of them was a large shadow against the trees.

James turned abruptly in his path, heading in its direction.

It was no shadow. It was the small conservatory Violette had noticed against the trees, though as they approached it, she could not see the leaves and branches of wintering plants within. Still, there was little doubt as to its purpose. She had already decided she would follow this man anywhere, but would be forced to reconsider if he intended to set in the bulbs for spring or pull out the pruning shears.

"Where are you taking me, James?" she asked, tugging on his hand.

"To the one place at Evergreen where I have always been assured of privacy. You are the first woman I've brought here."

She supposed she should be flattered, though it was not enough to compensate for a small knot of disappointment. If this was not his accustomed trysting place, there would be no lovemaking on this starry night.

James released her as he stepped up to the threshold of the building. He turned the knob once and again and then kicked the door in with his boot. "Stay here," he said, and disappeared into the darkness.

Violette stood tentatively, one step beyond the doorframe. She heard James moving about, knocking over things and cursing softly. It was tempting to just turn away from him and whatever he intended here, for she could simply retrace their footsteps in the moonlit snow. But just when apprehension was about to win out over anticipation, Violette heard a faint scrape, and then a torch sputtered and caught fire, its growing light outlining James's large form as he walked toward the far wall. In a moment, the large fireplace there was lit, and seasoned wood crackled in the still, fresh air. He hung the torch on a sconce on the wall.

"It will be warm in minutes," he said, and emphasized his point by shrugging off his greatcoat. "The servants know I may come here at any time, and always have the makings of a good fire set in the grate."

But Violette hardly heard him, for she now gazed in wonder at what could only be seen by the brilliant flames. On every surface of the room, and dangling like snowdrops from the ceiling, were dozens of crystals, reflecting light from the fire and from each other, sparkling with exquisite beauty.

"You are thinking you have come to the sanctuary of a madman," said James, sheepishly.

She turned to face him, and saw nothing of the confident, rakish man who was ever known for his misdeeds and wild ways. Instead, she saw someone who seemed younger and a little doubtful, offering a gift he valued to a friend, a man utterly unsure about the reception that gift would receive.

He needed not have doubted her, or the wonder of the gift.

"James," she said clearly, hearing his name echo in the warming air. "It is the most extraordinary thing I have ever seen. It is like a magical crystal cave, a dragon's lair, an ancient cavern in the frozen north."

He laughed. "I did not think you prone to hyperbole, but I think you have gone too far. There is nothing magical about it. This is merely the place where I work, experimenting with glass and quartz, grinding lenses and prisms. It is all very ordinary."

"If you believed that — if you thought I would believe that — you would not have brought me here." Violette studied him, watching the ways in which little sparks of color and light glanced off his dark reddish hair and the planes of his face. He was quite right about the warmth in the room, for she felt like her face was burning. "It is the most extraordinary, wondrous thing."

Violette caught herself, knowing she was now talking about something else altogether, and grateful he could not see her blush.

"You are wrong about that," he said, and started to come toward her. "It is not the most extraordinary, wondrous thing."

"It is not?" she asked faintly.

"It is not. You are that," he said, and caught her at the moment she thought her knees would give out.

He kissed her as they had not kissed before, as if no one in the whole world had ever kissed before and they were the ones to have discovered this extraordinary pleasure. His lips were warm, as were hers in a moment, and Violette felt she was drinking in his passion and his strength, filling herself with the same. She arched her back and pressed against him, while her fingers played havoc with his hair and the rough flesh at the back of his neck. His body answered hers with a hardness that might have alarmed her, but so lost was she in sensation, and so desirous of claiming him, she rejoiced in everything of the moment.

Somehow, she was out of her heavy cape, and James's hands were on her arms, waltzing her backward to a corner of the room, until the backs of her legs pressed against a low cushion. James urged her downward, murmuring reassurances as his lips moved down her neck to her shoulder to her breast.

"You have a bed here?" Violette whispered, amused. "Now I know what sort of work you do here."

"I sometimes sleep here," he said impatiently, his cheek scratching the soft flesh over her collarbone.

"Is that your intention this night?" she asked.

He looked up and stared down at her in the shifting light, sparks of color flashing in his hair. "Perhaps, but not before we do other things, much more pleasurable. This is the time to tell me to stop, Violette, to remind me of the unalterable bond already between us, and how this will only make our lives more complicated. I will do what you wish, tonight and always. But this is the time to tell me if we are not to go any further."

"Dear James. Surely you must know that I will go anywhere in the world with you, and share every adventure, even if we go no farther than this narrow bed."

He smiled, in that way he had that she was coming to know and love. She knew her words, though spoken in the heat of passion, could not be more true. For she would go anywhere with him if he would just smile like that.

"I have been dreaming, in recent days, of visiting the volcanoes in Italy with you at my side, or sailing the calm waters of the Mediterranean," he said. "But, for now, on this cold winter night, we shall have to find adventure enough right here."

CHAPTER 5

Though James had woken up with various women in his bed, it took him several minutes to realize where he was and why someone's soft hair was tickling his neck when he opened his eyes in the early morning light. Without raising his head, he knew the fierce fires of the night before had burned out in the grate, for the air was chilly and his nose was painfully cold. And then he turned just slightly, to the riotous curls spread across his shoulders, and buried his nose against them.

Violette squeaked and pressed her naked body nearer to his. Not all the flames had burned out, it seemed, and he was tempted to see how quickly they could ignite, but her gentle, steady breathing reminded him that she was exhausted. And with good reason.

It had been a long night, one of exploration and great delight. Violette had not been a virgin, but certainly was not a woman of much experience either, and she made good on her vow that she would follow him anywhere. What was most extraordinary was that they went to places that were new to him as well.

How had this happened? How was it possible he had never dared to reach out and lay claim to the sister of his sister-in-law, who had been dancing and ice-skating and dining right before his eyes for nearly all his life? She was always a little beauty, uncommonly clever, and truly tempting. Whereas he had been a fool.

His arm reached above her head to a small side table on which he had several of his favorite prisms on display. He picked up the smallest of the group, one he'd fashioned when he was no more than a boy. It was somewhat irregular but did the job for which it was intended. James held it aloft, catching the pale sunshine, and watched as slivers of light danced on the glass ceiling of the old conservatory. Still experimenting, he turned it toward the woman still snuggled against him, and cast rainbows of color on her naked shoulder.

That was it, of course. He only needed to look at Miss Violette Makepeace in a different light, through a prism, seeing things through the glass that had never been apparent to him before. It was not merely that they were now thrust together, though that accounted for much, but their shared tragedy had changed them both.

And in this, he realized with a fair share of guilt, he had evolved a good deal more than she. If he turned the glass on himself, he would recognize that the loss of his brother made him finally appreciate the fragility of human life. And the guardianship of three young children made him see the need to become a man. His life had never been as reckless as rumor would have it, but it was bad enough. He found pleasure with women with whom he had no future, and spent his fortune on frivolous wishes.

And now there was a woman who somehow had never been in his past enough, yet might become everything for his future. This is what he saw in the reflection of his glass.

"James?"

She startled him, and he dropped the prism on her head.

"What was that?" she asked, rubbing her scalp. Her hand groped about on the pillow and she found the unintended weapon. "A piece of glass?"

"A prism, my dear. And I am sorry if I hurt you."

Violette turned in the bed until her breasts pressed against his chest. Her lips looked reddened and bruised and her eyes were heavily shadowed. He had probably hurt her in ways having nothing to do with dropping something on her head, but could regret none of it, except this most recent assault.

"Did I interrupt your work, James? I have never before awakened to find a man at my side, but I hoped it would be more romantic than this."

Beautiful and uncommonly clever. His assessment was entirely accurate.

"Do you not find this romantic, my love?" he asked, his tone matching hers. "Even if I replaced my prisms with diamonds and placed them in your hands, you would not see a sight more wondrous. Here, hold it to the light at the window, and behold the beauty of the day."

Violette did as she was told, shifting the glass between her fingers, creating a universe of suns across the plain white ceiling. Then, as he guessed she would, she turned the light on him.

"I think you are beautiful," she said.

"And I think you are a lady who has looked too admiringly of marble statues, which bear very little resemblance to a man's rough body," he said.

She blinked into the prism, undoubtedly contemplating his words. She bit down on her lower lip, stifling an answer. But she would not be stifled for long. "You are right, James. I daresay, I will see things differently in the stronger light of day." She dropped the glass onto the floor and so slowly he barely knew what was happening, the warm quilt under which they lay started to edge down.

Her tongue traced a path down his chest to his stomach, pausing just one aching moment before she went further.

Dear God. Just when he understood where his future lay, this woman would kill him.

"What will Mrs. Bligh and the other servants say?" Violette asked as they walked toward the great house. Her hair was tangled and loosely piled beneath her shawl, and she had an uneasy feeling that James had missed a button when helping her dress.

"What do servants always say when the master and mistress present themselves after a spot of lovemaking?"

"I have no idea, James. I have not a lot of experience in this regard," Violette said, vaguely bothered by his casual acceptance of the situation. "And we are not the master and mistress, which is very much to the point."

"I suppose I never cared what anyone had to say, but you are quite right," he said, suddenly serious. "I would not have your reputation damaged, even among the servants. But it is not our inclination to make excuses for what is not their business, so we shall have to allow them to imagine what they will."

"We have been out of the house all night, so I believe they will imagine a great deal."

"You shall have to marry me, then, and put all speculation at an end."

Violette turned away, knowing he might not

be serious for all his appearance of being so. She wished she could be as easy in her manner as he was. James could not possibly understand how everything had changed for her in this one night, how everything she dared dream about what went on between men and women was as extraordinary as she'd hoped and as illuminating as the many crystals in his cottage. Her body ached just thinking about what they did last night, and she wondered what the servants would say if the master and his sister-in-law's sister stayed in that little conservatory for a week or so. She was tempted to find out.

"Or perhaps they will simply guess that we have been crafting some Christmas surprises in your workshop and will only speculate about what we have planned," she said instead, her tone light and her voice surprisingly steady. And then, a moment later, she stopped and touched his arm. "James, that is precisely what we should do!"

He looked at her with an expression, part confusion and part disappointment, that beguiled her. She wondered if she misread the moment, and he had indeed been serious about offering her marriage. But she would not accept a proposal given after a sleepless night and for the sole purpose of saving a reputation that was already ruined. And, in any case, if the moment ever existed, it was gone for now, pushed away because she thought it so unlikely.

"Let us decorate the dining hall and parlor of Evergreen with your lenses and crystals. No one will ever have seen the like," she said, her voice now faltering a bit. What if he had indeed been thinking of marriage, and she of interior decoration?

"I cannot imagine why our few guests would have any interest in bits and pieces of polished glass, my dear. It will only be the family and the Whittiers and the servants," he reminded her.

"James, please recall that we would not be here at all if we did not hope to give the children one last Christmas of joy before telling them the dreadful news about Wilson and Olivia." She glanced at his solemn face as they walked along together. "Well, I would not have been here at all."

"Never before has such tragedy led to such joy," he said.

Violette faltered, understanding that what he said only minutes before must have come from his heart. He did care for her and perhaps he did truly wish to marry her.

"And I am interested in your bits and pieces of polished glass," she said softly. "I did not know where you were bringing me last night, but your workshop is a wonderful place. I viewed everything there with more pleasure that I could ever imagine."

He stopped on the path, only yards from

the great house, and Violette went no farther. She turned to meet his eyes, and nodded in agreement to anything he silently asked her. She had no doubt he understood her perfectly.

"I daresay we have an audience," he said.

"And you have given me strict instructions that I am not to care about that," she answered, realizing she did not.

He leaned closer and kissed her on the lips, their bodies separated by the cold air and a respectable distance.

"Ah," he said, drawing away and licking his lips. "You are reminding me of how hungry I am."

Violette hoped he did not mean kippers and toast, because she suddenly found herself hungry for other things.

"And yet, I suppose we ought to eat breakfast," he said. Again, he understood her perfectly.

"Yes, indeed. We need our strength, for I believe we are to ice skate once again."

Though Violette had already pointed out to James that she was not the mistress of Evergreen, her role in the household changed subtly after the night they shared together. She supposed it had more to do with her behavior than anyone else's, for she was now sufficiently confident to invade the lower sanctums of the house, and discuss the

Christmas preparations with the appropriately named Mrs. Baker, the cook, and Mrs. Bligh.

"If you don't mind my saying so, Miss Makepeace," said Mrs. Baker, after some discussion, "you are the first lady I've met who seems to know the difference between a stewpot and a sieve."

"If you are trying to determine if I have ever served as a cook, I am sorry to disappoint, for I have not."

"Miss Makepeace, I am sure Mrs. Baker —" Mrs. Bligh protested, fully indignant on her behalf.

"It is quite all right. I do know my way about a kitchen, as you see, for I find it a diverting experience. More to the point, I am a collector of menus and recipes, and am planning a volume of cookery for those young women planning to enter service. Not every girl is lucky enough to have her mother's recipes, and must rely on the expertise of others."

"That is a most sensible idea," said Mrs. Baker.

"If one assumes that all girls with kitchen skills are able to read," Mrs. Bligh argued.

"Well, yes. There is that," Violette sighed. "Perhaps my next mission shall be the opening of a school."

"You are an ambitious one, that's for sure," Mrs. Baker said approvingly. "And I suppose you've come down here to ask me for my best recipes."

"Yes, of course. I hope you do not mind sharing them," said Violette.

"And I do know how to read and write," Mrs. Baker said, looking defiantly at the housekeeper. "I have so many recipes, however, and am not sure where to begin. I suppose you'd like to know the special favorites of the master? He has very rich tastes, you know."

She didn't know, but it did not surprise her. She blushed, thinking about his various appetites, and realized her two companions were watching her and grinning.

Violette cleared her throat.

"I imagine it is inevitable we will get to that, but I hoped to discuss your Christmas menu. In that way, we can both consider what is to be served on Christmas Eve and Day, and I can add recipes to my collection."

"We will have a goose, of course," Mrs. Bligh said. "One for the master's guests, and one for the servants."

"I dress the geese with sugared fenberry sauce, and put chestnuts in the stuffing. And I always bake the bread special for the stuffing, none of the stale stuff for this household," added Mrs. Baker.

The chestnuts reminded Violette of other things on the menu.

"Miss Rosella Whittier has promised to

bring minced meat pies on Christmas Eve," she said.

Mrs. Baker and Mrs. Bligh stared at each other, as if they dared the other to speak first.

"I understand from Mr. Whittier that she is a most accomplished cook," Violette said.

"She is most accomplished at poisoning the guests," said Mrs. Baker.

"Surely you do not mean that," whispered Violette, while yet hoping — most ungenerously — it might be true.

"I am sure it was just an unfortunate coincidence," said Mrs. Bligh, very sensibly. "The Whittiers arrived for Christmas Day luncheon several years ago, bringing those dreadful pies. They might as well have been made of boiled turnips, for all anyone touched them. And then Hercules, the groom's mastiff, helped himself to the leftovers and was dead by the morning."

"Good heavens. But no one was truly poisoned?" Violette asked.

"The groom loved that dog," said Mrs. Baker, dabbing at her eyes with a linen handkerchief.

"I understand. But I fear it is too late to relieve Miss Whittier of the obligation, if such it is. She seemed most enthusiastic about bringing them, and her father seemed most enthusiastic about promoting her talents."

The women nodded knowingly. Violette knew very well that she ought not gossip with the servants, and certainly not ask for any information about their master. And yet these two might be able to settle one lingering bit of discomfort for her.

"I suspect they wish to please Lord Green-lough," she said, matter-of-factly.

"My dear Miss Makepeace. If a certain fish wished to be caught, he would have opened his mouth to the bait years ago, poison or not. But he is no longer even swimming in the same pond and is not likely to be hooked," said Mrs. Baker.

"That is a most dreadful metaphor, Mrs. Baker, but I see your point," said Violette. "And I shall avoid the minced pies, in any case."

"You are quite right about this lady, Mrs. Bligh," said Mrs. Baker, speaking as if Violette had already left the room. "She is wise as well as beautiful."

Wils, John, and Anne were wet and cold by the time the sun was low in the sky, but they were not quite as wet and cold as they had been during the previous outing, and James considered the ice-skating lessons to be a huge success. This time, he brought several of the stableboys with him, who seemed to be as capable of graceful movement on narrow blades as they were on the back of a horse, and were happy to have an afternoon away from the monotony of the stables.

Nearer in size to the children, they made for excellent tutors.

James rewarded each of them with a coin, and rewarded his own aching muscles with a respite. In addition, he needed time to think.

He assumed Miss Violette Makepeace was his, in every way that mattered, for he would not have dared to love her as he did last night if he doubted it. And yet, this morning, she deftly bypassed his declaration, speaking some nonsense about Christmas decorations and suggesting he put his fragile crystals on display like the trophies at White's. Surely she understood that he would not trifle with her affections nor claim her heart and body if he did not intend for their relationship to endure.

But perhaps he'd blundered into the business too soon. Though they made a good show of Christmas cheer for the children and servants, they both knew they were in mourning, or would be soon enough. His beloved brother and her darling sister were dead, lost to those who loved them best, and the children they adored. It was only five days to Christmas, and probably only two weeks before he and Violette would be the bearers of bad news, and then called upon to be the pillars of strength to those who grieved with them.

She was right. He had spoken too soon. There would be time enough for formal protestations of love and fidelity, and all the months ahead to make wedding plans.

But then, he would marry her tomorrow, if possible. He did not wish to spend another night without her, and he wanted her by his side when he took three little orphans into his house. If they waited until they were out of mourning — which would be appropriate — months would go by, and anything might happen.

Anything could happen.

"My lord?"

James wondered how long Nanny Lind had been calling until he heard her.

"Yes?"

"I am taking the children back to the house. It would not do for them to be ill when their parents return."

"You are very wise, Nanny Lind. Yes, do take them back to the house, and I will join you soon. I have to gather some crystals for our Christmas table."

"Should you not wait until Christmas Eve to gather ice, my lord?" she asked.

"My crystals are more durable," James said. He watched as Wils threw a snowball at his brother's head, and knocked his hat off. "They will survive the heat of the room. I only pray they survive the children."

Nanny Lind shook her head as she walked away, scooping up Anne, and trying to keep up with the boys.

James watched them until he could no longer hear John crying or see Wils gathering up more snow to torment his younger brother. His own brother was an excellent father, attentive to his children and caring of their needs. James vowed he would be nothing less.

But it was going to be difficult. Uncles had the ability to pop in and have a good time, and leave when the going got rough. Uncles did not have to worry about discipline, or sending boys off to school or procuring a kind governess. But he was no longer an uncle, certainly not in the usual way, and would have to step in where Wilson had so unceremoniously left off.

And then there would be children of his own, at least as many as his brother and sister-in-law had bequeathed to him. Perhaps there would be more, and as they would also be little scions of the Hanford and Makepeace families, the whole collection would be a perfectly matched set, like the family china.

Dear heavens, but he was beginning to think like a man ready to embrace domesticity. All this, because he already embraced Violette Makepeace.

As James started toward his workshop to gather some of his prized prisms and lenses, he realized that the path was slowly being covered by a fresh layer of snow. He opened his eyes to what should have been apparent:

the dark sky portended another storm and the first flakes were rapidly falling on Evergreen. It would be a fine night to find refuge in the workshop with Violette, but he suspected she had other plans that had nothing to do with lying beneath him and a heavy eiderdown quilt on a narrow bed.

Violette looked up from her reading, though she had already taken the words of Walter Scott to heart and did not need to look at the page. Wils and John sat on either side of her, listening attentively to the story of *Ivanhoe,* and Anne had been taken up to the nursery.

James came through the door, his dark hair covered by a cap of snow. He held a long, flat box, so roughly fashioned that Violette thought he brought them logs for the fire.

"Where would you like this?" he asked, interrupting them. The boys, usually so eager to join him, sat quietly, for once too tired for games.

"In the fireplace, perhaps?" Violette ventured.

"I rather thought you preferred to decorate my home with them, to give one the impression that Evergreen is an overly large chandelier," he said, and gently slid the box to the floor.

"Oh, you have brought the crystals!" she said, and closed the book. How had she forgotten her only request of him, after a night during which she might have seized the advantage and asked him to do anything? She gently stood from her place between the boys, and walked toward him.

"Did you not desire them?" he asked, as she came close.

"You know I did," she said, in a whisper. It would be very easy to forget that two pairs of eyes watched from just behind them, and probably listened to every word they said, as well. "But I would like to hang them in the windows, and am not certain how to go about it. I need you. To help, you understand."

"I believe I do," James said, looking over her shoulder. "I do not know what you were reading, but it seems to have made quite an impression on the boys."

Violette turned around and saw that Wils and John leaned into the seat she only just vacated, their heads meeting so that their bodies formed a triangle. "There is nothing boring about *Ivanhoe,* it is only that they are exhausted. And it is just as well they are not watching us, as they may get certain ideas."

"I cannot imagine what you mean, but let us take advantage of this fine respite, and do what we can with my little offering. If you think my pieces of glass will make our holiday more festive, then I believe you." He opened the great box, in which he had carefully laid out an assortment of prisms. "My idea is to wrap each one in wire, so they might be tied to the boughs and hung from the draperies. Is that what you envisioned?"

Violette gazed at him, at the fine straight line of his nose, and his curiously-shaped eye. She looked at his fine wool jacket, fitted to perfection, and the diamond stickpin in his cravat. Oh, yes. This is what she envisioned all her life.

"I am speaking of the glass, Violette," he said softly.

She blinked, and returned to more practical concerns. "Of course. Whatever else would you possibly mean? I thought we might ask Mrs. Bligh to have some set about on the dinner table as well. Do you not think the effect would be extraordinary?"

"Almost certainly," he said.

James took a small knife from the box and cut several strips of the copper wire. Then, very carefully, he twisted the wire around one of his crystals at the widest point, intent on doing the work properly. This was a side of Lord Greenlough very few people were likely to see, Violette realized. There was nothing of the rake here, or even the cheerful uncle. Instead, here was a serious man, in pursuit of knowledge and willing to experiment as he worked things to perfection.

"Will you show me what to do?" she asked.

"Of course," he said, "though you must be careful with the knife."

James held her hands in his, working the

wire around the glass, testing an edge for sharpness, and showing her just how to tighten a knot without breaking the fragile pieces. With anyone else, she would have pulled away, confident that she could handle the task by herself. But as was also true in his bed, she learned from his hands, accepting experience and greater knowledge, and finding pleasure in it.

"You do know, I hope, that I have truly cared for very few women in my life," he said suddenly, as if they were discussing the weather. "My general indifference made me move from one affair to another."

"You should not be discussing this with me," said Violette, her hands suddenly cold, though he still held her.

"You are precisely the one with whom I should be discussing this, for there is no one else to whom it could possibly matter." He removed the prism they both held, and placed it on the table before he caught her hands again. "I want you to know that everything has changed."

"Because you require a mother for the children, and I am uniquely suited for that role?" Violette asked, unwilling to let go of her doubts.

James looked surprised, even amused. "Because the role for which you are uniquely suited has nothing to do with the children. It does, however, have everything to do with me. I want you to marry me, Violette. I love you."

Heat suffused her body as she stepped back.

"That is quite a different thing, as well I know," she said.

His amusement was gone. "Do you mean, because you loved your bigamist French count?"

"I do not think he ever intended to marry me, so whatever his faults, he was not a bigamist. But I did not love him. I only know that because I love you, and it is altogether a different matter."

"Yes, I rather think it is." James studied her and Violette met the intent look in his curious eye, and considered how everything looked different to her in this extraordinary season. "I did not expect it, or even consider it before. I only know that I have been a fool, looking everywhere for love, when I need not traveled farther than my brother's house on a festive eve."

"And I was there," Violette nodded. "But I was not looking for you either."

"Then we have both been blind, though I must take the greater blame. A gentleman has a certain freedom to be adventurous, and a warrant to experience what he wishes of life until he finds what he most desires."

"There is no blame to be assigned, James. My only regret is that we have been finally brought together by shared tragedy, and the most poignant task of raising three children not our own. If we had not lost Wilson and Olivia, we might not have found each other." Violette smiled. "Though we remained in plain sight all these years."

"You doubted me, did you not? I sensed it from the start, and not more than a few minutes ago as well. I would have thought that by now you had every reason to believe me."

"I do believe you, truly. But you cannot blame me for suspecting this was to be a marriage of convenience. You become guardian of three little children, and those children need a mother. Who better to take up the task than an aunt who already adores them?" Violette drew a deep breath. "And then I realized that might be a sacrifice I was prepared to make, in the name of love."

"I hope I have managed to convince you that you need not sacrifice anything," James said. "I hope you will continue to pursue the things that interest you, with the exception of other eligible gentlemen."

"Might I ask the same of you?" Violette asked.

"I have no interest in eligible gentlemen," James quipped.

"Yes, I suppose you have made that abundantly clear," Violette said, stifling a giggle. "I am speaking of the ladies, of course."

"You are my only lady, far surpassing even

the heavenly goddesses visible through the great lenses at the great observatory in Greenwich."

"I see," she said solemnly. "I think I should like to meet those heavenly goddesses."

"It would give me great pleasure to introduce you. I have never had a female companion who demonstrated any interest in their acquaintance," James said, just as seriously. "Perhaps they feared they would pale in comparison."

Violette smiled, realizing her love for him had made her utterly fearless.

The snow that punctuated all their days at Evergreen resumed in earnest on Christmas Eve day, covering their tracks and trails with a stiff white counterpane. The birds found shelter in the trees and beneath the eaves of the buildings, and the servants ventured forth only out of necessity. Violette stood at the window and wondered if the Whittiers would even be able to join them this night. She would be perfectly happy if they did not. She certainly no longer saw Miss Whittier as a rival for James's affections, but realized she wished only to reflect on the blessing of solemn grief now mitigated by unexpected joy. This strange duality truly seemed a perfect reflection of the holy night.

"Will the Whittiers be buried in the snow as they make their way here?" James asked so suddenly that Violette jumped.

She turned from the window. James sat in the most comfortable chair in the parlor, where he had been reading her copy of *Ivanhoe,* though not aloud. The children were sitting on the floor, setting up their dominoes. This domestic life was now hers, though granted to her under the most unfortunate circumstances. Tears welled up in her eyes.

"Surely, I did not startle you so as to make you cry?" he asked. Wils looked up, curious at the conversation that went on above his head.

Violette wiped her cheek with the back of her hand. "Of course not," she said. "It is only that I am standing so close to the cold window that my eyes started to tear."

"You need not worry about the Whittiers, you know. They will manage to get here in time for dinner."

"I have no doubt. I daresay Miss Rosella Whittier will shovel the road the whole way from town to Evergreen, as that is a very remarkable quality in a wife."

"I can think of several others," James said. "But our friend Rosella tries very hard to please, and her father tries even harder, so something will come of it eventually."

"I will not pity her, for she is young and healthy. But surely you realize there are many excellent women who never find a husband. It is a fact of which I was reminded with increasing frequency."

"You exaggerate, Miss Makepeace," James said, himself with exaggerated formality. "Who would utter such a thing?"

"Why, nearly everyone I know."

"I would not have said such a thing."

"I see. And this, coming from a man who never seemed to notice me."

"Uncle James noticed you," Wils spoke up. "He told me you were very beautiful."

"Now, there's a good lad," his fond uncle remarked. "Remind me to instruct you in the art of discretion about the conversations that pass between men."

"But I am not a man," Wils argued.

"Remind me of that as well," James said. "Your aunt's great beauty quite deprives me of all sense."

"But —"

"That is quite enough, Wilson," James said, putting his book down on a small table with unusual emphasis.

Violette studied him, never having witnessed this stern aspect of his character, but also realizing it a necessary trait in a parent. James met her eyes and shrugged just perceptibly, perhaps a little surprised himself.

"If Miss Whittier is to shovel the road, I shall help her," John said, ever the peacemaker.

"It will not come to that, John," said Violette gently, trying not to laugh. "We are lucky to have servants to help us, and they will see to the roads if they become too deep with drifts of snow."

"And then my parents will be able to come as well, for they promised to be here for Christmas."

A log sizzled and fell in the fireplace, but the room was otherwise silent.

"Promises are made with the best intentions," James said. His voice was steady and sure, revealing how well poised he was to stand at the head of a family. "We trust in them, and in those who made them, but circumstances sometimes make the fulfillment impossible. A man may promise to love and marry a woman, but then discover that he cannot."

Violette thought her heart had stopped in its course, so unexpected was this startling defection. Yet, returning his gaze, she realized he did not speak of his own promise and protestation of love, but of the man who preceded him in her affections. He seemed to be telling her that her odious Frenchman was no more than a man trapped by circumstances, speaking words he hoped might someday be true. Looking at the situation through a different lens did not make a false promise more honorable, but it did pardon the lady who believed it.

The burden she had borne for several years, weighted with guilt and anger, slipped from

Violette's shoulders, finally abandoned. She would not carry it, and James would not carry it for her, for it no longer mattered to anyone.

"And your parents would wish for nothing more than to be here with us this night," James continued. "But they may have encountered obstacles beyond their control."

"Like Odysseus," Wils said. "But I hope it does not take them ten years to come home to us. They would not even recognize me."

"They would know you in an instant, no matter how much time passes, for you are the very image of your father. And your uncle, for that matter," Violette said.

James started to rise, just as Rosella Whittier marched into the room. Violette's surprise was tempered by some gratitude that she had interrupted them before the conversation became too maudlin.

"Lord Greenlough. Miss Makepeace," the young woman said. "We have arrived!"

James cleared his throat, and Violette knew he was as much affected by the conversation as she had been. "And you are most welcome, Miss Whittier. But did we not expect you this evening?"

Miss Whittier's parents followed her into the parlor, already joining in the conversation.

"We were most concerned that the roads would become impassable, for it is such a storm," said Mr. Whittier. "Knowing full well that there are more bedchambers at Evergreen than you can possibly need, we decided to pack some belongings, and set out a bit early so we might stay the night. And of course, we brought the minced pies."

"Thank goodness for that," muttered Mrs. Bligh, trailing after the Whittiers.

"Did Mrs. Whittier come with you?" James asked, looking past his agitated housekeeper.

"She is already with Mrs. Baker, advising her as to her preparations," said Mr. Whittier on a note of pride.

"My dear friend," James said, "it is not necessary for your family to see to our Christmas Eve dinner. I am certain my staff will manage as they always have."

"We have come to help," said Miss Whittier. As she looked around her, at the greenery and glinting crystals in the parlor, her expression sobered. "But it appears all is quite done."

Violette felt a surge of sympathy for the woman, ready to forget the somewhat ungenerous thoughts she had entertained not many days before. She was cheerful and lively and reputedly talented, and would surely make some man an excellent wife. But James Hanford was not that man.

"It is all done, Miss Whittier," said Violette gently. "But that is all to the better, so we might sit at ease and become better acquainted."

James turned to face her, looking like a man who needed rescue. Violette knew perfectly well that he could capably handle nearly any situation, but his gesture of supplication was nevertheless satisfying.

"That would be lovely, Miss Makepeace, for I have much to tell you."

Violette caught the young lady's hand and pulled her to a corner of the large room, just as Mr. Whittier descended on James like a cat to the milk.

CHAPTER 6

"I hope you realize he loves you," Miss Whittier said sometime later.

She stood with Violette on the second floor landing of the grand staircase, gazing up at an elaborately framed Elizabethan gentleman who looked very much like James. Her words did not seem to have the slightest bit of regret or sadness and there was no resentment in them.

Still, Violette felt compelled to respond with something like an apology. "I have known him as long as you have, Miss Whittier," she murmured, as if that explained anything.

Rosella nodded. "I have said as much to my parents, who nevertheless maintain their highest hopes in that regard. While I would have been perfectly happy to spend my evening working on my embroidery and singing a few carols, they were quite insistent we set out for Evergreen and make a great show of celebrating Christmas with the family here."

"It is an old custom, I understand," Violette said, feeling particularly generous this night, and it was only in small part to the nature of the season. "Along with your fine offering of minced pies."

"I hate minced pie," said Rosella.

Violette laughed. "Surely you are not serious?"

"I am always serious. I have not the talent to appear light and witty, much to my parents' dismay."

Violette thought upon her own experience of the past few years, in which she sometimes had to remind herself to smile. Even when one's life appeared privileged and comfortable, there were often other invisible demons with which one had to wrestle. With luck, and with love, they could be vanquished.

"I do hope you and Lord Greenlough will soon announce your betrothal."

Violette turned away from the old portrait, wondering if Rosella was able to read her mind. "Why do you wish it, Miss Whittier?" Violette asked, genuinely intrigued.

"Because once the matter is settled, my parents will be perfectly pleased if I accept Mr. Birch's proposal. He is a good man, and has a most beautiful home. We have known him for many years. But he is not, you understand, Lord Greenlough." Rosella looked away from the portrait and studied her instead.

504

Violette sighed with relief. "But then again, no other man is."

"You love him, too," said Rosella, and nodded her head in satisfaction.

"Indeed, I do. I scarcely recognized it until I was quite lost with loving him, and now wonder why I did not see it sooner."

Rosella shrugged. "I suspect it is a little like looking through Greenlough's little pieces of glass. One thinks one recognizes something, but through a glass it takes on a somewhat different appearance. It is possible to see the flaws, of course. But then, sometimes, things just sparkle."

"What a clever way of describing it, Miss Whittier. I believe you are possessed of a wit greater than you will admit." Violette took Rosella's hand, wondering if she would become a friend. "And do you love your Mr. Birch?"

"Much more than I do minced pie," Rosella said, barely able to stifle her joy.

"Oh, come, Miss Whittier! I will have the truth from you!"

Rosella laughed out loud, tossing her own assessment of her self out the window. "I adore him," she said. "Only someone who feels this way can recognize it in another."

Looking at this young woman, so willing to please her parents, and yet so certain of her own mind, Violette knew she was absolutely right.

■ ■ ■ ■

The minced pies were not to James's liking, but the children seemed to enjoy them, and Mr. and Mrs. Whittier would eat nothing else, nor speak of anything but their taste and texture, heartiness and suitability for a cold winter night.

Violette and Rosella, sitting on either side of him, seemed to favor Mrs. Baker's stuffed pheasant and oyster pie. Wils, John, and Anne, unaccustomed to sitting at the formal table, were quite in awe of the whole scene and managed to behave themselves with some level of decorum.

"My lord?" Mr. Whittier sounded a bit impatient. "What do you say about the matter?"

James looked past Rosella to her father, and wondered what it was to which he ought to respond.

"Lord Greenlough has discussed the matter of preserving the old buildings in Littleton, with some enthusiasm," Violette said softly. "And I daresay, some mortar as well."

James shot her a look of gratitude, and realized this is what it meant to have a partner in one's life. She would match him, step for step, and catch him when he slipped. And so he steadied himself and launched into a discussion which provided the answers that

Mr. Whittier apparently hoped to hear.

"Then you are likely to spend more time here at Evergreen, my lord?" Mrs. Whittier asked, after a while.

"I should like nothing more," James said. "But I find that I am happy anywhere, as long as I am surrounded by those I most love."

Looking around the table, he realized that not only did he speak the truth, but had managed to satisfy everyone in the room. Even the servants looked rather pleased by his pronouncement, though their lives would be infinitely more peaceful when he left with his entourage. However, the two youngest members of that entourage looked like they might fall asleep and slip down into the food on their plates.

"Shall we retire to the drawing room?" James asked a bit too loudly.

John's head shot up and he opened his eyes. "Will we receive our presents?" the boy asked, fully awake.

James pushed back his chair and stood. "I believe some of the presents might be as impatient as you are, my boy," James said, and avoided Violette's questioning gaze. He signaled his intention to one of the servants.

They soon regrouped and stood in the large room, where the many crystals caught the light off the flames in the fireplace and cast them onto the ceiling and walls. He had spent so many years considering the practical use of glass and lenses, but decided the beauty of their reflections was perhaps of equal value.

"The room is quite lovely, my lord," said Mrs. Whittier, who so rarely commented upon anything without prompting from her husband.

"We have Miss Makepeace to thank for the effect, for she seems to grace any setting in which she finds herself," James said, and felt Violette's hand tighten on his forearm.

Mr. Whittier opened his mouth to say something undoubtedly predictable, when the unmistakable high-pitched bark of a puppy came from the foyer.

"Oh, dear God," Violette murmured and her fingers dug into sleeve. "Please tell me you have not purchased a dog for the children."

"I have done better, three times over," he said proudly. "There is one for each of them."

Mrs. Whittier shrieked and gathered her skirts close around her as three little black and white creatures scampered into the room and were immediately chased by the children. Rosella closed her eyes, as if willing herself to be anywhere but here. Mr. Whittier backed away toward the door, perhaps calculating his escape.

"You will spoil these children," Violette said, with no hint of censure.

James looked down into her face, catching her smile and the glint in her bright eyes.

"We certainly shall," he said, as a nearby chair toppled onto a small boy and dog.

Violette would not have the evening end, fearful she might sleep and then wake to the lonely life that was hers for too many seasons. She sat on a plush tuffet, nursing a cooling cup of chocolate, reflecting on the events of the night.

The children had received several presents, including her own carefully wrapped playthings and warm vests, but nothing could compete with three misbehaving puppies. Mrs. Whittier was happy with a bright pin cushion, and Mr. Whittier with leather gloves. James gave Rosella a book about the fossils of Eastbourne. And both she and Rosella, proving they were more alike than they first imagined, had each knit a scarf for James.

There was much excitement and admiring comments, and more food to follow their Christmas feast. But finally, the Whittiers had retired to the guest rooms, and the children were carried off to the nursery. The puppies, just as exhausted, were brought down to the kitchen. And James waved off the servants, wishing them the joy of the evening.

The great house was silent. Outside, the heavy wet snow had turned to sleet, tapping an insistent rhythm against the windows. The flames had died down, but the coals still flashed heat like rubies revealing themselves against dark stone.

"Did you like your gifts?" James asked.

Violette looked across the room, to where he reclined on a chair, rubbing his forehead. He had slipped off his jacket and his ascot hung limply from his neck. She was merely exhausted, but he looked as if he had just run from Marathon to Athens. Or, at the very least, chased after three puppies that threatened to destroy his drawing room.

"Vi?" he asked.

He never called her that before, but she did not know if he meant it affectionately, or was simply too tired to utter her whole name.

"I am here," she said. "I received a beautiful little box from the Whittiers, painted by Miss Whittier. The children gave me a pretty muff, though I suspect it speaks more of your taste than theirs."

She paused, realizing she had not received anything from him, wondering if the muff was a gift from them all.

"Anne picked it out, though I do not know if she thought it alive or dead. I have my own gift for you, though I did not require the children's help in choosing it."

"We have enough puppies in the house, James," she said wearily.

"That is true. And yet, as must be self-evident, I do enjoy puppies. But I have other interests, and thought you might better appreciate a token of something else about

510

which I feel rather passionate."

It was not so much what he said, as how he said it, that made her senses spark and her curiosity aroused. Violette watched as he reached over the back of the chair, and blindly felt for where his jacket had been carelessly thrown well over an hour ago. He patted the several pockets until he spoke again. "Ah, excellent. I feared it might have dropped, and gone out with the remains of the wrappings."

Whatever he had was surely not very valuable, Violette reflected, as he had not taken much care with it this evening. But then he stood, tightened his cravat and smoothed down his rumpled shirt. And Violette realized that if his offering was not very valuable, it was nevertheless important. She straightened in her own chair and watched as he came toward her, for once looking unsure of himself.

"The box is not anywhere as beautiful as the one you received from the Whittiers, but it has the distinction of bearing the name of a friend of mine, who has taught me many things about the cutting and grinding of crystals." James knelt before her and opened his hand to offer her a plain black box tied with a green ribbon.

"James, I —"

"Open it, please. Say nothing until you see what it is."

The green ribbon was removed in a moment, and Violette's fingernail released the tiny clasp.

She said nothing, though she knew precisely what it was. It was a ring, a large green stone set in gold in its center, surrounded by clusters of tiny red brilliants. She tilted the box one way and then the other, watching the way the light played off the faceted surfaces, reflecting light on the porcelain saucer still in her lap.

"It is not glass, you realize," James said, a bit impatiently.

"Dear James, I realize that even a man of your particular tastes and sense of artistry would not likely present a lady with a ring made of glass stones. I am not an expert of course, but even I am able to recognize an emerald. It is exquisite." She sighed, overwhelmed by its beauty. "As are these lovely little garnets."

"Rubies," he said under his breath as he took the box from her hand and removed the ring. Once released from the bed of velvet, its reflected light glanced off the ceiling and wall. But then the fire was once again subdued when he slipped the ring on her finger and the light was for her alone.

"But why?" Violette asked, looking at him, at the warmth in his dark and unusual eyes, at a small muscle twitching in the corner of his mouth.

He started to rise, and pulled her up with him. "I should think the answer to that is obvious," he said.

Without warning, he suddenly lifted her up into his arms, and sat down on the chair she only just vacated. It was suddenly warmer, and infinitely more comfortable. Violette settled back against his chest, and trifled with his ascot. Really, if this was his intent, he ought not have bothered to straighten it before approaching her. He should know better, where she was concerned.

"I love you and want to marry you," he said.

Violette abandoned his ascot. "This is your proposal, then?" she asked, lightly, teasingly. And yet, she felt just the slightest bit of disappointment that he did not present a formal declaration, as the authors of romance — and her own poor sister — had led her to expect.

He laughed, which did not make her feel much better about it.

"I would say that we have already betrothed ourselves by word and deed throughout the days of Advent, heralding the wonder of this very night. But given the circumstances of our coming together, and the sadness of our loss, we must delay any announcement of our own joy. So let us not say this is a betrothal ring, but rather, this is a Christmas Eve promise: when time and the dictates of propriety permit, you shall have your formal proposal, Miss Makepeace. And if I somehow neglect to deliver, you have my permission to flash your bright emerald and ruby bauble into my eyes, and remind me of what I promised on this evening of the twenty fourth of December. Though by now, it must be the twenty fifth, and Christmas Day."

"And I have only given you a scarf, not nearly as evenly stitched as the one you received from Miss Whittier."

"You, my dear, wonderful Violette, have given me everything, including those things for which I never dared hope. It is difficult to rejoice in all that has come to me in the past month, when our double loss has been so great, but I have never felt more settled and satisfied in my life. Neither my words, nor that glittery ring, can express what I feel tonight."

"It is the same for me, James," Violette sighed and her fingers returned to the business of his troublesome ascot. He pulled her closer, which made her task more difficult, but brought her mouth to his jawbone, where her lips tasted the rough texture of his skin. Her hand dropped to his shirt, where she was just able to slip her fingers through a gap between the buttons, and warm her fingers against the smooth muscles of his chest.

The storm raged outside and in, but Violette knew she was safe and at home, at last.

James heard the insistent drumbeat of the

regimental band, and wondered what brought the King's army to Evergreen and why on Christmas Day? Then someone punched him on the chin, knocking his teeth together, and he opened his eyes to meet the attack.

Violette, still seated snugly on his lap, was rubbing the top of her head and scowling up at him. The fire had nearly burned itself out in the grate. The room looked very much the same as it did when he had finally closed his eyes in the early hours of the morning, strewn with paper and ribbon, and decorated with fresh green boughs sagging slightly under the weight of his large glass crystals.

The drums, now recognizable as banging on the door, continued.

"Someone must be locked out of the house," Violette murmured. Her loosened hair toppled to her shoulders as she pushed herself away from him.

The banging stopped, replaced by shouts and cries. It did not sound like the return to the house of someone who had to spend the night in the stables or in the orangerie. James was torn between setting Violette aside while he protected his property, and holding her tighter, protecting her.

"There must have been an accident on the road. Or one of the tenants has an urgent need," he said. He pulled her close.

The cries in the hall grew closer, and one deep, resonant voice — so similar to his own

— was suddenly at the door.

The great oak panel was thrust open, and people spilled into the parlor like water over a sluice gate. James blinked and shook his head, certain he still lived within his Christmas morning dream. But the scene before him was real enough. He started to rise, forgetting that Violette remained on his lap, and then fell back into their chair.

"Why, what is this?" Wilson said, gleefully. "Have you no strength to rise and greet your only brother?"

"Violette? What one earth are you doing? What is this about?" Olivia Hanford said, at precisely the same moment.

Two brothers and two sisters stared at each other with equal parts of disbelief, during which time the servants silently retreated from the room.

Violette was the first to find her voice. She slipped off his lap, and made an obligatory if useless gesture of tucking up her loosened curls. She stood in front of him, partially blocking his view. "Olivia!" she cried.

Her older sister started to unfasten her woolen jacket, though her eyes never left Violette's face. "What is this about? We have come to Evergreen to be with our family, just as we promised. We have endured storms and illness and the rolling waves of the fierce Atlantic to be with you and our children."

"We went first to Curzon Street, where the

servants told us that the two of you packed up the household to come to Evergreen," Wilson continued. "Instead of sending a courier out into this storm, we decided to risk it ourselves and made haste for Kent. I barely stopped to shave," he added, rubbing his jaw.

James mimicked his action, though his jaw was still smarting from its impact with Violette's head.

"We were told you were dead," he said, at last, the awful words sticking in his throat. They were tripping through something like conversation, when the only thing that mattered was that they had thought Olivia and Wilson drowned at sea and now, here they were, very much alive. He walked toward his brother. "Mrs. Hamilton, of Nevis, wrote to inform us that you were lost at sea."

"I fear she was very much mistaken," Olivia said in a very small voice.

Violette squeaked and hiccoughed and ran past him into her sister's arms. James just had time to notice this, when Wilson grabbed him and started pounding him on the back. His brother smelled of salt and snow, of pineapple and pine.

"We thought you were dead," Violette sobbed. "She told us you were dead."

"We did not tell the children, so they would have one more joyous Christmas. It was Violette's plan," James admitted, realizing he sounded like a dunce. "We planned to raise them, of course."

"Of course," Wilson said. "But are you not delighted to be free of that obligation?"

"Oh, yes." Violette said and then contradicted herself. "No, not at all. That is, nothing is more wonderful than that you are alive and well. But we love the children and would have had them with us always. Truly, though, it may be our lot, in any case. You may wish to return to the Caribbean without them when you learn that your brother has given them each a puppy."

"Wilson, let us leave at once," Olivia said, "before anyone remarks on our presence."

"Not yet," said her husband, laughing. And then they changed partners, so each hugged an in-law and agreed that this was the most extraordinary Christmas ever.

Many hours later, after warm baths were drawn and the children were awakened by their parents, and the Whittiers made their way downstairs to eat breakfast, and the puppies tracked melting snow through the marble foyer, and Wils slipped on a puddle and was comforted by his parents, the exhausted Makepeace sisters and the equally tired Hanford brothers finally settled down to a recapitulation of all that occurred in the time they were apart.

"We thought you were drowned at sea," Violette said for the hundredth time. "Mrs.

Hamilton was most clear on the matter."

"Mrs. Hamilton is a lady with somewhat disreputable connections, who is always looking for some reason to stir up excitement. Ever since her hotheaded nephew died ten years ago or so, she has been the most infamous of all of the Nevis gossipmongers. Her nephew, by the by, was someone who mattered in the Colonial government in New York, but got himself killed in some foolish duel," Olivia said firmly. "As for our story, there was a small fire on board ship soon after we set out and some things had to be thrown overboard. Mrs. Hamilton must have found my charred handkerchief box and drew her own conclusions."

"But we will not be too harsh on her because we will soon be neighbors," Wilson said pointedly. "Olivia and I have found a lovely property, with good water and fertile soil. The children will enjoy the monkeys."

"Monkeys! I did not realize they lived in the Americas. Are they anything like the apes in Gibraltar?" James asked.

"No, these are little fellows, gray in color. They apparently like the climate there as well as we do." Wilson said.

"When do you plan to take possession of the property?" Violette asked, clearing her throat. Now that her sister was home, she did not want her to ever return to Nevis.

"We already have, but will wait to return

for the good weather," Olivia said. "There is much to be said for the climate and lush foliage, but we truly prefer the social climate of London. We intend to cross the Atlantic several times each year, with or without the children, and hope you will visit us there as well. I expect we will not return until after the hurricane season."

Violette could not be happier knowing she and James would continue to be a part of their nephews' and niece's life.

She cleared her throat. "The puppies will have grown a bit by then, and I daresay they will protect your bananas and mangoes by chasing the gray monkeys off the property."

They all laughed and somewhere in the house a dog barked. Violette, acting as hostess, poured them all fresh cups of coffee and passed around the silver tray still laden with small pastries. They sat companionably in silence for some minutes.

"And what have the two of you been up to?" Wilson asked, his voice slicing through the still air.

Violette studied her cream puff, wondering how Mrs. Baker had managed to get the soft confection into its little shell. It was a most intriguing little problem, but not one that was likely to provide an excuse for conversation for more than a few moments.

"Why do you think we have been up to something?" James asked, saving her the trouble of doing so. "We have been entertaining your delightful children, packing up an army of servants to make this Christmas trip to Evergreen, teaching the next generation of Hanfords how to skate, and allowing them to decorate the halls with greenery and prisms."

"Ah yes, I noticed," Wilson said. "You have scarcely allowed me to touch your precious crystals in all these years, so I am rather amazed that my children, who can barely make it through a room without incident, are entrusted to dangle them from the ceilings."

"If nothing else, these past weeks have taught me to treasure the things that truly matter," said James quietly.

"I suppose that is why my sister appears to be wearing several of them on her finger," Olivia pointed out.

Violette knew her ring would not go unnoticed, and she suspected Olivia had noticed it the every moment they burst into the room last night. She could never hide anything from her sister.

"My ring is not made of glass," she said softly.

"Of what is it made?" Olivia asked, acting the innocent.

"It is made of promises that are now likely to be kept sooner than anticipated," James answered. "I suppose I am in the strange position of asking my younger brother for permission to marry his sister-in-law, for Wilson appears to be the head of her family."

"I shall have to consider your prospects, Lord Greenlough," Wilson said thoughtfully.

"But he will not consider them for long, for we have been ever hopeful that such a thing would happen," Olivia rushed on.

"Whatever do you mean, Olivia?" Violette said, frowning. "James and I have hardly said a word to each other in all these years. When he showed up at my house weeks ago, with his wretched news, I could not imagine what he could possibly want with me."

"But hope has nothing to do with the way things really are. We perceive the truth of some situation but then go on, against all odds, to imagine circumstances might be otherwise, as we wish them to be," Olivia answered, philosophically. "You see, I have had many hours to think of these things while crossing the Atlantic."

Violette frowned. "You are making me feel quite guilty. I should have had hope all these weeks that Mrs. Hamilton would be proved wrong, that you would be returned to us. James had the right of it, from the very start, because he told me we should wait for definitive proof. But still, it was impossible to erase that keen sense of despair from everything we did."

"When we broke in on you, last night, you seemed to have found some consolation," Olivia said, laughing.

Violette blushed, thinking they must have drawn some obvious conclusions. And she was grateful that, at least, she was fully dressed when they arrived.

"We have found more than consolation," James broke in, saving her once again. "But if you are about to tell us that you concocted this scheme to bring the two of us together . . ."

"Never, James!" Wilson protested. "How can you even think we would be so cruel? Or so Shakespearean, for that matter. For, indeed, the plot elements are all there. A shipwreck, misinformation, brothers and sisters, the Christmas season. By the way, have you already received the folio from Coimbra that you so much desired? Perhaps we shall consult the text of *Twelfth Night?*"

"Violette has brought her own copy along with her to Evergreen, as I recall. Though I doubted she anticipated we would be acting some parts in the flesh. For now, let us just say that *All's Well That Ends Well.*"

EPILOGUE

But even on that wonderful night, in the season of light and love, Violette knew that it was not an ending but a beginning that would be reckoned so well. The family — for they were truly one large family now — spent the snowy days of Christmas in a whirlwind of planning: the eventual journey back to the Caribbean, the children's education, the outfitting of a large manor house, clothing to be ordered, a wedding.

By June, all this was memory, and precious enough to last a lifetime. Her marriage to James, a simple ceremony in the small stone church in Littleton, was attended by all those they held dear, and a good many others besides. In the Christmas season, Evergreen had seemed aptly named for the conifers that surrounded the great house, evidence of life when all else on the landscape was dead. But now, Violette reflected that the name suggested the perpetuity of life, rebirth, and regeneration.

Even without the advantage of endless hours onboard ship, she had become as philosophical as her sister.

"I thought we might journey to the Caribbean in late winter," said her husband, looking up from his examination of a recently-delivered codex. "The winds are calmer then, and the heat is not yet oppressive. Wilson has purchased a small boat and I thought I would teach you to sail, if my poor eyes can endure the sun on those blue waters."

Violette looked into those eyes, which looked perfectly wonderful to her, but said nothing.

James frowned. "I have not yet taken you on a wedding journey. We could go to Italy, of course. And I believe I once promised you a visit to Portugal, to Coimbra. But would you not prefer to see your sister's new house? And the children, of course."

"And your dear brother's fruit groves," Violette reminded him.

"Yes, yes, and even the dogs and the monkeys, if any have survived the onslaught of little Hanfords," James said impatiently. "Why do you hesitate?"

"It has to do with the matter of little Hanfords," Violette said. "Or, at least, one in particular."

"If you are speaking of Wils going away to school . . . oh!"

" 'Oh,' indeed, Lord Greenlough," said Violette, and smiled.

"Oh," James repeated, but the single syllable was somehow replete with joy. "Were you not planning to tell me, Lady Greenlough?"

"I thought you would notice, in time. And I wanted to be very sure before saying anything. Even when a slight suspicion became hope, I dared not imagine that what I most wanted could possibly be true."

James abandoned his book and rose from his seat, coming around the table to pull her into his arms. One hand dropped, hesitantly, to the folds of her gown, which might have effectively disguised a carpetbag, let alone a tiny growing baby.

"And yet we have learned that such things could happen," he said.

"My love, we have learned that such things do happen," Violette said, and kissed her husband, deciding that enough had been said on the subject.

DEDICATION
(*IN THE SEASON OF LIGHT AND LOVE*)
To welcome Leah Beverly Valenzuela
With Much Love
And with Blessings for every Season
Of your life
To be one of
Light and Hope.

A Season for Giving

by Shereen Vedam

Chapter One

December 20, 1812, London, England

Christopher de Wynter skimmed his hand across the page as he wrote down the time, date, location, and purpose behind this final experiment. Flickering candlelight from three lit candles accented his perfectly-written script. His mama used to say his writing was a work of art. It was in Christopher's nature to be precise, a useful trait for his work with volatile mixtures.

And important work it was. He designed trigger mechanisms for guns that soldiers in combat could use in a dependable and safe manner. He had recently been inspired to use a small canister linked to a braided rope-type fuse in place of the less reliable fuses made of straws or quills filled with black powder. He hoped that one change would greatly reduce the hazard of accidental explosions.

With the war still raging, the navy had gone to great lengths to ensure Christopher's work was kept top secret. If successful, his new fuse could hasten the end of the war and save numerous lives. Still, such an invention was best kept out of the hands of the enemy. Only his family and his naval commander, Sir Trigg, were privy to his work.

Christopher had been given permission to use the Royal Arsenal's laboratory in Woolwich to work on his theories. Its location, on the outskirts of London, was far from his family home in Mayfair, so on those nights when he worked late, he stayed in the barracks nearby.

While there, he still took pains to ensure his most dangerous work was conducted only when no one else was likely to be nearby. He scheduled his tests when his colleagues had left for the evening or were at church on Sunday when the adjacent offices were certain to be empty.

Despite painstaking precautions and triple checks of his routines, occasional unexpected explosions did occur, and they were hard to keep quiet. Come daybreak, neighbors nearby were known to complain about the loud blasts at night and charred debris spewed on the streets. Those annoyances were tiny compared to the stir that would be caused if such disruptions were to happen in his laboratory at his home in Mayfair, where the ton of London, with strong connections to members of Parliament, resided.

As for his own safety, Christopher, with an

insatiable thirst for knowledge and a predisposition for working with chemicals, had spent the last couple of years surviving the dangers of his chosen profession. It helped that he had a special family talent that enabled him to escape an imminent blast. An unusual inheritance passed down over many generations had kept him out of harm's way.

The story went that one of his ancestors, a Spanish gypsy, had been a tightrope dancer in a circus until, in retaliation for a perceived wrong, a witch had cast a curse that clashed with the gypsies' protection spell. Christopher was unclear about the specifics and uncertain if he even believed in such far-fetched tales, but all direct de Wynter descendants could race like a gazelle, scale walls as nimbly as a squirrel climbed trees, and leap like a startled Yorkshire hare. On occasion, a de Wynter was known to even defy gravity and rise straight up in the air.

Whatever the source of his uncommon talent, Christopher's ability to clamber over barricades and race along long corridors in a blink had kept him alive on more than one occasion. His talent had also helped him to stay true to his single-minded goal to create a safer explosive fuse. Now he was on the brink of victory. His new fuse, once proven successful, might save countless lives, perhaps even his brother's.

Post Captain Everett de Wynter was home

to heal after a firing accident during a gun battle aboard his vessel. But too soon, he would be well enough to return to the fray. Christopher's invention would hopefully reduce the chance of his brother being involved in another such accident. If his new fuse worked as designed, Sir Trigg planned to have it installed on all British ships' guns, land cannons, and howitzers. The ultimate result: this endless war against Napoleon might end in British victory.

"I am about to make you proud, Mama," he whispered into the shadowed room. If only she could have been alive to witness his success. He shook off his sorrow and focused. He could ill afford distractions today.

Yesterday, Christopher had checked every detail until he was satisfied all was ready for a preliminary test today with gunpowder. He had set up his experiment with enough explosive mixture to guarantee to Sir Trigg on Monday morning that his new fuse would not fizzle out before it reached detonation point. So many current fuses did fail, which endangered sailors who patriotically inched closer to fix the problem, hoping to turn the course of a battle. Since sleep eluded him, Christopher had returned to carry out the test. The early start meant he could enjoy his moment of triumph in private.

He rested his pencil on the open pages of his book. Time to light the fuse. He dug into his pocket for the flint and his fingers brushed against a flat, sharp-edged object. Christopher took out the hand-sized bone fragment and looked at it in momentary confusion. *What was this?*

Then he remembered his conversation with his father the previous day. The old man had been droning on about two fossil pieces a friend had lent him to verify authenticity. His father, in turn, had asked Christopher to have a scientific colleague who was an expert on bones test the samples to see if they were truly from an ancient crocodile skull, or was, more likely, a recently deceased animal's remains.

Christopher had accepted both pieces, but later reconsidered the wisdom of that action. Safer to separate the two in case one became lost or misplaced. Yesterday, he left one fossil in a drawer here for retrieval on Monday, but held on to the second piece, which he intended to leave at his other workroom in his father's Mayfair home. Mystery solved, he shoved the fossil back into his inside pocket and retrieved his flint.

Excitement built as he leaned toward the curved cylinder housing the gunpowder, focusing on the four inch wick. He had measured it yesterday to ensure it was the right size so he could record the speed of burn. As soon as the wick sparked, he retreated, dragging his book to the long workbench's far edge. Despite the use of gunpowder, the explosion would be mild since he only used a tiny quantity. No more than a loud "pop." He doubted anyone sleeping in the nearby barracks would even hear it. Pencil poised to note every step, he checked his timepiece; the fuse had burnt half way to the canister, on schedule. A sparkle of black powder on the lid caught his eye.

Christopher gulped in shock as that discrepancy registered. He had wiped the lid clean before he had left last night. He hurried over to open the casing's cover and check on the gunpowder. The lid refused to budge. In fact, he could not move the canister at all. It was as if someone had sealed the cover shut and nailed the canister to the table. And the only reason for that would be if the canister had been packed with gunpowder. Obviously, someone did not want this death trap disturbed. The fuse continued to burn.

Christopher looked around for scissors to cut the burning fuse. He slammed his hand against the empty worktop where they should have rested. In shock, he jerked back and hit the scales where he measured his gunpowder. The bronze plates swung wildly and sent candlelit shadows gyrating. Where the metal disks struck the central stand, an alarm sounded, disturbing the quiet night with a discordant clanging.

Heart thudding in terror, he rifled through

his limited options. To escape, he would have to race upstairs and out the landing. He checked his timepiece. Ten seconds to impact — an impossibly short time for a normal human to cross such a distance. But Christopher was no ordinary human.

One. He raced for the door. The empty rooms nearby meant there would be no other casualties if the fuse reached that canister faster than he expected. *Impossible.* It was designed to burn at a set rate.

Two. Pulse pounding, he broke through into the nearby stairwell, his talent sparking along his arms and legs, indicating his body was ready for action. Energy flared through his muscles as he bypassed the stairs and leaped straight up into the air.

Four. In one smooth motion, he landed twenty feet up one wall and clung to the vertical surface before he leapfrogged to the opposite side a further twenty feet up.

Six. He bounced off the wall as questions and second-guesses mimicked his zigzag motion. *Who could have gained access to my workshop? Why did I not re-check that test canister before lighting the fuse? Next time, I must include a quick disarm switch to that set up.*

Eight. He blasted through a door and rolled across the concrete surface. The chilly, winter night was silent.

Ten. The building behind him exploded. He was racing off the landing, his ears ringing, when the door flew off its hinges and walloped him across the backside.

For the second time that night, he sailed through the air, this time involuntarily, and over a steep staircase. Ignoring his throbbing back, he stretched out his arms to establish balance. About to twist in midair so he would land safely on his feet, he spotted the night guard standing below him, over by the street lamp.

Alger. What rotten luck! The elderly gunner, whose noticeable lisp normally made Christopher smile, was out on patrol. He was watching Christopher's impromptu journey with open-mouthed astonishment, a whistle held in his raised hand.

There was no choice now but to make his landing seem natural. He swallowed a curse and crashed onto the unforgiving stone staircase. With a painful thump, he rolled over the last few steps and came to an ungraceful, jarring halt on the snow-covered pavement by Gunner Alger's boots.

The old, slightly bent gunner from the Royal Artillery Invalid Battalion assigned to guard this facility shut his mouth, stood to attention and saluted. "Morning, sir!" After a beat of silence, he added with a lisp, "Been working late again, have we, Mr. Christopher?"

Far from amused, Christopher was about to hotly deny that the blast was his fault, at least, this time. Then he reconsidered. Whoever had instigated that explosion might be watching. He wanted the culprit to be disappointed at his failure to kill him but not so alarmed he would flee London. So with his silence, Christopher accepted blame for this "accident," but his fists clenched. When he discovered who was behind this sabotage, he would make them pay for the aches and pains his body was currently complaining about. A quick check showed no one nearby. The area was deserted.

When he attempted to rise, his left ankle protested. He cringed and, swallowing his pride, allowed Alger to assist him up. Once on his feet, he took silent stock: tender ribs, sore back, stinging left ankle, and blood trickling from a cut on his chin, which would likely ruin his cravat if that crisp confection had not already been crushed and covered in dirt from his inglorious fall. His jacket and breeches, too, looked fit for the dustbin. His valet would be displeased.

"I gave the alarm soon as I heard the 'boom,' sir. 'Elp should be coming."

Christopher nodded and shifted sideways. He instantly regretted the movement. And something rattled in his pocket. *The fossil!* He cringed at the damage he must have done to that bone and tentatively stuck his hand in to check. Several jagged pieces pricked his fingers. Instead of one, there were now three, no, four smaller pieces. More powdered bits littered the bottom of his pocket. He shook his head. The fossil had survived hundreds of years . . . until he laid hands on it. And the other piece in his lab was most likely destroyed. His father would be furious.

Watching him with concern, Alger pointed toward the barracks where men ran out. "Here come the boys."

Shouts went up to form a bucket line, and to grab blankets to smother spot fires.

"Never fear, sir," Alger said, "we shall have your workshop all cleaned up in no time." He observed the smoke billowing out windows and the broken door splayed half over the top of the stairs. With forced cheerfulness, he added, "Should be able to have you back to work in under a month."

A month? Broken fossil forgotten, Christopher surveyed the damage and groaned. That explosion had destroyed his prototype so he would need to begin work on a new one immediately if he hoped to have it ready in time to be fitted on his brother's ship before Everett returned to sea. He could not afford to simply lie about for a whole month.

I need another place to work.

The only one that came to mind would bring this danger into the heart of his family — his father's home in Mayfair.

Sailors ran past them to the building and a bucket line formed to the nearest well.

Christopher limped out of the way, watching as men ran by him.

Scrutinizing the activity, Alger said in a conversational tone, "So what are your plans for Christmastide then, sir?"

That seemed an incongruous question. *Unless* . . . "Alger, what day is today?"

A beat of silence followed his request, and then with a bland countenance, the tactful gunner said. "Sunday, sir. Five days afore Christmas Eve."

Less than a week before Christmas? He had written the date earlier in his notebook and yet not twigged to the number's significance. He took a deep breath and the crisp air stank as if a hundred chimney sweeps had all started working at the same time. Of course, it was Sunday. That was why he had put the second fossil in his pocket, because when he returned home today, he had meant to leave the fragment there for safekeeping. The broken pieces in his pocket mocked that plan.

Well, there was no point lingering here. He was in no shape to help, so he might as well get on with his day. After this setback, he had a great deal to accomplish. But first, he had to visit his father. His family's Sunday breakfasts were sacrosanct — a tradition instituted by his late mother, and fastidiously maintained by his father. The dark horizon stirred hope that if he hurried, he might make it in time for breakfast and avoid a lecture on tardiness. *How much time do I have?* He pulled out his watch from his waist pocket. The glass front was shattered and the casing fell apart with a metallic clatter in his palm.

Before he could ask, Alger pulled out his own watch. "Nine minutes to the hour." At Christopher's blank look, Alger patiently elaborated. "Afore six in the morning, sir."

Six? Already? The snow clouds blanketing the sky made it seem closer to midnight than daybreak. At mid-winter, sunrise was a couple of hours away, but his papa was an early riser. Sunday breakfasts at his table were always at seven thirty sharp. And this close to Christmas, his father would expect his three sons to accompany him to church afterward. There was something else about this year's Christmas he was supposed to remember, but the detail eluded him.

The more pressing matter now, was how to get from here to Mayfair in a little over an hour. He needed time to change into appropriate church attire before presenting himself at his father's breakfast parlor. He despondently straightened his wet, wrinkled jacket. "Alger, have the warrant officer inform Sir Trigg that I will give a full briefing on the morrow about what happened here tonight. Oh, and" — he gestured at the smoking building — "kindly add my apology."

He gave the guard an absent pat on the back and, in the guise of seeking out a hackney, painfully limped through the snow toward a main street. In truth, a public vehicle would not be fast enough to get him home in time for breakfast. Better to rely on his talent. It was a risky proposition, since anyone out and about this night might see him, but this was an emergency. His father insisted on punctuality. Since it was still an hour before daybreak, he hoped that most Londoners were still abed under their warm covers and would not notice a dark shadow leaping over their rooftops.

Once out of Alger's line of sight, and ignoring his aching leg, Christopher broke into a lopsided sprint down the lane.

Ahead, a man pushed open a window shutter and leaned out. "Lad! What was that blast?"

"I heard nothing," Christopher said. "You must have been dreaming."

"Why are you limping then?" The gent hugged himself in his nightshirt as a cold wind fluttered his white nightcap. "Was it them navy blokes messing about again? If they hurt you, you can complain to the magistrate. Even if we are at war, we have rights. They cannot go about blowing people up every night."

"I tripped on the ice."

"Papa, who are you shouting at?" a young

boy asked, squeezing next to his father at the window. He seemed as scrawny as his father and Christopher wondered if either of them had eaten more than one meal today.

"Nothing for you to worry about, Thomas. Apparently, I dreamt about a bomb going off," the man said, though he gave Christopher a look laced with skepticism. "Go back to sleep." After shooing the boy away, he said, "Well, be careful on these icy streets, lad."

Christopher nodded and hurried on, shrugging aside his concern for the pair's welfare. His mother would have said attending to those who were less fortunate was everyone's concern. That reminder jogged his memory about what was special this coming Christmas.

Their vicar had arranged a Christmas play. In addition to collecting food baskets or old clothes, the vicar had requested the church's wealthier patrons to bring something the parish's poorer members could not afford to purchase in the normal course of their lives. Along with the three wise men's gifts, the offerings would ostensibly be laid before baby Jesus. The next day, however, the vicar and his helpers planned to leave the presents on the doorsteps of the parish's most disadvantaged families.

Now with a saboteur on his trail and an experiment to recreate, there was no time for shopping. Releasing a sigh laden with regrets, he slipped into a dark alleyway. Using his talent to travel swiftly was the only way he would make it to breakfast. And time was a commodity he could no longer waste. But there was an added advantage to traveling by rooftop.

A particularly wonderful windfall of the de Wynter "curse" was that whenever he used it, he grew stronger and faster, bones mended and wounds healed. With each leap, his abused body would become whole again.

He called on his talent, and his fingertips and toes instantly tingled. In one leap, he reached the third story building's midpoint and clung to its side. His next jump took him to the rooftop. He crouched over the slate tiles and observed the vast city. The night was quiet and dark. Nothing moved except for a few stray cats chasing scurrying mice. Out on the river, ships and boats were at rest in berths.

Chimney smoke rose like signal fires and led him onward. With each jump, his ankle healed, his sore ribs quieted their complaints, and his body thrummed with revived energy. He kept the Thames River to his right until he reached Westminster Bridge. Wrinkling his nose at the stench of the river, he then raced across the bridge before resuming his rooftop leaps.

Once again back high above the city, he sailed over buildings. The journey gave him time to consider why someone might have sabotaged his work. Had news that he was close to a revolutionary new discovery somehow leaked out? If so, a French spy might be behind this villainy.

Christopher's labored breaths added white puffs to the rising morning mist and chimney smoke. By the time he arrived at Grosvenor Square, he was out of breath and famished.

It was time to break the news to his papa that he would have to bring his work home in order to finish on time. But doing so would put the whole family in danger if the saboteur struck again before Christopher caught up to him.

CHAPTER TWO

It was too early in the morning to deal with this! Honoria trailed her *horrid* younger brother, the Honorable Mr. Henry Gilbert, second eldest son of Viscount Locke, around the breakfast table as he waved her private letter to God. She had tucked it under her pillow, so her brother must have gone into her room and rifled through her bed to find it.

"Dear Lord, please find me a gentleman who is just right for me," he read, holding the page above her reach.

What could they have fed him this year at Eton that he had grown so tall? She could not even reach his ears for a good tweak. Honoria, or "Honey" as her papa called her in trying moments, was not feeling the least bit sweet toward her pilfering younger brother.

Honoria had never been able to control her Henry, although she had tried. As a result, he had become a tormenting horror that her parents refused to punish no matter how fervently she insisted that penance was essential to build solid character in a young lad. And the Christmas holidays had only made him worse.

She held out an imperious hand. "Give me that letter this instant, sir!"

"He must be fleet of foot," Horrid Henry read on as he skirted around the breakfast table, eluding her grasp.

"What does 'fleet of foot' mean?" Henry asked his older brother, William.

Honoria's cheeks flamed.

"It means he should be swift enough to keep up during a dance tune," William, her father's heir and Honoria's junior by a year, said, taking a mouthful of crumpet.

"Do not speak while you chew, William," their mama said. "And being good at dancing is a necessary ability for any gentleman to possess. Sound request, Honoria. However, as remarkable as that letter sounds, what I wish to hear from each of you is a suggestion on what we should take to church on Christmas morn. I thought a doll house might suit. I saw a pretty one at a shop on Bond Street last week."

"Chadwick's wife is rumored to bring one of those," her husband said from behind his newspaper, and then added, "Ladies do not like it when men step on their toes, Henry."

"Adequate dancing is a sign of a man's agility," Honoria said past clenched teeth. Though that was not why she had included the wish to her list of requirements for a proper suitor. She had added "fleet of foot" because she wanted a man like the one she had seen leaping with such grace over London's rooftops early this morning.

Of course, that must have been a dream. No man could ford such vast spaces as she had seen the man in black manage, especially on slippery rooftops. But, if she brought up what she thought she saw in front of her two brothers, she would never hear the end of it. However, the sight, vision, dream, whatever it was, had left an indelible impression on Honoria. Enough to make her squeeze that late request near the top of her full-page letter filled front to back.

She had tucked her missive under her pillow, and then, while still in her nightgown, she had raced upstairs to her attic studio to draw her man in black while he was still fresh in her memory. After lighting several candles, she had spent two glorious hours at her easel sketching that figure. His movements had spoken of ultimate freedom, of someone who lived life without a care, no responsibilities, no encumbrances, nothing to weigh him down. He did what he wanted, whenever he pleased. Without any annoying brothers to gainsay him. Even gravity bowed to his command.

Once finished, she locked her studio door. She had wanted to ensure a maid did not stumble across her scandalous interpretation of a man with a stunning physique in fluid motion.

Now that pilfering Henry was home until after the twelve days of Christmastide were over, she was doubly glad she had locked away her sketch from prying eyes. But she must retrieve that list before he reached the most embarrassing part!

Her papa put aside his newspaper and addressed his cooling breakfast. "It is good to make a proper list, Honey. Wise to be clear about what you want."

"But what are we to take to church for the play?" her mother asked. "That is the list that concerns me."

"Sometimes you are too particular." William frowned with concern at Honoria. "Fellows do not like to be found wanting. Else you may find yourself without a suitor next Season, too."

"I had plenty of suitors!" Honoria said in hot denial.

"None who came to heel by Season's end." Will's tone was adamant. "Burn your list. How about a ship in a bottle, Mama?"

"Chadwicks have ships in bottles covered," her papa said.

"Locke, do not be difficult." Her mama's face was flushed. "At this rate, we will attend church on Wednesday empty-handed."

Honoria crossed her arms and pressed her lips tight. Her brother had made an unarguable point — while four of her friends already planned their marriages, no one had offered for her. But her suitors had been so dull that she had not encouraged any. "I have grown more mature this autumn."

"Aged," William said, with aplomb.

"Wiser!" That, too, stung, for two months ago, she had turned nineteen. She was almost on the shelf!

"Please Lord, let him be taller than I, but not so tall that he resembles a lamppost." Horrid Henry's mimicry was so uncanny, Honoria's face burned. But the careless lad had stepped too close to William, who snatched the letter from the young scamp's grasp and handed it to her.

"Oh, thank you, Will!" Honoria hugged him as sweet relief coursed through her. Thankfully, Will had saved the letter before Henry reached the part where she mentioned that she wanted a suitor who was pleasing to look at, but not too studious about his appearance.

Men who were overly concerned with their looks tended to find a style they deemed smart and then followed it religiously, resulting in the dandy set who looked so similar, it was hard to distinguish one from the other. Then there were those who showed little interest in perfecting their attire. They tended to sport garish waistcoats that attracted too much attention. She wanted a man who dressed discretely but exhibited exquisite taste.

She sauntered triumphantly past Henry and, once seated, folded the note and tucked the page close to her bosom inside her gown. *Let the toad try to get it now.*

"All of you hurry up and finish your breakfasts or we shall be late for Sunday service," her mama said. "And while there, I hope everyone prays for an idea of what we can bring with us to the play."

"Why must we go to the early service?" Henry asked. "The pavements are probably still icy."

"Once we return, we have a great deal to accomplish for our ball tonight," his mama said.

"Could we not postpone church then, Mama, so you do not tax yourself?" William asked in a suspiciously solicitous tone.

"To my recollection," his mama said in a disapproving tone, "most of us have missed services the whole year through. *Today,* on this fourth Sunday of Advent, we will *all* be present. And Henry, wear your purple vest to represent your penitence. And take this rare opportunity to be in God's presence to beg His forgiveness for your transgression toward your sister."

"He will be more forgiving than I." Honoria glared at Henry, silently promising retribution.

Laughing with unconcern, he slumped into his seat across the table. "I shall make amends to Honoria by seeking out a *pleasing-looking fellow* to lead her onto the dance floor. One who is not too concerned with his looks but still cares."

She instinctively kicked out and struck his shin so hard he cried out, while her toes thrummed with pain. Her big toe complained as if she had broken the thing. She cursed herself for her vile temper and worried she might not be able to dance at all now. Fighting back angry tears, she nibbled on her cold buttered toast and wondered if William was right.

Should I burn my list? She could trim it. In fact, she was ready to strike out every requirement but one. *Fleet of foot. Oh, I would love a chance to race across London's rooftops in my man in black's arms.* Her throbbing toe called her a daydreaming fool. She did not care. She wanted to fine-tune her sketch, but there was no time. After church, her mama would conscript her to decorate the house with holly and other greenery for the ball.

Her drawing did not show any facial features. The man had been too far away and the sky too dark for her to see him clearly. All she had gleaned was an outline of his body. *But what a body!* Tall, lean and muscular. Honoria toyed with her eggs. *What would it be like to be held in his arms for a dance?* The image stirred a shiver of excitement. That was the type of man she wanted, and no words conveyed it more succinctly than "fleet of foot."

All of a sudden, she was anxious to go to church, for it would be nothing short of a miracle if she were to find a man that stirred her as had the one who had leapt across London's rooftops this morning.

"A winter ball?" Christopher said with utter dismay. "Tonight? Papa, I have no time for such frivolities."

"Make time," his father said in an adamant tone.

His father was still in a foul mood after being informed about the explosion. Even though Christopher said he had not been harmed, he could tell his father had been shaken. Very few people were aware of Christopher's connection to the navy engineers because his father and Sir Trigg had gone to great lengths to ensure Christopher's association remained hidden. As far as most people were concerned, Christopher de Wynter was no more than a navy clerk.

While he ate, Christopher reviewed his list of colleagues, considering the most likely suspects. A stranger would not have been able to get past Alger's vigilant watch. So the culprit was most likely someone who worked there.

He crossed off those he was absolutely certain would never harm him. In the end, he was left with four viable suspects. One, in particular, troubled him. *Allen.* The man's mother was French. And dead. But that family connection might have influenced his actions. It was worth taking a closer look.

Monday, he had a meeting scheduled with Sir Trigg and could ask him to hire a Bow Street runner to investigate Allen's whereabouts Saturday night, while Christopher interviewed the other three men whose names were left uncrossed on his list. He also wanted to return to his ruined laboratory to check for clues that might point him in the right direction.

His pencil snapped in two.

From across the table, Nicholas, Christopher's eldest brother, gave him a worried glance. With a heavy sigh, Christopher dropped the broken piece still in his clenched fist and lifted his cup of hot chocolate. It was empty. Unfortunately, there were no footmen in the room to refill it. This lack of service was a standard rule for Sunday breakfasts, so father and sons could speak in absolute privacy. No servant would enter this room until all four had left it.

He strode over to the sideboard to refill his cup. He had even less time to socialize now, which suited him fine since he found most of his society's entertainments overrated. And he had more serious things to ponder. Aside from the mystery of who had interfered with his equipment, he had to tell his father that his fossil fragments had been destroyed.

Back at his seat, Christopher sipped his refreshed hot chocolate in melancholic silence, for thoughts of the fossil brought back memories of his mama.

Her favorite refrain used to be, *If your papa had been born an ordinary gentleman instead of an earl's only son, he would have happily spent his days on the beaches of Cornwall on the hunt for old bones instead of crafting laws at Parliament.*

Perhaps that was why his father had taken such an interest in Mary Anning, the young girl from Lyme Regis who had discovered the fossils in the first place.

But now Christopher had this winter ball to contend with as well. He set down his cup too hard and liquid sloshed up the sides, threatening to spill over. He gave his two brothers, Nicholas and Everett, imploring looks and received no discernible sign of compassion.

While Nicholas looked hale and hearty, Everett's left arm was tucked into a sling. At four and twenty, Ev was Christopher's senior by a year and two months. He sat in morose silence and stirred his spoon around his full porridge bowl, but did not eat a bite.

Lines absent a year ago were now etched onto Ev's youthful face. Since the age of twelve, his brother had been at sea with his closest friend, Arthur. The two lads volunteered under a captain to gain experience and through the years, they had both risen in rank. Last November, with their ship under fire, Ev had attempted to save his friend's life, and failed. Though he was now home to heal, Ev's loss had left him with a wound more agonizing than a broken arm.

When his brother had first returned home, Christopher had asked Ev why he had not used levitation to heal himself. One or two trips up the side of their home at night and his brother would have been whole again. Ev said he preferred to have his body heal naturally. But Christopher thought his brother nurtured his pain, in atonement for his friend's death.

Ev had even refused to take laudanum to ease the pain. He had said that it left him dull-witted.

Across the table, Ev now doodled on a piece of paper.

"What do you draw?" Christopher asked in curiosity.

Everett's distracted gaze seemed to look

right through him. "This is a bear. Arthur's favorite animal. He used to carve it on the ship's sides. I told him that he was defacing the wood, but he would never listen. He said that while I might one day be remembered as our ship's greatest commander, this was his way to make sure that he, too, left his mark on the vessel."

Greatest commander. That suggestion had a ring of destiny. His brother would one day achieve that standing. *If he lived long enough.* Christopher might not be able to keep Ev out of danger, but every glance at his brother solidified his determination to help the British forces end this infernal war. Ensuring their fighters had more reliable firepower was his best bet for keeping his brother safe. But to do that, he needed to catch this saboteur, and then get back to work.

Since logical reason had failed to win Christopher his freedom from attending this ball tonight, he tried an emotional plea. "Surely dancing will aggravate Ev's injury?"

"Nonsense." Everett's pain-filled blue gaze turned stubborn. "After a year spent on a battleship, dancing and lighthearted conversation with beautiful women suits me fine."

Defeat nipped at his heels and Christopher turned to Nicholas, his eldest brother, but had little hope of rescue from that quarter. Less than four years after completing his degree at Oxford, Nicholas de Wynter's carousing had earned him the nickname, "The Mayfair Rake," by the protective mamas in Town. Christopher would not have put it past Nick to have been the one who suggested attending a winter ball in the first place.

"You work too hard," Nick said, with a grin, confirming Christopher's suspicion. "Come play with us tonight. I know a beautiful filly who can help you forget about guns and fuses and such folderol." Then he became serious. "I do not care for the idea of you chasing after the villain who blew up your equipment. It is bad enough that one family member is intent on putting himself in harm's way without you joining in his folly."

Christopher blinked and Nick's carefree expression returned. *Did I imagine Nick's unease, or is he truly more worried than he pretends?* A grain of concern wedged itself into Christopher's heart. His eldest brother often acted as if nothing bothered him, but lately, he had noticed subtle hints that suggested Nick's blithe demeanor was a façade. Unfortunately, Nick was as difficult as decipher as his father. Or Ev.

Christopher scraped the dregs from his bowl, surprised to discover that he had finished every last bite of his delicious porridge. His race to get here must have spurred his appetite.

Well, he needed all of his energy. The room

downstairs had to be suitably set up for his work. And in the next few nights, Christopher hoped to sift through the rubble left by the explosion, in search of clues. He had no time for a ball.

"You can spare one night to humor me," the earl said with finality. "Now I have another disagreeable matter for us to consider." He paused, as if uncertain how to proceed. Then he obviously decided to just admit it. "I have been, well, hounded, by a certain female for the past few weeks."

That caught Christopher's attention and he swerved in his seat to study his father. The earl had shown little interest in women since Christopher's mother had died two years ago. The old man had been mired in grief for so long, it had begun to feel like a natural state of affairs. *Now a woman has broken through that morass?* To Christopher's mind, this was good news.

"Her name is Mrs. Helen Beaumont. Since we have never been formally introduced, I refused her requests to meet." His father picked up a crinkled piece of paper that looked as if it had been scrunched up and straightened several times. "Then she had the temerity to inform me that she knows about our abilities."

"What?" Christopher straightened from his slouch. Annoyance was one thing; this sounded dangerous. "How could she possibly know about us?"

"Apparently she witnessed Nicholas thrown into the air during a carriage accident — fourth one this year, was it, son?" He gave Nick a stern look. "She asserts that he leapt up, twisted and then settled to the ground as if carried on angel wings."

Nicholas had the grace to look contrite.

"So, now I have no choice but to meet the infernal woman, if for no other reason than to uncover her intention on how she plans to use this knowledge. I gave her permission to approach me at the Locke ball tonight."

The earl shoved away his empty bowl and it clattered across the mahogany table. "Mrs. Beaumont accepted, though how she plans to gain an invitation is beyond me. She is not of our set. But that is her dilemma. Ours is that she is adamant there are others like us, 'shifters' she calls them. People she has gathered to form a group named the Rue Alliance. Rue it we will, if anyone discovers our association with such a cult."

He crumpled the offensive letter. "And she dares put her ravings in writing. That alone convinced me we deal with a lunatic. Imagine, sending this information in the Royal Mail."

The news turned Christopher's stomach. This woman was threatening his family's whole existence. His saboteur problems paled next to this new threat.

"Is it not prudent for us to at least find out

how much she knows, Papa?" Nick asked.

Christopher nodded. An enemy was easier to defeat once its weaknesses were known.

"Is this even possible?" Ev sounded more curious than concerned. "Could there be others like us, sir?"

"It matters not whether what Mrs. Beaumont says is true," their father said in a hard tone. "It is best that we keep our secrets sealed tight. It has been that way for three hundred years, ever since your thrice-great grandfather had the bad sense to bed a cursed Spanish gypsy. Then he showed an utter lack of discretion and married the chit, passing on her unnatural heritage to his heir."

Christopher was not touching this subject. Even his beloved mama had been unenlightened on the subject of her sons' talents. When each of his sons was five years of age, the earl had taken each boy aside and put the fear of God in them to keep silent about their talents. Practicing was done in strictly controlled settings. This need for privacy partly explained why Christopher and his brothers had yet to marry.

It is hard to think about committing to a marriage when truth will not, cannot, be a part of it.

Worse, the lady would be excluded from these family breakfasts. His mama had never sat at this table on Sunday mornings. His father had told her it was a special "men only" time.

Christopher had never cared for that arrangement, but he had not dared counter the earl's ruling. He pushed his empty bowl away. Sunday breakfasts always left him hungry for more.

"If I have any say," Christopher's father said, "our ability will remain a family secret for the next three centuries. So, it is best if each of you limit your progeny to the absolute necessity for carrying on our line, or there will be deWynters leaping all across England, instead of only in this room." He gave his eldest son a stern look. "Are you listening, Nicholas?"

"No need to worry, Papa." Nick offered an unrepentant grin. "There is more than one way to plunder hidden treasure."

"Just because none of the gels you have seduced has begat a child does not mean that run of luck will continue."

Christopher grinned. The reprimand about Nick's deplorable behavior with ladies was long overdue.

"And racing across London's rooftops is no way to keep our talents hidden either, Christopher. Anyone could have seen you."

"Sorry, Papa." His humor dying, Christopher sank lower in his chair, afraid his father's ire was now well and truly aimed at him. Seeing his eldest brother's smirk mimic Christopher's earlier enjoyment did little to cheer him.

Their father marched over to the hearth and flung the re-crumpled missive into the flames. "If Mrs. Beaumont's hope is to extort funds from me, she will not gain one farthing. Tonight, we will show a unified front to dissuade this woman from ever broaching this subject with any of us again. Understood?"

"Yes, sir," all three responded in unison.

"Now that it is settled, Christopher, have you made any progress on the fossil?" his father asked.

He gulped down his distress at disappointing his father on this subject, too. After he explained what had happened, he noticed that his father seemed worn and tired. The earl brooded over the four tiny pieces of broken bones that Christopher had returned to him.

"I will write to Miss Anning to request another sample." He handed the bits back to Christopher. "For now, see what, if anything, can be discovered about the age of these pieces. And try to keep them safe. I heard some misguided Presbyterian fools from Scotland were caught destroying precious artifacts at the British Museum on Montague Street."

"Yes, Papa." Consumed with guilt, Christopher tucked the bones back into his pocket, but thought there was little chance anyone else would want to get their hands on them. After all, there was little left to destroy. He

had already made sure of that when he fell
on them.

CHAPTER THREE

With hardly a limp, Honoria hurried outdoors with her family. Her fight with Henry had left no repercussions other than a bruised self-image.

As she stood on the landing outside, dressed in a red spencer over her morning gown, she was toasty warm with her hands tucked into a wide fur muff and her toes encased in knee-high boots. She took a deep delighted breath of the crisp winter air. The steps to the pavement were icy so she grabbed the railing. She must not risk a twisted ankle before tonight's ball.

Inside their carriage, her papa took the seat opposite her and her mama, while Henry and William rode on horseback. Her parents engaged in playful chatter on the way. But once they entered the church beneath its vaulted fanned ceiling, talk hushed.

William was late joining them because he had stopped to speak to a friend from school. When he did arrive, Henry scooted over to allow his brother to sit between him and his sister, acting as protection from what he termed "Honoria's dangerous feet."

She leaned toward Will. "Who is your friend?"

"Callum Finley. Scottish. He hopes to be ordained and gain a living at a parish. He is from a good family, but is too serious-minded to interest you, Honoria."

His description did put her off Mr. Finley, but she rolled her eyes at her brother's presumption that any interest she had in a man was as a prospective match. Simply because she was now of marriageable age did not mean attaining that lauded state was her sole interest. "How do you know him?"

"He is a year ahead of me at Eton. He is after an invitation to our ball so he can beg Papa to sponsor him as a vicar at one of our country parishes. I have arranged an introduction after services."

Singing began and Honoria stood with her family. She was enjoying a rendition of *While Shepherds Watched Their Flocks by Night* when a strong baritone caught her attention. The voice belonged to a gentleman three rows ahead of her and across the aisle on her left. The man was of a good height, five inches taller than her.

The gentleman on Mr. Baritone's right was similar in height but built broader. The gentleman on his left was a head taller. She would have a crick in her neck if they conversed while dancing. He had an arm in a sling, suggesting an injury.

Sadly, there were many injured soldiers about Town. Henry, with his impetuous behavior, had threatened to buy a commission once he finished school. She had a couple of years yet to foil that foolish plan. She only hoped the war ended before then. Thankfully, Will, as the eldest and heir, would never receive her papa's permission to go to war. So he was safe.

A row behind Mr. Baritone stood Mr. Finley. He appeared to sing, but she suspected that he might be mouthing the words since she could not distinguish his voice from any others.

Once they sat, she tapped Will's arm. "Who is that man? On our left three rows up. Just ahead of Mr. Finley." She refrained from adding, *the gentleman who is beautifully lean, sings like an angel and is just the right height for me.*

"Do you mean one of the Earl of Berrington's sons, dear?" her mama asked. "The whole family is made up of eligible men. The earl is the one with silver hair. Since his wife's passing, he has shown no inclination to marry again. Since all his offspring are sons, I suppose he no longer worries about fathering an heir."

Her mother gave a sniff that sounded as if she disapproved of such shortsightedness, but then she continued with her litany of the Berrington clan's assets. "His eldest son and heir, standing to his immediate left, is a rake. I would not see you hurt at his callous hands. Also, he may not live long if he does not change his sporting habits, for he has been in several carriage accidents this year alone."

Now Honoria remembered him. She had met Nicholas de Wynter once, briefly, and despite her friends calling him The Dream, she agreed with her mama's estimation. A man who could not settle on one woman was unlikely to settle at all.

"His next younger brother is in the navy," her mama continued. "He was injured this past autumn, poor boy."

A lady ahead of them turned and said, "Shhh!"

Undeterred, her mama leaned closer and spoke even softer, her warm breath brushing Honoria's cool left cheek. "Everett de Wynter recently returned from the war."

"He was captain of the *Esfuerzo*." Her father leaned around her mama to add that bit of detail.

"It means 'Endeavor,' " William whispered in a revered tone. "Our forces captured the ship from the Spanish in 1802. Her captain is a hero."

Her mama continued the tale. "As second in line, he would do better than his elder brother. Worthy of your attention. I sent them all invitations for tonight."

"And the other young gentleman in that row, Mama?"

"Christopher de Wynter?" Her mama waved a careless hand. "I would not bother with him, dear. He is unlikely to attend. He rarely goes to social functions. I have been told that he is wrapped up in his work. Though I cannot understand what could be so fascinating about a low-level navy clerk position."

Honoria nodded her understanding but her heart sank with disappointment. The youngest de Wynter was the one who interested her most.

The vicar began the Lord's Prayer and the parishioners stood to recite it along with him. Honoria raised a hand to her bosom where her hidden missive to God still resided and reverently closed her eyes.

A *shhh!* from the opposite aisle a few rows back drew Christopher's attention and then a vision in curls captured his attention. "Ev, who is that golden-haired beauty?"

"Viscount Locke's gel," Ev said, "Honoria Gilbert. Her mama attempted to marry her off last Season but failed."

His outlook on tonight's ball immediately improved.

Miss Gilbert's well-endowed figure was encased in a high-necked gown that constricted his breathing the longer he stared.

567

Were all the men in Town blind? Locke had deep pockets, so a lack of dowry could not be the issue.

"Is she bookish?" he asked, but that hardly diminished her allure. He liked his women to be widely read on more matters than the latest fashion.

"Particular," Ev whispered back.

"That is an impediment?"

"Since she judges every fellow she meets as undeserving, yes." Nick sounded piqued.

If Nick had tried to win this diamond's favor and been rebuffed, Christopher understood his eldest brother's peevishness. It was a rare occurrence. But that lack of success shot the lady higher in his estimation. Christopher took another look.

Her eyes were closed, as were everyone else's, for prayers were underway. Her fist clenched beside her luscious bosom, she appeared to genuinely entreat the Almighty on an important matter. Then her gaze snapped open and swung to clash with his.

Christopher de Wynter is staring at me! Honoria's heart pounded with excitement as his dark gaze bore into hers. The contact felt as if it had lasted hours but could only have been for a few seconds, for the vicar said, "For ever and ever, amen." Then Mr. de Wynter turned away and Honoria was left breathless. Her heart boomed from that extraordinary meeting of glances.

"Stop staring!" Will said in her ear. He might as well have grabbed her scruff and pulled her upright. "Especially while you clutch at your bosom like a gothic heroine."

Honoria dropped her arm, mortified that she had appeared to slaver after him, which was exactly what she was doing, but, as Will said, it did not do to make such ardent emotions obvious. Why had she not tucked her Christmas wish into her reticule? That would have been the sensible thing to do, but she had wanted to hold the blasted note close to her heart.

Oh, and now I also swore while in church.

She bit her lip in consternation and sent up a silent prayer for forgiveness, then added an apology for kicking Henry at breakfast.

During the remainder of the service, despite Will's admonition, Honoria could not help but seek out the youngest de Wynter several more times. Yet, not once did he look her way again.

To make matters worse, as she repeatedly sought to recapture the younger de Wynter's interest, she kept skirting around Mr. Finley's curious gaze. She worried she might have inadvertently encouraged the would-be curate. She expected to receive a harsh lecture from Will on the matter of flirting with his friends, especially after he had warned her off.

After the service, Honoria followed the rest
of her family as they filed out of the church.
Mr. Finley approached them in the churchyard and Will introduced him. He presented
well, appearing handsome and well dressed.
Honoria took in his tall figure, reddish wavy
hair and gray eyes and deemed him a suitable height for dancing.

Past him, the youngest de Wynter entered
his father's carriage, his movements liquid.
Honoria could not help thinking that the man
was probably a born dancer. But he did not
seek her out. Miffed, she smiled warmly at
Mr. Finley. Immediately, she realized her
mistake as he took her smile as encouragement and requested a dance tonight. She
graciously agreed, but inwardly vowed to
make it only one set.

"Mabel Chadwick crowed about how divine her doll house is," her mother said as
she entered their carriage. "And then she
asked what we planned to bring. Since we
have yet to decide, I was tongue-tied."

Will helped Honoria climb in, offering her
a stern warning. "Forget Finley." He then
returned to his mount.

"What was that about?" her mama said as
the door shut.

"William's right, Honey," her father said. "I
had words with Berrington earlier, after William told me his friend wanted a parish. The
earl mentioned that Finley had approached

him, as well, but he had found the lad possessed of strange notions that he did not care for. I suggest you turn your sights elsewhere. I have."

Honoria said not a word. Her brother and papa's warnings were unnecessary, for she had no interest in Mr. Finley. And she refused to be bothered by the youngest Mr. de Wynter, either, for he had looked keenly at her and then apparently decided she was not right for him. That conclusion stirred a painful twinge in her chest but she shook it off. If she must dwell on unattainable men, then she much preferred to think about her man in black.

Christopher was late for the ball. At least the venue was close by. He only had to walk past seven houses to get to where the festivities were being held. Though it was the middle of December when gentry normally returned to the country, the road to Viscount Locke's home was lined with carriages. Overhead, heavy clouds threatened either snowfall or sleet.

Inside the Locke residence, festivities were well underway. A footman led him upstairs to a series of interconnected rooms with blazing candles, heavy perfumes, and chatter. He strolled leisurely, keeping an eye out for his father and brothers. The largest room was arranged for dancing with chairs pushed to the edges. A small ensemble made up of a pianist, three violinists, and a lad with a flute, played a lively country tune.

The first lady to capture his attention was the one he remembered from Sunday's service. No woman should look that enchanting, for it was unfair to the rest of her gender and a danger to his. Her pink ball gown with lace netting overtop a long white satin undergown flowed like a river with each step she took. Above that, her bodice hugged her in a peasant style with silver ties that sparkled under candlelight, crisscrossing between her bosom. If she kept wearing such enticing gowns, no matter how exacting her standards, she would not remain unattached for long.

Christopher wanted to request a dance from Miss Gilbert, except a court of steady suitors were already lined up, reminding him of the string of carriages outside her doorway.

Several other young women were not as fortunate, hugging walls or their mamas' sides, so he requested their company for dances. On his third turn about the floor, he found himself before the ball's most sought-after temptress.

Her welcome smile was reflected in her dazzling green eyes. No wonder every man here had sought her out. As they took their turn, she moved like a dream, kept perfect timing and never missed a cue while she gave him her undivided attention during each twirl.

They might as well have danced above the rooftops with naught but air beneath their feet.

He was loath to release her, for her fingers felt right in his clasp, as if she belonged with him. His heart pattered and he sensed a smile played across his lips as joy rushed through him. It was a feeling he only experienced when he sailed across London's rooftops.

Her startled green-eyed glance suggested she, too, sensed a connection, but it could not be anything like the wrenching reluctance he felt at releasing his hold on her. The exasperated sighs of nearby dancers, however, said he had monopolized her for far too long. He flashed an apologetic smile and stepped away. After a courteous bow, he moved on down the line of waiting young ladies in a fog, the dance's joy gone.

With supreme effort, he steeled himself to not glimpse backward and kept his focus on his new partner. Once the dance ended, he thanked the young lady and escorted her to her mama. Then he left the room in search of his family, for after that incredible twirl with the golden goddess of dance, any other partner would fade in comparison.

He located Everett surrounded by his navy friends. With a tilt of his head, his brother indicated a bevy of women, and Christopher deduced Nicholas's whereabouts. He left the Mayfair Rake to his play and wandered to an adjoining room in search of his father. He found the earl beside an unknown older brunette and a younger ebony-haired female.

The elder lady stood a head shorter than his father, but looked him straight in the eyes without flinching. *Mrs. Beaumont?* Her forthright demeanor suggested so. The younger lady hung back and tilted her spectacles with a forefinger as she scanned the room with a suspicious frown.

Christopher sent a footman to fetch his brothers and made straight for his father, his protective instincts on high alert. It was as he had feared — something was very wrong.

CHAPTER FOUR

Honoria hurried to William's side and dragged him away from a group of uniformed officers.

"Honoria, I was listening to news about Napoleon's retreat from Moscow from Everett de Wynter! Now there is a fellow who would make you a good husband."

"He is too tall and I could not care less what Bonaparte is doing in Russia. I want to find my man in black. Not only is he real, but he is in my home and he danced with me! There he goes into the other room, Will. Come on, hurry!"

"A 'man in black' describes half the fellows in our home tonight. The rest are in regimental colors. Be more specific."

Honoria clamped her lips. What if speaking his name aloud jinxed her, or if Will said Christopher was not right for her? Such worries kept "his name is Christopher de Wynter" from wriggling out of her tight throat.

Her brother stared backward at Everett de

Wynter. He and the other gentlemen were laughing about something. "Also, I take leave to inform you, sister dear, that you have an abominable sense of timing."

She saw Christopher moving through the crowd. "There he goes, hurry! Go and tell him . . . tell him . . . never mind." She gave him a shove. "Find him and bring him to me."

"Honoria, you look flushed." Her mother came over, frowning with concern, as William left on his vital errand.

"Mama, I have found him! The man in black is here. He is not a vision after all. He is utterly and completely real and he dances like an angel." She froze as a startling thought arose.

"What is wrong?"

"Mama, my Christmas wish has come true. I shall never again grumble about going to church."

Her mama placed a hand on her forehead, "Are you feverish, dearest? It is too hot in here. I would have a window opened but the moment I do, someone is bound to catch a chill."

Honoria removed her mother's hand from her forehead, for she had never been so clearheaded. But then a wave of fear swept over her, toppling her confidence. "Mama, do I look all right? Am I pretty enough? He never asked me to dance. Not once. It was only by the merest chance that we had a turn on the floor, and then only for one brief heart-stopping moment. Most every eligible man here has asked me to dance at least once, but he never did. Why not? Is my gown displeasing?"

"You look beautiful, Honoria. Pink suits you. Now stop fretting, or you will give me the megrims. My head pains me enough because your papa insisted on inviting the Chadwicks to our ball. Of all the years for them to stay in London for Christmas, why did it have to be this one?" She searched the crowd. "Where is your papa? He should be here, by our side, during this crisis."

"Oh Mama, do not worry about what the Chadwicks are giving the poor. I promise to find something to take to church on Wednesday."

"I have not given that problem one iota of thought. What do I care if that woman brings a doll house, one every young girl dreams of receiving? It is the act of giving that is important, not the gift. What does trouble me is your vision. If that is not a crisis, what is? Wait here while I fetch your papa."

She hurried off before Honoria could correct her that she had said her man in black was *not* a vision. Though if she truly believed Christopher de Wynter was the man she saw racing over rooftops, then her mama might be right to be worried. How was such a thing possible?

But there was no time to dwell on it. Moments later, William returned. Alone.

"Well?" Honoria said, as disappointment settled over her stiff shoulders. "Where is he?"

"Obviously, I lost him," Will said with a frown. "Though I doubt I ever had the right 'him.' This place is brimming with gentlemen in black."

"Oh, Will, how could you!" She dragged him into the next room but a frantic search showed no sign of her rooftop leaper.

"Told you," Will said. "May I return to de Wynter's tale of the war effort now?"

Honoria hugged herself as she shivered. Disbelief as cold as snowfall washed over her. He could not have abandoned her a second time. Had he not felt their connection? Had she alone experienced their electric touch on the dance floor? "Will."

"What?" William had gazed off to where he left his newest hero, Everett de Wynter.

"What do you do if someone does not care for you the way you care for them?"

Slowly, her brother faced her, his eyes drenched with worry. "Honoria, you cannot possibly care for this man so deeply, so quickly. You have seen him how many times? Once? Twice? And you danced with him for half of one set."

"I know enough."

"Then describe him." William crossed his

arms and leaned back. "And it had better be more than, *he is my man in black!*"

"He is five inches taller than I, with deep blue eyes that rival starlight twinkling in twilight. His touch is quicksilver for it makes my heart speed up, my palms dampen and set my toes to tingling. Oh, also, while we twirled, it felt like we might have risen over the green room's floorboards."

"Hah! You and your fanciful imagination. Do you know anything concrete about this man such as, say his *name?*"

"Christopher," she said in a soft shuddering voice. "His name is Christopher de Wynter."

Will's pale green eyes widened at her succinct answer.

"What about Christopher de Wynter?" a man said. "You danced with him earlier, did you not, Miss Gilbert?"

Honoria swung around and found Mr. Finley behind her. *Oh, what rotten timing.* He was probably here to claim his dance. She had no wish to partner anyone else except for Christopher. And if he did not feel about her as she did about him, then he had better say so to her face. She was done with his running away.

Her back straightened and she lifted her chin. Before this night was over, he would partner her for a full reel. No more half measures that merely tempted without assuaging her deeper needs. But that would require losing Mr. Finley so she could be free to track down the elusive Mr. de Wynter.

She moved as if to walk toward Mr. Finley, but after taking a few steps, she grabbed hold of Will's arm and cried out, "Oh! I have rolled my ankle."

Her brother gave her a concerned look until she winked. His lips thinned in disapproval as he helped her totter to a chair.

"Well, horseradish," she said in a mournful tone. "That puts an end to my desire to dance the rest of this night away."

"We are all heartbroken," Will said, in an unsympathetic tone. "Shall I get Mama?"

Honoria grabbed his sleeve. "No! I mean, I will be fine if I rest here a moment. Stay with me, Will?"

His scowl told her that was the last thing he wished to do, but being a gentleman, he nodded and dragged over a nearby stool on which to rest her foot and then found a chair for himself.

Mr. Finley hovered beside them with a frown. "I hope you feel better soon, Miss Gilbert. Were you searching for Mr. Christopher de Wynter?"

"Yes," Will said, as Honoria said a flat, "No."

Mr. Finley frowned in obvious confusion.

"What my sister means is that she needs her mama. Would you fetch her, Finley, while

I keep Honoria company?"

"Of course. I shall be right back." Mr. Finley turned on his heel and made his way back into the other room.

The moment his friend was out of sight, William turned on Honoria. "Your ankle is no more hurt than mine!"

She jumped up, proving him right. "Hurry, Will, we must find Christopher de Wynter before your friend returns."

Will reluctantly trailed after her. "Honoria, I looked around here earlier and do not recall seeing him. Are you truly infatuated with him?"

As they wound their way through the crowd, Honoria dug in her reticule for her sketch. "He looks like this."

William laughed. "You do take the wildest turns. This might indeed be Christopher de Wynter, but it is hard to tell since this drawing does not have a face."

"We might have better luck finding him if we separate," Honoria said. "I shall go left, you go right. Meet me back in the green ballroom. Will, do not let me down."

With that entreaty, she hurried away and left William in silent study of her sketch.

Still bemused by his dance with Miss Gilbert, Christopher arrived at his father's side and bowed to the two ladies attending the earl. His father introduced Mrs. Helen Beaumont and her companion, Miss Nevara Wood. Mrs. Beaumont, in her mid-forties, wore a holly-berry red gown, while her companion wore white.

Miss Wood had a foreign demeanor. She was young. Nineteen, possibly twenty. Her features were similar to his trice great grand-mother, which put her in the Spanish camp. With her black hair and eyes and those rose red lips, she would have been stunning if not for her bespectacled and severe-gowned disguise. No doubt she did not wish to outshine her employer.

Mrs. Beaumont was also pretty, but in a manner that suggested she had spent years learning life's lessons the hard way. She conversed with his father without fawning and that alone set her apart from a hundred other women. It also explained why the earl had such a difficult time shaking her off his trail.

"Mr. Christopher de Wynter." Mrs. Beaumont curtsied. "I am glad to meet such a renowned scientist. Your work is legendary."

He started and his pulse sped up. It was like coming across a garden snake while he strolled across the lawn. In two short days, someone had stolen into his secret Royal Arsenal laboratory to rig his experiment to explode and now a stranger seemed well versed with his hidden accomplishments. *Were the two incidents related?* The earl's frown suggested he was wondering the same thing.

Before Christopher could question her on where she had heard of his work, Ev and Nick joined them. Not surprisingly, Nick immediately responded to Miss Wood's unenhanced beauty and positioned himself closer to the captivating young lady. After introductions, the earl suggested they remove themselves to someplace more private to continue their discussion.

"I scouted out a suitable room earlier." As he spoke, Nick's gaze lingered on the stunning Miss Wood with a suggestive gleam. "After a turn off the outside corridor, there is a room two doors down. We will not be disturbed there."

When had Nick found this sanctuary? His brother's wicked grin suggested Nick had not only found it, but had also tested the site as suitable for a rendezvous. He took Miss Wood's arm in his. "Shall we go?"

Mrs. Beaumont agreed but the earl stopped them. "We will speak with Mrs. Beaumont alone."

The look in his father's eyes brooked no argument.

Without hesitation, Mrs. Beaumont nodded her agreement and asked Miss Wood to await her return. When Miss Wood appeared ready to object, Mrs. Beaumont took her companion's hand and led her away. They had a heated discussion before the elder lady firmly sent her companion off. Their trek to the chamber Nick had scouted out took only a few minutes. Once at their destination, Christopher was the last to enter the secluded room. About to shut the door, he spotted his golden-haired dancer hurrying around the corner from the ballroom. She was unmistakable in her bosom-laced, pink gown. Ever since their short dance, he had been plagued with the desire to unlace that silver cord to release its tight hold on her velvet bodice.

Then she spotted him and her lips stretched into a satisfied smile.

Unable to walk away from Miss Gilbert's challenging look, Christopher offered an excuse to his father and stepped back into the corridor, shutting the door behind him. "Searching for a dance partner?"

She came closer but stopped a respectable five feet away — close enough to show interest but far enough back to impress his father that she was more of a lady than Mrs. Beaumont. "My dancing partners do not normally race away, sir, leaving me alone."

"Hardly alone." He kept his focus on her apple green gaze that would tempt a wary Adam to shed his reservations about biting into forbidden fruit. Harder still was avoiding that tantalizing, crisscrossed silver cord at her bosom. Her father should flog whichever dressmaker designed that blatantly enticing

584

artifice to draw a man's attention toward his innocent daughter's greatest assets. Then the young lady's mother should reward the dressmaker for crafting such a successful ploy.

He narrowed the gap between them to four feet. "If any more men vied for your attention," he said in a teasing tone, "there would be none left to partner every other lady."

They stood assessing each other, leaving little enough room for anyone to traverse this corridor either behind or between them. As if to test that supposition, a servant girl rushed down the corridor with a tray of sliced oranges. She came to a startled halt, hesitant to brush against either of them in her desire to go past. The standoff continued for five heartbeats, with neither giving way.

Then Miss Gilbert took a bold step forward, bringing her scent within reach. She smelled of succulent apples. He took a deep breath and held it, savoring her aroma as the maid slipped past them.

"Anne," Miss Gilbert said.

The maid stopped short and her tray tilted to the side. Oranges slithered across the flat surface toward her. She shifted her grip to restore order. "Yes, miss?" she said breathlessly.

Keeping steady eye contact with him, Miss Gilbert said, "After you deliver that tray, please inform William of my whereabouts and that I have found what I sought."

"Yes, miss." The girl scurried off.

Neither the lively chatter that spilled out from the nearby ballroom doorway, nor his father awaiting his presence in the room directly behind him, could weaken this lady's hold on him. If anything, the danger of being caught with his fingers tugging at that beguiling silver cord at her bosom merely enhanced her pull.

"We have not been properly introduced." Miss Gilbert sounded incredibly prim, considering she neither ran away nor retreated to put proper distance between them now that the maid had left.

She might not be so different from the bold Mrs. Beaumont. If so, Christopher pitied his father.

"I hoped my brother could oblige and introduce us, sir," she added, "but he has probably returned to his worship at your brother's coattails."

"Which one?"

"The overly tall one."

"With a broken arm?"

"In uniform."

"Not the one who is favored by the ladies?" He wanted to be crystal clear they spoke of Ev. It was important.

"Mama disapproves of your brother, Nicholas de Wynter, and my brother William is an excellent judge of character."

"Are you, too, an excellent judge of character?"

She blinked and tilted her head, considering her answer. Then her Garden of Eden gaze returned to tempt him. "I always know what I like."

"And do you see what you like now?"

A slow smile crossed her full lips and Christopher ached to take possession of that luscious mouth. He swallowed hard and clenched his hands to keep from pulling her to him and scandalizing them both.

She watched him intently. "I liked what I saw last night."

Since he had been nowhere near her last night, disappointment seeped in as he said, "What did you see?"

"I saw a man streak across London's rooftops as if he were leaping over obstacles at a frost fair on the Thames."

CHAPTER FIVE

Honoria's man in black moved with lightning speed. He crossed the three feet separating them and, with his hands on her waist, he impelled her backward and upward until she dangled midair under a wall sconce. Mistletoe hung from that lamp. She had tethered it there earlier today, determined that, before her mama's winter ball ended, she would have her first kiss.

All signs of playful interest were gone as he demanded, "Who are you? Are you in league with Mrs. Beaumont?"

Her pulse pounding in terror, she stared into his furious countenance and realized he held her up as if she weighed no more than that kissing vine tied to the sconce. His ability to keep her airborne reminded her of him racing across the rooftops. *Does gravity have no effect on you, sir?*

"Answer me," he repeated roughly.

"I do not know a Mrs. Beaumont." Despite fear coursing through her veins, she understood his sudden change in mood. If she could do what he could, she would keep it hidden, too. Instead of viewing it as an incredible talent, some in Society might consider it otherwise. And she had blurted out that she knew his secret. She hoped he never discovered that she had also drawn him leaping across rooftops, or that she had shown that sketch to William. *But who is Mrs. Beaumont?*

Her pulse settled into a steady thumping as fear receded and logic returned. She loosened her white-knuckled grip on his strong shoulders. Though his hold was firm, it did not punish. In fact, it was almost as if his fingers caressed her. And they were so close, she could practically taste him. What would it be like to be held against him instead of the wall? To feel his lips on hers? And then she remembered the mistletoe.

Dare I? The mistletoe gave her courage. What were the chances that, of all the places he could have held her, it would be below a kissing bough? If that was not a Christmas miracle, she did not know what was. Anticipation overrode her qualms and she leaned forward and boldly kissed his firm lips.

He responded instantly, consuming her in a delicious dance of desire. Her blood soared, flowing faster than when he had first taken hold of her. In fact, she was no longer held against the wall, but pulled tight against him and slowly, exquisitely, lowered, inch by tormenting inch. Every part of her that brushed a part of him relished that moment of intense, intimate, togetherness. *If this is what a Christmas mistletoe kiss is like, I want more.*

"Christopher!" a voice commanded. "What are you doing?"

He released her so quickly, Honoria's feet hit the ground with a thump. He swung around to face the one who had interrupted them and, Honoria suddenly realized he was floating an inch off the floor. With a grip on his jacket, she pulled him down.

He landed and his knees buckled before he regained his balance. He extended a hand at his back, as if to shield her. It was a gentlemanly gesture that thrilled Honoria as much as his kiss had.

"Christopher!" a second voice said, but this man sounded entirely approving of their scandalous kiss.

A peek around Christopher's shoulder showed Nicholas de Wynter's smiling countenance. The disapproving figure beside him was none other than Christopher's father, the earl. She could have died on the spot, for his lordship's expression promised that her papa would soon hear of her outrageous behavior. The earl's entire family and an unknown lady were there to witness Honoria's downfall.

"Explain yourself!" the earl said in a tone

that would have made her intrepid brothers quiver.

Since Christopher seemed tongue-tied, Honoria gently tapped his shoulder and pointed a forefinger straight up.

Everyone's gaze shifted up to the mistletoe.

Christopher's shoulders dropped their tense stance. "It is simply a seasonal custom, Papa."

"Hah!" With that one exclamation, Nicholas de Wynter conveyed both disbelief and admiration of his brother's attempt at a plausible explanation.

"If that is how those in your scientific circles address a holiday tradition," Everett de Wynter said, tucking his good hand under the broken one as if to give it support, "then I have been entirely mistaken in your friends' social prowess."

The lady with them chuckled and turned to the earl. "I shall leave you and your sons to your Christmas entertainment. I have much to discuss with my friends, my lord. Thank you for your time. I look forward to receiving your answer."

With a nod in Honoria's direction, she bid them goodnight.

At that moment, the sound of running footsteps heralded a newcomer. William raced around the corner and almost ran into the departing lady. He sidestepped her and then came to a halt at sight of the crowd in the corridor. He still held her sketch.

591

Honoria wished she was close enough to snatch it back.

William first focused on Everett de Wynter. He saluted and the paper crinkled against his forehead. He quickly switched the page to his left hand and did a proper salute. "Captain."

The wounded officer acknowledged him with his good arm as Honoria edged around Christopher to reach her brother's side.

Finally out in the open, she curtsied to the earl, ignored his sons and hurried over to Will's side. In one swift move, she had the page in her possession and hidden behind her back.

"There you are," Will said, though his wide-eyed gaze remained trained on his hero, Captain de Wynter. "Mama is searching for you everywhere."

"Everett," the Earl of Berrington said, "as you are acquainted with this young pup, please make the introductions."

His son did as his father requested and then William introduced Honoria. She curtsied again and then on impulse, held out the sketch, face down, to Christopher as an olive branch for getting him into so much trouble. "This belongs to you, sir." It was her way of telling him she would keep his secret.

As Christopher reached for it, Nicholas whisked the paper out of Honoria's grasp. "Are you sure this is not mine?"

Before she could object, he turned the page

over. In a snap, he folded it and extended it to Christopher. "My mistake," Nicholas said in a quiet voice. "It is yours."

Honoria breathed a sigh of relief.

Grim faced, Christopher reached for the page. But Everett, obviously caught up in the mischievous spirit of the season, stole it out of Nicholas's grasp. "Then it must be mine, surely." One look and he went absolutely pale.

Honoria cringed at the thought of Christopher's family discovering how much she knew of his talent. Their reaction confirmed that they were very much aware of what Christopher could do. She bit her lip hard. By drawing attention to that sketch, had she landed her man in black in more trouble than with her kiss?

William was glancing from Honoria to the de Wynters and back.

Everett extended the sheet, face down, to Christopher and said in a grim tone, "Not mine at all."

This time, Christopher did not reach for it, and instead glanced at his father. The earl took the sheet and Honoria gripped her brother's hand in horror. His lordship studied it in silence, and then he said, "I believe it is mine."

Was levitation a family talent? Even with the *earl*? Goosebumps rose on her arms at that shocking thought. Anything she said now would only add fuel to this raging family fire.

Even if she had created this mess, Christopher would have to be the one to resolve it. It was time for a strategic withdrawal.

She bid the de Wynter family good evening and pulled her brother with her as she made a hasty retreat. At least she had confirmed the identity of her elusive man in black. For when they kissed, they had *both* risen off the floor.

The earl could keep her sketch, for not only was his son's image indelibly etched into her brain, but she now knew what it felt like to be twirled around a dance floor in his arms . . . and how delicious it was to be kissed by him!

Honoria glanced back and then wished she had not, for all four men stared at her with varying degrees of interest or, in the case of the earl, censure. Christopher de Wynter's thoughtful gaze, however, remained with her long after she joined her mama and listened to her scolding about the dangers of running off alone, even in her own home.

Still, it had been worth it. She hoped he would contact her again, soon.

"So no one saw you yesterday morning?" Christopher's father asked. Sarcasm dripped off each word.

"This is not the place for this discussion, Papa." Christopher wanted to defer this argument until after he finished his interrupted talk with the lady. And next time, he would not be distracted by her kisses. Not until *after* she answered all of his questions. "I am sorry I missed our meeting with Mrs. Beaumont. It was short. Was it constructive?"

"Unexpectedly so," Nicholas said, under his breath. "Unlike us, her talent is to change her features. She was like a veritable chameleon. Uncanny to watch. She and her Rue Alliance members have more to hide than we do."

"She hinted that the talents of the Rue Alliance members included more than that of merely changing features," Everett said. "And she is not interested in our money. She genuinely wants us to join her alliance. Says we will all be stronger and safer together than apart. The lady made a compelling argument."

"I do not care what she wants," the earl said. "We are not joining her ridiculous alliance." He thrust Miss Honoria Gilbert's sheet at Christopher. "I am more interested in how Locke's daughter knows of your activities, Christopher. Kissing her is not the way to discourage her."

"It seemed ingenious to me," Nicholas said.

Curious about what this sheet contained that had so unnerved every member of his family, Christopher ignored Nick's teasing and took the paper from his father. Cautiously, he turned it over and his heart skipped a startled beat.

Miss Gilbert had an eye for detail. Her charcoal lines had captured him in mid-leap, his sense of joy etched in a few fine lines. How could she have seen straight into his soul like that when she had never even met him when she drew this?

"This does not identify me, Papa," Christopher said, squelching a twinge of regret at what he must now do. "This sketch lacks a face. It is immaterial." He strode over to the wall sconce and held the drawing up to the flame until it caught fire.

"Then why did she hand it to you? And why kiss her?"

Christopher sidestepped that last tricky question by focusing on the first. "She is merely speculating. I can persuade her otherwise." He stomped out the last embers.

"See that you do, and tell her to stop these infernal drawings. We cannot afford such public mistakes or all of London will soon know of our secret."

"Yes, sir." He did not add that he had made several mistakes, aside from being seen on the rooftops. The first was dancing with the enchanting Miss Gilbert. And the second was kissing her back.

Except, when he had held her, his pulse had thudded like a racehorse that anxiously awaited the signal to go. Their kiss left him yearning for a second one.

He took a deep calming breath. "I will contain this crisis, sir."

"We will finish this discussion at home, later." His father strode back to the ball.

Nicholas followed his father, grinning. It was not often that Christopher was the one causing a problem.

Everett gave him a sympathetic pat. "Oh, by the way, since you have enough troubles on your hands, and Nick will likely be too distracted by his pursuit of the Spanish beauty to bother, I will deal with the presents we must bring to church. I have an idea that might suit and it might give me some peace."

Christopher nodded his thanks, happy to go along with anything that could wipe away the anguish in Ev's gaze. He wandered toward the stairs, deep in thought. Somehow, he must convince the astute Miss Gilbert that what she saw early this morning was not real.

For their next skirmish, he would be better prepared. On impulse, he raced back to the corridor. After checking that he was unobserved, he rose until he could reach the sconce. Then he plucked the mistletoe and tucked it into his breast pocket.

At two o'clock the next morning, Christopher found himself clinging precariously from the Lockes' rooftop, like a bat, as he checked one room after another in search of Miss Gilbert.

In the west wing, guests slept the night away rather than risk the dark snowy roads. In the east wing, the youngest Gilbert snored while in an adjacent room, William read by candlelight. Their rooms were decorated with frames of inviting country landscapes.

A few doors down, her parents were engaged in a passionate embrace in bed — a scene that left Christopher's cheeks burning as he hurried away.

Finally, he located an empty bedchamber and gained entry through an unlocked window. Inside, he detected the delightful apple scent of his quarry. He took a big whiff, enjoying her fragrance, but there was nary a sign of the luscious Miss Honoria Gilbert anywhere. There were, however, more paintings by the same artist whose works adorned her brothers' and her parents' walls.

A closer study of one painting revealed no signature. He made a note to ask Ev to inquire of his adoring fan, William Gilbert, about this popular artist, so he could acquire a piece.

Since she was not in here, he stole into the corridor to plan his next move. She could be anywhere, from a stillroom in search of a sleeping draught to the library, deciding on a book to read, or even in the kitchen, assuaging an empty stomach. His scientific mind suggested that systematically checking all rooms, floor by floor, should net him his prize.

An hour later, he was ready to wave the white flag of surrender. Soon, the chambermaid would come around to light fireplaces and find him. Discouragement nipped as he made his way to the topmost floor, where he found rooms stacked with dust-covered boxes and trunks. He was out of time and rooms and had still discovered no sign of Miss Gilbert.

He was about to abandon his search when a sliver of light under a doorway drew his dark-sensitive eyes. Surely she could not be there? It was more likely a chambermaid having a tumble with a footman. Yet, he could not leave the possibility unchecked. He eased open the door, stealing himself for the piercing scream of a startled maid. But there was no sound. The room's lone occupant did not detect his intrusion. From the prim white nightcap to the warm shawl over her pale blue evening gown, from the bare toes curled around the lowest rung of her stool to the paintbrush she flicked across a painters' palette, this was no chambermaid.

Among blazing candelabras that sent shadows dancing across this studio, Miss Gilbert presented a breathtaking profile of an artist at work. She sat hunched over a wooden easel as she raised her paintbrush, now well loaded with crimson. The window before her had its shutters flung open, as if awaiting the morning light. The white puffs of his breath suggested that those shutters should be closed tight, but the young lady seemed undisturbed by the cold.

The painting she worked on was hidden by her stance but her concentration intimated that she was involved in intricate work. Along every wall were canvases, leaning against each other like old friends. Directly beside her was a long wooden table; much like he had had in Woolwich. On this surface was housed her palette, paint-smeared rags, colorful paint bottles, a cup with various sized brushes, and a mortar and pestle.

He had stepped into a serious artist's workshop. Tiptoeing behind her, he gently tipped paintings to see her scope of work. Landscapes and country life were favorites. They showed a joy for life, an appreciation of simple pleasures, and most shocking of all, common folk. How could Miss Gilbert, who lived amid the wealthiest in her society, be familiar with her subjects?

"I painted them," she said.

He swung around and the frame he held slipped from his hand. She had twisted around to face him, one leg crossed over the other, her arms resting loosely over her knee and red-tipped paintbrush still in her hand. She was as delectable a vision as an artist as she had been as a dancer. The only incongruity she presented was that she lacked an artist's smock. He had discovered that earlier, stuffed haphazardly behind a stack of landscapes to his left.

But why had she not screamed when she discovered him in her private sanctum? Or questioned his ability to enter her locked home? There was only one viable explanation for the intrigue that was Miss Honoria Gilbert. He would bet his latest fuse design that she had expected him to come tonight.

He straightened, pretending that invading a lady's studio late at night, uninvited, was an everyday occurrence for him. "I beg your pardon?"

"When strangers view my work," she said, "they wonder if the pieces are mine, questioning how I would be familiar with such themes. Not that many strangers see my work."

"*Are* you familiar with such scenes, Miss Gilbert?"

She twirled her brush in thoughtful silence before she met his gaze. "If I say yes, you will think me disreputable for frequenting unsavory places, sir. Yet if I say, no, you will believe me a liar for claiming these paintings as mine." She paused. "It is as much a conundrum as unexpectedly finding yourself alone at night, with a gentleman, unchaperoned."

When he did not say anything, she continued. "I did expect you, sir." She hopped off her stool. "Though I thought you would come through the window."

He glanced over at the wide arched opening with its window latch left hanging open. "Do you often expect men to enter your studio through the window so late at night?"

"Only men who can scale high walls." She tilted her head in challenge. "That window has a direct drop of some fifty feet to the snowy ground."

She stepped away from her easel and the painting she had been working on came into view. Christopher's breath caught. There was no mistaking his face this time, for it was as clear as the moonlight that shone onto the black rooftops, depicting each slant, each tile, each brick of a chimney in vivid detail on her canvas. He skirted her to gain a closer view of her work.

She had to have been slaving away on this piece since she had left the ball. Since she had left him. It was only half completed, but still, the intricate lines linked him directly to her midnight leaper.

Regretfully, he whispered, "I will have to burn that."

"Not until after I have finished it," she said.

She offered no objection. No, get out. No, over my dead body. Anyone else this talented would have lashed out at the suggestion of destroying her creation. "You will allow me to raze it?"

"After I am done," she said in a soft voice

that was painful in its absence of anger. "By then, it will be etched into my mind. Every nuance, every stroke of my brush, every shade and shadow. This painting will have become a living thing, much more than just a girlish dream. No one will be able to take it away from me then."

Her words evoked such profound sadness that his chest tightened painfully. He wanted to wrap her in his arms and take away her hurt. Though it came out as a question, he spoke with certainty. "Your paintings have been destroyed before?"

She gently set her brush on the table. "When I first began to paint, the subjects were what my tutors taught me. Red apples. Delicate white daisies. Pristine green lawns."

Leaning against her worktable, she gave him a bemused smile. "But when I began to add in a child in torn trousers biting into that stolen apple, or a daisy crushed by a dairy maid's bare feet as she raced across a field with a lad who chased her, or the lawn tended by a weary elderly gardener in old clothes with scars on his face, my papa was afraid his friends would not understand."

She traced her canvas's edge and he took her hand, squeezing it in sympathy. She linked her fingers with his. "It took Mama years to convince him that my paintings were a reflection of the truth as I see it, that they were something to be treasured, not feared."

He brought her hand up for a closer inspection, but instead of long delicate fingers with paint smears, he saw paintings by the unknown artist in her brothers' and parents' rooms. "So now your work is proudly displayed by your family."

"Yes," she said, with an irrepressible smile, "but they are all unsigned. It was a compromise. When I turned fifteen, Papa gave me this room for my studio because he said it had become apparent that my penchant for painting was unlikely to wane."

"Wise man." To avoid the temptation to hug her, Christopher dropped her hand and put some distance between them. Then he turned to study the artwork. By the time he tipped a frame from the third stack, he was determined to have one.

How could he convince her to sell to him? Especially after he had declared that he intended to burn her current creation? He knelt before an ice-skating scene. Tables on the shoreside were heaped with loaves of bread. On the ice, ropes cordoned off where a skating competition was underway. "Where is this from?"

She came over and bent beside him, bringing with her the scent of apples. The lady was as tempting as her paintings. "That event took place in the Fens. Papa took us there for holiday one winter when we were children. We were invited to witness a race among the farm workers."

She pointed to the skaters' feet and her arm brushed against him, sending tingles shooting up his arm. Christopher had a hard time concentrating on the skaters. "They used animal bones for skates. I doubt they could afford metal blades. The game's prize was a loaf of bread provided by the local squire."

He picked up the frame for a closer study. This, too, was unsigned and that left a bad taste in his mouth. "I would like to purchase this. With one stipulation."

"Which is what?" Her forthright glance had not a hint of shyness. The lady valued her work.

He liked that. Holding her gaze, he said, "I would like you to sign it. You should not hide your gift." His words were said as much for her, as for himself. It had always bothered him that his mother had been kept in the dark about her children's incredible aptitude for playing with gravity.

Miss Gilbert looked away and Christopher wondered if his request had crossed a boundary. She had been taught since childhood to hide her true self. He would wager that none of her suitors were aware of the brilliant artist behind the heavenly dancer, any more than his navy friends saw past the earl's youngest son who tinkered with volatile mixtures to the man who could leap through air.

She blinked a few times, then quickly wiped

away a tear before she stood and put the room's length between them. "I shall consider your request, sir."

He laid the skating portrait against the others and rose, too, but kept his distance. It was time to broach the main reason for his visit. "You must stop painting me."

"No," she answered flatly, with no room for compromise.

He began to understand her needs, but she could not or would not grasp his. "Miss Gilbert, be reasonable."

"After this one, I promise not to paint you climbing over rooftops, Mr. de Wynter," she said. "But I refuse to agree to never painting you in any other manner I wish."

"Ah," he said, warmth stealing into his heart. If these works were any indication of her normal subject matter, she rarely featured anyone from their social circle. He, therefore, took her insistence on this stipulation as a compliment. It meant that their kiss had been mutually cherished. *Good.*

Although he had technically achieved his aim in coming, he lingered, wanting more. "If it is acceptable to you, Miss Gilbert, may I call on you on the morrow?"

At her arched eyebrow, he added with an enticing smile, "Through your front door. My colleagues tell me there is a pond in Hyde Park that is currently frozen over and I would dearly like to take you there to skate."

"I would enjoy that, sir." Her gaze turned speculative. "But you surely do not plan to leave before showing me how you make yourself airborne?"

CHAPTER SIX

A gate slammed shut over Christopher de
Wynter's features as clearly as a castle draw-
bridge being pulled back. Honoria's heart
pattered in alarm, for he was headed toward
the window. If it was not such an unladylike
gesture, she would have stomped her foot. "I
shall give you my skating painting in exchange
for one flight." *Stay. Please.*

He stopped, his hand on the window latch.
Slowly, he turned around, but resignation was
clear on his face. "I cannot do as you ask."

She took a step closer to him. "Why not?"

"I cannot take another with me."

"You did it before."

He shook his head. "That is impossible."

"You drew me above the dance floor, downstairs."

His smile grew wider, making his eyes
twinkle in candlelight. "I am glad you enjoyed
our dance, Miss Gilbert, but we were ever
earthbound."

"For a few moments, as you held my hand,

I floated."

He took a cautious step toward her. "I, too, treasured our dance, Miss Gilbert. We can dance like that again, perhaps on the ice."

"I wish to dance with you again, Mr. de Wynter, on air as well as ice."

His smile vanished like the morning mist and he sliced his arms in a display of frustration. "You ask for the impossible."

How could he not realize what they had done together downstairs? She quickly moved aside her stool, pushed her wooden easel toward the wall and then put away a stack of paintings scattered on the floor. Once there was adequate space, she turned sideways and held out her right arm, palm up. "Prove me wrong. Dance with me."

He stared in silence and then said, "We have no music."

"I need none."

Still, he hesitated, wearing an endearing frown. She liked this man. All of his reactions were genuine. He was someone whom one could trust to say what he meant and do what he said. To entice him closer, she tilted her head in challenge. "If indeed you cannot raise me up, sir, what harm can one dance do, more than your presence here, at this time of night, has not already done?"

"You, Miss Gilbert, are incorrigible."

But he had relented, she saw. For as he spoke, he walked toward her with purpose that set the nerves in her spine tingling with anticipation. Her fingertips prickled long before he touched her and then power shot up her arm as if she had been struck by lightning. She reflexively gripped his hand and his wonderful smile returned.

By mutual accord, they began the steps to a country dance, similar to the one they had danced downstairs but this time, with no others with whom to switch places. Music rang in Honoria's ears, as if they were indeed in a ballroom and the orchestra played a lilting tune. On their third turn, she rose.

Her heart thumping with excitement, Honoria kept her gaze locked on his. He seemed intrigued, but unconcerned.

He does not realize that we are floating! It was an amazing discovery, one she kept to herself for the time being. She wanted to savor these thrilling moments of rising up every time they touched. At the end, as the music in her head died, she curtsied while he bowed.

Now she was ready to show him the magic of their touch. She took a step closer and held out her hands. He gazed at her in surprise and then took her fingers in his. Holding on to him, she raised their arms and together they did two turns. Keeping hold of his hands, she checked below. They were a foot above the ground.

With a nod, she indicated that he should

look downward. He followed her line of sight and with a gasp, released her. They landed, arms flailing to balance themselves.

"That cannot have happened!" he said.

"Yet, it did," she said, pleased to have made her point. "Thank you, Mr. de Wynter. The dance was all I had hoped for. Though, next time, I would like to travel over London's rooftops with you."

Shaking off the lure of her apple scent, Christopher stared at Miss Gilbert in stunned silence. He had thoroughly enjoyed their dance and would have been happy for it to go on all night long. But this rising above the ground while she was in his arms was impossible to comprehend. He had touched many a young woman, some in intimate ways, and never once had any become airborne.

He shook his head in denial and extended his arms toward her. "That cannot have happened. Show me again."

Her smile had Cleopatra's confidence as she took hold of his fingers. His heart rate sped up, as it had during their dance. The woman was seduction personified, and a beautiful dancer, but she could not have levitated with him. He stood holding her soft hands, happy to be touching her again. His feet remained firmly on the ground.

He gave a sigh of profound relief at that reaffirmation of his gift's set rules. Still, to be on the safe side, he did a twirl with her. They remained on firm ground. A tiny traitorous part of him regretted that outcome. "See. No flight."

Her confident smile did not waver. "Why not try to rise, sir, and see if you leave me behind."

It was a daring proposal, for he would not only be admitting to his ability to defy gravity, but verifying with a physical display. There would be no denying he had this ability afterward. His father would disapprove. He took a deep breath and decided that he did not wish to be his father.

Christopher called on his talent and it tingled in response like a well-trained puppy, springing from the tips of his toes up to the top of his head. He recognized this exciting feeling. It came before each of his leaps. It could not have been there during their dance, however. He was sure he would have noticed. Unless . . . no, she could not have entranced him so much that he missed this familiar yet unique sensation.

Yet, suddenly he was rising up toward the room's high angled ceiling. And she had come with him!

"This cannot be happening." His head brushed the ceiling. Unable to swallow his delighted smile, he ducked and brought them both downward a little. He twirled her above the workbench that held her brushes and

612

paint jars, thrilled at sharing this extraordinary experience with another person. His brothers took their skills for granted, never seeming to delight in this exceptional feat, while his father never wished to speak of it, as if their abilities were a foul secret, best kept hidden.

Unlike his family's reactions, her answering laugh was playful and carefree. "I knew this is how it would feel."

The lady was full of surprises. There were no screams, no clinging at him to keep from falling, no calling him an unnatural beast. "How does it feel, Miss Gilbert?"

At his serious tone, her green gaze met his, and her smile softened. When she finally answered, it was in as serious a tone as his. "As if I have the world at my feet, Mr. de Wynter."

Her fingers were gentle but firm within his, not clutching but a force to be reckoned. He had to ask about her fearlessness. "Why are you unafraid? Do you sweep men off their feet so often that this is commonplace?"

"I am quite certain it is you who has swept me off my feet, sir." She glanced down. "Five feet, to be precise. I have never been afraid of high places." Her charmingly confident gaze tangled with his bemused one. "Even if I was, I would not be in the least bothered as long as you held me."

She knew what to say to make a fellow feel

exceptional. No wonder so many other ladies at the dance had been abandoned in her favor. "I wish we could —" he said, when a boom shuddered outside. A windowpane splintered, sending spider veins across its surface, though the glass did not shatter.

"What was that?" Now she clutched at his arms.

Worried that he knew the source of that blast, he flew them over to the window and settled them on the floor. Together, they peered outside. Seven doors down and across the street, his home was ablaze. Fire licked out the downstairs windows and, on one side, there was a gaping hole.

"Not again." Terror and anger mingled as Christopher struggled to unlock the frozen window. He cursed himself for dallying here when he should have been home to stop the fiend. "My family is inside that house, and the servants."

The window burst open and cold air rushed in.

He had one foot slung over the ledge when she grabbed his arm and held him back. "Look, sir." She pointed to his house. "Is that not your father?"

Indeed it was. The earl was helping female servants exit an attic window, one by one and then came the men. Finally, Ev stepped out. There was no sign of Nick, but he could be scouring the house for others to save. Including a younger brother who might be found in a basement room with his experimental paraphernalia. Equipment that someone had again used as a weapon against him.

"They need my help." He tried to shake off her grip.

She held on tight. "Look, there are people coming out of homes below," she whispered. "If you go down, they will find your landing beside them more astonishing than the fire."

Neighbors were indeed emerging out of doors to investigate, and a bell sounded the alarm through the night air. She was right. He stepped away from the window. But he could not go through the front door either and risk getting caught. By the sounds of it, her household was already awakening to the nearby danger. "I have to inform my family that I am not trapped inside. I cannot risk my brothers lingering in the burning house to search for me."

"I see William, below," she said. "I can ask him to inform your family that you are safe."

"And how will you explain my presence in your studio?"

"I will think of something."

"Wait."

Looking again at his father's home, he saw that an effort was being made to get people off the roof, and below, several bucket brigades were already forming lines to put out the flames. He looked closer. Yes, there was

Nick, crawling out the attic window.

His pulse steadied as he re-thought his options. Now that he knew everyone was safe, his best bet was to scout out the villain who had caused the fire. He might have lingered to enjoy his handiwork.

Miss Gilbert was right on one count — there were too many people who might witness his descent. But windows allowed for more than one means of escape for a de Wynter.

"Sir, do you know who is behind this explosion?"

Her paintings had told Christopher that she was a perceptive young lady, and that question confirmed his hypothesis. "This is not the first attempt on my life."

"Someone wants to *kill* you? Who would want to do that? And why?"

"I do not know who. But the reason might be related to my work." In for a penny. "I am not a navy clerk, Miss Gilbert. I am designing a weaponry aid. Someone appears intent on stopping me." And then a distressing thought intruded. "It is not safe to be near me until this man is stopped."

"We should tell a magistrate about this. My father will know of a good one." She tugged him toward the doorway.

He held her back. "Miss Gilbert, you should join your family outside, and allow me to attend to this matter," he said with a heavy heart. He had to leave her. Not only for tonight, but until he captured this saboteur. But what if she found someone else before he returned to claim her? The lady seemed determined to marry if her use of seductive gowns and mistletoe were any indication. "You will be safer outside in case this fire spreads. Wear a coat. It will be cold."

"What do you plan to do?"

He took her in his arms again and kissed her as a silent plea for her to wait for him.

She returned his kiss by opening herself to him and claiming him as completely as he wanted to claim her. She was kindling to his coal. Sparks blazed between them and he pulled her tight, kissing her cheeks, eyes, neck, and tugging at her confounded cap so his fingers could roam in her golden locks.

A shout from outside broke through the spell. He pulled back for a much-needed breath and found that they were airborne again, her limbs tangled with his as they twirled above the floor. This could not keep happening! What power did she have that she could tap into his talent with a mere touch?

He shook his head in wonder and brought them to ground. If he was not careful, there would come a day when he would end up floating with her like this in public. That brought him up short, for the idea suggested years stretched ahead, with her by his side. He stared at this woman who made no attempt to straighten her gown that now half-exposed her delectable bosom. Had he done that? His fingers clenching at her back with remembered pleasure shouted, *Yes.*

She made no move to pull away, though their feet were now firmly planted on solid ground once again. Instead, the lady ran her hands through his hair, leaving his scalp tingling with joy. Sounding breathless, she asked, "Sir, what was that for?"

In answer, he did as she had done the last time they kissed. He pointed his forefinger upward.

She spotted what he had seen earlier. A sprig of mistletoe was tied to a nail directly above the studio's only window, the opening through which she had expected him to enter.

He straightened her gown and tenderly stroked her cheek. "How often do you plan on employing that tactic, Miss Gilbert?"

A delicate blush stole over her face as her wild green gaze met his inquisitive one. Now she stepped away, slowly disentangling herself from him and arousing him all over again with her sensual withdrawal. Her impish grin returned as she tidied her gown. "As long as necessary, Mr. de Wynter."

Then the bewitching minx raced across the room and away.

Christopher stared at the closed door for a long moment. She was a woman like no other. He could clearly picture her at his family's Sunday breakfast table, where no woman had ever sat since the de Wynters began to streak across rooftops. Yet, he felt that Miss Honoria Gilbert would be at home there.

Half bemused and half fearful of his father's reaction to that daring notion, Christopher retrieved his cravat. He was sure that she would wait for him. Now all he had to do was discover the villain who wanted him dead.

He left her studio by the window. But rather than go down to the street below, he rose toward the roof. In one leap, he reached the crest and balanced himself. It was a great vantage point for hunting down a criminal.

Honoria ran to her room to comb her tousled hair, straighten her delightfully disheveled gown, and don a warm coat and boots as ordered. There was nothing she could do, however, to suppress the rosy pink blush of exhilaration on her cheeks. After his last incredible kiss, there was not a shred of doubt that he wanted her.

The moment she came out her front door, her mama waved her over, as if she had been watching for her. The night rang with alarm bells and frightened chatter.

"We did not wish to disturb you, dear," her mother said. As if anyone could sleep through this racket. "Your papa planned to find you if the fire looked to be spreading, but for now, it seems to be contained to the de Wynter household."

"Where is William?" Honoria asked.

"He, Henry and all of our servants are assisting with the bucket lines. You look flushed, Honoria. Did finding the house empty frighten you? We should have woken you."

"I am fine, Mama. Has the fire brigade been called?"

"Yes," her papa said. "The phoenix fire mark was on a plaque beside the de Wynter's front door, so we sent for that insurance company's fire brigade."

"I have to speak with William, Mama," she said. "Which bucket line is he on?"

Her mama pointed to her brother but warned her to stay away.

"But this is urgent, Mama." She raced over, ignoring her papa's, "Honoria, no!"

Lines stretched from nearby wells and Honoria went to the one where her brothers were helping. Since most houses in Grosvenor Square were closed for the winter, she was surprised to see so many people out fighting the fire. Although, she guessed that many were probably servants left behind to keep homes aired and dusted.

"What are you doing out here?" Will asked when she reached his side. Waves of heat buffeted her from the burning house. "It is too dangerous. Return home, Honoria."

"If this fire spreads, it will be dangerous at home, too." She had to shout to be heard above the din. A man with a torch strode by, roaring instructions about where to shift the bucket line.

The smoke was thick, making breathing difficult. "Have they removed everyone off the roof, Will?"

"All except for Christopher de Wynter," a man beside William said. It was Mr. Finley. "Good evening, Miss Gilbert," he added. "Once everyone was safely off the roof, his brothers had to be restrained from returning to search for him."

She nodded. "Will, you must take a message to the earl."

"What about?" Henry joined in on the conversation as he took a full bucket from his brother.

"I have news of Christopher de Wynter," she said softly.

"What news?" Mr. Finley asked.

Drat. She had hoped he would not hear. She tugged at Will's forearm. "I must speak with my brother, sir. Pray, excuse us. We will be right back, Henry."

She dragged a protesting Will away. Henry took his brother's spot beside Mr. Finley and gave her a concerned look over his shoulder. To her eyes, Horrid Henry suddenly looked incredibly brave. Honoria was loath to leave him, but for now she had no choice. A few

621

steps later, she came across her father. Relief bathed her in a cool wave. "Papa, oh, thank heavens."

"Honey," he sounded uncommonly brisk and winded. "I had to leave your mother with neighbors to come fetch you."

"I am sorry, Papa, but I must speak with William. Would you please watch over Henry?" With a gentle push, she sent him on his way before he could argue.

"What is Mr. Finley doing here, Will?" she asked absently as she pulled Will along. "The ball ended hours ago."

"He came to discuss Papa's cool response to his request for a vicarage. He was also upset that you reneged on your promise to dance with him. I told you not to encourage him."

"Does it not seem odd, though? His coming to visit at this time of night?"

"Honestly, Honoria, you have a suspicious mind. It is no wonder you have no suitors if you treat your admirers to such speculation."

Honoria bit back a scathing denial and when Will pulled away, she tightened her grip. "Never mind Mr. Finley then. But we must inform Christopher's family that he is safe."

"You are on first names with him?"

"Where is his family, Will?"

"At Baron Larson's." He pointed in the direction of the house and then hurried after her as she dashed across the street. "How do you know he is safe?"

"Because he is ensconced in my studio."

"He is *where*? I shall call him out!"

Honoria swung around to glare at her brother. "You will do no such thing, William Gilbert. He only sought me out because he was worried I might spill his secret."

They had stopped by a street lamp. Honoria saw Will's expression change from incensed to intrigued. "What secret?"

"It would not be a secret if I told you about it."

Her brother frowned. "Honoria, you cannot really believe that he can leap across buildings?"

Though William spoke with supreme disbelief, a boyish wonder in his eyes suggested a tiny adventurous, imaginative and wildly wistful part of him wished it could be true.

Honoria grinned, for he reacted exactly as she had when she spotted Christopher race across London's rooftops. She gave a wink. "No, of course not. No one can do that. Now come along."

They hurried toward the Larson residence, which was only two houses from the de Wynters' smoldering home. From the dwindling bucket lines and the reduced volume of chatter, the fire must be almost contained. Perhaps most of the house could be saved after all.

"Honoria?" Will turned her around to face him.

"Hmm?"

"What draws you to Christopher de Wynter, when so many other men have failed to make an impression?" Her brother sounded truly curious. Did he wish to capture a lady's interest?

"I have met many admirable gentlemen this past year, Will. Some of whom Mama and Papa would approve. But love makes its own inexplicable snap decision. Later, discoveries can taint, or cement that initial judgment."

She gave him a complacent smile, for she was now sure Christopher reciprocated her feelings. "Many little things have added weight to my initial conclusion. At church, I loved his heavenly voice. At the ball, dancing with him was akin to floating on air."

"Truly? As in your drawing?"

"Shhh!" Honoria warned.

Raising his arms, Will formed a roof peak with his left hand and with two fingers, mimicked someone walking overtop.

Honoria lowered his hands and looked around nervously. But everyone's attention was on the charred house down the road. Then, meeting her brother's gaze, she said, "Will, when we spoke outside the ballroom, he defended his family fiercely. I could tell that Christopher de Wynter would lay down his life for those he loved. I want him to feel such passion for me."

She left out the most amazing reason. *His kiss touched my soul.* "Now we must inform his father that his son is safe."

Once at Larson's front door, Will inquired about the earl's whereabouts. A footman led them inside to be presented to the lady of the house. A plump woman, Lady Larson looked as haggard as Honoria's mother had been by the night's events.

"My husband helps to coordinate the fire response," the baroness said as she led them upstairs. On the first floor, they stopped at a door where a guard had been posted outside. "The de Wynters are worried about the missing family member."

"We have news about Christopher de Wynter, Lady Larson, that should allay their fears," Honoria said.

Lady Larson walked in and then cried out. "They are gone!"

She called to the guard as Honoria and Will entered. The guard denied any knowledge of the de Wynters' whereabouts. Honoria noted the room's open window had curtains that fluttered. She pointed out the likely escape route to Will. A ten-foot drop would have been no problem for soaring de Wynters.

"I believe they have left to find Christopher," she whispered. "We must return to their residence." Grabbing Will's hand, she rushed him out the door.

CHAPTER SEVEN

Christopher knelt on the far side of his father's neighbor's house, his hands and feet clinging to tiles to keep him in position. From the roof's crest, he observed the crowd below. To his right, smoke billowed from his father's home, but fires no longer burned. On his left was Baron Larson's place, where his family had taken refuge. Across the street and seven houses to the left was the Gilbert residence.

The Phoenix fire brigade had finally arrived, towing a water engine placed over a wooden trough. Men filled the trough with buckets of water as fast as the pump pushed it out through a long hose. They were too late to be of any real service, but would no doubt take credit for the hard work the locals had done in putting out the fire.

He studied the crowd gathered around the water engine. One among them could be responsible for setting off this latest explosion. He was searching for someone who looked to be enjoying the spectacle. Too often, however, Christopher's attention strayed to the golden-haired beauty whose kisses still left him breathless.

"The crowd is on your right," a man said from beside him.

Christopher started and his feet slid off, dislodging tiles. He grabbed the roof to keep from ignominiously falling off and levered himself back up. Once his heart stopped hammering, he said, "Evening, Nick."

"Chris." His eldest brother settled on the roof's peak, as if resting on his neighbor's rooftop at four in the morning was as normal as taking a carriage ride down Park Lane.

A soft *thunk* on his left announced Ev's arrival. He, too, knelt beside Christopher. He then shook his wounded arm and stretched the newly mended limb. "Chris."

"Ev." Pleasure swept up Christopher's back to see his brother's arm healed.

"Is that Mrs. Beaumont over there?" Ev asked.

"Yes," Nick said. "Unlike our dear brother, she and that divine Spanish beauty, as well as a thin, shifty-looking fellow who joined the pair have been here since the fire began."

"I am surprised Miss Wood was not in your bed when the fire broke out," Christopher said.

"The lady's heart had already been stolen." Nick sounded disappointed, but he did not elaborate.

"Since Mrs. Beaumont knows about my work," Christopher said, "she seems the most likely suspect."

"She could be our French spy," Nick said. "Miss Wood intimated that her employer had travelled widely in Europe."

"If Mrs. Beaumont is allied with the French, her knowledge of our talents becomes as much of a concern as her interest in your work," Ev added. "If Papa is unhappy about people in Britain finding out about us, imagine his reaction to the French learning our secrets."

With a loud *thump,* the earl landed behind Everett.

Christopher was stunned to see his father using the family talent. Other than when his father had showed him the basic moves, the old man had never, to his knowledge, used his levitation ability. Wearily, he said, "Evening, Papa."

"Christopher, is there any sign of the bounder who blew up my home?"

"No, sir."

"But then, Chris has been distracted," Nick said.

Christopher clenched his fist to keep from shoving his brother over the edge.

"Distracted by what?" his father asked.

"The lovely Miss Gilbert." Nick pointed to where the young lady spoke to her papa and her brother.

"She is the one you kissed tonight," his father said. "What is she to you? And no more tall tales about mistletoe!"

When I touch her, she flies with me. Since Christopher had no logical explanation for that amazing reaction, he settled for, "I plan to marry her, Papa."

That statement produced profound silence as they all studied the young lady who crossed the street with her brother. The two were headed this way. Even Nick did not offer a quip.

Finally, the earl said, "We shall speak of this later."

"There is nothing more to say, Papa."

"There is everything to say, sir! Have you forgotten who you are? Who we are?"

"She knows who I am."

"And she still wants you?" Nick sounded surprised.

"You fool!" his father said. "It matters not what she wants, or what you want. Our family security is paramount and you have compromised that."

"No, I have not, Papa. She will keep our secret."

"Even if you do not offer for her?"

"She is honorable, so yes, she will keep my secret."

His father held up a hand, and then pointed downward.

A few houses away, Honoria and her

brother had halted and her brother was making a hand gesture with two fingers that made Christopher's blood run ice cold.

"As if that Beaumont woman's interference was not enough," his father muttered.

"I have been thinking on this and have concluded that Mrs. Beaumont is unlikely to be the culprit here," Ev said.

"Explain," the earl said.

"If she meant to impede Christopher's war efforts, sir, she could simply have pretended to be someone else and shot him at close range. It makes no sense for her to go to the trouble of blowing up his laboratory or our home."

Christopher stepped away from his family, his thoughts in too much turmoil to focus on useless speculation. How could Honoria have told someone about him? He had been on the verge of inviting her into his heart, into his home and even his family's treasured Sunday breakfasts. It did not matter that her confidant was her brother. He gulped past a swollen throat, hands shaking with disbelief.

His colossal mistake rained over him like a shower of hot ash. *My father did not even trust my mother with this information and I spoke of it with a complete stranger.* Someone he had barely known for twenty-four hours. He wanted to shake her and shout at her for betraying him. Betraying them. Betraying any chance of a future for them.

"All may not be lost," Ev said in a consoling tone. He came over to lay a hand on Christopher's shoulder. "William Gilbert is a sensible fellow. I will speak with him."

Christopher shook off the comforting touch and strode to the roof's edge. Raging over his idiocy, his thoughts came to a crashing halt at a sudden movement below. He leaned over for a better look. Forty feet below, a man with a drawn pistol was watching the two Gilberts as intently as his family was.

"All of you have done enough damage to our family name," the earl said. "Christopher, what are you . . . ?"

Christopher raised a warning hand.

Will hurried after Honoria, shouting his thanks to Lady Larson over his shoulder. The door shut behind them and he said, "Would they have returned to a burning home?"

In a rush to reach the de Wynter residence, Honoria spoke over her shoulder. "The most logical place to check would be their roof, Will."

They had taken no more than a few steps from the Larson residence, however, when Mr. Finley stepped out of the darkness.

Honoria skidded to a halt and William crashed into her back. Her pulse rocketed in alarm when she saw the dueling pistol aimed directly at her ribs.

"Both of you, come this way." The would-be

curate jerked his weapon toward the servants' stairs between the Larson and de Wynter properties. "We have much to discuss."

Will pushed her behind him. "What is this about, Finley?"

"Your sister has information I need. Now move!" He shoved a lantern at William. "Raise the shutter. We will need light."

Will did as he was bid and then with the bright lantern lighting the way, he took Honoria's gloved hand and led her down the wet stairs. At the bottom landing, they sloshed through puddles that had drained there. Her skirt hems were soon soaked and she began to shiver from cold as much as fear. She gripped her brother's hand tighter. He squeezed back, a silent gesture that was incredibly comforting.

"What is this about?" Will asked.

"Quiet," Finley said in a harsh whisper. "No more talk until we are inside." He jabbed the pistol at her back.

Honoria gave a startled yelp. From above came a hiss.

"What was that?" Finley looked upward.

"I only heard my sister's cry," William said in a tight voice. "Touch her again, and I will thrash you until you can no longer grip that gun or anything else."

"It might have been a cat," Honoria said in a shaky voice, but her backbone stiffened because she suspected the hiss had come from something a lot larger, angrier and more lethal than a harmless kitten. She almost felt sorry for Finley. Because she would bet her last painting that Christopher de Wynter was on the roof.

Will opened the door and they shuffled into a narrow corridor. Finley shut and locked the door behind them.

That will not help you. Honoria squeezed her brother's hand, this time in encouragement.

William gave her hopeful expression a suspicious glance.

"Go straight down and to the left." Finley prodded them along until they reached a large kitchen with a long scarred worktable, cupboards, and a range. No pots hung on hooks, the shelves were empty, and the air smelled stale. Like many aristocratic families, the one that owned this townhome must have gone to the country after Parliament ended. A lonely mug on the table was the only sign of habitation.

"This is not your house, sir," Honoria said as she faced the false curate with a hard expression. "Why do you inhabit it as if it were yours?"

"I needed a place in this square so I could keep an eye on the de Wynters," he said. "This was the closest empty home, and a servant only comes here once a week."

Behind Finley, a beloved face descended in the window well, hanging upside down.

633

Honoria barely suppressed her scream. Not so William, who let out a startled shout.

Finley swung around but Christopher was already gone. "What did you see?" Finley raced to the window.

Honoria elbowed William before he spoke.

He gulped and then nodded in silent understanding. "Sorry, it was a cat. Jumped past the window."

Finley peered out, his hot breath misting the cool glass panes. "Are you sure it was not a person?"

As Finley continued to search, Honoria grabbed her brother's hand and raced for the door. A shot rang out. A bullet whizzed past her cheek and struck the wood. Honoria screamed.

With a furious cry, Will swung around. He would have charged his friend, but Honoria held him back. Finley had already drawn another weapon from his waistband after throwing away his spent pistol. His hand was shaking so hard, she was terrified he might fire by accident and kill her brother.

"Listen to your sister, Gilbert," Finley said.

"What do you want?" Will asked.

Finley swung the gun at Honoria. "Where is Christopher de Wynter? He was not at his home tonight."

"How do you know?" Honoria said. "Were you there?"

"Very clever, Miss Gilbert. Yes, I was there

to take what should have never been given to him."

Her eyebrows shot up in surprise. Was this not about Christopher's experiments? "What was he given?"

Finley extracted a flat bone from his breast pocket. It was jagged at one end. Finley shook it as if it was evidence in a terrible crime. "This!"

"A bone?" Will asked, sounding confused.

Finley rushed toward him. "A fossil! The devil's creation."

As he drew closer, Honoria recognized what had always bothered her about Finley. There was madness in his gaze.

"It is just a bone, Callum." William used Finley's given name in a gentler tone, as if he, too, had noted his friend's fragility.

"No, not only a bone." Finley's hand began to quiver. "It is a tool that can be used to destroy the church. Lord Berrington has already succumbed to its evil powers. When I approached him to beg a living on his estate, he proudly showed me this abomination. Me? A man of God! He talked and talked about how it might be from an ancient crocodile. One that purportedly lived millennia before God created the world."

His laugh held a hysterical note as he paced the small room. "I realized then why the earl had balked at considering me qualified to be his vicar. The man was beyond reasoning. I had to take action."

"What did you do?" William said, again shielding Honoria.

"Once he told me that he planned to give the devil's bones to his youngest son to authenticate, I had to act quickly. I followed Christopher de Wynter to his laboratory and entered the building by convincing an old lisping guard that I was a curate come to visit a parishioner. De Wynter is not a clerk, you know, as he pretends, but a scientist. I hid and waited as de Wynter set up his experiment. He took forever to check every detail two or three times. I thought he would never leave."

Honoria could clearly picture Christopher at his work. He would be that thorough. Finley must be talking about the other explosion Christopher mentioned. She shivered at how close she had come to never having met him.

"Finally he left. That is when I searched, retrieved this bone and then filled his little canister with gunpowder. I was certain the explosion would hide my theft."

Honoria came around Will to face Finley, her fists clenched. "You almost killed him!"

"He should have died!" Finley frowned at her. "I did everything in my power to ensure it, yet he survived the explosion. I do not understand how, unless the devil aided him. And tonight, I went to find the other half of this bone in his home, but it was not in his new workroom. With little time to search, I realized the only way to destroy it was to raze the building."

"Callum," William said, his arm out in front of Honoria to keep her from rushing the lunatic, "you almost killed the entire de Wynter family and their servants. Do you not see that what you are doing is wrong?"

"I had to burn that house, William. Do you not understand? The other piece of this bone had to be somewhere in there. But Christopher de Wynter was not inside. And then everyone else escaped. That should have been impossible. I nailed all the downstairs windows shut."

Honoria sucked in her breath at the evil in this man. And he believed the de Wynters were aligned with the devil?

"We must be ever vigilant, William. Now, make your sister tell me where Christopher de Wynter is. He could still be in possession of the other piece of fossil."

"He is right here," Christopher said from behind Finley.

Finley swung around and fired.

Christopher dropped to the floor.

"No!" Honoria cried out in horror. She shoved her brother aside and charged the madman, bringing him down. Landing on his back, she pummeled him in fury. "You killed him, you fiend. How dare you kill the man I love!"

CHAPTER EIGHT

She said she loved me! Christopher lay on his neighbor's kitchen floor in stunned astonishment as Honoria Gilbert pounded on the man who had fired a pistol at him.

Her brother dragged her off Finley. No longer able to use her fists, she flailed at him with her lower limbs.

Joyous laughter churned in Christopher's belly.

"Ow!" Finley cried out as one of her kicks landed soundly on his ribs.

William pulled her away from Finley, who crawled across the floor to cower in a corner. *Coward!*

"Let me go, Will!" Honoria was still kicking.

"Settle down, Honoria!" William said, holding her tight.

Christopher's amused gaze met her brother's and the young lad began to chuckle.

"How can you laugh when Christopher has been killed!" Honoria cried.

"Because he is not dead. Look to your left."

Christopher stood and slowly approached Honoria. *She loves me!* His brothers melted out of the shadows to join him.

Finley made a dash to the door, but Nick nabbed him.

"I will take this one to a watchman, Papa," Nick said.

His father finally stepped into the light. "Inform the magistrate that I shall make a full report in the morning."

"Yes, sir," Nick said and left with his prisoner.

His father let out a bark of laughter. "Well done, Miss Gilbert, on capturing that malcontent." His approval thrilled Christopher as much as Honoria admitting she loved him.

As her gaze finally met his, she stopped struggling. William released her and she rubbed her arms where his hold had left finger impressions. He wanted to kiss those bruises better.

Ignoring the onlookers, she stepped closer and poked his chest with a forefinger where that bullet should have pierced. "You are unharmed? Can you deflect bullets as well, sir?"

"No," Christopher said, "but I am adept at avoiding exploding projectiles."

His father stepped up to the kitchen table and scraped a chair across the floor. Offering it to Honoria, he said, "We have much to discuss, Miss Gilbert. Everett, light more candles."

Christopher wished he could tell her that he loved her, too, but a better idea formed. One that might solve two of his problems at once. He could show Honoria how he felt about her, and prove to his family how right she was for him.

Honoria sat, but kept hold of her brother's hand, as if to ensure he would not leave her among so many possibly hostile de Wynters.

Christopher's temper had cooled since he spotted Honoria's and William's exchange on the street, for he realized she would never intentionally hurt him. Her brother had seen her initial sketch and could have guessed at Christopher's part from the way his family had reacted.

Nick returned as Ev finished lighting the kitchen as brightly as a ballroom.

Christopher strode over to Honoria. "Miss Gilbert, may I have this dance?"

"Not so fast." Nick shoved him aside. "Miss Gilbert, may I have this dance?"

As she studied Nick, Christopher stepped away without rancor. Perhaps this would work out better.

She glanced at him, and her tentative gaze made his chest swell with pride, for it said, clearer than words, that she would never betray him without his permission. "I have told my family about the effect you have on my talent," he said gently, "but they do not believe it."

"Miss Gilbert." Nicholas held out his elbow. "Shall we?"

She finally released her brother's hand and stood.

"I do not understand," William said. "Why do you wish to dance with my sister? And without music?"

"You are quite right, Gilbert." Everett ran over to grab a couple of ladles off the wall and handed them to William. "Use the handles to drum us a tune, lad, while we all take a turn about the floor with your sister."

"We need more room." To Christopher's surprise, his father, too, stood and gestured for his sons to move the table to the wall. The adjustment effectively blocked the doorway, guaranteeing no one could enter and witness what was about to occur.

William then began to drum the rhythm for a cotillion and Christopher leaped up to sit cross-legged on the table, adding his humming to the musical notes. His heart was racing for he, too, was anxious to see if her amazing effect on him extended to the rest of his family.

She curtsied and her three partners bowed. Together, they turned in a circle and then alternated, turning right to right, left to left. She took turns with each man, twirling twice and then exchanging partners. Christopher watched her feet. Not once did they leave the floor, other than in a deliberate skip.

The dance ended and William dropped his ladle and clapped. Honoria looked crestfallen. His brothers and father were complacent. Christopher was euphoric. *She only flies with me!*

"Seems a normal gel to me," the Earl of Berrington said.

"I disagree," Nicholas de Wynter said. "She is a superb dancer. Thank you, Miss Gilbert."

"Here, here," Everett said in enthusiastic agreement.

Honoria looked tearful.

Christopher jumped off the table and sauntered over in a slow measured walk. He stopped three steps away. "Miss Gilbert, may I have this dance?"

A smile tilted her lips up and she wiped away a tear. Gilbert's drumming began and his family added their baritone humming. Christopher bowed. On rising, he took both her hands. The contact was akin to coming home. This was the perfect woman for him. Christopher knew it and it was something his talent had recognized long ago.

Before they had danced two turns, gasps came from below. The drumming stopped. Christopher continued his dance with Honoria, because for them, the music carried on.

The earl cleared his throat. "If this is how you carry on, you two are never to dance together in public again."

The morning after the fire, Honoria sent William to speak with Christopher. Upon his return, he informed her that Christopher was engaged in delicate negotiations regarding the Gilberts' knowledge and asked her to be patient, to trust him.

Honoria expected Christopher to find her at her studio that night or even the one following. But he did not come. At the end of two days, she asked William to take her to Christopher at his father's home. Her brother refused, telling her it was unladylike to chase after a gentleman.

That was all well and good, except that Christopher did not get around to chasing after *her.* She hung mistletoe all around her studio and bedchamber, but gained not one kiss in return.

Finally, it was Christmas Eve. Too restless to sleep, Honoria paced in her studio before her window, partly because the de Wynters' smoky front door was in perfect view, and she could see who came and went from that half-burned house. Worries that had kept sleep at bay trailed her around the room. What if Christopher's father decided she was unsuitable for his son? Or a bad influence?

She wanted a chance to convince the earl that despite her past behavior, she could be trusted. After all, she had not spilled the de

Wynters' secret to any other member of her family. And she needed Christopher. He made her believe in herself, taught her to be proud of who she was. She held up the skaters' painting to the candlelight. And suddenly, a delightful idea pushed aside her concerns. She might not be able to convince Christopher's family that she was good for them, but she could show Christopher how good he was for her.

On Christmas morn, she hurried her family outside and into their carriage so they would be on time for the service. It had snowed all night and the sky was a blanket of heavy clouds that threatened to release more white powder throughout the day.

Honoria impatiently brushed away flakes of snow that had landed on her nose as she entered the carriage and sat beside her mother.

Henry rode inside this time, beside his father and directly across from Honoria, braving a strike from her lethal limbs. William rode up top alongside the coach driver to ensure none of Honoria's Christmas presents slid off the carriage roof.

"Finley has been arrested," her papa said as the vehicle lumbered forward.

"William's friend?" Her mama moved her knees closer to Honoria so her husband could stretch out his long legs. "How extraordinary. William usually has excellent judgment about people. What was the young man's crime, dear?"

"Apparently, he was the one who set Berrington's house on fire last Sunday."

"He wanted to kill the whole family, Will says," Henry added.

"Sir Trigg is to testify at his hearing," her father said. "It appears he tampered with naval equipment as well, but all ended well. The engineer whose work was destroyed was able to successfully recreate his new fuse. It is to be tested on ships' guns on the *Esfuerzo*, Everett de Wynter's vessel."

So, Christopher was back at work. Honoria scrunched her handkerchief. *What about me? Has he forgotten me?*

At least there was a chance she would see him again at church. He had to be there. She was counting on his presence.

They finally arrived and she rushed out and dragged her mother up St. Mark's snow-laden steps.

"Honoria, what is your rush, my love?" Her mama puffed as she struggled with her package. Behind them, the groom and two footmen unloaded the rest of packages from the roof under Will's surveillance. Honoria took the one her mother carried. It was one of her paintings, one of many being unloaded.

Last night, she decided that Christopher was right — it was time she shared her work with the world, rather than keep them hidden in her attic. And who better to share them with than the people of London who had inspired them? When she timidly broached the idea with her parents, she was surprised to see tears in her papa's eyes. He said it was a splendid idea. Her mother, for once completely speechless, had simply hugged her.

"In this weather, we are likely the only ones who will be here, Honoria," her mother said as she carefully climbed up the icy stairs. "The vicar has probably postponed the gift ceremony, so though I understand your excitement, dear, I do not believe there is a need to rush."

"I merely look forward to the service, Mama."

"There is someone in particular she wishes to see inside," William said, joining them at the church's front door.

"Who is that, Honey?" her papa asked.

"No one, Papa." She glared at her brother.

Her mother had been correct. The church was half empty when they stepped inside, but the most important people were present. The de Wynter men had come to church.

He is here! She breathed a sigh of relief.

Christopher, however, did not turn around.

She stomped her boots so loudly they echoed. At her mama's shocked look, she muttered, "Snow was clinging to them, Mama."

They took their places and before long, the

play began.

When it was the de Wynters' turn, each brother carried a different object. Nicholas de Wynter placed a square child-sized tent. Captain Everett de Wynter set down a cage beneath the tent that appeared to hold three animal carvings. Christopher de Wynter hooked a line of rope between two of the tent poles.

"Are those bears in that cage?" her mama whispered.

"The de Wynters have contracted with Bartholomew Fair to host a circus event specially designed for all the poorest children of the parish, Mama," Will said in a hushed voice. "There are to be a variety of acts from dancing bears, to equestrian feats, and even pantomimes. The earl is arranging transport for the children and their families to the fair and has hired Bow Street runners to guard the area on the day of the event, so everyone will be safe from disturbances so often prevalent during such performances."

"What is the meaning of that rope the youngest de Wynter lad added?" her papa asked.

"It represents acrobatic acts." William made eye contact with Honoria. "Christopher de Wynter says it is in homage to one of his ancestors who was a tight-rope dancer."

She smiled in understanding of that odd family connection. When it was her family's turn to give their present, Honoria's papa proudly walked her down the aisle, carrying her autographed painting. She set it beside the caged bears. On impulse, she released the latch and opened the cage door, and then rose to gaze with awe at the bounty of offering.

The front of the church was packed with baskets of food and stacks of warm clothing. The doll house was there, as were several ships in bottles and numerous frilly dolls. And at the center, lay a baby in a lowly manger on a straw-laden floor. The child's parents in long robes bid them welcome and graciously thanked them for the gift.

Returning to their places, Honoria sought out Christopher's gaze and found him fighting a proud smile. His approval warmed her heart. Without a word being said, she believed all would be well between them, after all. Honoria and her papa had barely returned to their pew when the vicar announced that a special request had been made that required Viscount Locke's assistance.

Her papa seemed as surprised as Honoria, her mama and Henry. William, however, wore a smug grin that infuriated her.

What is he up to?

Christopher de Wynter stood and crossed the pew to the middle aisle, one hand at his back. Hushed whispers erupted all around the church.

Honoria's heart thudded as Christopher strode to her papa's side and knelt on the wet carpet. "Sir, I have a request to make."

Her papa cleared his throat. "Here? Now? Well, of course. Pray, proceed, Mr. de Wynter. I shall be happy to be of any assistance. If your family needs a place to stay while your home is being repaired, you are all most welcome at our home. We have plenty of room."

"Oh, yes," her mama said. "You may move in any time."

Honoria slid a glance toward Christopher. His lips were twitching with a suppressed smile and all her lingering qualms vanished.

"Thank you, my lord," Christopher said, "but my family is managing adequately. My request is regarding your daughter."

"Honoria?" Her papa sounded surprised.

William elbowed her in the rib and then winked at her.

"Yes, sir," Christopher said. "My father informs me that I am forbidden from offering for any lady whom I have known for less than three months. He says I cannot possibly know my mind, never mind my heart, in less than that time. As such, I request your permission to court your daughter for the next three months, exclusively."

"Exclusively?" her mama said, in a soft trembling voice.

"Exclusively?" her papa echoed, in a confused tone.

"Yes!" Honoria said, and then added in a quieter voice, "I mean, if my parents have no objections."

"This is all very sudden," her papa said, looking around the church at the many grinning faces.

"I believe this situation is exactly as it should be, sir," William said. "Do you not agree?"

"I agree," Henry said from his other side, surprising Honoria. "Christopher de Wynter is top of the trees."

She mouthed a silent "thank you" to them both, and squeezed William's hand before she turned to her parents. "Papa, I am perfectly agreeable to this arrangement."

Her parents exchanged a silent look and then her papa held out his hand to Christopher. "Shall we shake on it, sir? Details can be discussed later."

Christopher brought forward his left hand, the one he had kept hidden behind him and raised it high. In his fist, he held a sprig of greenery. "If you do not mind, sir, I would rather the lady give me her word that she will seek no other suitors from this day forward, so help her God."

Seeing the mistletoe in his grip, Honoria chuckled. It was droopy, crushed and missing a few leaves. She knelt on the ground and leaned forward, and very circumspectly, kissed Christopher's warm cheek. "I promise."

His lips touched her ear and he whispered, "In exchange for my waiting three months to propose, Papa agreed to invite you and William to breakfast with us every Sunday from now until Easter."

Honoria squealed in delight. This is what he had been negotiating — her inclusion into his family. It was the best engagement present he could have given her. And she knew exactly what to bring for that first auspicious Sunday breakfast as a thank you to the de Wynters for their generous invitation — the one painting she had retained of her collection. The one of skaters in the fen, also duly signed.

Before she could tell him, Christopher kissed her on her mouth, right there in church, before her parents, the avidly watching parishioners and the vicar. The moment their lips touched, she began to lift off the ground. William's hand hastily descended on her shoulder to keep her grounded.

Wrapping her arms around Christopher's neck, Honoria returned his kiss. She sent a silent prayer of thanks to heaven for making her Christmas wish come true.

DEDICATION
(*A SEASON FOR GIVING*)
Thanks to the late Linda Kichline,
for her faith in my writing.

ABOUT THE AUTHORS

Jo Ann Ferguson has been creating characters and stories for as long as she can remember. She sold her first book in 1987. Since then, she has sold over 100 titles and has become a bestselling and award-winning author. She writes romance, mystery, and paranormal under a variety of pen names. Her books have been translated into nearly a dozen languages and are sold on every continent except Antarctica. You can reach her at her website: joannferguson.com or by email: jo@joannferguson.com.

Karen Frisch writes Regency romances for ImaJinn Books, among them *Lady Delphinia's Deception.* With two nonfiction genealogy books in print, she began tracing her family history as a teenager and discovered she is a cousin of Edgar Allan Poe (removed by six generations). A lifelong resident of New England, she is also a portrait artist. Follow

Karen on her website at: KarenFrisch.weebly .com.

Sharon Sobel is the author of eight historical and two contemporary romance novels, and is the Secretary of Romance Writers of America. She has a PhD in English Language and Literature from Brandeis University and is an English professor at a Connecticut college, where she co-chaired the Connecticut Writers' Conference for five years. An eighteenth century New England farmhouse, where Sharon and her husband raised their three children, has provided inspiration for either the period or the setting for all of her books.

Shereen Vedam writes heartwarming historical and fantasy romances that have a healthy dollop of mystery, with a pinch of magic. Though born in Sri Lanka, Shereen's roots are firmly planted on the west coast of Canada. After thriving for five years in friendly Winnipeg with its −40°C wind chill factor, she decided sandals and shorts for nine months of the year was infinitely preferable to six months of parkas, snow boots, and frozen nose. Now Vancouver Island's magical rain forest, with its ancient cedar, red-barked arbutus and giant weeping sequoia, inspires her writing.

Follow her on Facebook and shereenvedam
.com.

The employees of Thorndike Press hope you have enjoyed this Large Print book. All our Thorndike, Wheeler, and Kennebec Large Print titles are designed for easy reading, and all our books are made to last. Other Thorndike Press Large Print books are available at your library, through selected bookstores, or directly from us.

For information about titles, please call:
(800) 223-1244

or visit our Web site at:
http://gale.cengage.com/thorndike

To share your comments, please write:
Publisher
Thorndike Press
10 Water St., Suite 310
Waterville, ME 04901